MW01595124

To my world of dreams, where sunshine dances and love conquers.

Contents

Day 1

A scream shattered the peace of my chamber, awakening me. Opening my eyes a sliver I scanned the room wondering whether I was dreaming. Light streaming in through the window signaled it was morning, and as the material world around me became clearer I could hear multiple voices coming from outside through the slightly open pane. Rubbing the sleep from my eyes I tried to make sense of the jumbled sounds, and then there was another sharp scream. A chill ran down my spine. I recognized who it was. It was N screaming in extreme pain, but she was not alone. I could hear someone cursing in a heavy voice, and with my mind completely alert I rolled out of bed careful not to stand up and peered out of my small room's window. There was nothing on this side of the building, the alley was deserted. My room was in the back and probably this was taking place in the front courtyard. The loud male voice was gruff and unidentifiable. I could smell danger hanging in the air; slowly I crawled to the door leading into the main room of the small clinic. It was empty, and the front door was open. Our clinic was poorly furnished with a single table for the medical staff and a few chairs, nothing worth stealing. Whatever was transpiring surely wasn't about that. The door to the sole examination room was closed but it was clear the sounds weren't coming from there either. I moved forward staying close to the wall, meanwhile more male voices had joined in cursing and yelling,

"Where is the American girl?!!" that single question resonated in the air. They were interrogating N about me, but they didn't receive an answer and then there was another scream. I could hear the distinct sound of slapping. They were hurting her because of me. Blood rushed to my head, but I controlled my anger. I knew a rapid and calculated response was required with no time for any rash futile actions if I wanted to help her. The window facing the front was a little far from me. Creeping near it, I peeked out. I saw N in the middle of the courtyard surrounded by five men in black clothes.

"Rebels! militia" my mind went blank. Naively, I had hoped for someone else.

They were holding her by the arms, her lips were bleeding and her cheeks looked swollen. It was evident by the cold looks on their faces that if she didn't cooperate with them, they would torture and kill N without a second thought. Fury seethed within me pushing fear to the distant corners of my brain. These thugs were hurting her on my account; they wanted me, and I was going to give them what they had come for.

"Think fast Sarah." I was calculating the odds,

I slid back near the floor and crept over to the table, a plan was forming in my mind and I just hoped it would work. Careful to make the least possible noise I opened the drawers and found what I was looking for in the middle one. Grabbing it in both hands I stood up and rushed to the half open door slamming it open against the wall. Silence fell across the courtyard as everyone looked in my direction. N screamed for me to run and tried to pull herself free from the man who was holding her by the arms. The man facing her raised his hand to slap her again,

"Stop or you will regret it. I am the American you are looking for." I yelled before he could finish the task. He paused and looked at me sarcastically,

"What are you going to do; you should have run when you had the chance, she is right. Not that it would have done you any good, but it would have been good sport." The corner of his mouth twitched in a mock smile.

"You shouldn't underestimate anyone before you have made their acquaintance. Let her go or I will blast the grenade in my hands." Raising my hands, I showed them the small bulge and my thumb crossing through a small round pin. The expression on the leader's face changed, I could see anger paired with contempt.

"Are you going to pull the pin and kill yourself for her?" He pointed at N.

3

"Yes! And this is the last time I am telling you to let her go." My voice was stolid, with my eyes fixed on him.

"No, you wouldn't. Your type are all cowards, and you are not going to die for her." His voice was steady, but I could hear the hint of doubt,

"Sarah please get out of here, before they take you." N pleaded with me.

"I will detonate this, and you will lose your precious American hostage. Do you want to risk that?" My eyes were locked with his cold stare and it took all my will power to do so, trying hard to win this game of wits. His men stood around staring at the both of us confused about the next move and he himself indecisive.

"Let me spell it out for you, if you let her go I won't blow myself and all of you to pieces, ... I know in any case you will kill us both, so I have nothing to lose. It's your call." I tried to keep my tone flat and matter of fact, but internally I shook and my throat stung.

I wasn't sure how long I could keep the charade going and was praying he would take the bait and let N go. There was nothing else I wanted more at that moment then for her to get home safely to her newlywed husband and I was ready to do anything for that.

The group's leader was a surly man with a creased face and a furrowed brow, he had all the markings of a seasoned soldier, cold and merciless. Silently he kept his eyes fixed on me sizing me up. My desperation and the urge to just attack them to get N free grew, but my brain was warning against it. Even if my emotions took over and I jumped

4

them there was no way I or N could get out of there alive. He had to take the deal, he just had to.

The few seconds that had passed felt like a century as he kept trying to assess me.

I raised my hands once more, one of his commanders came close to him and whispered something in his ear, they looked at each other and then at me standing in the doorway of the small building of our clinic.

Silence weighted down on us all as we waited, I for him to let N go and him trying to evaluate the conviction of my threat. Then as I held my breath trying to keep myself composed, he cued for his men to let go of N's arm. She almost dropped to the ground; her face was ashen with tears streaming down her cheeks. With shaking legs, she tried coming towards me, but I stopped her,

"N get out of here and go home, Run!!!" She stopped in her tracks; questions lingered in her eyes as she looked at me incredulously. I smiled weakly at her and turned my attention to the thugs' leader,

"You will let her go unharmed and I will come with you. If anyone goes after her I will pull the pin." My face was blank as I spoke to the commander of the militia. He nodded, and N stumbled out of the courtyard at my cue and disappeared behind their SUVs parked in front of the small metal gate of the clinic, a mere bar of metal.

As N walked out, I waited a couple of minutes, calculating her distance from the clinic, ensuring she was deep enough in the labyrinth of streets to be out of the militia's reach. When I was satisfied that my purpose was

5

achieved, and she was safe I turned and sprinted, 'grenade' in hand, to the back door. The gruff commander cursed loudly and ran after me with his men.

Our clinic was comprised of four rooms altogether, first was the main room after entering from the courtyard and then there was an examination room on one side of it and a bathroom on the other. My room was in the back, next to the tiny pharmacy behind the main room. I aimed for the pharmacy's back door leading out to the rear porch and then the street. There was a slim chance of getting there because I suspected the soldiers of the militia to be on either side of the building by now and it wouldn't be hard for them to reach the back door before I got to it, and woefully I was correct. As I ran out two men jumped me from both sides and grabbed my arms twisting them, the 'grenade' dropped out of my hands. I screamed in pain and stood on my toes trying to balance my body so that my arms wouldn't break.

Their commander came running out behind me and stopped at the edge of the door where my "grenade" lay in pieces, one misshapen medicine bottle and a single metal hoop used for hanging keys. He spat on the ground as he came close to me. I was pretty sure he was going to strike me but instead he caught hold of my face and looked directly into my eyes, there was utter disbelief in his. Then he let go of my face and said something to his men and they loosened their grip on my arms. I let out a sigh as the pain in my arms eased, he scooped the pieces of my grenade and waved them in the air showing his comrades.

They were all unbelievingly staring at me, and I suddenly became very uncomfortable.

The adrenaline rush had worn off and I became fully aware of the gravity of my situation, being at the mercy of these men while having no clue of who they were, and what they wanted from me. The leader barked some more orders and I was dragged to the SUV parked in the front street, next to a big pick-up truck with an automatic machine gun mounted on it. The street was completely deserted, I wasn't surprised, people here had learned the hard way to avoid men like these in any manner possible. They stopped me before shoving me in the back seat of one of the two vehicles tying my hands and covering my head with a black bag made of coarse cloth. In the vehicle I was stuck between two men; I couldn't see them but could feel their thighs squashed next to mine.

I sat there staring into the cloth, thinking, what had I gotten myself into now?

The ride began with a jerk and we were off. None of my questions were answered, despite my annoying persistence. The surly soldiers simply pushed me in and rode towards their destination, wherever that was. Silence ruled as I contemplated my next move, more accurately their next move. They had asked for me as the American girl, they didn't know my name and that meant they had been sent here by someone, this wasn't some personal vendetta.

But in this country every American was an enemy, we were hated and considered a curse unleashed on these people, but that didn't explain why come after me. I was a nobody, working in a small village north of Baghdad with no prominence or consequence in any one's war. I and N had hoped that we were not on anyone's radar, but apparently, we were proven wrong, they had eventually come.

The journey was dark and gloomy; I knew there won't be any escaping these people, their guard had been very tight after my stunt in the clinic. The car ride gave me time to think about my abduction, concluding that I was taken hostage for a particular reason which probably had something to do with my government. As minutes turned to hours my back became stiff as a board and my bodily necessities became of urgent concern. I shouted through the cloth for them to stop, but there was no reply. I screamed again, same silence was in response, I really had to go and my patience was at its end. I blindly stood up and leaned forward towards the driver's seat scrambling to get his attention, the goons next to me tried to pull me down but I started yelling that they had to stop for their own good. They probably got the message and the car came to a stop. Someone pulled me out and removed the bag off of my head. The noon sun blasted in my face making me squint as I tried to look at the man holding the cloth bag.

"I have to use the bathroom, I am not lying, I really have to." My voice was shaky, the guy scowled visibly unhappy about stopping; the other pick up had also stopped a little far from us. The commander popped out of it and started yelling at his men in Arabic, and from what I could understand he was pissed at them for stopping without asking him. They explained that the crazy American was jumping all over the car and that she had to use the bathroom. He stepped closer to me, almost in my face,

"If you are lying and try anything I will personally whip you." He warned in a harsh voice and I didn't doubt a word he said,

"One of my men will go with you inside and rest assured the others will be outside surrounding the building and windows." He pointed to the rundown petrol pump they had stopped at. I walked a little dazed after being in the dark for hours. The bathroom was in the back as usual and was adequate, with soap and towels. I took care of my needs and then washed my face straightening my hair a little. My reflection in the mirror was of a girl with long deep gold blonde hair and a face paler than usual.

I had always been weary of my milky complexion, trying to tan it to be like the other girls.' Lying in the sun once I burned my skin so bad my mother freaked out and that was the end of my tanning experimentation. The memory made me smile, my mother's horrified face and her long lecture about being happy with who I was and what I looked like played in my mind like a movie.

Here I was standing in the middle of nowhere in a rundown petrol pump, held captive by some blood thirsty soldiers of fortune and waiting for my sentence, only if my mother knew. I pulled back the blonde locks and bound them in a rough half bun with my trusty hair slinky always wrapped around my wrist. Somebody banged at the door,

9

"Hurry up, we don't have all day!"

"I am coming." I hurriedly shouted before they decided to come in.

Their English language proficiency was astonishing, almost all of them could speak it fluently and some of them had a flawless accent. They had been quite vocal around me during the trip when they wanted, probably to show me that I was not dealing with amateurs. As soon as I was out their leader came and personally put the bag on my head.

Once again, we were off, with my world covered in darkness. I didn't know how many hours we had traveled, dozing off sometimes or just staring in the shadows. They did make another stop and everyone ate including me. Although I felt like throwing up, I was forced to swallow some of the food on the "insistence" of the commander of the pack.

My journey had been fraught with memories. Remembering my mother in that lonely bathroom had dredged them up from the depths of my heart. Memories I had tried so hard to bury deep in a place where no one could stir them, but maybe life and death experiences had the capacity of digging out the remotest of our thoughts that we have banned from our consciousness.

My mind had reeled back penetrating every detail hidden in the cage of it. My father's farmhouse in the middle of West Virginia and the laughing face of my mom; the mischievous smiles of my two younger brothers denying their hijinks, and my dad, a soft, tender authority in the middle of it all. I was their pride, my mother's

10

special flower, her confidant, and she was my best friend. I had never searched for any companionship outside of my own cozy house because mom was always there to be the one listening to my jokes, stupidities, triumphs and losses. As time passed, mom and I had grown closer as she was always there for me. After I went on my first date in tenth grade, my mother accompanied me during the night to throw tomatoes at my poor date's car for trying to get fresh with me. My father knew about our escapade but he never admonished me or mom. Later in eleventh grade when dad's friend's son Jake asked me out, they both were incredibly happy. I dated him oblivious to what was transpiring. Jake was genuinely nice and sweet like a huge marshmallow, and he was the only child and heir of dad's good friend, a business marvel who had made his farm into an industry. Our dates continued until we both were in the last year of high school. We had been going "steady". He was a wonderful guy and everything but I didn't love him, although my parents did. They had been so happy for my presumptive future that I didn't have the heart to let them down.

"If Jake would ask me to marry him, I would say yes." I had decided.

Sometimes I would think and plan a different kind of life, but it was only a dream. Eventually Jake popped the question just before graduation. His intentions were to get engaged and join his father in the family business, and to get married after a little while. It had felt nice to be asked, there were no booming crackles of lightning or rainbows stretching across the sky but it was nice. ᵛ⟍⟋

Anyone and everyone in the school heard and gave their opinion about the union. Consensus was that I had definitely become pregnant and Jake had to marry me to keep himself out of trouble. It was jealousy I knew, and I almost doubled over laughing when I had heard the rumor. If only these people knew Jake and I had never been intimate, we were saving it for the wedding with the restrain coming predominantly from my side. First, I wasn't sure about the whole affair and was going along for the sake of my parents. It wasn't that I didn't like Jake, he was a sweetheart but there had never been any sparks, as they put it. Secondly, I had seen some examples of young pregnancies in my small town. It was not pretty and I was not taking any chances. I intended to live before getting bogged down by anything like an unwanted pregnancy. Mom had been a little dismayed after I told her about the rumors, but she was strong as always and laughed it off.

Graduation day came with all the fanfare a small place like ours could muster and everyone was happy at the presumed freedom of eventually being recognized as grownups, ready to take on real life. I rather felt sad; it was a chapter of my life which had closed permanently. What lay ahead was comfortable and secure, but was it for me?

I had stopped asking myself that question pushing it into the recesses of my consciousness, trying to be happy in the joy of my parents. I kept myself busy with my mother's different projects for the wedding. My wedding had joined the ranks of her passions along with baking and decorating the house.

Three months after graduation the first bomb fell. Jake died in a fatal car accident coming back from one of the many parties he had started going to. His sports car crashed into a heavy eighteen-wheeler on the highway and he had not even made it to the hospital, dying at the crash site. His parents were devastated and so were mine. I, on the other hand was numb, the emotions inside of me were scattered and confused. I wasn't strictly in love with him, but we had been planning a wedding and it was the only topic my mother and I had been talking about for months.

Suddenly, he wasn't there anymore.

Life became boring after that. My mom stopped talking about my wedding and everything which had been brought out for the occasion was packed in the attic. She returned to her baking and I started thinking about a future without Jake. A future where I was going to a university and leading a completely different life. On the bright side, I was happy to disappoint all who had been waiting for an impending birth.

In the months following Jake's accident, my mother's occasional headaches had become more frequent and severe and she would rest more than usual. Our family doctor advised her to get further investigation done, worried about the continuous migraines. He had been advising my parents on that for some time, referring mom for medical tests but she had always slacked, calming my father with her assurances and never complaining about the headaches, brushing them off as minor inconveniences until the pain had become unbearable. Dad eventually took her to a bigger hospital in the city. They kept her there for a few days running every kind of test; no one anticipated any serious problems.

The day they returned home, it was bright and sunny. I was working on the patch of flowers in the front yard, November was cold and I was striving to save my flowers, covering them from the night frost and providing them with good manure. Dad had driven in the driveway very slowly, more than his usual style. I got up from the dirt and approached the parked car as my parents emerged from it. There was something wrong, I could tell. Although they were smiling at me, but I knew.

"What's wrong?" I took the gardening gloves off and threw them on the side.

"What do you mean, Sarah." Mom sat on one of the chairs on the porch, tired.

"What is it mom?" I hadn't even let them cross the threshold of the front door.

"I mean what did the doctors tell you. Is everything okay? I stood next to the chair placing my hand on mom's shoulder. Dad stepped closer, he sighed and placed his hand on mine,

"Sarah, we need to tell you something. William and Mike are at school, and I don't think they need to know at present." Dad's voice was hollow. My heart sank. I knew that tone. It was the same when he had told me about Jake's accident, only more solemn.

The news shattered my mind, "How could anything like that happen to my parents, to my mother!" It was inconceivable.

Her headaches were due to a tumor which had spread through her brain like a parasite sucking the life out of her every minute of the day. She was dying. I looked at my mother, as she sat frail and tired with a look of defeat on her face. I didn't know what to do. My whole world was falling apart in that split second of a moment. Like a scene from a movie, the weather had changed from sunny to stormy in matter of minutes. Little dewdrops started forming in my eyes, stinging like hell,

"What are you going to do dad, mom, we can do something can't we. Dad!" My voice was breaking and the pricking in my eyes was getting unbearable.

"No darling we can't, it has spread too much." Mom said in a soft voice.

"I don't believe you, I don't, I am going to call the doctor myself, you are not giving up." I ran to the kitchen and dialed the number of the neurologist she had been seeing. My heart was pounding with every click of the phone; his front desk answered. I was not in the mood for waiting and my tone conveyed my desperation, and they connected me with the doctor right away. When he heard my mother's name, his voice changed, speaking volumes to me, he didn't have to say anything; I knew what he was going to tell me.

I stumbled back in the den with feet heavy as lead; mom and dad were sitting next to the fireplace, quiet. I couldn't speak or think, the words were lost as I slumped on the sofa next to them.

It was found that mom had only a few months left. I lost interest in everything, my brothers became very obedient and orderly, and dad, I couldn't make out how he felt. He worked all day as before, later sitting with her laughing at movies and being just as helpless at finding his socks as always. I was angry and assumed he was being callous, insensitive. She was dying, and he seemed unmoved. One day I couldn't take it anymore and caught him out in the barn as he was tending to the horses.

"Dad why are you like this?

"Like what? He didn't pay much attention to me,

"Like this, don't you care she is dying, you act as if nothing has changed." My voice raised as frustration spilled out of my mouth,   should've hit her

He looked up from the bale of hay in his hand, directly into my eyes,

"That is exactly why I behave like this, I am not going to take her life before it's her time, she needs to be happy while she is here. There will be enough time for sorrow when she is gone. Sarah, she needs to be happy and normal not tucked away in a room until it happens. I am trying to let her enjoy life till her last day. Do you think I don't die every minute I think of a life without her, but I can't hurt her, I have to comfort her even if it kills me." Dad's voice broke into tears by the end of it.

I saw what he meant, what he was doing, his strength, his love for my mom. It just dawned on me that very moment that he was the one who was going to lose the most. Mom had been his soul mate; how could I not see it.

"I am so sorry dad, I just don't know what to do, I don't want it to be true. How do I get through this?

I hugged him and he lovingly patted my head,

"Sarah be brave for her; we have to make her happy. Don't think of these as her last days think of it as an opportunity to give her all you can." And I understood what he was asking me.

That day was the last day that I sulked in my room. I didn't exactly know how much time she had but I was going to make it the best. I convinced dad to go on a road trip, taking mom all over the country, every place she had never been, creating memories. Will and Mike were all for it, they didn't like their school anyway.

We left home in the beginning of December driving through different states eventually spending Christmas in New York City. My mom loved it. The big tree in Rockefeller center and............

"Wake up sleeping beauty!! A harsh voice jolted me out of my dreams, the memories disappeared into the dark shadows around me.

Were they memories or my dreams? Was I sleeping? Bewildered I opened my eyes.

Without realizing it I had fallen asleep on the way to wherever. The cloth bag was still covering my head, blindly I tried to get out of the back seat and follow whoever was calling me, but the bag on my head was proving to be a challenge. I almost fell flat on my face but my knees and hands broke the fall. Thankfully, my hands were tied in the front rather than the back. I stumbled to my feet as another voice laughed and yelled at me. Whoever was walking beside me pushed me in a certain direction. I was taken into a building and locked in a dark room without any windows or light. They had eventually taken the bag off and given me some food which I couldn't eat and the room where I spent the night in darkness had no bed or even a blanket. I lay on the dirty floor with my hands under my head to protect my face from any creepy crawlies. The whole night passed without a second of sleep.

Day 2

The leader of this pack of thugs opened the door of my cell letting a few rays of light in. I suppose it was morning. He looked rested and in good spirits,

18

"How was your night, I hope comfortable?" He had a mean smile on his face.

"Yes, thank you, I almost forgot my stay at the Ritz." I replied unperturbed, that probably got to him wiping the smile off his face.

"Today we are taking you to the people who have paid for you. You should be thankful that they wanted you unharmed or we could have had a very good time." He surveyed my body from head to toe making me writhe.

"Aren't we lucky, praise the lord." I just couldn't shut up, could I.

He scowled at me and stamped out of the room instructing his men to tie me up tight and this time hands on the back not the front. I instructed myself to be careful stepping out of this place and in the car as the bag had returned.

Bagged again and riding in just one car with the boss in the back with me and three others, I hardly had room to breathe, let alone move. This trip was not as lengthy as the previous day, still I was relieved when they stopped and let me out at a gas station. After a brief stay, we started again and didn't stop anywhere until we were at our destination. The boss pulled me out of the back seat and stood me up.

Hours of driving for the past two days had left my legs and back strained, and on top it off lack of sleep and nutrition made me woozy, I almost crumpled a few times before they finally led me through a door. This time they hadn't removed the bag from my head adding to my misery. There were more men here, I could hear lots of noise and commotion and could feel the movement of many people. The guy who had brought me in was talking feverishly with someone in Arabic, and I just stood there like a dummy hearing the whole tale of capturing me from his mouth, picking up bits. Living in this country I had learned scraps of the language. He accused me of being a sneaky bastard, I could understand that much, he was narrating his version of what had happened at the clinic with some added color and I just couldn't help but smile under my bag. Whoever was listening was quite patient because I didn't hear anyone interrupt him. When he was finished, a heavy voice asked someone to pay him and then it instructed him to leave the place. The thug thanked the sound and I assumed he left after the transaction was over. I didn't hear anything further from him, suddenly there was silence and then the voice spoke again, in clear fluent English,

"You will be held captive not because of any fault of yours but because of the crimes of your government, and if they meet our demands, you will live but if they don't you will die and we will broadcast it all over the world." There was no introduction or any side talk, he had come right to the point. His voice was very calm and ice cold. It was apparent whoever this man was he would have no quarrels about cutting my throat in a second.

"Now you will be taken to your room in one of our buildings and I have assigned my best soldier to look after you. If you have any special requirements, you can tell him and he will make sure that you are provided with whatever you need. We are not barbarians but we do not forgive anyone sullying our land."

The conversation was over and I was escorted out, my face was still covered but someone was holding my arm. Supposedly a guide to take me to the place intended as my prison. Whoever this person was, remained quiet until we were inside the building, but as soon as we stepped out his manner changed. He released my arm and let me wander before setting me in the right direction evidently enjoying the mistreatment; his intentions became clear when he whispered about the enjoyment of killing me when the time came.

This guy really detested Americans I suppose. In a few minutes we were entering another building where I tripped over the threshold of the door, luckily the door frame broke the fall but this second fall bruised my knees, bringing temporary tears to my eyes. My hands were still tied behind my back, incapable of any assistance. There was clatter inside, with multiple voices speaking over each other. As I stepped in silence fell across the room. I suppose everyone was staring at me, the strange feeling of being watched by many eyes was highly unnerving, especially when I couldn't see anything. Someone asked a question in a loud voice and the guy who had brought me in answered in English,

"We should not talk in a foreign language; let's respect the guest we have." Sarcasm dripped from his tone. The other asked again,

"Is this our bargaining chip?"

"Yes, this is it." There was silence again, I felt sweat running down my spine. The weather was hot, but that was not the reason. Suddenly the tone of the silence changed; someone else was there. I could feel it. The others started greeting the newcomer; this was probably my keeper. I didn't hear him say anything, waiting blindly for something to happen as I stood there. Suddenly someone pulled the bag off my face and pushed me forward with a jerk making me stumble, this time there was no doorframe to stop my fall. I helplessly closed my eyes tightly, anticipating a bloody broken nose and bruised face after hitting the ground, but instead my face hit someone in the chest sliding downwards. Two hands caught me before I could further descend.

"Jabbar behave yourself." A stern voice uttered from the body I had fallen into,

"Thank you." I whispered involuntarily.

The light in the room made my vision blurry. After remaining in darkness for so long and with all the stress, I was about to collapse anyway and this stunt kind of pushed me over the edge. I tried standing up, but my legs were buckling and whoever was holding me helped me stand, not letting go. This was the first time. Since my capture that anyone had given me a hand and been nice. Trying to keep my balance I looked up to see him but couldn't. His face was hidden behind a black checkered scarf that covered his head and most of his face only leaving his eyes visible.

"I was just giving her a hand, Ali." Said the smug guy who had apparently pushed me, smiling at him and me. My savior's name was Ali. Was he the one their leader was talking about? The one who was responsible for me. I looked again; he was tall and clad in black, and there was little else that could distinguish him from the others except that they were all intimidated by him. Everyone was mute and stationary,

"I don't know why he prefers you over me; I should be the one taking on this job." The smug guy, Jabbar, was right in my face. He wasn't wearing anything to hide his face. I wished he had been, he was young and good looking but with a mean countenance and eyes full of hatred.

"He didn't for a reason." Ali was composed and concise,

"Now if you don't mind, I need to get to work." Ali wasn't looking at me.

He cut the ropes around my wrists and gave me a few minutes to get my bearings. I straightened my hair and shirt trying to look as decent as possible. The men in the room stared at me like I was from a zoo, adding to my discomfort. Ignoring them I went into a narrow corridor leading inside as directed by Ali. By now my eyes had become accustomed to the light and environment. The building was old and in bad shape. Paint was peeling off the walls and at other places the plaster was broken off, creating holes. He led me to a small room that had an iron barred door with a window like opening in the wall across it bringing in some light. A wooden bed graced one side of the room and a door the other. There was a dim light bulb hanging very close to the ceiling, most definitely to keep it out of reach from people like me.

"This is where you will stay. That door leads to the bathroom." He pointed to the door in the wall, saying plainly.

"My own bathroom. Wow what a treat." The words slipped out uninhibited like a flowing ravine. He looked at me strangely, squinting a bit.

"I should thank you again for not letting me fall." I quickly changed my tone and the topic.

"You are welcome. Being our prisoner doesn't mean he should misbehave." His voice was devoid of any emotion.

"It is afternoon, soon it will be dinnertime and I will bring something for you." Saying this he left and locked the iron barred door behind him. It was obvious that there would be no privacy in this room; I would be under constant surveillance I suspected. 'But my own bathroom' that was at least something to be happy about and at that moment I had to go. I rushed and opened the door to find the bathroom alright, but it was in shabby condition. There was an old toilet and a small wash basin with no shower in sight. I did find a water cup and some old toilet paper stacked on the commode tank. Soap was provided but there was no mirror, they probably wanted to make sure no one could use it as a weapon.

"How am I supposed to take a bath? The thought ran through my mind unintentionally,

"Why am I considering things like that when I am in captivity awaiting death." Admonishing myself, I sat on the bed. It was covered with an old but clean quilt, a sole pillow lay on the head and a folded blanket on the foot, but my mind was wandering. I was sure the government would do something and get me out of this; after all I was their citizen, what could be more important than saving my life? But then again, ...

With that thought, my father's face flashed before my eyes. He would be devastated by the news. I felt so sorry for him and a pang of unnerving guilt. First to lose my mother and now this. I realized that I had been very unfair to him, but when I had left, I couldn't think of any other options to keep myself sane. I had hoped this would save me. Moments of my past reflected in my memory as I laid down on the bed.

Mom had traveled with us. We had driven all the way to Washington state and then her health started to deteriorate very quickly. We had to cut our trip short. She never got to California and was airlifted to the hospital near our place. Her last weeks were spent in the hospital; we all stayed with her, sometimes dad, sometimes me and sometimes one of the boys. Our lives had become an embodiment of endless misery as the month of February came with heavy snows and further despondence.

Mom had stopped responding to anyone, she lay in a state of coma and the doctors were at the end of their treatment and waiting for the final day. I just sat next to her bed watching her wither away, my mother, my friend, my safe haven being lost in every passing second. I sat there reading to her, talking nonsense, and telling her events of

25

every day. It was my solace to be there close to her, but it was short lived.

When it ended, we brought her home as calmly and quietly as we could. I had her favorite dress laid out for her. She was buried in the old graveyard next to the church which was one of her favorite places. Every Sunday and in between she liked going to church, praying there in solitude. My father made sure she got a spot there.

I didn't cry neither did anyone in my family, our tears had dried up, we couldn't even grieve. We had all lost our soul, the anchor that had kept our lives in place was no more, and our hearts were crushed. We had been mourning for months, mourning the failure of our prayers, of our love.

A slinking sound jerked me out of my thoughts. I felt my cheeks. They were sticky with tears, I hadn't realized it but I was crying. Quickly I cleaned my face, before the intruder could see me.

"I have brought some food for you." Ali, my keeper, placed a tray on the bed next to my feet; there were no tables in the room. The food comprised of some pita alongside some vegetables and water in a cup next to some plastic utensils. I could feel his gaze fixed on me. I didn't care at that moment whether he thought I was wuss or an Amazon. All I wanted was to be left alone in my misery,

"I am not hungry." I pushed the tray away,

"You need to eat, if you don't there will be nothing. After this the next meal will be in the morning." I saw his finger pointing at the food.

"Why, so you could have a fat sacrifice?" I said clenching my teeth, my depression had to come out somehow.

He didn't answer, just stood there,

"What, you are not going to force me to eat like the others. Don't you like a good show? Why don't you try, maybe it will make you feel like a man?" My words dripped with contempt as I looked up for the first time since his arrival, his face was hidden but his eyes, his dark intense eyes were fixed on me. Despite my instigation he remained silent. I wanted to throw the food in his face but suddenly I lost my vigor to fight, I just wanted to close my eyes and sleep. Moving the tray to one side I laid down facing the wall and closed my eyes. I knew tears were brimming at the corners, ready to spill but it didn't matter. I wanted to sleep.

Keeping my eyes closed I ignored him, and eventually I lost consciousness. I had no idea how long I was asleep but when I woke up the tray was sitting on the floor next to my bed and he was gone.

I stared at the food. It was there and he hadn't taken it away as he had said. Why?

Getting off the bed I went to the bathroom, washing my face made me feel a little better. Coming out I fully scanned the room for the first time, it was small and had one six by twelve barred window high above in the wall facing the main iron door. Sunlight streamed through it and from the corridor on the other side of the iron door. At that moment, there was partial darkness and the dim ceiling

27

bulb was illuminating the room with a weak sickly light. Just enough for me to see where everything was. It was barely more powerful than a night light. I came and sat on the bed. There was nothing for me to do but to wait for morning and see what was in store for the next coming day. I didn't touch the food tray. I just kept staring at the six by twelve hole in the wall above on the left side of my bed.

"Maybe I could see through that, I could pull the bed there and that could give me enough boost to reach it." Thinking that, I got off the bed and tried pulling it under the window. But then I discovered that the bed was fastened to the ground. I couldn't move it. In all of this, morning light started to streak in from the small window, which meant the window faced east. With nothing fruitful to do I lay on the bed pulling my hair above my head letting them hang loose off the bed helping me relax. My eyes became heavy as the room grew cooler making me sleepy again.

Day 3

I was about to drift off deep into dream land when an agitated voice broke my nap session,

"I left the food but you still didn't eat it." He was standing next to the bed; I almost jumped out of it, his entry had been quiet as a cat.

"I wasn't hungry." I tried to straighten my long shirt,

"That's okay, but going on a hunger strike will not help, don't worry no one is going to hurt you as soon as your government yields, we will return you." He was trying to sound convincing.

Ah! Yes, I had forgotten that part, maybe there was still hope. I looked up at him through my tousled hair, his face was still covered, except for his eyes again. Their intensity made me uncomfortable. I looked away fixing my hair after struggling with my shirt.

"So is there anyone who has been contacted." I asked,

"Not yet they will be called next week." He answered,

"Why not now, that would end this soon, and we could all be on our way." I said irritated, not comprehending.

Why were they going to take that much time? My complaint seemed completely legitimate to me.

"It's not my decision; it's the commander who decides about the strategy." He walked over to the bathroom door, "Do you need anything in there?" He waved his finger in the direction of the bathroom.

"No, I don't need anything! Why will they take so much time?" I had no interest in the bathroom supplies at that moment.

"I can't answer that, but we will let you know when the negotiations start." He came back to the middle of the room "I have to go now and bring some fresh food soon." He picked up the tray.

"But I don't want to stay here anymore then I need to. You people have to contact whoever you have to now!!" I stood up restlessly. He didn't say anything, just turned and left.

I wanted to bang the door and irritate anyone who might be out there but then I decided against it, deeming it a futile effort on my part. First it would hurt my hands and secondly it was not possible due to the bars. I knew it was not going to make me feel better, but I had to do something for myself. I was not going to let this get to me. I had to keep my head cool and think about a way out of this place. Sitting on the bed I combed my hair with my fingers trying to calm my nerves. It was the third day since my abduction and I was quite positive that the Americans were aware of it by now. I didn't know if my father was informed of the situation or not. I hoped he was not; I didn't want to think about his despair. The thought agitated me, I sat there blank,

"What if these bastards go after N again?" A thought occurred to me,

"But why would they? She didn't do anything and she has no value for them." Random ideas purposelessly ran through my mind.

The door opened and my lovely handler came in with another tray of food. The room was well illuminated by now as the sunlight from both ends had lit it up nicely. I could see him much better. His clothes were simple, a loose khaki pant and a worn-out blue shirt. He was no more in his black attire, but his head and face were still hidden behind a blue checkered scarf (keffiyeh).

I wondered why they wore it. Nobody was going to recognize them. They were here, where no one dared oppose them or question them. What were they afraid of? Most of the men I had seen until now wore the keffiyeh covering their faces and to me the need felt like a wasted effort.

"Whatever, who cares!" I huffed. It made him look at me, and with a hint of interest in his dark eyes he said

"I have some breakfast for you and this time I will advise you to eat it." He placed the tray on the side of the bed as before. It contained a roll of bread and some white porridge kind of stuff in a plastic bowl.

"What is this? I pointed at the bowl,

"That is oatmeal."

31

I had never seen oatmeal like that but if he said it was oatmeal it probably was. I was hungry by now, so the food didn't look so bad. I picked up the tray and took a bite of the bun. A sigh of relief uttered from his mouth, audible through the cloth of the keffiyeh. A smile spread across my lips involuntarily; it was amusing to hear him sigh. Quickly I checked myself and lowered my head to stay out of his scrutiny.

"Are you going to contact anyone today? I questioned him chewing the bun slowly; astonishingly he hadn't just dumped the food and left.

"I told you it will be done in a few days."

"Why? Are you making them sweat, what good is that going to do? Eventually you have to contact them why not sooner than later."

"The only thing I can tell you is that it is a strategy of my superiors and I don't question them." The way he answered meant end of discussion on that topic.

"Then why are you waiting here, I don't need a butler, and I won't use this bowl as a weapon, I assure you I am not trained for that." I chewed out the words sarcastically.

He didn't leave rather he started to pace, there was a hint of uncertainty in his manner,

"I wanted to ask you something.........I heard what you did when they went to capture you. Why?"

"Why, what?" I couldn't understand his question.

"Why did you save the life of that girl?" He had stopped pacing and was facing me,

"Why do you want to know?" I raised my eyebrows, dismissing his curiosity,

"Because I think your kind comes here under precise directions to sabotage whatever you can and cause as much chaos as you can. There is nothing that matters to you people, you and your government have only one purpose, to exploit us and our riches." His voice was full of disdain,

"Just to let you know I work for the Red Cross, my job is to help people, not exploit them. I took the job from the Red Cross not from the government and I work as a volunteer. As far as N is concerned, she is my friend and I wouldn't let your thugs harm a hair on her head if I could help it." Answering his accusation with the same contemptuous voice as his I had kept my gaze lowered to save myself from his reaction. I knew he believed that I was lying; it was evident what their perception of me and my presumed role was. I didn't want to clarify my position any further to him or anyone.

I finished my food and handed him the tray without another word. He was quiet as well, perhaps finding it fruitless to make me confess about my real intentions in his country.

He walked out of the room and I lay down to rest. There was not much to do here but to rest.

"What will be their next move? How would they broadcast my capture?" My train of thought was random.

It would be in the most dramatic way possible, I assumed. Pulling my hair back I let them hang loose as before pushing the disturbing thoughts out of my mind. I

33

knew this practice would only drag me down; I had to divert my attention. The window in the wall! Maybe if I could reach it, I could see what it was out there, and possibly could prove helpful in any escape plan. "Escape plan!", a weary smile twitched at the corner of my mouth. Still, I had to try, it was only human to do so. I had a strong hunch that they were going to kill me anyway, being under no illusions about their intentions.

'Only if mom could see me now, planning an escape from a prison cell, instead of practicing ballet, isn't this a twist of circumstances.'......... 'And maybe I could practice my ballet here; it would keep me busy and drive these people nuts.' The little curl on the edge of my mouth broadened into a smile. It was utterly crazy but maybe abduction and imprisonment did strange things to one's brain. I had forgotten about the window. Getting up I gave myself a twirl standing on my toes spreading out my arms, graceful as a swan.

Like a machine I kept practicing jetés and pirouettes; spinning until my head became dizzy and I collapsed on the bed. Just then a clinking sound drew my attention to the door. He was standing there, silent with his eyes fixed on me. For reasons I couldn't fathom, my breathing which was already unsettled, became more so, but within a fraction of a second, he was gone, leaving me alone in that cell once more, trying to settle my nerves. He didn't look angry rather seemed amused.

Afternoon came with the dimming of light in the room. I had been sitting or pacing in it since the episode in the

34

morning. Later, I had tried to reach the window but no matter how much I stretched I couldn't reach it from the bed. I had to devise another plan if I ever wanted to have a glimpse of the outside world. Climbing on the bed once more I leaned towards the window edge nearest to the bed and caught hold of it, pulling myself forward I was able to peek out, almost hanging sideways in the air just barely able to balance against my own weight. The scene outside wasn't too different from what I had seen before, it was definitely a rural area. There were other rundown buildings in the vicinity and I could hear people. Only a few were visible from my point of vision and I got tired of hanging like that after a few minutes. Getting off rather actually almost falling off, I came down from the bed. The insight I got from my small scanning mission was that where I was being held was probably in the middle of a small settlement and there were a lot more people around than I was aware of. Only a miracle or some kind of commando action could get me out of there in one piece. None of which I was capable of, with all my girly habits and training. What I pulled off for N had me just as surprised as my assailants, but that was more of an accident then planned. My situation here was different than that; it was immensely more difficult.

There was nothing but to wait on others to decide my fate now, and hope that it wouldn't end in tragedy. By the time I came down from the window edge, the sun had started to set and I was expecting my keeper to come with the evening meal.

The sound of the opening door had me standup; it was Ali, clad as before with his face hidden. He had a worn tray in his hands, I peeked at the food, same as in the morning, "It's not breakfast time, why the porridge again." I rolled my eyes,

"It's all we have right now." Ducking a little he bypassed me and placed the tray on the bed. His side arm touched my leg as he passed,

"Why do you carry that gun, do you think I can jump you or something." I said in a sardonic tone,

"No, it is a habit, that's all." He calmly answered,

"I have to ask you for a favor, can you provide me with some books or something to read. Since morning I have been sitting or walking around to kill time." Sitting next to the tray I placed it on my lap.

Ali was standing in his usual place, the middle of the room, waiting for me to finish my meal. I could never exactly decipher what he was thinking with his face covered but his eyes were so expressive, when I asked about the books, I could see a flicker of light in them. He didn't commit to it, but I hoped he was going to bring something for me. Finishing the oatmeal, I drank the water and handed him back the tray. Taking it, he locked the door after leaving.

His answers had been short and there wasn't much conversation, but I suppose there wasn't much to say in this situation, both of us bound by our own worlds.

I leaned against the wall with the pillow placed behind me and closed my eyes. The sound of the door clanging again made me sit upright; he was back with something in his hands. I saw that he had brought two books. It was unexpected; in a way I had wanted to believe that he would do that, but my head had questioned the anticipation, "Why would he bring anything for me?"

He came close and handed me them,

"You can read these, maybe you will like them." He said in a muted voice, as if trying to hide something,

"Thank you; I wasn't expecting this, when you left without saying anything I thought you didn't care." I took the books from his hands. For the first time I saw his hands with long slender fingers and clean well-manicured nails with smooth tanned skin.

"It is not about caring. You wanted something for passing time and I obliged as promised by us. Whatever you need will be provided." His response was dry.

I looked directly into those dark intense eyes, exploring, and for the first time his gaze lowered avoiding the inspection. I turned away keeping the books in my hands and leaned against the wall. He left.

Turning over the books I eyed the Jane Austin's collection and Tolstoy's *War and Peace*. The selection of books confused me, why these? How did he get these? They didn't seem the kind of books anyone like him would be reading or possessing for that matter.

"Maybe he stole them from somewhere." The thought disturbed me, "but he doesn't seem the sort."

"Why not, these people kidnap others for their own gains and kill them, stealing books is a trifle." My brain shot back at the naivety of my heart.

Night fell and the room got darker. My eyelids started to droop and my limbs felt heavier. The books would have to wait until the next day.

Day 4

Sunlight was weak in its efforts to break through the gloom of my cell where I lay staring at the ceiling and at the dim bulb hanging in the middle of it. My sleep at night was choppy with nightmares and chasing shadows occupying the depths of my subconscious as the haunts of my past and the demons of my present surrounded my conscious hours. It was daybreak, the fourth day of my captivity; I turned on my side to take in more light as it came through that hole in the wall with its rays falling on the bed. I folded my legs so the rays would fall on my toes and waited for the light to skirt away as the sun kept rising. It was a game that lasted for some time until my toes couldn't reach the sunlight.

The room was warm. The month of June was one of the hottest I was told and this was first of mine in this land, but sadly imprisoned. I counted the days on my fingers; it was the second week of June. Only fifteen days ago N had tied the knot with Hamid, the young man who had been courting her for two years. She was so happy, stars shone in her eyes in the days before the wedding. All the preparations reminded me of another wedding planned by another eager mother across the oceans. I remained astounded at the commonality of the sentiments of those two mothers thousands of miles and two worlds apart, just happy in the bliss of their daughters' eminent unions.

I raised my hands to see the remnants of the henna I had been wearing on them since the wedding day, all of her friends had to. We had helped her prepare for the big day, striving to make everything perfect. Even in these difficult times all of us forgot about the miserable surroundings with hopes for the future, believing in love and happiness. She had been my family since my arrival here when I joined the small health clinic as assistive staff, where she worked as a nurse providing care to the little village in the war-torn land. I had come broken, trying to piece my life together possibly by helping the destitute and deprived, looking for solace. Noor-ul-Saba, "N" was the first person to greet me when I landed; she was there to take me to my new home. I had been reserved, all the loneliness and depression had built walls around me, not ready to let anyone in. She never pushed her way into my heart but slowly entered its treacherous territory with great care.

I couldn't pronounce her name properly so we came up with "N". The first days I spent with her she gently showed me how to cope with the new world of her country and to find the beauty in the hidden corners of it. My fear evaporated and my confidence built as I grew closer to her, a bond formed between us which was stronger than the conventional ties of friendship. She was like a sister to me.

In the short time that I had been there since my arrival in early April I had settled into my little place in the clinic and grown accustomed to her presence in my life. The day she had brought me to the village she had insisted on my stay at her house as a guest, but the small room in the back of the clinic had caught my eye, and I decided to reside there. She had respected my decision and supplied me with every necessity, despite my protests.

We worked together in the clinic from morning till late evening. At first, I got overwhelmed by the number of people who came seeking help. N guided me through the challenging initial period and slowly I grew accustomed to the new life, and she became my confidant, someone I could lean on. Then one day in mid-May she announced the news of her marriage which made me both happy and sad, because I didn't want to lose her. N was in a state of absolute bliss and I didn't want to dampen her joy by letting on about my fears of loneliness.

I would have to cope with her loss, it was bound to happen someday, but then before the wedding I found out that she was not going anywhere. Her husband was going to move to the village and help us with the clinic as he was a nurse too. The day I learned that she was not leaving I actually cried and N had just hugged me and scolded me on not letting her know about my angst.

After that the days passed with such glee and festivity that everything else happening around in the world eclipsed. Helping out with the decorations, clothes and every knickknack I was happy as a lark, not even realizing that I didn't have any special clothes for the wedding however N had a surprise for me. She had dresses made for me along with her own. I couldn't believe it when I saw the beautiful garments she handed me a few days before the wedding,

"This is for you Sarah; you are going to be with me as my sister." N lovingly held my hands and I couldn't do anything but look at her with tears. I had never imagined she would want me to be her sister and yet she did. That had been the day when my soul finally rose from the ashes. I called dad and told him about everything and he laughed, deeply happy at my joy. He had also sent a gift for N which arrived a day after her wedding, thanks to the efficient mail service, but she was content as always.

The door clanked and my thoughts faded, morning light had spread all over the room as usual from both ends. Ali came in as usual with a tray in hand. I sat up pushing my hair back,

"I brought breakfast for you." He tried to give me the tray,

"But I haven't washed up yet. You will have to give me a few minutes." I hid my hands behind my back and stood up, leaving him standing with the tray.

"I will leave it here with you and get it later." He ducked past me as I walked to the bathroom and placed the tray on the bed. I had almost reached the door of the bathroom when suddenly the question which had been bothering me popped again in my head and I had to ask it before he left,

"Where did you get those books, I mean the Jane Austin collection. You don't seem the type." I bit my lip to stop the smile,

"It's none of your business, you wanted books and I gave you what I had." He had reached the iron door when my question stopped him in his tracks. His answer was abrupt and almost rude, but I was expecting that, obviously the books weren't his and my comment clearly conveyed my insinuation. Replying he strode out and locked the door. I washed up and ate the same oatmeal as the night before, only the cup of tea was new and it was refreshing for a change. Finishing everything I put the tray under my bed next to the wall, concealed from plain sight, just to mess with him. He would have to kneel and get it. That should bring him down from his pedestal. As the day progressed the room grew hotter. I lay on the bed and tried reading one of the books, but the heat was too much. Since the day of my abduction, I hadn't taken a shower and it made me feel filthy. I wanted to bathe more than anything and the room temperature wasn't making life any easier. The question was how could I? there was nothing in the bathroom for such "luxury." I suppose they wanted their prisoners dying of crud than anything else, saving them the trouble.

The heat was excruciating and I wanted to take a bath and cool myself off by any means possible. Exploring my options, I had made up my mind by midday on how to accomplish that. The plan was to use the long night shirt I

43

wore, ripping pieces from the edges to make wash cloths and rub myself clean with them. I was desperate, the heat was getting to my head and I had to do something to cool off and clean myself. This seemed like a plausible plan. "Take that!" I was quite satisfied with my intelligence. Ready to fulfill my goal I ripped strips off the edges of my shirt with great difficulty, it was a tough cloth but eventually I was able to do it. Armed with two wash cloths made out of the ripped fabric I went in the bathroom triumphantly ready for my bath. The bathroom was not very big and I had to stay close to the wash basin for water and soap. Assessing the available space, I decided to do my top half first and then my legs. Closing the door, I took my shirt and bra off and carefully hung it on a nail sticking out of the wall. I stood facing the wall opposite the bathroom door, next to the broken wash basin serving as my container for water and soap. I had closed the door behind me but it was not locked as there was no lock on it, but I wasn't expecting anyone. Ali was supposed to come in the evening with the second meal.

I wet both cloths and started my "bath", one cloth with some soap on it and the other soaked in plain water to clean it off. It was blissful to feel the cool water against my skin rubbing it clean, I was so occupied with the whole affair that I didn't hear anything outside in the main room. After finishing the front, I twisted and swung my hair over my shoulder making them fall on my chest and started on the back. While I was trying to reach the middle of my back to wash it, the door burst open. I was stunned, my hands froze in their positions, one on the back reaching from the bottom and the other wrapped around my chest trying to do the same from the top. I didn't dare move in my condition, being completely at the mercy of whoever was there. Fear gripped me and I started cursing myself for being so foolish. Who needs a bath in captivity Sarah?

Silence filled the air; the invader hadn't said a word. I hoped it was Ali for some reason, but I wasn't sure and didn't have the courage to turn my head and see.

"I can help you. You missed a spot." It was Ali, his voice was flat and emotionless but what he said utterly caught me off guard.

I didn't know what to do standing there with my naked back facing him. At that moment I was so thankful for the wash basin for being where it was and my decision to do one part of the body first and the other later, I was thankful for so many things.

How was I supposed to respond to his offer? My mind was not able to think coherently and my heart felt like it was stuck in my throat. I could barely make a sound. Silently I moved my lower hand from the back and handed him the soapy washcloth.

He took it and gently wiped my back careful not to touch me with his hand. I couldn't breathe, couldn't move, acutely aware of his presence. Finishing with the first wash cloth he handed it to me and took the other with plain water and as careful as before wiped the soap off my back. The water was cold but I was burning hot, every inch of my skin was on fire. Completing the task he handed me the second wash cloth and stepped out of the bathroom closing the door behind him. I almost collapsed on the floor, except for holding onto the wash basin steadying myself.

What had happened was something I couldn't even fantasize.

Quickly I got dressed and came out. It was not very late in the afternoon; how come he had come to the cell at that time? And then I saw the missing tray from under the bed.

My heart was still racing as I lay down on the bed and closed my eyes trying to relax, but I could feel his hand moving across my skin. Although he hadn't touched me but the sensation of him being so close was enough, his dark eyes occupied the sanctuary of my closed eyes. Frustrated I sat up and started to comb my hair with my fingers, braiding them and twisting them into a bun. That done, I started pacing in the room to settle my nerves with every turn I stared at the door of the bathroom. This wasn't helping. Eventually I stopped and stood in the middle of the room, motionless with a blank mind. God knows how long I stood like that, but my senses returned to the present when the shadows got longer and the room darker. It was almost time for him to bring the evening meal.

With my heart slowing down to a beat commensurable to a coma I waited for him, and for the sly looks and abrasive behavior.

He came at the same time as always after sunset. I had made up my mind to ignore him. The door opened with the same clanking sound. I didn't raise my head but his shoes were visible, coming close and finally approaching me.

46

At last, I was face to face with the dreaded encounter, "Here's your dinner." His voice was toneless,

I didn't look up as he placed the tray in his usual manner. I knew he would not leave until I was done with the food but at that moment, I couldn't swallow anything, I was barely able to swallow my saliva.

"I am sorry for barging in, I wasn't thinking. I had come to take the food tray and couldn't find it and then you were also nowhere. I waited for a few minutes and called out your name as well but you didn't answer. Then I had to find you. I did find the tray later standing against the wall under the bed." His voice was dead serious, there were no smirks or any insolence.

I had to raise my eyes, just to meet his, sharply dark and guileless. As our eyes met, he averted his gaze and moved to the wall containing the small window for air and light, looking out of it he remarked at the increasing heat. I then realized how tall he was. The window I had to reach hanging sideways on my bed post was at his vision's level.

I quietly ate my dinner, this time it was the same oatmeal but no remarks left my lips, too worn out by all the stress.

He waited patiently leaning against the wall. I didn't look at him a second time but I could feel his gaze fixed on me. Finishing the food, I handed him the tray keeping my eyes cast down. Silently taking it, he walked out. I fell on the bed sighing heavily keeping my vision fixed on the ceiling, not ready to fall asleep but without any strength to even lift a finger.

Day 4 (Ali)

Slamming the door behind me I pulled off the keffiyeh, it was choking me. Sweat ran down my back. My heartbeat like a wild stallion, and I had trouble inhaling. Taking a few deep breaths, I stabilized my nerves and leaning on the table looked at myself in the small mirror of the clock on the wall, my face was the portrait of what was going on within me.

She had been here for only three days and I couldn't get the scent of her body out of my senses after she had crashed into me on the first day, thanks to Jabbar's 'civility'. My spontaneous reaction was to hold her by the arms preventing her fall. She was confused and disoriented after traveling with that cursed cloth over her head but the first words, she said were to thank me for just giving her a hand.

Her hair wildly haloed around that face of hers. There was no arrogance or fear in her as she tried to orient herself with her surroundings. But she was crying when I went back with dinner that night, and I couldn't sleep that night; her face and her tears kept me awake. It wasn't that I hadn't seen a beautiful woman, there were several around fawning over me, I could have my pick of the lot but I never wanted to, but this girl...... I couldn't understand what was about her that tugged at my heart. I had announced to bring her meals even though Jaria could have done it easily but I didn't let her.

She wasn't like anyone I had ever met, the second day I found her dancing in the cell completely oblivious to the world around her. Why would she? Shouldn't she be afraid? I suppose she hadn't expected for me to see her, but I had just gone to check on her and accidentally discovered her. She looked taken aback but not intimidated.

The next day she asks me for some entertainment and I furnish her with my books. I still couldn't understand why I gave her my books, my most prized possession. I could have asked Jaria to find something for her but strangely I didn't. I wanted her to have mine. What was wrong with me?

Unbuttoning my shirt, I sat on the chair; what had happened today? I had decided to keep my distance, not to indulge her anymore. The books were given and I didn't want them back yet, but what happened today............. I closed my eyes making the cardinal mistake, as her image came haunting.

I had gone to get the tray from her room to bring her dinner, deep down I knew it was an excuse to see her, but when I got in, she wasn't there. I panicked, where had she gone? I remembered the stunt she had pulled with the soldiers who had gone to bring her in. It was rumored around the whole camp; people wondered how she found the courage to defy those men just to save the life of one of her co-workers.

Had she ditched this cell as well? I had to find her. It never occurred to me that akin to any normal person she might be in the bathroom. Like a mad man I had to barge in, while she stood there naked waist high, trying to reach her back to wash it. God had been merciful that she wasn't facing me. I stood there, incapable to think sanely as she froze in her spot. Then I offered to help clean her back, like it was the most normal thing in the world. She didn't utter a word and simply passed me the washcloth.

I couldn't fathom what might have been going through her head, but I could barely keep my hands steady. Quietly I did it and bolted.

Now I was looking at the reflection of a man whose face looked like he had been beaten hard without sustaining any wounds. The anguish was visible in my eyes. I could read it. Would she see it? I didn't want her to. She had been so clear in her indignation about 'my kind' almost ridiculing me for having those books, how could she ever know what they meant to me. Maybe I should take them back.

I turned around and stared at the gun and the holster I had thrown on the bed along with the keffiyeh. She had asked me why I needed to bring it? I had no rational answer for that question. This burden was too much for me, I carried it in front of everyone but not in the privacy of my chambers; here I was the same as before, my father's dream, my mother's shining light and my little sister's big bear. Wretched I got up and opened the drawer of the table, their picture was in there, along with the only book I had left, the beautiful fairy book. The others I had given to her. The last ones my parents were reading and the small fairy comic book my sister had been insisting on me to read to her before my world was destroyed. Holding the fraying book I stared at the colorful pictures, which had started to fade now after so many years. Her innocent smiling face peeked out of the pages as I turned them. A storm wrecked my mind; I closed the book and placed it back in the drawer, next to the sole photograph of whom I had lost so long ago.

Pressing on my eyes I helplessly attempted to calm my throbbing head. I wasn't ready to feel anything. I never would be. I had to be just the guy everyone knew. The ruthless soldier who was never stirred by anything or anyone. Then why did I feel the walls around me shaking and cracking?

I had to stop it. Picking up the holster I tied it around my waist blocking the memory of her skin next to mine. I was going to take her meal and there won't be a hint of what had happened. I was determined to keep my path unchanged, there were promises I had to keep, and nothing in this world would deter me from what I had to do.

Day 5

Sleep had come easing my tension and I woke a little later than usual. The first thing I wanted to do was to wash up before his appearance. As soon as I came out all clean and fresh, he entered with breakfast. I had my hair still tied up in the bun from the last day. Sleeping with that had cricked my neck. I had decided to take my meal without indulging in conversation today, but my plans changed when I saw what he had brought with him, a plastic bucket and cup for bathing.

"You brought a bucket!" I couldn't keep from exclaiming loudly.

"Yes, I can see you require one, and I apologize for not realizing that earlier." He put the pail and cup next to the bathroom door.

"Why did you have to get the tray, is that the only one you've got." My embarrassment from the previous day eventually spilled out.

"Yes, that is the only one we have here, we live within our means, which are not extensive." His glance gave me a clear sign that he wasn't joking plus his worn and faded clothes told the tale of their limited means as well.

"Oh! Okay, thanks for the bucket." Discomfited once again I got busy with breakfast.

Today I would take a proper bath after he left.

"Today I will come again in the afternoon to take you; a message will be recorded about you." His statement brought me back to the ugly world of my circumstances and the childish excitement at seeing the pail vanished.

I looked at him, his face was hidden and his eyes conveyed nothing. How could they remain so indifferent to the people they held? I felt like throwing up.

"When will you come?" my voice was hardly perceptible,

"In the afternoon."

"What time, so I can be prepared." It was absurd of me to ask him all that, as if I had a watch or a clock to keep time.

"I am not sure." His minimal syllable answers were just as my questions, pointless. What was going to happen was not in his control or mine. He was their puppet and I was their prisoner. We both lived in the limits of our boundaries.

I turned away and waited for him to leave. I had lost interest in a bath, the pail stayed next to the door. Instead, I opened up one of his books to read. The Jane Austin collection, the first page had a name written on it in beautiful cursive handwriting. I tried reading it, "Amara", a nice name I thought, probably the real owner of the book.

Flipping through the pages I couldn't concentrate on it. I had read Austin many times back in the day when life was carefree and the stories of these maidens finding true love midst all the restraints and obstacles captivated the heart, not anymore. I put it down and picked up the other one "War and Peace". The first page had a name written on it in the same handwriting, beautiful cursive spelled out "Zain". These books had two different names but the handwriting signified that their owners were related somehow. I started reading Tolstoy, aware of his place in history, being one of the greatest authors of our time but this was the first instant that I had an opportunity to read his work.

The book was a simple hard cover with frayed corners just as the Jane Austin collection, seemingly of same age. The story narrated about the Russian aristocracy and their bizarre lives. The text caught my attention and took my mind off the eminent meeting with the leaders of this militant group. I lost track of time as I slowly read through the book, it was worn and had all these markings in it as if read by someone many times until I heard the door open once again. Ali was stationed at the door looking at me. I put the book on one side and stood up, he didn't have to spell it out for me, I knew it was time to go.

We walked through the same corridor to the room I had been brought in four days earlier. There was a man clad in traditional Iraqi clothes holding a video camera and two other men clad in black with their faces hidden behind black keffiyehs. I was seated on a chair and then they started their work. I looked out through the window in the wall on the right side, trying to block out what was going on, the sun was blazing and I could see men in the compound walking around, the sounds I heard through the small window in my room had faces now, at least some of them. I also saw a few women walking about, everyone was busy. It didn't seem like a military base but more like the residential quarter of a rural old town.

"Look at the camera." Someone addressed me; I turned my head and saw Ali watching me as always but when our eyes met he looked the other way, probably afraid that I might see something hidden in the depths of his dark eyes.

I straightened my back and stared into the camera lens, nothing else was said, I was videotaped for a mere five minutes and then Ali escorted me back to my cell.

I had decided "Cell" was a well-suited word for my abode. I noticed that the narrow corridor had another door on the same side as my cell before we reached it. There were no doors on the opposite side of the wall meaning these were the only rooms in the building along with the one in the front. This building was kind of similar to the clinic I was working in, a room in the front and two in the back, but did they have another prisoner?

"Do you have someone locked up in this room?" I pointed to the closed wooden door of the room before mine,

"No, that is my room." His answer was short as usual; I would have never guessed that his room was next to my cell, but it made sense, considering his job to keep an eye on me.

He wanted to leave as soon as I was in, but my question stopped him,

"Why do you do this?"

"Do what?" He turned around,

"Take people like me and use us, like we were sacks of flour you could trade for your own goods."

"It is the same that your people do, treat us like we are dispensable commodities not humans with lives and a society of our own." His voice was bitter,

"My people, what do you mean my people. I don't know anyone who would want this war imposed on you and your people." I suddenly got angry, what did he mean people like me,

"Your people are your government who you work for." Anger was visible in his eyes as well,

"How could you measure everyone by one stick?" My response was quick and curt.

"Just like they do, killing people without "measure" as you put it, collateral damage isn't that what we are called." .... "Do you think a child who loses his parents in an air raid or bomb attack understands the meaning of collateral damage?" The pain and bitterness in his voice muted my argument.

Since my arrival I had witnessed the misery these people were living in, wreaked upon them not only by foreign troops but by their own militias and so called liberation groups. They lived in fear of the next day, of the destruction of their livelihoods, and the security of their families. It was a torment to see ordinary people being crushed in the middle of a war that they had no part of.

I had no answer to his remarks, politics not being my forte; quietly I sat on the bed with my head lowered. He walked out.

What pained me the most was the insinuation that I was part of some elaborate conspiracy. My short explanation the other day hadn't convinced him of my sincerity or innocence, but I didn't intend to clarify my position to anyone. It was not what he or his comrades cared about. They had me for a purpose and to justify that they would always have their reasons.

I sat there looking at the bucket sitting next to the bathroom door, and the memory of the past day made me blush, questioning his sternness,

"Why would he behave like that?"

"Does he believe me...... but keeps the pretense going for some other cause." Confounded, my mind was in disarray.

I didn't want to dwell on it; whatever he was up to wasn't for my sake.

Day light had receded to the last corner of the room, it had been a hot day but the warmth felt good like an enveloping fog, lukewarm and comforting. Unexpectedly the heat helped me relax after the strain of the day, I got drowsy and lay down on the bed. Sleep was quick to come but it wasn't peaceful.

I was running in the dark towards a single flame burning in the distance. It became more distant as I ran faster and faster towards it, stretching out my hands to catch it but it was fruitless. Suddenly I was standing in a room full of people with sad and gloomy faces, I didn't know anyone of them, then I heard my dad calling me, his voice was frantic. I could see him at the end of the ocean of faces surrounding me. He was calling my name. I shouted to him, but he couldn't see me and suddenly fire roared all around. People who stood around me were burning, their bodies melted in the flames without a sound. I could see my parents standing far away on the other side of the sea of fire, drifting backwards as I called out for them, then they disappeared and there were just hot flames around me, choking the breath out of me.

I woke up with a scream holding my throat, perspiration beaded my forehead.

Someone caught me by the arms; I completely freaked out, blindly fighting whoever it was,

"Take it easy nobody is going to hurt you." Ali's voice brought me out of my frenzy, he was still holding my arms. His grip was tight but not painful. I looked around, bewildered by my surroundings and the dream, where was I? Was I still dreaming? Was this all an elaborate nightmare?

Apparently not, the same deteriorating cell walls around reminded me. I pulled myself away from him, why was he here? A little disoriented I strained to see him; he was standing next to the bed silent. I wiped my forehead as my sight fell on the food tray sitting on the floor. It was supper time!

"Are you alright now?" he sounded concerned,

"Yes, I just had a bad dream." I pushed the hair back from my face,

"I brought your dinner." He picked up the tray and handed it to me.

"Why do you feed me, when you eventually are going to kill me. What is the rational of this nice treatment? You don't have to waste your food on me." I put the tray on the side.

He didn't reply,

"Please take it away and give it to someone who needs it more than me. I am the enemy, a conspirator, why are you being nice to me, bringing things for me. I am a leach not to be trusted and believed, isn't that what you think. If it's your boss you are worried about, I promise he wouldn't know about anything. I am not going to tell anyone." Frustration poured out of my mouth, agitated at this charade.

I was the enemy then why all this courtesy, they hated me and where I came from; I was part of the murdering band of intruders who were the cause of mayhem in their land.

Why be cordial to me?

I stood up restless and walked to the wall with the window in it, my face turned away from him. I couldn't see his reaction to my comments and frankly I wasn't interested.

"You should eat, I am not taking the food away, and no one is going to kill you. We are not monsters."

"That's not what your leader told me, that's not what the video tape is for. I am the bargaining chip in this ploy and no matter how much you deny it that is the truth. How can you do this? Even if I was working for the so-called agencies, how could you kill an unarmed person without mercy?" I turned around to face him, to look him in the eye, why was he hiding the obvious; he knew it as much as I what my fate would be if his boss didn't get what he wanted.

He nearly threw the tray on the bed,

"Nobody showed mercy to my parents when they were shot down in front of our house, they were not soldiers and neither was my seven-year-old sister. Nobody showed me mercy when I was scrounging the streets for shelter and food. This war has destroyed not just homes it has killed our souls, what do you expect from people who have suffered like that to do." He was almost shouting.

I was shocked by his revelations, the resentment and grief in his voice seemed infinite. His abhorrence had roots deep in his painful past and I was astonished at his decency towards me in spite of all that. Lowering my head, I sighed at the loss he had suffered and the life he had endured. The losses I had experienced were true but his were entirely different.

Ali and I were at the opposites of a spectrum, my life from his, the tragedy of his life was irrefutable, it had made him who he was but I couldn't accept that for his misfortune he would murder others. Perhaps I was naïve on my part, where my tragedy was not inflicted by other

61

people but by the creator who had left me helpless. I couldn't find solace in fighting a war with the presumed enemy.

His outburst quashed any words stirring in my head and I silently went to the bed, his hands were clenched in fists, the strain visible by the veins in them.

"Just to let you know I have never killed any unarmed person. I have fought in many missions but I am not an uncivilized brute. I fight for a cause and that doesn't give me the right to kill indiscriminately, unlike your people." Why was he defending himself to me, he didn't have to?

"And I am not going to be part of killing any innocent people." His last words were a puzzle, being contrary to what his leader was planning. His attempts to defend his position confused me.

We stood there for a few minutes inarticulate, and then he left. Night fell as the light dimmed inside the cell. I wasn't hungry or sleepy, climbing on the bed I sat leaning against the wall adjacent to his room next door, waiting for morning.

Day 6

I hadn't slept most of the night, that and everything which had happened resulted in a splitting headache. It hurt like hell, washing my face didn't improve it, then as a last resort I took the bucket inside and bathed hoping that would alleviate the pain, but it was useless. The tray was still on my bed, I didn't have the energy to move anything. Curling up next to it I lay down holding my head, while my sleeves and the bed were getting wet by water dripping from my hair. I had forgotten about not having a towel to dry myself after the bath.

Lights flashed in front of my eyes as I pressed my head between the heels of my hands in vain.

The door opened with a clink and I could guess who had come in, he stopped a little far from the bed. I was sure, to assess the situation whether I was trying to pull a fast one on him. I stayed motionless as he came close and removed the tray from the bed,

"Are you okay, what's wrong?"

"My head really hurts." I replied in a weak voice,

Without a word he turned and left, tears welled up in my eyes.

Why? I had no idea, maybe because somehow, I was expecting sympathy from him but he had just left, then the door opened again and he was back,

"I have this medicine it would help." He was leaning on the bed with something in his hands.

I pushed myself up, my vision was blurry as flashing lights sparked around, the pain made my surroundings spin. I couldn't sit straight. I suppose the malnutrition and headache both could be accounted for my condition. He leaned a little more and holding me by the arms pushed me against the wall for support and handed me the pills with the glass of water he had brought in. I swallowed the pills and fell on the pillow, semi-conscious.

His presence was unknown to me until I came about, I guessed a few hours had passed because the sunlight had shifted, he was sitting on the floor next to the door with his knees drawn to his chest and his hands dangling from them, his gun holster was on the ground near him.

My head felt better, and I could open my eyes without squinting with pain.

"Why are you sitting there?", Was the first thing I blurted out,

"I was waiting for you to wake up; you need to eat something, it's imperative for your health." He said without moving.

"What do you care about my health." Another blunt remark passed my lips, I tried getting up,

"I do! .... I mean you need to eat so I don't get in trouble." He still hadn't moved from his place.

"What if I don't...." I stubbornly replied as my dry and ruffled hair teased my face. I knew I was being childish; he could make me eat if he wanted to, but my mind wasn't operating on full cylinders at that moment.

"Please you need to." He got up and came close,

"I am sorry for being so harsh, I shouldn't have bullied you. I apologize." His tone had completely changed from the other day, I wasn't expecting this. It made me forget what I wanted to say. I was up by then, sitting on the side of the bed with my feet dangling in the air and he was standing a little far. Only this much activity had fatigued me, raising my hand I signaled for him to give me the tray he had put next to himself. The food was cold, but I ate it and he waited as usual. I always tried not to look at him, there was nothing much to see except for his dark eyes and the verve in them always disturbed me in a strange way.

Finishing the bowl of oatmeal, he had brought I handed him the tray and our eyes met. His dark eyes were mellow today, not a trace of anger rather I could see something in them that made my heart race. I had caught him searching my face and he didn't get the chance to avert his gaze quick enough, the emotions in their depths stirred something in me which I couldn't understand, an emotion I had never felt before. I was relieved when he turned his gaze sideways and left the room.

Feeling better I got up and started pacing the length of the room, random silly thoughts running through my mind,

His room was next to mine, was he in it when I was stuck in here?

But he couldn't be, he was a soldier, he would definitely be out there with others training as I had seen some of them do. I had also seen a few women train with them.

These discoveries were made by the few glimpses I had caught looking through the small window in the wall.

Confused by some of my emotions I wanted to look outside to divert my attention, the window was my link to the world, which was inaccessible for me presently and perhaps forever,

"How to reach it without breaking my back............ the bucket!" the idea made me jump, I ran and got the bucket, plopping it upside down I got on it. It elevated me enough to easily see outside, my dilemma was solved. No more hanging on the side of the bed, but to my dismay the small window didn't show too much.

I could see there were other buildings next to ours and the compound in the middle was filled with people, mostly young men. I was astonished by the hustle bustle; my first guess was correct. It didn't have the appearance of a military base rather it was more of the likeness of a poor rural settlement. This was a good cover for them to keep prying eyes away. All the men in my range of visibility were with weapons and training in some way. I kept watching, there were women as well practicing in a similar manner which I had seen before. Then I saw him coming out from our side. As he approached the middle of the compound, most of the soldiers stopped.

What was going to happen? My curiosity grew; he picked few of the men and a young woman from the present crowd. They assembled around him as he instructed, and then began his lesson in combat. The soldiers were taught strategies and ways to handle their weapons, everyone seemed impressed by him. The training went on in the blazing heat of the afternoon, and I kept watching until my legs started to ache like crazy from standing on the bucket.

With cramping legs, I got off it and put it back in the bathroom. I didn't want him to know my secret. He was still out there working with his men and "women", somehow the women made me uncomfortable. The room was hot. I terribly felt the lack of a fan but had to endure. Sitting on the bed I opened the book he had given me. I had gone through half of it and was sure that I could finish the rest of it by the evening before he brought my dinner. But I didn't intend to return the books yet and wanted to keep them to pass the time. It was obvious I wasn't getting out of here anytime soon.

'No way I'm returning these. They aren't his, so I don't have to.' Like a stubborn toddler, my mind was made up.

I had always been a fast reader. The book was finished by the evening as I had predicted, and after finishing it I put it under my pillow with the other.

It was almost time for him to bring the evening meal. I hadn't combed my hair since morning. Hurriedly I ran my fingers through it and unsuccessfully tried to braid it, but my hair was wavy and thick, utterly unruly. After trying a few times to tame it I gave up and let it fall around my face in a mess of waves and soft curls, anyway I never liked braiding it, this was way more comfortable.

My next plan was to bring the bucket out and take a short look through my window at the world again, but it was cut short by the clinking of the door lock. I rushed to the bed but was stopped in my tracks as he came in and saw me standing in the middle of the room.

The expression of his face was hidden by the keffiyeh, but I could see wonder in his eyes,

"Did I come at a wrong time, were you going to the bathroom, I can come back later." He tilted his head towards the door of the bathroom. I was a little embarrassed but then I decided that there was nothing to be embarrassed of.

"No, I wasn't going to the bathroom; I was just walking around the room, stretching my legs." I smiled nervously; this surprised him even more because I had never smiled at him before.

"You seem to be better; I hope you will eat your dinner." He came closer and gave me the tray. I took it quietly and sat on the bed, I knew he was going to wait on me.

"Can I ask you a favor?" I asked him between swallowing the oatmeal, again!

"Yes, what is it?"

"Can I have some clean clothes; these are dirty and smelly? I can wash them, but I need another pair plus I need a towel, please." I stopped eating and searched his eyes for a reaction. There was nothing there; he was very good at hiding his emotions, with a few exceptions though.

"I will see what can be done." Short as usual,

The meal finished I handed him the tray, drinking the whole glass of water in the end. He made a sound under his scarf like he was deliberating at my level of thirst. How could I explain to him that the small plastic jug of water provided was insufficient in that heat and the water got warm and was hard to drink, so I tried to drink all the cool water he brought with my meals.

He left, there was no more conversation. I hoped he would bring the things I had asked for, not sure whether he would, still it was worth a try.

I pushed myself on the bed and thought about my bucket again, it was dark outside; it wouldn't do any good to spy on anyone now. I thought about washing up once again to refresh before sleeping. I went to the bathroom and as I was coming out, he was back, a stack of clothes in his hands. I looked at him amazed, he had literally listened, but then he had done that before when he had brought me the pail and books.

"Try these they might fit you." He handed me the pile and walked back to the door,

"Please stay I will try them on and see if they fit, if they don't you can take them back." I called him from behind, stopping him where he was. He didn't turn around,

"Okay, I will stay."

I went in the bathroom with the clothes, they were faded but clean. Taking off my dirty ones I wore the ones he had brought, which was a traditional Iraqi women's dress not like the long shirt and pajamas I was in. It was a soft pink tunic with beautiful embroidery around the neckline in blue and green and along the seams, it came with a pair of soft long pants to be worn under it.

"Where did he get this?" I thought as I changed, "Possibly asked someone in this settlement." I concluded.

As I stepped out of the bathroom, he turned around and his eyes got lost in me, apparently forgetting to avoid staring for a minute. I positively blushed,

"I think this is fine, can you thank the person who gave you this on my behalf." I said feeling awkward.

"I will," his response came in a hushed voice like he had trouble speaking.

We stood there trying to avoid staring at each other, both of us immobile. I wanted to get to my bed and hide under the covers, his deep dark eyes unsettled me,

Why was I blushing, I never blushed even when I was with Jake?

Ali had an effect on me which I wasn't able to explain or comprehend. He was my captor, I should have hated him, but I didn't, maybe it was the prisoner captor

70

relationship shrinks talk about. I probably would be a textbook example for them.

But I was sure it wasn't that, sitting alone I had pondered on his comments about his past and I wanted to know more, it was curiosity I suppose,

But why was he looking at me like that? I wondered.

He came out of his state and moved to the door, and I walked to my bed and sat on it, watching his back, when he suddenly turned,

"I will get the towel you require tomorrow." His voice was normal now,

"Thank you, I appreciate what you are doing for me, even though I am your prisoner and you might not even like me." I had a way with words, I was told by my mother, and evidently, I was proving her right.

He stopped instead of leaving; there was something in my words that had pinched him, but I couldn't assess his reaction because of the darkness in the corner where he stood.

"I don't hate you, ... you are our prisoner .... and I know that you assume we hate you, ... that you are in danger, and I am sure nothing I say can convince you otherwise, but this was not a burden. I should have thought about it myself; it was my fault." he stood in the shadows, but his voice was soft and reassuring,

Still, I couldn't understand why he wouldn't acknowledge the fact that his leader was bent on killing me.

I sighed at his ignorance and my helplessness, he was trying to be nice, but it was futile, it wouldn't be of much use in the end if his leadership didn't get what they wanted. "If you say so." Was my simple reply, he stayed there for a minute longer and then left.

Sleep was miles away as I lay contemplating about my future, dread filling my heart. Ali was different, I could feel it but he was part of this militia, their trained soldier, What was his past?

What would he do if they tried to kill me? Would he remain complacent, or would he try to save me? But why would he? He had no incentive to do it, what was I to him but another intruder.

How would dad feel? Did they tell him about me; am I on the news by now?

Questions filled my head and images of everyone I knew flashed before my eyes, even my hairdresser.

Why would I be remembering her? It was weird; maybe it was normal for people in confinement waiting for imminent death to recall every little detail of their lives.

Vivid images of the happy days before mom's illness, of my brothers and parents danced in my memories.

I couldn't stay at home after she had passed away. My plans to join a university in the fall were a promise I kept making to myself but my life had become a drag. Dad had gotten busier with his work, Will and Mike went back to high school and immersed themselves in studies, they were young, and school kept the hollowness at bay. I stayed at home, alone most of the time, cooking and sometimes chatting with the housekeeper Mrs. Dillard. That was the extent of my interaction with people other than my family. Dad asked me to go out and spend some time with the girls I had known in school, but I couldn't take their pity. Always treating me like the lost youth.

By March I was completely going insane, I had to get out of there. Responding to the Red Cross pleas online for help for the displaced and tormented civilians in Iraq, a place ravaged by war, became my new mission. It was a moment of reckoning for me; I made up my mind to join the Red Cross and work as a medical support staff for them in Iraq.

My dad didn't know about it until I was ready to leave in the beginning of April with my basic training as a medic complete. I was given a short basic course to administer first aid and assist in a rural clinic or any small emergency set up.

Dad almost blew his top; he had never expected that I would take such a leap when I had declared that I was going to join the Red Cross. He was anticipating a move to probably South America or somewhere in East Asia, not Iraq.

I didn't yield, I had to do this. Dad couldn't understand my desperation, but he gave in by the end. My brothers on the other hand were excited trying to train me in using a gun, taking out dad's old hunting rifle, showing me all its parts and how to load it. I was least interested but to indulge them I "learned everything" there was about guns.

The day I was to catch my flight from Pittsburg my dad and brothers drove me to the airport. Dad had always been a strong man, the only time I saw him shed tears was when he put my mother in her grave, but as I walked to the check-in line tears glistened in his eyes,

"Take care of yourself for me." were the only words, nothing more but that was enough. I could feel his heart break and my heart went out to him, but I knew I had to leave.

And then I met N as I landed in Baghdad, she had come to pick me, and my life took a new turn. I came to the village where she lived and ran a small clinic for the general populace. She was a trained nurse and the sole service provider in the clinic with no doctors to devote any time there. The country had a shortage of medical staff and facilities. The rural clinics were run by the local nurses, if available, with the help of NGOs. There weren't too many volunteers, because of the fear of aggression against foreigners.

N was startled when she first saw me; my deep gold blonde hair, pale skin and bright blue eyes took her by surprise. She gave me a big scarf to cover my head and face as soon as we were out of the airport,

"You are not what I expected when they told me I was going to get help; you are so young and pretty." She had a worried expression on her face,

"Why, I have the training and I can help, and I am not afraid." I replied with conviction.

She smiled and held my hand, something I wasn't used to,

"You will be fine; I am worried for your safety, that's it. You stand out like an apple among oranges."

Her analogy made me laugh, I was an apple! And she laughed too. N wasn't much older than me, but the tough life she had lived had matured her past her years. She had recently completed her training as a nurse and had started working in a government clinic with the help of the Red Cross. We hit it off instantly; although it was hard for me to open up to her initially. She on the other hand was very easy going, like an open book. I loved being with her, no pretenses only friendship. Work in the clinic was difficult with very limited resources and huge volume of patients but it was my solace, the one thing which brought me comfort. The content faces of patients even when we couldn't provide them with sufficient medicines and treatment made me feel blessed. At least I was given the opportunity to help in some way.

Sleep eventually came as the pictures of my past life ran through my head.

Day 7

Waking up wasn't easy, sleeping so late had me unfocused but the clanking of the darn metal door woke me anyway.

"Can't you come later, I am trying to sleep," I grumbled and turned on my side, ignoring Ali.

There was no answer, which was more annoying than getting one of his short ones,

What was he up to?

I had to turn over and see. He was standing close to the door, mute with tray in hand.

"Why can't you just leave it and go, or if you think I am going to blow it up take it with you and come back later when I am awake." I was leaning on my elbow, trying to keep my eyes open.

"It will get cold," he spoke softly,

His reply made me burst out in laughter. Just the thought of that lumpy oatmeal they had been giving me since my arrival, getting cold and stale was hilarious.

He was surprised by my burst of laughter, now I was definitely awake,

"Oh! I forgot about that! Yes, you are right if I don't eat it now, it will get cold and all lumpy and bland and yucky; we don't want that, do we. It will be a shame to let all the work of your gourmet chef go to waste. I am sorry I will wash up right away and dig in." My mouth was still curled in a huge smile, the idea of that breakfast getting cold was just too much. I couldn't keep myself from laughing.

Ali stood where he was, completely baffled by my gabble. It was quite unexpected for him; I could tell by the immobility of his limbs and his widening eyes. I sat up in bed with the morning light illuminating the cell and my bed as always. It was time to get up, there was no chance of me getting any shuteye anymore.

Eventually he stepped forward, I raised my hand to stop him right there,

"I have to wash up, can you please bring this later or leave it. Take your tray later I assure you I won't eat it."

"Yes, I can, let me just put this on the bed," he moved towards the bed but before he could do that, I grabbed it from him and signaled for him to leave, like he was my personal butler or something.

It was amusing to see the changing expressions in his eyes, especially when I gestured for him to leave.

After he was gone, I went to the bathroom.

Breakfast was not what I was expecting, no wonder he was worried about it getting cold, he had brought orange juice, eggs and toast for me. I hadn't even paid attention to it when I took the tray. He was right it wasn't as tasty cold but it was better than the oatmeal, which was a food not to my liking even at home.

I ate the whole lot washing it down with juice and then sat combing my hair running my fingers through it untangling all the knots until they were smooth. Content with the satisfactory completion of that task I brought out the bucket to spy on the compound. Maybe something interesting was going on. Even though it was early I could hear a lot of mixed sounds. My hunch was correct, today they were not training, most of the men were playing soccer with two makeshift goal posts on either side of the compound.

It was an interesting match with all the players displaying good skill; strangely no one was wearing any keffiyehs. Most of them were in T-shirts, soccer shorts and sneakers, a good choice considering the weather. I was so engrossed in watching the activity that I forgot to stay cautious about Ali's return to retrieve the tray sitting on my bed.

I had picked a favorite team and was rooting for them from my cell, but I wasn't the only one, the teams had a load full of spectators comprising of women, other men and some children. They were standing on either side of the ground watching and cheering. I was happy that I was inside rather than outside as my cell was not as hot.

"If you are done, can I take the tray now?" His voice made me jump; he was standing right behind me.

Startled, I tumbled from the bucket and would have fallen flat on the floor if he hadn't caught me in his arms. In a low voice cursing the precarious pail and myself for my obvious stupidity I moved away from him. The fall and then his embrace was all unnerving enough to temporarily cloud my senses and judgment.

I was still shaking by the time he left me standing in my place and picked up the tray. I could imagine the expressions under that keffiyeh of his, probably smirking at the dumb blonde. I wasn't letting him go that easy,

"Why are you not playing, don't you know how to?" my tone was satiric,

He stopped at the door,

"I had other things to do, I couldn't join them." His face was in the shadows of the door,

"That's a good excuse, probably those players would beat you in a minute, they are pretty good." I didn't know what I was doing, annoying him was not a good strategy but as usual I couldn't hold my tongue.

Now he turned and came back, stopping in the middle of the room. I realized my mistake; he was probably annoyed. I waited for him to snap at me or do something harsh but instead he pulled out a large handkerchief from his pocket and taking the Styrofoam cup from the tray put the tray down on one side. Next, he placed the cup in the middle of the handkerchief crushed it and wrapped the cloth around it making it round like a small ball, I was puzzled by his actions, what was he up to?

What happened next left me speechless, he bounced the makeshift ball on his knees and then like a pro spun it on his fingertips and ended the demonstration by rolling it over it his shoulders, catching it on his foot and kicking it in the air.

I stood there agape, while he picked up what he had come for and left.

My face probably had gone red with embarrassment, mortified at my behavior and remarks, because he was good and he just showed me a demo of his skill without saying a word.

After his departure I got back up on the bucket to see the conclusion of the game outside but it had already ended. Coming down from it I sat on the bed and pulled the books out from under the pillow. I leaned back against the wall and endeavored reading Jane Austin, but it was hard to put Ali out of my mind. The words in the book were jumbled as I couldn't concentrate on it. I wanted to do something to keep myself physically busy.

"Ballet! I should practice. If he is good so am I."

Stubbornness pervaded my brain. Putting the books in their place I stood up and stretched like I always did before my lessons back home. Slowly rising on my toes, I started dancing. My mind was empty, at peace and the world around me disappeared. It was just me, my favorite tune humming in my head and nothing else.

Minutes became longer and I became tired, sweat trickled down my back as I bent and twirled careful not to make a mistake as if my mother was watching me, keeping time. At last, my strength waned and I stopped.

Sitting I pulled my hair up in a bun in an attempt to cool down when there was some commotion outside. I got on my pail to inspect, finding vehicles armed with guns in the compound and men who had been playing soccer a while ago were all in their typical military attire, getting ready for some kind of offensive.

The black garb was in stark contrast to the light clothes they had on for the soccer game. I was abruptly thrown back to reality, no matter how they spent their time this was a war camp and I was a prisoner of this militia.

I came back to the bed and picked up a book waiting for the noise to die down. Eventually there was silence and I could concentrate on reading, but it wasn't easy. My mind was wandering, what was going on? Was there some kind of attack or was this usual practice? The vehicles were no longer there when I peeked out of the window again, the afternoon sun was hidden behind clouds and a cool breeze was blowing, giving respite from the blazing heat.

But in the cell, I was tired and hot, courtesy not only of the weather but also my dancing. Deciding to take a bath I took the bucket and went in the bathroom. Water dripped from my hair and the tunic stuck to my skin when I came out because I still didn't have a towel. Ali had said he would bring one and I was expecting it in the evening, which was arriving soon.

I stood on one side and straightened my hair taking out the tangles.

My attention turned to the books which were under my pillow, I had kept them there since receiving them, it seemed like a good place to store them. I didn't want to put them on the floor. Finishing with my hair I came and sat next to the pillow taking out Austin again. "Maybe I should walk and read like Churchill, which might be helpful to keep my attention on the book." The thought was funny.

I slowly walked and read, it wasn't too bad, just that I got not only tired after about half an hour but also dizzy. This called for some rest, putting the book I lay on the bed and soon fell asleep.

A loud sputtering sound of a big vehicle woke me. It sounded something like a bulldozer outside making all that noise. The cell was dark except for the meager light from the small bulb hanging from the ceiling. Getting up was hard but I had to go to the bathroom so I slipped out of bed and went. Washing my face before coming out refreshed me. Dinner would be coming soon and I didn't want to eat with a stale mouth. But Ali didn't come; I waited for a while and then gave up. Eventually they had probably realized their folly about wasting their precious resources on me.

I sat staring at the wall, it was the first time he was late and it felt strange, like something was missing.

Suddenly the door lock clanked with a familiar sound and he came in bearing the tray.

"Why were you late?" the phrase burst out of my mouth without check, catching him off guard. His eyes widened in amazement.

"I had come earlier and you were asleep so I didn't wake you. You weren't very happy about it in the morning." He raised his eyebrows at me.

I remembered my reaction earlier in the day, and the abruptness now made me bite my lip, attempting to hide my awkwardness.

"Sorry for that, sometimes I just ramble on, my mother used to call me a chatterbox."

"Used to, why?"

"She died some time ago."

"I am sorry to hear that."

I softly pulled the tray closer, for I was at a loss for words. It was oatmeal again. I dumped it down and then emptied the glass of water to take the taste out of my mouth.

I was certain he knew that I didn't like oatmeal but he never remarked about it. Once finished I remained seated on the side of my bed, observing the long dark shadows on the walls. It was much later then his usual time and the room was darker, I didn't know the hour but it appeared to be fairly late in the night. He took the tray but didn't leave as he always did.

I got apprehensive, why was he not leaving? Then my fears were answered by his question,

"Have you read the books I gave you?" He scanned the room as if I had hidden them in a nook or cranny somewhere.

"What books?" the words slipped out of my mouth before I could stop myself,

"My books!" his tone changed suddenly, the calm in his voice was gone replaced by urgency. He looked around the room again, clearly striving to find them. I quickly pulled the books out from under the pillow and hid them behind me scooting back on the bed. I held the books tightly in my hands with my back pressed against the wall and looked at him insolently,

"Where are my books? His voice was harsh this time,

"I threw them away." I just couldn't stop, I could see the changing color of his eyes even in the dim light and it was obvious that this might get out of hand but I couldn't stop myself for reasons unknown,

"You what!! No, you didn't, you have them." Fury reigned in his voice,

"I don't have them, what do you care, they're not yours anyway." My voice also rose,

"What do you mean they are not mine?" His tone was getting deadly now,

"I know that because, seriously Jane Austin and Tolstoy, I can't imagine you reading them. When do you get time between shooting people and kidnapping them?" My last comments did the job, he threw the tray on the floor and dashed towards me.

"Oh my God, what have I done, I should have given him the books." I closed my eyes waiting for the worst. But he came near the bed and only threw the pillow and blanket on the floor in an effort to find the books, and then he observed my hands behind my back.

"Give me the books, you are hiding them, they are mine." He stood towering over me as I sat crisscrossed on the bed, my back against the wall. This was the occasion when I should have relented, but not me, fear was a characteristic I lacked.

"They are not, and to prove it there are names of people on them which are not yours, so you probably stole them from somewhere, and definitely keep them to impress others of your literary skills." My voice was quivering, but I didn't want to give him the books, how could he claim someone else's things as his own. I knew it was absurd but my mind was made up and I wasn't going to let him have the books. Rationality had completely abandoned me at that moment.

"I know you are hiding them behind you, I am asking you for the last time." He looked menacingly at me,

"No!"

My answer was the last straw for him, he leaned forward and thrust his hands behind me trying to snatch the books out of my hands. Everything went crazy after that, we were struggling like little kids, as he tried to grab the books, I pushed myself further in to the wall holding them tightly. In all this his face was practically inches away from mine, his body bent on top of mine trying to keep his equilibrium while fighting with me to get the books out. Eventually he lost his balance and crashed into me with his face resting on my neck and his hands behind me.

I froze so did he, his breathing was labored and warm, sending a shock wave through my body. I was in his arms with his whole body weight on me. I could hardly gasp, my heart slowed and then raced like it would break out of my chest. Slowly he straightened up pulling out his keffiyeh tangled in my curls.

"Please give me those books."

"You need to understand they are very important to me, please." His voice had lost its fury and he sounded beaten,

"Why?" keeping my eyes lowered I asked, I could scarcely speak, the closeness of his body had made my head spin like it had never before, I could hardly think or breathe. There was a strange sensation pulsating through my whole body.

"The names you see on them are my parents." He said in a broken voice,

"These were their books, and one of the few possessions I have of them. You are right I am not the type to read Jane Austin or Tolstoy. In your opinion I am a brute and maybe you are right. But the people these books belonged to were one of the most loving and beautiful people in the world. I could never measure up to them but I have to live this life which I was dealt by fate." His speech was fragmented as he turned away.

Those books belonged to his parents, the parents who had been killed along with his little sister, I remembered. How callous of me, I had been so cruel, so quick in my judgment. Taking out the books I stood up next to him and handed them to him. He just took them and held them close to his heart, which was enough to tell me how much I had hurt him.

"I am so sorry, I was very mean to you, please forgive me." I placed my hand on his shoulder, an involuntary instinctual action, but that made his body tense, I could sense it. Removing my hand, I sat on the bed giving him space.

"Please tell me about them, I would like to know." I asked him sincerely.

He didn't move for a few minutes and then he came and sat next to me on the bed. This was the first time he had done anything like that.

"My father was a teacher. He taught history in a college and we used to live in the city, my mother also taught but she was an English teacher. She loved to read books; her particular favorite was Jane Austin's work. This was one of her most cherished books; it was a gift from my father. She bought Tolstoy for him as a gift so he would feel obligated to read it. I remember he wasn't very happy about it. You see it's a long book and nothing to do with his subject, but to please my mother he read it and once he had, he loved it." Ali spoke in a low voice, his mind wandering through the past. I sat motionless listening as he continued,

"My sister was five years younger than me, always running around the house and playing. She was a very happy child; her favorite things were fairy tales and dolls. We played hide and seek inside the house and outside, sometimes hiding in the street. My mother stopped us many times especially when the war broke out." Ali's eyes were staring blindly at the wall across us.

"We weren't supposed to play outside that day when they came for my father because he spoke against tyranny and division. I think they didn't like that, him challenging their agenda. They killed him and my mother and my little sister. I was hiding, because we were playing hide and seek, they didn't get me." Ali's voice sounded hollow as he got lost in the depths of desolation. His whole body stiffened, struggling not to break down.

"Ali I am so sorry to hear this, I know nothing I say can heal this wound but I hope they are in heaven smiling down at you." Somehow, I wanted to make him feel better, to take away his pain, regardless of the fact that I was his prisoner.

He turned his head and looked at me, a myriad of emotions in his eyes. The sheer intensity of emotion in them made me lower mine. Then he stood up agitated, his mood changed,

"My parents died at the hands of someone who I have been searching for all these years and once I find him, I will take my revenge. Then I will be able to die in peace. My parents never wanted me to become a soldier. They hated violence, they wanted me to be an engineer and you know what?....... I have an engineering degree, a degree that gives me an edge in warfare, isn't that funny" he laughed caustically, "and I fight because I have to, I have to settle the score." The cold tone of his voice gave a glimpse into his tormented soul.

He was pacing in the room, haunted by the ghosts of his tragic past. I didn't say anything, there was nothing to say.

His life had been a living hell since his childhood, the time I had spent in the loving environment of my parent's shelter he had been on the streets destitute and then had been picked up by this militia to do their bidding.

Since my arrival in Iraq, I had worked with families, who had suffered similar losses, in the clinic but I had never seen someone so up close. N's family had been lucky, only a few friends had suffered at the hands of the intruding forces and then the local militias. But I had always seen her worried about her family and husband to be. Security wasn't a given for these people. They had to fight for it or leave their homes to find it.

Ali's story was similar to some of the others I had heard but his was so close to me and I could see firsthand what that violence had done to him. His education and his talents were all a waste because of his obsession with revenge.

"How did you get your degree?" I wanted to distract him,

"These people were instrumental in that; I am a chemical engineer; they have me trained in many things for their own purposes." Sarcasm dripped from his voice.

I could imagine what he might be trained for, but I didn't want to delve in the subject more. Suddenly he stopped and stared at me for a while and then darted out of the room leaving the tray lying in one corner. The door closed with a loud bang and it was locked with a clanking sound.

I knew sleep was a privilege I wouldn't be enjoying that night, dwelling on all that had transpired between us.

Day 7 (Ali)

Why did I pour my heart out to her, I couldn't even begin to fathom? For the first time in my life, I had told my story to someone and this someone was the enemy. I loosened the keffiyeh around my neck and took it off.

It seemed like a noose around my neck, but we had to wear it per our leader's orders and we had to obey orders. She didn't understand that, whenever I tried to assure her of safety, she confronted me and refuted it, although against my nature I had divulged to her what I knew. I still couldn't reveal to her that this was all a strategic game.

'She will be safe.'

I removed the gun and went in the bathroom to splash water on my face.

I had promised myself that I wouldn't get close to her, wouldn't indulge in conversation after the bathroom incident but when I took her the bucket, the sheer joy on her face to be given such a trivial thing was enough to undo any of my vows of silence. That was the day we video-taped her for the message Daanish was planning to send. I saw the light extinguish from her bright blue eyes when I mentioned it. During the recording session and after it she was very passive as if it was happening to someone else. But her questions, why did they hit me so hard? I wanted to clarify myself so desperately to her, why?

"But she thinks that we are monsters, she doesn't believe that she won't be harmed."

I sat on my bed leaning on the pillow thinking about the coming mission, but my mind wasn't in my control. Images ran rampant, she was troubled by something, I looked at my hands which had held her to calm her after she had that nightmare and now when we had struggled for the books. Stretching on the bed my head commanded me to stop but then I wound up recalling the day after the video tape, how she had asked for a change of clothes and later thanked me for the old dress I provided her. She never blamed me for keeping her, only questioned why it was so.

My room was lit better then hers with two light bulbs which were turned on now as I tried to divert my attention from her thoughts to the upcoming mission and its preparations. Dragging myself I got up and checked the weapons, everything was in order, then I checked the plans lying on the table and they were complete, ready to execute. I went to my closet and took out the loose pants I wore to sleep. Changing into them I laid on the bed shirtless, feeling hot. Maybe it was the heat of June or the temperature rising in my veins with her image taking over my consciousness. The dress I got from Jaria fit her well, hugging every curve of her body. I couldn't take my eyes off of her, she had noticed but instead of getting apprehensive she blushed making it even harder for me to keep focus. Why couldn't I leave her side that day? Even though I tried. I slapped my forehead, why was I turning into a softy? I couldn't let this happen; this obsessiveness had to stop. I got up and pushing the table with my feet made it tumble and fall on the floor with a loud clang. My first instinct was to look at the wall adjacent to her room, 'did I disturb her?'

'What is wrong with me, I need to focus on more pertinent issues like the next step in my quest to locate the murderer of my family',

Daanish had promised that he had found some clue about the murderer and we could catch him after the operation. But as my head hit the pillow the image of her watching the game outside, standing on that flimsy bucket made me smile. It was funny the way she balanced herself on that thing and cheered for the teams outside. I just had to watch that innocent display. She didn't look like a subversive intruder at that moment or in the morning when she kept jabbering on about the food and laughed with such spontaneity at my insistence on eating her breakfast. It was the first that I had heard her laugh. Closing my eyes, I reveled in her laugher as it melodiously rang in my ears. This was maddening; I couldn't stop myself even if I wanted to.

My eyes flung open as the day replayed within them down to every little detail, how she felt landing in my arms unexpectedly after I startled her and to the sensation of her skin against mine when I crashed into her trying to get my books. Raking my fingers through my hair I staggered out of bed, recalling my agony when she ridiculed me about having those books. I couldn't endure it and divulged the truth about them for the first time. I let her see through me, bared my soul to her, letting someone in for the first time. How was it possible? It was against everything we were trained for and made to believe. I had allowed her to enter territory which was off limits to her, but she was in and I was powerless to stop her. She knew my story even more than the leader of our militia, the one who had picked me up from the streets, educated and trained me.

The clock on the wall softly chimed the hour as I stood resting my head on the wall and promised myself that I will stop this. I was treading on dangerous ground that could turn to quicksand at any instant, swallowing me and her. It had to end, all of this was not possible, it was unheard of and completely unacceptable.

Straightening I paced in my room in the dark turning off the lights trying to bring focus to my mind. Tomorrow I had to lead the attack and I couldn't do it with my head in the clouds.

Day 8

Light was piercingly sharp that morning or maybe I was waking up later than usual. The night before created so many doubts in my mind and yet so many questions were answered. Sleep had eventually caught me by the early hours of morning. It had been heartbreaking to hear Ali's story. I could relate to his pain in a small way. My mother was taken from us without any violence and it hurt, but to have his whole family murdered in front of his eyes. I couldn't even begin to measure the trauma he suffered at such a young age, being left all alone in this world so cruelly.

Still, I wasn't in the mood to be awakened by him for his breakfast brigade, and I wondered how he would bring the meal without his precious tray, as it was lying in one corner of my room since the past night.

I turned on my side to face the wall and avoid the light, but my mind kept replaying the scenes from the other day. It had been an unusual one in every respect, the game being played out in the compound, the trucks brought in and then driven somewhere, Ali and I, our skirmish and his opening up.

'I definitely should get up and wash' because I was positive, he would be on his way. But a surprise awaited me when I came out of the bathroom; an older woman was in the room holding a platter of food for me. Disappointment griped my heart,

"Where was he?" Maybe I could ask the old woman,

She was a tacit person and my inquiries went unanswered, she ignored my queries and simply took the tray and the empty plate after I was done. There was something ominous about her presence, her scrutiny of me and her complete disregard of my questions. After she departed from my cell, I couldn't concentrate on anything, pacing in the room aimlessly. I didn't climb on the flimsy pail to scan the compound, and I didn't try to read the books Ali had left behind.

Interestingly last night when he was done pouring out his heart, he had walked away without the books. The reason for all the commotion between us and now he was missing.

This emptiness was a first for me; I had a new sensation of loss which baffled me, it was unlike anything I had experienced and I wasn't ready for it.

Was it him? I should have been happy if he was gone, one less enemy to deal with but regardless of what I told myself he didn't seem like the enemy and I couldn't shake this strange new feeling. At last getting tired of pacing, I sat and opened one of the books with a new respect for them, now that I knew who they belonged to and how important they were.

Tracing the written name with my fingers, I imagined Ali as a young boy running after his sister being lovingly scolded by his mother and then his father. I could visualize them sitting in a small comfortable house with books piled up in shelves and light curtains hanging in the windows, gently swaying in the breeze. A household full of love and security. As I turned the pages the scene in my mind changed to a violent disastrous episode of people running in the streets and his parents lying in pools of blood, his little sister........... I couldn't dare to think of what had happened to her. An innocent young life snuffed out mercilessly. Amid all that I saw Ali standing, a young boy with his world shattering to pieces around him, his life extinguished before his eyes leaving behind the shell of a human being with his being crushed.

I couldn't take it anymore, putting the book down I got up again and dragged out the bucket scraping it over the floor with my foot. Placing it upside down, I stood on it trying to occupy myself with the scene outside. It was midday but unusually there was not a single soul in the big compound. Wind swept the sand under the burning sun in the empty space.

Where had everyone gone?

Clank! The sound made me turn around to see who it was, hoping to see the hidden and familiar face, but it was the same old woman. She was staring at me severely; I jumped off the pail, a little embarrassed.

"You won't find him there." Her tone was stern; this was the first thing she had said to me. Her cold voice and insinuation made me wince, "him who?" I pretended not to understand,

"You know who I am speaking of, he is not for you." Her language skills weren't like Ali's or the other men, she spoke with a clear accent, but was very much able to convey her hatred.

"I don't know what you are getting at; nobody has anything to do with me." I swallowed to wet my dry throat, suddenly it had gone bone dry and I had trouble uttering words.

"The dress you are wearing, I gave it to him. It was my daughter's." her eyes were fixed on me in a gloomy stare,

"Oh! Thank you, can you give her my message that I really appreciate her giving me this dress." I knew now how she knew about me being with Ali.

"She doesn't need it anymore, she is dead. She was killed in an air raid. My beautiful daughter!" Her eyes were glassy with her mind back in the past.

I went mute, how could I have known her daughter was dead, no wonder she hated me.

"It looks good on you, I heard what you did for that girl, it is hard to believe but if Ali believes you, I do too." Her expression mellowed as her attention came back to the present.

Thank God! She didn't hate me; I couldn't take this burden of guilt hearing everyone's stories and tragedies.

"Please believe me when I say this, I am very sorry about your loss and everyone who has suffered. I joined the Red Cross because I wanted to help ordinary people who have no voice, who become collateral damage when these so-called liberators clash. We are the ones who pay the price of these horrible wars with our lives and blood. I wish so hard that this never would have happened." I stepped closer to her to console, but she took a step back and I stopped.

"It is what it is and we have to live with it, so will you, he has to let go of you and let justice be done." Her tone changed again; I couldn't understand her riddles. What did her comments mean? One thing that struck me was her numbness about all that had happened and what might be my fate. In her eyes it would be an act of justice, but could I argue with that? Convincing her that I was innocent was useless.

I turned and sat on the bed, at a loss of words, blank and fatigued.

"What is your name? Mine is Sarah." I said a few minutes later when she didn't leave, something to start a normal conversation.

"I am Jaria, I know your name, he talks about you." Her answer was short and again confusing.

"Where did everyone go today? The whole place is empty."

"They are not here; if you need anything you can tell me." Talk about pointing out the obvious.

"No thank you, are you in this building also?"

"No, this one only has you and him." She was good at being short syllabled.

I sat quietly for a short while waiting for her to say something, but she stood near the door silently. This was awkward, if she had left, I would get back to spying on the compound or try to rest, do something other than be the focus of her sharp scrutiny.

"Do you want anything from me?" Eventually I had to ask.

"No."

"Would you like to talk?"

There was no answer from her. I gave up and pushing myself up on the bed leaned against the wall and closed my eyes.

"Do you like him?" This sudden inquiry startled me by the bluntness of it. It took me a few moments to reply to her bizarre probing,

"Like whom? I am a prisoner, if you have forgotten that. I can't like anyone; this is not a TV drama. I am waiting for the verdict of your leaders whether I will live or die. I don't have the luxury to like anyone." I spoke with my hands raised in exasperation, what did she want from me? Asking me about irrelevant things.

"You didn't answer my question." Her stare was undeterred. I was done with this, closing my eyes I tried to shut her out. After a couple of minutes, the clanking sound of the door closing made me open them. She was gone at last, leaving me in peace. I came to the door and looked through the bars, nobody was in the corridor, she had left the building. I came back to my bed contemplating what had happened, her strange inquisition and then the insinuation that I liked Ali. Why would I like him or he fall for me? We were from two opposing worlds pitted against each other. It was absurd to think about such an occurrence, but what did she mean by "he would have to let me go." I credited that to the ramblings of a grieved soul.

Still the question remained what was I supposed to do with my time? I was done with reading and peeking out of windows, nothing was interesting enough to keep my attention. I lay on the bed imagining what the leaders of this pack had planned for me. Different scenarios materialized in my mind's eye and none of them were pleasant. I was positive these people had no intention of letting me go alive, but ironically, I wasn't bothered as if by some miracle I would be saved. There was this sense of conviction that it would be okay in the end. Still my dilemma remained, it was hot and I was restless the only sane thing left was for me to do was to take a bath and cool my nerves.

I did that and came out dripping as always due to a lack of towels. At that point I was sincerely inclined to call on that old lady and ask for a towel, but I was out and my clothes were already wet so there was no need to invite trouble. I walked around the hot room letting my long hair dry, combing and untangling them with my fingers. Dusk was visible through the small window in the wall. After walking like a zombie for a while frustration set in and I wanted to bang the door and get someone's attention even that old woman. Giving in to the urge, I started banging on the metal door, shaking it wildly, making a lot of racket. No one came, I felt that I was the only living soul in that whole place; the old woman had also disappeared. There was no sound outside or inside, complete silence surrounded the place as darkness spread.

A hint of fear crept into my mind, "what if all of them had left and forgotten about me.

'What a way to go!'

I got back to the bed and tears welled up in my eyes. I hadn't cried for 'me' since this ordeal had begun, but tonight I was crying. Bizarrely I was crying on being left alone. Imprisonment was an odd thing and it played games with your mind. Solitude was my only companion and I should have reveled in it, to be rid of all, but instead I sat on the bed with tears running down my cheeks watching the shadows darken in the cell. The dim light bulb unsuccessful at illuminating it.

Suddenly there was a clinking sound and the door opened, I jumped to my feet, expecting the old lady but it was Ali, he was back from wherever he had gone, carrying the tray of food.

"Where were you? Why did you leave without telling me?" I yelled uncontrollably, extraordinarily happy to see him, which was even more confounding than my outburst.

His eyes enlarged in wonder and then the color changed as they became deeper and darker.

"I didn't know I had to inform you about my travel plans." There was a hint of marvel in his voice as he walked over and handed me the tray, then he noticed my tear stained cheeks and red eyes,

"Were you crying? Did someone hurt you?" his voice had anger wrapped up in it as his eyes explored my face. I quickly wiped my cheeks with the sleeve of my tunic,

"No, I am fine, nobody hurt me, and your friend Jaria was here. She brought my meal earlier. She is a nice lady." I didn't want anyone getting in trouble over me, his tone sounded alarming.

"Please eat, I have to go and rest, it has been a long hard day." He turned and leaned his tall frame on the wall next to the door. His keffiyeh was dusty and so were his clothes. He was wearing black today and it seemed strange on him. I sat and started eating. I wasn't very hungry, swallowing slowly I was taking my time; he changed his posture and tried to stand straight. I was deliberately not paying much attention to him, but his voice made me look up from the platter,

"I have to go, you can keep the tray, I will take it later." I nodded and straightening up he stepped towards the door. I was watching him, there was something wrong because his feet were trembling and his gait staggered, I attributed it to fatigue, then before he could cross the threshold he actually swayed and hit the wall,

I quickly put the tray on one side, "Was he drunk?" It didn't seem like it, his speech had no slur in it, but he was definitely woozy because now he was holding the wall trying to keep himself from falling.

Instinctively I ran to him and putting my shoulder under his arm gave him support to stand. He tried to stand on his own and move me aside but his eyes were closing as he tried. I almost fell under his weight as he finally passed out; his tall and wide frame making it very hard for me to hold his weight, and I had to lay him on the floor. Rushing to the bed I fetched the pillow and placed it under his head, he had fully lost consciousness. Suddenly I realized if he was unconscious, even if it was for a short period, I could escape.

"But why had he collapsed?" I asked myself standing next to him. Me and my inquisitive brain! My curiosity was answered when I saw the floor being painted red with blood under his right leg. He was hurt badly I could assess that by the amount of blood on the floor. Bending down I checked his leg; the cloth was ripped from one side and a deep wound was visible with a blood soaked makeshift bandage around it. My eyes looked passed him. I could escape but if I left him there, he could and probably would die because of the blood loss as we were alone in this building. I had to make a choice quickly either to get out of there or save his life, and peculiarly the decision wasn't hard.

Kneeling I took the knife from the belt of his trousers and tore open his pants on the right leg to expose the wound on his thigh. There was a wide gash, caused by a bullet I guessed, which was poorly bandaged with blood oozing out of it like a fountain. I had to stop the bleeding if I wanted him to live, for that I required cloth or bandages. But I was short on both, scanning the room I saw the pile of my clothes lying in one corner and the light blanket on the bed and the belt around his waist. I pulled out his belt and tied it around his thigh above his wound and then rushed to the bathroom to get some clean water in the bucket. After washing the wound, I wrapped the strips of my blanket around his thigh. It stopped the bleeding to a certain level but he had lost a lot of blood and I realized an infection could set in the wound if he didn't get further medical attention. I had to find someone to help me, securing the wound I dashed out to see if I could find Jaria. As I emerged from the building, I saw her coming from another small edifice, her mouth gaped when she saw me running towards her, lifting her hand she stopped me, and then I saw she had a small gun,

"Please come quick and bring some medicines and something to drink he is badly hurt." I stopped, gasping for air,

"Did you do something." she hadn't moved an inch from her place,

'What was wrong with her?' we had to rush,

"Are you listening to me I was coming to look for you. Ali is severely hurt. I bandaged his leg but he has lost a lot of blood and will lose more if we don't hurry. Get the first aid stuff now!!!" I rambled on franticly. I wasn't waiting for her, turning I sprinted back inside to check on him and to see if the bleeding had stopped. If she wanted to shoot me, she could do that in the back.

He was lying on the floor, his face still covered with the checkered scarf, I hadn't even gotten a chance to remove that and see his face, but there was no time for such trivialities. I checked his eyes and his pulse; the blanket strips were holding but I wanted to suture the wound and apply medicine.

"Where was Jaria?" I came back out of the cell to find her rushing towards it with a bag in her hands. She entered the room and was caught by surprise at what she saw. I signaled her to hand me the suture and medicines in the bag and clean bandages. We got to work, by the time we were done, his leg was wrapped in clean bandages and he was propped up in my bed with an extra pillow under his head brought in by Jaria. He was still unconscious but the bleeding had stopped and I was hoping he would wake up soon.

At first Jaria was stunned by my behavior, possibly because she had witnessed an inconceivable event. I hadn't tried to run or escape rather I had stayed to help despite the fact that my life was on the line.

We stood next to the bed after securing his leg,

"Do you have anything to drink, like juice or something stronger?" I asked her, keeping my eyes on him,

"I will fetch some juice." She got up and left,

"I know you don't drink alcohol but, in his condition, a little bit can boost his energy." I called from behind.

He had been out for more than half an hour now and I was getting worried as I had no idea how long he had been losing blood.

'Why had he come when he was hurt like this, he could have had his wound taken care of and rested?' His actions were irrational; they made no sense to me, 'Why endanger himself?' Jumbled thoughts knocked at the boundaries of my reasoning, but I let it be. Thoughts like that would only make things more complicated than they already were.

I sat on the side of the bed waiting for Jaria. Ali's face was still covered, Jaria also hadn't removed his keffiyeh, but now we would have to, if we wanted to give him something to drink or eat.

She was back before long, her hands full with juice packs.

"Can I remove his scarf? I will try to wake him and have him drink some of this." I pointed to the juices.

"I think you know what to do. I will leave you to it. I didn't bring alcohol as we don't have it, but the juice packs should work too. I am tired and need to rest for a while. All this running around has fatigued me. If you need me call me, I am where you found me." Jaria had not sat after dumping the juice packs in my lap. It was clear she trusted me for keeping him safe and was leaving him in my hands.

"Okay I will call if I need you." I replied simply, putting the juices on the floor next to the bed. Jaria walked out, locking the door behind her,

'How was I supposed to call her? Maybe scream at the top of my lungs!'

The corners of his eyes twitched a bit due to the pain, but he still was unconscious. I needed to awaken him and give him some liquid, it was essential. It was obvious I had to remove his keffiyeh which filled me with a sense of dread for some reason, but in all honesty, I wanted to and had to.

The anticipation of finally being able to look at his face made my stomach twist, to see him after so many days of imagining what he looked like under that thing was daunting. Apprehension filled me as I reached for the loosened keffiyeh and my heart pounded in my chest loud enough to be heard in my ears. Slowly I touched his scarf and carefully pulled it down, revealing the handsome face of a man in his early twenties, but his face was pale due to blood loss. He had a contoured jaw with full lips and his stubble made him look older than he probably was.

I got lost in his face my hand still holding the keffiyeh until his eyes flew open and he tightly caught hold of my hand, staring directly into my eyes baffled, his lips parted but no words came out. He was still holding my hand from the wrist.

"What happened? How....... why did you take this off?" eventually questions came rambling out in a whisper. He jerked my arm pulling me close, frightening me a bit, but then I saw the utter confusion in his ever expressive eyes.

"Everything can wait you need to drink something." With my free hand I picked up a juice pack. My calmness made him loosen his grip around my wrist and relax.

He needed to sit up and I could prop him up further from the front but the mere idea of getting so close to him while he was awake sent a warm tingling down my spine. Handing him the juice I gently released my wrist from his grip and went behind to push him up. Using the pillow, I was able to raise him a bit so he could easily drink the beverage. There were no more queries; he silently drank the juice finishing it in a few gulps.

At this moment I strictly directed my mind to view him as a patient and nothing more. After he had finished the juice, I checked his pulse and his wound. He had completely settled down and normalized. I could observe the color returning to his lips and cheeks but he needed more nourishment so I gave him another pack and called Jaria from the cell. Just as I had anticipated, I had to scream her name loud enough to wake up the dead.

Ali was silently watching me; he hadn't said a word after his initial questions and quietly finished the second juice also. I waited for Jaria to come, which she did after a while bearing a platter of food. She had somehow guessed he was up and in need of nourishment, and then strangely enough she gave me the meal and left. I had thought she would stay and relieve me of the responsibility as he was awake now, but she had no such intention. She did lock the door behind her, which was clue enough that she did trust me with his life but not with an open cell door.

I came to his side once more. Jaria hadn't even stayed to talk to him, 'What kind of friendship was this?' I shook the thought and sat on the side of the bed,

"You need to eat something; the loss of blood has left you weak and this should help." I placed the platter on the side next to him. He had to sit up if he wished to eat and that meant I had to push him up further, or 'maybe he could do it on his own'. Without my help he did try but the pain in the wound made him grunt, clenching his teeth he pushed himself to sit up right but it was hurting him. Instantaneously I went behind to help him sit. Once he was upright, I returned to my position on the side of the bed as he picked up the plate of food.

I sat there motionless while he ate. Talk about a reversal of roles! He was restrained to the bed and I was the delivery guy. It was later in the night and the room was cool, because the temperatures at night fell, and it was usually the time when I felt a bit of relief with the room getting more comfortable.

He was done with the food in a few minutes; nothing passed between us as I waited on him. He had become very placid; it was a little unnerving to be there as he reclined back on my bed. Aware of the oddity of the situation I stood up, not in the mood to sit.

"Do you need anything? I can call Jaria." My voice came out a little shaky, this whole episode had drained me in a way, and now I couldn't even sit to rest.

"No." a concise answer as usual,

'Maybe I could bring the bucket out and sit on that.'

"Are you going to stand all night?" He had reclined, a slight smile on his face,

"No, not really I was hoping to get the bucket and sit on that." I said plainly.

"You can sit on the bed. I won't bite." He replied in the same manner pointing at the corner of the bed,

"Why did you do it?" He started to pull the remaining part of the keffiyeh off his head, revealing a full head of dark hair, not long but not very short.

"Did what?" sitting on the place pointed out by him I replied innocently like he had just asked me about the weather,

"Save my life and not escape." His eyes were fixed on the blood stain on the floor where he had collapsed.

"I don't know, I wanted to run, but I couldn't. I can't explain it. I just didn't." I had a difficult time answering that question myself since the inception of the night, but there was no clear answer. And now I didn't want to find one. I knew it would take me to a treacherous territory, somewhere I wasn't ready to go yet.

We both sat there without a single word passing between us, until a loud racket outside caught both our attention.

"They are back. I should go to my room." He looked at the flashing lights streaming in through the window casting sharp rays of light on the wall opposite it.

"But you won't be able to move."

"I have to, you need to stay here."

"Well, I didn't have any plans for my vacation." I made a face at him; he didn't pay any attention to it concentrating on getting up from the bed.

He was trying to stand up but it wasn't easy, he groaned loudly and held on the wall as he scooted down from the foot of the bed. 'Why was he so worried about the people making noise outside?'

112

I stood in the middle of the room watching him walk slowly holding the wall and approaching the door leading to the corridor. I wished to help him but being near him made me feel strange and wonderful at the same time, a feeling I had trouble acknowledging. It was better he walked alone. At the door he found out that the key was missing, Jaria had taken it when she had left, but before he could yell her name she was there, 'was she psychic?' God knows but she opened the door and let him out locking it again as he hobbled to his room next door leaning on her.

There was something about the arrival of those outside that had both of them in a panic, "Why?" I thought.

Dragging out the pail I climbed on it to see what was so special about the people outside. There were trucks mounted with heavy machine guns, like the one which had escorted me here, and more pick-ups with rocket launchers. There were dozens of men dressed in the same garb as I had seen before, running around yelling to each other and busy with different tasks. It was a surreal scene like in a Hollywood movie with warlords and their men bearing automatic weapons getting ready for battle. The whole compound was lit up with lights from the scattered buildings and the vehicles. I kept looking; it was simultaneously frightening and interesting. The hours were pushing past midnight when they started to disperse, packing things and winding up in a way. There was one man in the middle of it who had been the main driver of all the soldiers around; he was distinctive in his appearance and behavior. The way he carried himself made it clear that

113

he was the leader of this lot, although it wasn't discernable whether he was the topmost brass. Eventually the noise died out and the compound was deserted except for a few strays. I got off the bucket. The muscles in my legs were terribly strained and my feet hurt. I hadn't realized how long I had stood on that flimsy thing. Worn out I came to the bed and straightened the pillows, now that I had two, fluffing them and setting them just right for a good night sleep hoping to drift into dreamland as soon as my head hit them. But contrary to my hopes my mind was awake and sleep was miles away as I lay in the very spot Ali had been occupying. It was an awkward situation with a distinct feeling of being cozy yet uncomfortable with an acute awareness of his presence there earlier.

Day 8 (Ali)

It had been a bloody battle and I was prepared for it, but we took a severe beating. The other militia had better weapons and was ready for a counter offensive before we were even there. According to our calculations it should have been a surprise attack but actually it turned out to be a surprise for us rather than them. They had been informed. There was no other explanation; it was obvious they knew about our imminent arrival. It was only instinct that some of us had made it out of there. The attack was a lost cause and I had to re-strategize to save as many of us as possible. It paid off but not before I got shot and narrowly made it out alive. The mission was far from our base and the ones who survived had a long drive back. I left for medical assistance with some of the other wounded. The plan was to make camp at the interim base a little far from our site and then move back to our actual base. Once at the short-term station whoever required it received medical treatment. The solider treating everyone had worked with a doctor somewhere, and after he patched me up and he advised me to stay put. Everyone had returned to regroup at the mid station. I was supposed to rest there for a while and keep pressure off of my leg but as I sat in the recovery of our small operating room my heart was restless, pulling at me to leave. My brain advised me to drop the idea but there was a force within me relentless and obstinate, wanting to get back as soon as possible. I waited for the sun to set and then without telling anyone took one of the jeeps and drove back to the base before the others. On the way I justified my stupidity with being vigilant and cautious about the captive or that the prisoner was my responsibility and I had to answer to Daanish if there was trouble or that it was vital to keep surveillance over her. She, who was going to prove instrumental in achieving our goals. I could have found a million reasons, but regardless of whatever rationale I gave for taking that risk, the end result was always the face of Sarah appearing in my mind. Finally defeated I stopped conjuring up reasons.

As soon as I was back in the base, I went to see her, by now I was convinced of my madness because my leg had started bleeding during the hour's ride and the bleeding had increased by the time I had gone to her cell. But her reaction after she saw me completely shocked me. I had thought my absence wouldn't concern her in the least but she was practically yelling at me for disappearing on her.

Somehow it felt good, her abrupt anger and agitation. Was she worried about me? I wasn't certain, it might have been anger at Jaria or because of something else. I didn't want to live in illusions, still it felt heartwarming. She had no clue of my escapade and ate her dinner quietly after the initial outburst but by then I was excessively bleeding. I knew it was imperative that I should return to my room and do something about the wound in my leg but I had misjudged my own endurance. Instead, I had passed out in her room. And surprisingly Sarah didn't escape, she didn't leave me there to die rather she gave up the only chance she had to live to save my life. I looked at myself in the mirror hanging above my wash basin. She had removed the keffiyeh and seen my face, the face of a soldier, of a lost soul, of the empty shell of my life.

I was not afraid about revealing my identity to her. I had wanted to take that scarf off many times but couldn't and now fate had done it for me. I leaned on my crutch and went to bed. I had to think, my life was becoming more complicated every day. Sarah had me questioning all that I thought was right and proper; she asked me things which I had no answer for. It was the first time ever anyone had the courage to talk about my parents and how my life would reflect on them. She brought to light the contradiction of my life, the parents I wanted to avenge and their dreams for me. I was helpless to defend my stance when she had pointed out that fact and I let her criticize me and to challenge me about my parent's will and their aspirations for me. It was clear as day that I had changed and if I could feel it, I was sure people around me were also getting the hint. Jaria had pointed it out to me a few times and she had warned me about the rest of the troops. There was no love lost among us; we were all soldiers of fortune in a way. Our allegiance was to the cause of the group, not to the individuals. Our betrayal was punishable by death and it was equally handed out to any soldier who was found guilty of treason. Jaria had been worried about me. I didn't blame her. I knew sanity was slowly deserting me. I had compelled myself to stay away from Sarah and had pushed hard to keep my mind occupied with other tasks but it was proving to be unattainable. Jaria lived on the base and keenly observed the changes in me, she scolded me for losing sight of reality but today Sarah had astonished her with her selflessness, proving many of her suspicions wrong. Jaria had kept me apprised of the growing suspicion within the camp of soldiers. She was alarmed and I trusted her instincts completely. She was one of my parents' old friends and had lost everything herself when her husband and daughter had died. Like me her life was empty. Somehow, she had come to live at the base and we had met by accident. I was the one who had recognized her; it took her a brief time to remember me once I reminded her of the old days. It was a moment of serene joy to find someone from my past who had known my parents. I cherished her company and heeded her advice and she treated me like family. Her life was ruined as mine because of her family's sympathy for the liberals and unionists. She blamed the outer powers for killing her family but I was sure that one of the militias was responsible for it. She was the one I could talk to and had asked for help when I needed anything for Sarah. I couldn't trust anyone else.

I was aware of the jealousy and rage of some of the other soldiers for me because of the preference given by our leader. I had risen in the ranks faster than anyone, some admired that and the others detested me. I had proven my worth to Daanish with my timely spontaneous decisions and hard work. He had picked me up from the streets a year after the murder of my parents. I still couldn't figure out how he had found me but he located me and took me in. He saw my potential, training me in warfare and sending me to study, encouraging me to become an engineer. My education and training made me who I was today. His righthand man, and some of the soldiers despised that. Since those days our small band had grown into a huge military group with Daanish leading us.

Daanish had promised me to locate my family's murderers on the day I had started training. We had a pact; over the years this was discussed on multiple instances and he always guaranteed that he would soon seek out the murderers. My agreement with him, when he had taken me off the streets, was to serve him in return for that information and we were still looking. Why hadn't we found them yet! Frustrated I slapped my leg and the sharp pain brought me back to the present.

The past was always with me, whenever I went on missions, trained and fought but since Sarah had come the lingering memories were replaced by a new face. Try as hard as I could to push it aside it stayed with me. Today I was convinced of the feelings I had for her; it was impossible to deny my heart the truth anymore. I had come back to the base for her and almost paid with my life to do so, if she hadn't saved it.

'But I cannot and will not let anyone know about this, not even Jaria and especially not Sarah. She has to go back and I have to get her to safety at any cost. My feelings are not relevant or important.' Firm in my conclusion I pulled myself up on the bed, the dull ache in my leg reminded me of the limitation of my bliss, I could want her, see her but could never have her. I lay on the bed with sleep distant and my dreams weary, regardless of the fact that I had taken an amount of pain medication that could put half the base to sleep.

Day 9

Jaria woke me from a pleasant dream where I was in a desert full of flowers. It was a colorful dream but there was no one there except me. I was all alone and wandering through the rainbows and flowers wondering where everyone had gone. Sands danced under my feet, and I could feel them carry me with them. Just when I was sure there was no one there, I saw the silhouette of somebody in the distance, far yet close enough to know it was a man. I recognized that shadow and wanted to call him, see him but just as I was about to, Jaria woke me up. Talk about rude intrusions.

I wasn't surprised by her being there, it was obvious last night that Ali won't be mobile for a couple of days. I got out of bed quietly and washed up.

It was the same ritual every day since my incarceration. I awakened, washed up and ate my meals but during that there were periods of rest and aimless pacing in the room or the looking about through the small window. Some days the activities outside held my attention and proved to be interesting but usually the scenes were similar, guys practicing their war tactics, honing their fighting skills, women sometimes joined them but mostly they were helpers and morale boosters. At times they were very loud making me uncomfortable, but this was their culture, I had experienced similar sentiments at N's wedding, which was a combination of colors and festivities. Reverting back to the past I recalled being given new clothes by her and being made a guest of honor as she considered me her best friend. I couldn't imagine being anyone's best friend let alone hers, but she had brought me into her life and made me a part of it. Unassumingly she had pulled me into her world, where I felt secure and comfortable. It was anomalous, in this land of turmoil I had found peace and friendship. Her wedding had been a beautiful event, with all of us dressed elegantly and made up to support the bride. N for the first time since our friendship didn't insist on me hiding my deep gold blonde hair, she even had a beautiful head piece made for me with beaded flowers and gold chains running the length of my long hair. I joked with her for turning me in to a Cleopatra wannabe but she dismissed the idea with a giggle and told me she wanted all her cousins to be jealous of her pretty friend and I didn't argue with the bride. Day of the wedding came with all the trappings and gaiety expected of such an event. I had been at her house staying with her for the last few days before the wedding; it was all the last-minute preparations and nervousness accompanied with it that had everyone jittery, including me. During one of the last days N had asked me reluctantly for wedding night advice assuming I had some experience in that respect, but my candid admittance to having no knowledge beyond high school health class made her break into a fit of laughter. She apologized later for her assumption but there was nothing to forgive. She was so nervous on the day of the wedding, I tried to calm her by reminding her that her husband-to-be was crazy about her, and he would love her and cherish her regardless of anything. But she was not concerned about that, rather was worried about disappointing him.

It was a little sad for me to see her so worried about him. Would I ever have anyone who I would care about so much that it would give me sleepless nights and butterflies in my stomach?

"Are you going to daydream or eat your meal." Jaria's shrill voice jerked me back to the present. I was in my cell sitting on the bed bleary eyed with a tray of food lying on my lap. I ate the meal and sat quietly waiting for nothing. Jaria had not stayed a minute more than she had to. I tried reading one of the books Ali had given me, but my concentration was off. I had to make myself busy, so I decided to take a bath and change my clothes, 'That was bound to keep my mind occupied.' I did that and wore my old clothes, which I had washed previously. After my shower, I attempted to wash the new ones Ali had given me but then I dumped them in one corner and sat on the bed combing my hair. My mind was going crazy. I couldn't understand why. This day wasn't any different than its predecessors but I couldn't focus on anything. I couldn't even calm myself.

"Ballet!" The word popped in my head as my mother's words flashed in my memory, that I had a gift, a talent that could keep me busy and satisfied when I had nothing to occupy myself or no one for company. I always argued with her trying to convince her otherwise, to avoid learning it, but she was persistent and I eventually ended up being one of the best pupils in my class. I had learned to love it and after she was gone it had kept me sane. Many mornings I had passed dancing, practicing my moves and just losing myself in it.

I remembered the second day after my abduction I had tried to practice it, being crazy as such but it had calmed me. I hadn't tried it after the second time. I wanted to show my captors that no matter how they intimidated me they wouldn't be able to break my spirit. We all have to die but I wouldn't die afraid of them.

Determined I stood up and tied my shirt to tighten it around my waist, and then I started dancing with a mellow tune playing in my head. I danced until I was dizzy and my feet hurt.

Tired I sat on the bed panting when I saw him leaning, with a crutch tucked under his arm, on the door frame outside, silently watching me. His face was not covered any more, the keffiyeh hung on his shoulder, but the features were obscured in that spot due to the shadows but I could imagine the expression of contempt and derision on his face. I lowered my gaze, not in the mood for any gibe and insults, not that he had ever been like that, still I wasn't in the mood for anything.

He didn't go away like the first time, just stood there making me upset, 'What did he want?' He should do whatever he had come for and leave me in peace.

"What do you want?" tucking the strands of hair behind my ears I asked him, a little irritated.

"Nothing."

"Then why are you standing there?" I was exasperated with his monosyllable answers,

"To watch you." A simple reply, lined with mirth, What was he so happy about? I had sensed the hint of laughter in his words.

"I like the way you dance; it has grace and elegance." He was still in the shadows.

Now I was dumbstruck. A compliment from him, a soldier in the army of devastation. I might be dreaming,

"Did I hear you right? You just complemented me on my dancing. Shouldn't you have rebuked my behavior?" My voice conveyed my bewilderment.

"What is beautiful should be acknowledged." He stepped in the light; his handsome face was visible with an expression that was inscrutable. What was he thinking? I could only imagine, 'Why compliment me?' Was there some hidden agenda or was this his way of saying thank you.

"You were supposed to rest. Jaria brought my meal you needn't worry." I wasn't going to give him the satisfaction of acknowledgement.

"I wasn't worried. I am trying to exercise my leg, don't want to be a cripple." His answer was flat, hinting on the futility of my assumption that he might be indebted to me in any way. I pulled back the hair sticking on my sweaty neck and forehead to tie them up in a messy ponytail which I had forgotten to do earlier and it had proved to be a mistake with my hair going wild with all that jumping and perorating. My sole hair scrunchy had lost its elasticity, I had to pull it hard to tie up my hair and prevent it from slipping out of it.

He watched my losing battle with my hair, a slight smile on his lips. I comprehended one fact. It was easier when his face was hidden, those eyes of his were very communicative but when there was a face to go with those deep dark eyes it was a whole new avenue to play havoc with my nerves.

Giving up, I lay down facing the wall trying to ignore him, 'Why should I talk to him?', 'What was there to discuss between us?'.

He got the hint and I heard him leave with his crutch. As soon as the sound faded into the distance I turned and laid straight on my back. His presence unsettled me in mysterious ways. The fact that I had given up my only chance of escape to help him, frustrated and baffled me even more than before. I should have escaped rather than help him live. He and his comrades were bent on killing me, 'Why didn't I?'. This question had bothered me since the previous day. I attempted to chalk it up to the training I had received and my own temperament. I couldn't let life

126

be taken when I could save it, even if it meant the life of an enemy. I wasn't that cold blooded. Turning my head, I stared at the dusty floor strewn with grass and dirt. I had been living in this hell for the past nine days and there wasn't any news of release. Perhaps that was what was driving me crazy that day.

The door unlocked and Jaria came in with some other men. Three to be exact. All with their faces hidden behind keffiyehs. I jumped to my feet alarmed, but Jaria put up her hand to signal me to stop.

"You need to come with us." She said in a low voice. I had no other option than to follow her and the three goons out of the cell. The door to the room next door to mine was closed. I went through the corridor to be stopped in the outer room once more. There was the camera crew and the same old chair waiting for me. They shot another film of me but this time I was asked to say my name and where I was before it was over. I looked outside the open window as before to find that the same vehicles were parked outside that I had seen arrive in the dead of the night.

First, I was thankful that these guys didn't come when I was practicing my ballet. I couldn't imagine what they would do if they had caught me, but then I scolded myself for being a coward, 'what do I care if they discovered me or not, my spirit wasn't bound by them'. They could incarcerate me but that is where their power ended.

They left me in my cell with a message that this was the second tele-message they were sending describing their terms and if my government didn't take the deal they would only wait for a fortnight before they executed me. It was evident that my government wasn't being cooperative and they were agitated by that. I just hoped that after the second message they might arrive at some kind of agreement, but I wasn't counting on that. Jaria left with them and locked the door. I stood in the middle of the room void of feeling, completely numb.

Jaria came back a little later with my meal and a surprise, new clothes and a bed sheet. She put them on my bed and picked up the others I had dumped in the corner. I wanted to thank her and explain about the dumped clothes but my mouth was dry and I was drained with no energy to speak. She probably could make out that much, without saying a word she tucked the clothes under her arm and left. I ate slowly, swallowing every bite with difficulty, I drank some water to sooth my dry throat but it didn't help. With great discomfort I finished the food and sat with my back pushed up against the wall, eyeing the set of clothing. It was of pale blue color, same as the other one in design I suspected, but it looked fresh and nice, better than what I was wearing. I picked it up and hung it, holding the shoulder seams in my hands. The dress was soft and pleasant. I would have appreciated it more if I wasn't to die in the next fifteen days.

Nevertheless, I appreciated Jaria's attempt to comfort me. I folded and placed it on the foot of the bed. I decided which was the foot my first day in the cell. I laid on the bed watching the shadows get longer by the minute with no clue to the exact hour. Not knowing about the exact hour was frustrating. I was always the one who ran life on a schedule until my abduction and here I had no idea of hours or minutes. I assumed Jaria would come again. I wasn't anticipating Ali since his visit in the morning, which was also unexpected. The room was warm and I didn't need the thin blanket I was provided with, so I drew it over my eyes rather than my body, pulling it tightly with both hands, trying to block out the anxiety.

"This will only hurt your eyes."

His voice made me almost fall off the bed, standing in the middle of the cell with his crutch he dominated the small space. How had he come in without making a sound? Or maybe I was so preoccupied that I didn't hear him.

Whatever!

Why was he here?

"What do you want?" I asked bluntly putting the blanket on one side.

"I was bored so I thought why not check on you." He tilted his head on one side; the corner of his lips was slightly curved up in a smile.

Today he stood there with a faded T shirt and jeans like any other young man of his age. With everything removed from his visage his appearance had completely changed, the short dark hair perfectly complimented his dark intense eyes, a clean-shaven jaw line more pronounced and his full lips pressed together, waiting for my response. I caught myself staring at him; he seemed amused by my interest and embarrassment. Trying to save face I quickly started studying the dress Jaria had given me.

"Do you want me to leave?" He was barely leaning on his crutch clearly his leg was on the mend.

"I have no say in the matter, dead people have no voice, they only listen and obey." Acrimony was audible in my words,

"You shouldn't call yourself dead, if you want, I will leave. I am not going to impose on you." He sounded sincere. It made me laugh, the irony of it all, he was nice and treated me like a human being but his boss had plans for me like I was a sheep for slaughter. Ali was surprised by my sudden reaction,

"Why do you pretend ignorance when you have full knowledge of what your boss has planned for me."

"What has he planned for you?" His question really drove me over the edge,

"What he has planned, as if you are unaware that he is going to kill me in the next fifteen days. I am his bargaining chip, a sacrificial lamb. He sent another message today to my government that if they don't yield to his demands, he will execute me on camera so that everyone can see." I was almost screaming.

Ali stood there like he was struck, not saying anything. Silence bore down on me and he didn't move. I half wished he would refute any knowledge of such a thing or try to deny being part of it all, but he was silent and expressionless.

"Why don't you say anything, did I spoil it for you, can't you still have fun playing with the dumb blonde?" My voice broke by the end.

I had trouble controlling my feelings in his presence. I had vowed that they won't break me but now I had given into the despair wrecking me internally.

"I didn't know he was going to do it now." That was the only thing he said. His countenance had a dark shadow making it stony hard. His statement struck me. It meant that he knew what were his boss' plans, only that his comrades were becoming hasty rather than taking time in executing me.

Why was I such a fool to believe that he wouldn't be part of it? My heart sank when he didn't deny knowledge of it, adding to the nauseating feeling in the pit of my stomach

"Who told you?" His question caught me by surprise, 'What?'. He wanted to know who had spilled the beans. His choice was for me to go to the gallows unaware so I wouldn't put up any fight or try to escape and remain naively hoping for the rescue which was never coming.

"That's it! You want to know who informed me of my fate. Why?! To punish the man who has been honest enough to tell me the truth and not let me linger in darkness!" I wanted to yell more but my energy gave away.

"No! not for that, but....... I know who it might have been, he likes to play with people's minds, likes to torture them." He kind of addressed me and himself.

"I am sure what he told you is not true; our leader has no intention of killing you. It would be a strategic mistake and no wise general makes a move that would jeopardize his plans ensuring future victory for him." Standing in his place he was lecturing me about military strategy, about keeping an ace up one's sleeve until it was time to take it out and make the most of it. How cruel and callous could he be? I had been mistaken about him, but stubbornly my heart still believed that he was better than that, he was compassionate. How could I be such an idiot? I actually slapped my head,

"Why are you hitting yourself?"

I didn't care to answer his questions; it had become painfully clear to me that I had been naïve. His mild manner was deceptive and alluring for good reason. No wonder he was one of their best.

Ignoring him I started looking at the solitary window where the moon light was shining, weakly filtering in through the small openings. Maybe he would go away if I disregarded him enough. Apparently, I was wrong in that respect as well,

"I know you are angry but you need to understand that some things are beyond the control of some." He had stepped a little closer now.

"Beyond control, how do you justify killing innocent people? Avenging the blood of innocents by spilling the blood of more innocents." My words flowed in slow motion as I turned my eyes on him. It was better when his face was obscured. Now I could see that his facial expressions conveyed nothing. The keffiyeh had been a blessing in keeping me immune to his stoic countenance.

"Sometimes you have to give up many things to achieve success. I am no different. I saw my parents gunned down mercilessly with no fault of theirs. I have to avenge their deaths and I will use any means to do it." Suppressed anger and despondence came pouring out as he spoke, his face stone hard with hatred.

"Your parents were killed by someone no different than these people whom you serve. How does that justify anything? Do you think your parents would condone this? You are bent on killing so their deaths can be avenged. How does that even compute? You will let these thugs kill innocent people and not lift a finger. Did they give their lives for this? For you to turn into a monster." I challenged him sitting up, having had enough,

"Don't talk about my parents. What do you know about pain and loss?! You haven't lost anyone like that." He snapped back at me.

Enraged I stood up and came face to face with him,

"How can you judge me?! I haven't seen my parents gunned down but I just lost my mother to cancer. She died slowly over a period of months and I sat beside her helpless waiting and watching as life slowly deserted her. If I could move heaven and earth I would've to save her but I couldn't. I couldn't do anything! I sat there watching her die every minute of the day painfully. The man I was engaged to marry died in a car accident just before the wedding. I saw him being brought in broken. It's not only you who has seen grief and suffering, but we carry our burdens differently. I came here to alleviate others distress, to find solace in their happiness. You asked me that day why I saved N, because I would not let a life be taken if I had anything to do with it and she is not only my friend but my sister and I'll be damned if I let anything happen to her.......................... You asked me why I saved you. You tell me why? You answer that question." I finished panting, my hands clenched by my sides,

With my last words he stood there looking at me shocked.

Minutes passed as I tried to compose myself and moved away from him. There was a storm reflecting in his eyes but his face bore none. It was indeterminable what was going through his mind. I stood under the window waiting for him to say something but turning on his heels he left without a word. Drained I fell on my bed and closed my eyes, but sleep was miles away.

Day 10

Nightmares haunted my sleep and I woke up exhausted, not only that, my stomach hurt like it was being drilled from the inside. I barely made it to the bathroom and back, "Maybe I was going to die?". The thought made me smile and then grimace as pangs of pain shot through my body. I wasn't sure what was happening but when I came back to bed, I felt something and I knew in an instant what the mystery was.

I had to see Jaria right away. I sat on the bed forcing myself to control it but it was as futile as pushing the wall behind me.

Clank! The door opened and a sigh of relief left my lips finding it was Jaria as I had hoped. I figured that the quarrel of last night, and the wound would have Ali indisposed. As soon as she was in, I called her to come closer but she got suspicious and stopped a little far from me. I stood up from my spot and it became crystal clear to her why I was calling her and what I would need along with new clothes. She rushed out locking the door behind her. I sat back in my place feeling awkward; as if being in this prison wasn't enough, I had to have the good old menstruation cycle catch me!

Jaria was back shortly with all the supplies I would need. I went in the bathroom and she started to change the sheet of my bed. It took me a few minutes but I quickly came out changed and with a pile of dirty clothes. She took it and silently left. I sat and finished the breakfast that had become cold during this. I also had wanted to ask for pain medication but in the process of changing had conveniently forgotten. Now the escalating stomachache reminded me of my mistake, but nothing could be done. She wasn't coming before the evening. I would have to tolerate it until then, evening seemed like an eternity away. I curled up on the clean sheets trying to block out the cramps in my stomach and legs, losing track of time with the mounting ache making me dizzy and nauseous.

"Are you okay?" Ali's voice seemed to come from a well,

The pain had shot up in the hour after Jaria's visit. I always had this problem and mom had multiple medicines for me at home but here there was no such luxury. I could feel tears running down my face but I didn't have the strength to stop them. I couldn't ask for help. I had been kidding myself. Here everything was a deception, the kindness, the care, all was a farce. I was exhausted by all of it and had lost hope. My efforts to persevere, to keep myself indifferent to all that surrounded me had failed, today I was beaten. I felt like dying right there, right then as depression clouded my mind.

Ali's voice made the tears burn my eyes even more. I didn't want him to see me like this. I didn't want anyone of them, but it was too late he was standing near the bed. I didn't move. I couldn't.

"Sarah, answer me, what's wrong?" he was leaning on the bed,

It was the first time I had heard my name from his lips. It made me look up at him. He was standing close with the crutch under his arm. Our eyes met and for the first time he didn't avert his gaze, they had the same sentiment I had seen before sometimes, when he wasn't quick enough to hide it.

"Ah!" groaning with pain, I curled up further holding my stomach, it was becoming unbearable.

"Jaria!!" he screamed from where he stood and then went out as fast as he could. My consciousness had become sketchy. I heard footsteps coming close and then voices but everything was getting muddled. I didn't care who was there or not, it was all a mix of distorted images for me until someone took my arm and poked a needle in it, after that everything went dark.

I woke up groggy and disoriented; it felt like I had been asleep for ages.

"Where am I?" I whispered to the form sitting next to me, the soreness in my stomach was gone and I could straighten my legs.

"You are in your room." Jaria's voice was unusually soft.

"My room." I scoffed trying to sit up, but it wasn't easy, my head was doing somersaults. Holding it I fell back on the pillow.

"You shouldn't, the medicine still has its effect, you must rest." She got up from a chair next to the bed. It was a new addition to the limited furniture.

"Can you help me go to the bathroom? I need to use it." I tried raising myself again and she assisted me. My head was wobbly but I was able to walk on my own. Jaria was next to me, ready to assist in the event of an accident, slowly and safely I made it back to the bed after the trip. Splashing cool water on my face had also refreshed me and reduced the residual effect of whatever medicine they had given me. Jaria took her place next to the bed on the chair.

"How do you feel now?"

"Much better." I was more conscious than before and sat on the side of the bed with my feet planted on the ground.

"Do you feel hungry?" Jaria was looking at me.

Why were they being so kind to me. I fumbled with the folds of my new dress. I liked this one better than the others, it was a combination of an orange and red print; Jaria had been smart in picking it, keeping my condition in mind.

"Would you like some food?" she inquired once more,

"Thanks for the dress, I forgot earlier. It was very considerate of you to help me out." I said without paying attention to her question.

"It was nothing; now tell me do you want to eat?"

"Eat?"

"Yes."

"Maybe later, what time is it, how long did I sleep?" I searched for the sunlight which had receded to a corner of the room.

"It is afternoon, about five o'clock." Jaria answered a little confused.

"Five o'clock, the hour my mom would make us snacks and send us out to play in the yard. She was very particular about that. She believed in getting exercise and fresh air. Sometimes she would play with us, it was fun, dad was mostly taking care of the farm outside and he loved watching us out in the fields running around going crazy. I was always the leader. The favorite of my parents, they always rooted for me not for the boys, who got jealous of me, but that was fake even they rooted for me." I spoke incoherently in a trance, as if my surroundings were not real, as if I was in a land of fantasy.

Jaria stood up and left the room with a strange expression on her face. I just sat there uninterestedly watching her depart. The room suddenly filled up with people. I looked at them as they walked around me impervious of my presence. My mother, my father and my brothers, N with her husband smiling at me. Perplexed, I closed my eyes to shake off the illusion, this was not real, but when I opened them they were still there surrounding me. I wanted to call them, talk to them, but my throat was choked and I couldn't utter a word. I stared at my loved ones slowly fading away with glassy eyes. My mom was the last one to vanish, becoming part of the mist. I had to stop her, screaming I tried to run after her but someone caught me before I could.

"No! Let me go, I have to go home." I yelled as someone held me tightly by the arms.

"Please let me go." Tears ran down my cheeks as I gave up and collapsed in the arms of my captor. The person holding me carried me to the bed. I heard the strained grunts from whoever it was. My brain was in a state of disarray, images and thoughts clamored against each other in it. I couldn't make out fantasy from reality at that moment.

It was Ali who prevented me from running and then brought me to the bed, he sat on the chair Jaria had vacated. I saw him but then I didn't. It was like he wasn't there. I looked past him at the wall as my mind catapulted into lost deep memories. I was probably losing it. My whole being seemed to be falling deep into an abyss of shadows with no one there to pull me out. Suddenly everything went dark again.

I woke up to the soft coaxing of someone,

"Sarah, wake up. Sarah."

'Was it dad?' I turned towards the sound but opening my eyes I realized that it was an illusion. Ali was calling my name trying to wake me up. Why did his voice sound so familiar and safe?

I closed my eyes once more,

"Sarah please wake up and eat something." He was gentle as he called my name again,

Why was he being so tender to me? Why were they keeping me here? Why doesn't he just leave me alone? Many questions confused my thought process.

"Sarah wake up." He tried again; it was clear he wasn't going away.

"I am awake, why are you here?" My mood wasn't cordial, the drowsiness and confusion were gone and the realization of my surroundings was back in full force.

"Why don't you leave me alone?" I said angrily,

"I can't, I mean....... it's my responsibility to make sure you are alright."

Pulling down the sheet covering me I sat up and looked at him. My eyes full of indignation.

"So, it's your responsibility to keep the sacrificial lamb healthy to have a great show."

"Sarah, please you need to understand there is no threat to your life. I am sorry for being so insensitive before. I was just caught by surprise and couldn't answer your questions properly." He was sitting on the chair again.

I scanned the room in the pale dim light of the bulb; Ali was the only person present. Jaria wasn't there. I didn't know how to respond to his explanation. I didn't trust anything he was saying, there was no reason for me to do so.

"Ali, you needn't explain yourself to me. I am not the one who can question you." The bitterness in my tone was evident,

"I am sorry if I made you feel like that. I didn't mean to hurt you, that man who told you that you were going to be executed was only trying to harass you. It is not going to happen, it's not what our leader told me, so I am sure that he was just trying to scare you, some of these men are complete animals." Ali's voice was reassuring and somehow, I wanted to believe him, but then again the words of their boss echoed in my memory.

"You are trying to tell me that he was lying and your leader has no such intentions, but you have forgotten one thing, your leader informed me himself that I would be executed if he didn't get whatever he wanted." I critically looked at him,

There was a puzzled expression on his face. He didn't answer me right away and then something occurred to him,

"I know the reason. It was to make his threat genuine because if you spoke of anything in front of the camera or weren't intimidated enough no one would take him seriously. I have asked him and he assured me that he has no intention of harming you." Ali was speaking fast as if he was going to run out of time with an urgency in his voice as if he wanted me to believe him more than anything else. His account had no substance, but I didn't challenge his assertion any further, even if I didn't, he believed that I was safe.

Well, we both would find out in a few days.

"You don't have to defend anyone Ali. I am fine, and I am not angry with you." I scooted off the bed, heading for the bathroom. There I could be alone and clear my head.

"Do you need anything? I can call Jaria." He stood up too.

"No, I am going to be fine." I answered without turning back.

When I came out, he was in deep thought and didn't pay attention to me. His face was lined and brow furrowed, something was bothering him but I didn't intend to probe him.

Standing in the bathroom I had objectively deliberated on my situation, my gut instinct was that his leader was lying when he denied any maltreatment towards me, but I had a strong hunch that Ali wasn't part of his grand plan whatever it was. Maybe it was wishful thinking about Ali but there was no doubt in my mind that his leader had every intention of killing me when the time came. I only hoped that I wouldn't have to find out.

I passed Ali sitting on the chair and sat on the bed straightening my new dress which was all creased and crumpled due to my bouts of sleep. At that moment I was lucid and acutely aware of my situation. I knew the negotiations would be only a delaying tactic on the part of my government and a testing strategy on the militia's part. If I wanted to get out of here alive, I would have to try on my own. I wasn't under any illusions about my captors or my government. The episode in the afternoon was done and over, I suppose the madness had to rear its head at some time as sanity and my patience reached its limit.

I was so lost in my thoughts that I didn't see him leave or return. I came to when he pushed the tray of food on my lap.

"You were so quiet I decided to get something for you without asking." Raising his eyebrows, he sat.

My brain was fast at work; I didn't want to annoy him because I could use him. His manner was deceptive so would be mine.

"I was not the only one quiet, still thank you, it's very kind." I smiled. Ali was a little surprised by my attitude. He nodded in return and sat quietly. I observed him as I ate, his face looked drawn and tired, there were dark circles under his eyes and his clothes were frazzled. It was obvious he hadn't shaved in a few days, the stubble was thick, but amid all this he still looked handsome. I wondered how many people he had deceived with his looks. Quickly finishing the food, I handed him the tray and scooted up on the bed leaning on the wall behind me. He was silent and so was I, we both were at a loss for words, a minute or so later he stood up and headed for the door. I didn't comment, simply watched.

"I think you should rest now, it's very late." Pausing at the door he pointed at the window in the wall streaming in the moon light. I nodded and sat where I was. He eventually turned and left.

The past two days had been a maturing experience. My silly optimism was gone along with my trust. I had become resolute that I would use any means possible to escape. My only dilemma was Ali, he was an enigma portraying to be principled in all this violence and chaos, but how could he be immune from it? It was impossible. He was their ultimate soldier. How was it possible that he wouldn't know the real plans of his leader? My heart wanted to accept his argument but my brain warned me, and I had chosen to listen to my brain for once. My plan was to win his confidence and then use him to get out before the fortnight was over. Thinking about different scenarios I fell asleep. The path to achieve my goal was something I was still working on.

Day 10 (Ali)

Jaria had taken over for the morning. I didn't mind. I and Sarah both needed a break. The message and then the harassment had really stressed Sarah and then I had not been able to handle the situation any better making matters worse. She distrusted me and was convinced of my dishonesty and my alliance with her tormentors.

When Jaria came back, I was sipping a cup of coffee washing down a bland breakfast. Jaria had never condoned my indulging behavior towards Sarah, positive that she was a spy and was not to be trusted. The story of Sarah, saving the life of her Arab friend despite the danger to her own life, had shocked Jaria. She couldn't believe it but she did when some of the other soldiers corroborated my tale. It was difficult for her to lend her only daughter's clothes when I had asked her; she had kept them all this time in the memory of her. She had given them because she regarded me as her family now, and cared for me, even if she didn't agree with me and I respected her for that. She trusted that I wouldn't jeopardize my mission and position with Daanish as he was my only source to finding the murderers of my family. In the past I had always been so focused and undeterred but now there was a change and she knew it. In the past few days, she had provided whatever I required for Sarah without question, but she was concerned that I was losing sight of my purpose and of the threat involved in doing so. When we were about to depart for the mission, her remarks stunned me; she warned me to keep my mind clear of Sarah if I wanted to live. She was severe but very direct when she said, "Ali you need to let her go. Justice needs to be done and you will let it happen if you want to succeed."

She had never hidden her dislike for Sarah but this statement confused me. Why was she asking me to let her go, and what was that about justice being done? Did she know something I didn't? What was going to happen?

Jaria's remark had shaken me because until then I had shunned the thought of anything between me and Sarah and fiercely suppressed the emotions stirring in me. It hurt like hell but me and Sarah, it was unthinkable and I was in no delusion. Still there was this thing about her eyes, the way she looked at me sometimes; it made my heart go wild.

Jaria had given me a riddle which I was still trying to solve when I had returned from the mission.

The mission had been a trap and I had come wounded seeking to see Sarah. I had conceded to the truth of my real feelings for her that day. That day all my doubts disappeared. I risked everything just to be there with her and she saved my life. She didn't have to, she had no reason to, it was her perfect chance to escape but she gave it up to save the life of her captor. I was baffled by her. Jaria's strict façade began to crack after that, she softened; it was visible from her caring attitude towards Sarah. Today she had asked to take breakfast for her and I had not objected. In the heated conversations after the injury Sarah had blamed me of deceiving her, and I was still working out the knots in my mind about her accusation. She was convinced that we were bent on killing her, but I knew that the plan was just to harass her government nothing more, make them sweat and get what we wanted.

Daanish had assured me before all this started that the prisoner wouldn't be harmed. We could keep her indefinitely but there was no intention to kill her. I had known him for nine years and trusted him, there was no reason for me to doubt him. Sarah's fears were fueled by the false information given to her by people like Jabbar just to tease her and cause problems for me.

Jaria stood at the door as I picked up the plate and put it in the sink. She was back and looked troubled watching me sip the coffee. Her expressions were stranger than usual. I waited to hear something but that was never the case with her. A little frustrated I asked her if there was a problem,

"You should be careful around her; she might not be well." That was all she said and got busy with the clothes in her hand, apparently Sarah's. I didn't understand what she meant by that, but if I knew her, asking anymore questions would be a wasted effort. I decided to go see Sarah myself. Our building was next to Jaria's and it would have been a short walk to it if I had not been called upon on the way by some of the new recruits to help them. They trained for about two hours. I was done instructing and they were done learning. Ready for a break we all dispersed and I got a chance to visit Sarah before lunch. I anticipated seeing her dance just as I had the day before, there was a grace and elegance about her which I had never seen. There had been instants when I had accompanied some of the men to places where they could get their fill of women and alcohol. There I had witnessed women dance but it was not beautiful or graceful. It was crude and lustful not like the way Sarah stepped in the clouds. I was amazed by the first sight of it and the second time it was even better.

Visualizing it I got to the room but found her curled up on the bed. Scared, I called her but she didn't respond and when I eventually called her name she turned and looked at me with a tear-streaked face. It was the strangest feeling; I had never been scared for anyone since the death of my family. I believed my heart had become frozen and would never be alive again but for Sarah I was frightened. Agonized I wanted to take her in my arms and comfort her but I couldn't. I had to control myself, hiding the misery of my heart within my soul. I ran to get Jaria. Sarah probably needed medicine and possibly Jaria knew what was afflicting her. Her comments in the morning made sense now. She came as soon as I called her and some others accompanied her too because of my indiscreetness. I had been so worried that it didn't occur to me that I had been screaming. Jaria had left her building immediately and reached me before the others caught on, then dragged me to my room. Leaving me there she went out to clarify other's suspicions.

"I told you that she might not be feeling well. Why are you screaming like a madman?" Returning she admonished me in a hushed voice.

"Was I screaming?" I just realized what I might have done.

"Yes, you were, now we can go to her. I have the medicines for her." she had her medicine bag ready.

"Jaria what is wrong with her, tell me or I will start shouting again." My logic was completely childish, but I knew she would never want me to get in trouble.

"She has what every girl in the world gets, don't worry it will pass in five to six days and then she will be fine." She headed out.

"What do you mean every girl has it, what do they have?" I was even more confused than before.

"You will know in time but right now believe me she will be fine." Jaria sounded frustrated by my foolishness.

Both of us were back in the cell where Sarah was still curled up in pain and crying. I couldn't take it but Jaria simply took out a vile of medicine and filling up a syringe gave Sarah a shot. Sarah was asleep within minutes, the strain on her face relaxed as the medicine took effect. Then I noticed her change of clothes, I guessed this was not the time to ask Jaria about that but I was relieved to see Sarah relax and sleep soundly. Jaria left but I didn't want to leave Sarah alone so I brought in a chair and sat with her. After an hour Jaria came and relieved me of my charge, she had a complex expression on her face. Taking the chair she advised me to go out and stay with the men. I left although my heart wasn't ready for it, seeing Sarah lying like that had torn me from inside like nothing ever had. Until Jaria had given her the pain medicine I was in torment, feeling helpless and devastated, unable to think or act rationally.

As advised, I came out to help the soldiers practice once more but my concentration was off. I couldn't direct a simple fighting sequence. I tried to but it wasn't working and I gave up dismissing everyone. During all of this I saw Jabbar watching me closely, he was also there when I had come rushing out for Jaria. He had been on the base since the night before. He liked to provoke me, trying to clash with me on different issues, but I always ignored him. I paid no attention to him then as well and came back to my room, I had forgotten about my leg in all of this, now it was hurting and I knew rest was required if I wanted it to heal. I stayed in my room lying on the bed waiting for any sound from the adjacent room. Jaria had stayed with Sarah, which was a surprise. I never could imagine that she would care that much for one of 'them'. A while later I heard low voices from the other room, Sarah was probably up. I was on my way to her room slowly when Jaria hurried out and caught me, a worried look on her face,

"Ali, you should come. I don't think her mind is working right." Jaria sounded very grave; I rushed in the cell to find Sarah sitting on the bed with a shattered expression on her face and eyes staring at nothing. I sat on the chair and motioned Jaria to leave but as soon as she walked out Sarah started to call for someone and then ran after Jaria, her hands stretched out in an effort to grab something or someone. I quickly caught her by the arms before she could run out, she didn't pay any attention to me just kept on crying and asking to go home and then she collapsed in my arms. I had to carry her to the bed where she became unconscious once again. Her face was pale and her eyes closed tightly as if she was in immense distress. My heart cried out to sit next to her, to straighten her hair and to comfort her but I wasn't supposed to, it was not for me.

I stood up agitated, why would I want to do anything like that anyway? What had happened to me in these days? I had to end this madness. She was a prisoner who was not a permanent part of our life and as soon as a bargain was reached, she would be gone forever. I would never see her again. Also, she was a foreigner and hated us. I had my own burdens to carry and I had just added her to my afflictions. Our worlds were not only poles apart but were each other's enemies. There were distances between lands and hearts that could never be bridged. I had to relinquish to that. Pacing the cell, I ran fingers through my hair pressing hard to soothe the nerves and waited for her to awaken. When she did, it became clearer to me that the differences between us were unsurmountable. She didn't trust or believe anything I said, she was convinced I had been deceiving her all this time, and it was becoming harder and harder for me to ignore her opinion about me.

I brought her dinner in the evening but didn't stay because although she was polite it was obvious, she was not comfortable with my presence and, for reasons I was painfully becoming aware of, I couldn't bear her indifference. But there was a consolation in all of this. I was satisfied that it was better this way that she detested us or me for that matter. Leaving her with the image she had of me was fine it would make things easier. I could move away without worrying about hurting her feelings.

Sitting in my room I recalled every word she said, every accusation, there was a hint of reality in them and my instinct was nagging me to explore what lay behind the apparent calm of Daanish. Her insistence on Daanish's plan to kill her bothered me and I wanted to dig deeper to find out for certain what was actually going on rather than following Daanish blindly. Incomplete and vague answers to my inquiries and the ambiguity of the whole affair had me questioning a lot of things that I had never before. My loyalty which had been unequivocally for the group was wavering now. I sought clarification which Daanish was not providing. The truth was hidden behind the shades of Daanish's friendship. I had to push through them and grasp it.

Day 11

When I awoke, I had a strong mind set to put my plan in motion to achieve freedom at any cost. I was not going to let these thugs use me as their victim.

My stomachache was back but Jaria had been very careful about me, she had brought some meds with breakfast. Ali hadn't come. I felt a little empty and sad but I wasn't under any illusion anymore. My sentiments weren't worth a dime to these people, everything was fake and I would be better off if I could comprehend that earlier than later.

I ate without making conversation which was easy with Jaria and took the medicine to alleviate the pain. Most of the time Ali and Jaria had been irrefutably kind to me and that made me feel guilty about what I had embarked on but there was no alternative. I had to consider the rest of the pack. Then again it might be a strategy to be nice to abate any escape attempts from me.

Jaria left.

I reclined on the pillows thinking about the irony of life, where I was being tested in ways I couldn't even fathom only a year ago. The events that had taken place would have been incomprehensible to the old Sarah. My chain of thought was broken by the arrival of a familiar sound. The door opened and Ali entered. He was still walking with a crutch. It dawned on me that he had carried me to the bed in that state, 'How did he manage that?' It made me feel a little ashamed of taking advantage of him but then the reality pushed me, hadn't he and his friends taken advantage of me, weren't they going to use me. Everything was fair in war and........, thinking I deliberately left the other word out; it could not be applied in these circumstances.

He came and sat on the new addition of furniture in the room. I remained silent as he started the conversation,

"Are you feeling better today?" He was a little hesitant in his question. I was a little embarrassed about it but he needed an answer,

"Yes, thank you. How about your leg? Any improvement?"

"It is much better. I need to thank you for that. If you hadn't done what you did, I wouldn't be sitting here." He looked at me earnestly,

I observed his face. Today he looked a little better, with the dark circles reduced and his face less stressed. His eyes were fixed on me so I diverted my attention to the chair's legs.

"I wanted to apologize again for all the pain we have caused you, hopefully this will be over soon and you will be able to go back home." Ali had his sight now set on the wall.

"I appreciate that you feel the need to explain yourself to me, otherwise who am I to question your treatment. I have no rights as a prisoner. I know how the game is played and can fully understand your kindness towards me." I was good. I could pat myself on the back, he looked at me and then again at the wall trying to avoid meeting my eyes.

"I am happy that you give me, I mean us that much credence."

"So, what are you doing to spend your time. I think war games and soccer would be out of the picture in your present condition." I was being friendlier than I had been since my arrival, his countenance relaxed,

I could start my work.

"Now that I remember I saved your life and I think that gives me the right to decide how we are going to spend our time together." My words first made him tense then relax again.

"Yes, I suppose you are right." He raised his hands in a gesture of defeat.

"So, do you have any games, like board games? Neither I nor you are in any way ready to go out for a basketball game one on one." Knitting my eyebrows I made a face, it made him smile broadly. It was the very first time I had seen him fully smile, he was handsome but with a smile on his face he could stop one's heartbeat. I looked away and to distract myself started searching under my pillow for games. He got the message and stood up,

"Wait I might have something or maybe Jaria will." He walked out slowly, leaning on his crutch, returning a little later with a checkerboard.

We started playing. It was an old, faded board and the pieces had edges breaking off, 'Which hole had he found this one in?' I wondered as we commenced with our first game.

I used to play checkers with my brothers back home. They were better than me but they always cheated and I also competed in the same way, only they were better at it then me. Ali had the red pieces and mine were the black, the game got really competitive as time passed and we got more involved forgetting about our surroundings. Ali didn't cheat but I was trained by my brothers. He just looked entertained when I pulled the tricks, I had learned from my siblings but didn't point them out, just kept smiling.

There wasn't much conversation during that time and we played until Jaria entered with the meal tray.

"I couldn't find you. They were looking for you, Daanish has to talk to you." Jaria was clearly worried.

"What's wrong?" Ali stopped playing. His brow furrowed and he got up, forgetting the game.

"I don't know, but he is in camp and is looking for you." She gave me the tray and took the chair. Ali quickly left the room. Jaria was quiet for a minute or two and then, to my amazement, uncharacteristically she started talking.

"Daanish is the leader of this group. He is a very ruthless man but he regards Ali greatly. He usually is never stationed in this place and moves around a lot with his soldiers. Ali mostly accompanies him but for the past two weeks he has stayed with you. I have lived with these people for seven years. After my life was ruined, they gave me a place to live and let me stay in return for my services in the camp because I know first aid and can cook." Finishing her account, she took a deep breath. I was chewing my food slowly paying attention to her tale, 'so she had been with Ali for a long time.' I could get information from her now that she had softened towards me.

"Did you meet Ali here?"

"No, I knew his parents but we had moved to another city before they were killed. His father was a friend of my husband."

"Are you a doctor?"

"No, my husband was and I used to assist him in his clinic. He taught me everything I know." Jaria was looking at her hands,

"How did you lose your home?", I knew it was a stupid question but it came out before I could stop myself. Jaria raised her eyes and looked at me with an expression of desolation and loss,

"Our home was partly destroyed in the bombing, my husband and daughter were there in the living room, I think, when it happened because that part was hit. I was at the market and when I came back there was nothing to come back to." Her face turned ashen. I cursed myself for asking her, 'why do I need to know whatever happened to her house, obviously she didn't run out of mortgage payments!'

"I am very sorry to hear that. I apologize for making you relive that." I stopped eating,

"It's not your fault and you can't remind of someone who is never forgotten." She said with a low voice. I was astonished to hear from her lips that it wasn't my fault; at least she was less severe than before.

"So how did you meet Ali?" I started eating again,

"When I was brought here, you see this is their central place, I saw him. He was still very young but he was being taken care of here. They made him study and trained him, he recognized who I was, I couldn't. After finding him I resigned that God had brought me here for a reason and he probably was it, so he became my family." Jaria was talking in a soft voice as she remembered her past, it was full of sorrow but she was composed. I watched her as she shifted on the chair and continued,

"He is the only family I have now and I don't want him to ever get hurt. You need to understand that. He is young and honest, not like the people he works with who are not as forthright as they pretend to him but he will be fine as long as he keeps his end of the bargain and doesn't interfere with their plans. They have promised to help him find the murderers of his parents and that's all he wants from them." Jaria was looking at me critically as if she wanted to get some message through. I lowered my eyes and finished the meal. I didn't want to discuss anything in depth with her. She had no use for me and could become a liability later if she caught on to my plans.

We sat there silently watching the empty tray, at last she left. I got up and brought the bucket out to inspect the compound. The military vehicles were moved somewhere else and there were soldiers all over the place engaged in different activities. I was looking for one familiar face but he wasn't there. I stayed in my position watching and listening, maybe I would hear something helpful but these men didn't really talk too much, mostly they practiced their skills in silence, except for the occasional outburst of someone. Standing on that pail was strenuous and my legs started hurting. I was about to come down when I saw him coming out from one of the distant buildings. He was walking with his crutch and it was easy to recognize him. Slowly he approached our building, his scarf hung on the shoulder swaying with the wind. He pulled it off and wiped his face not paying attention to the men around him. At the entrance of our building, he disappeared from my vision. Tired I got off the bucket and went to the bathroom, dragging it with me.

'Why had their leader called Ali? Why had he returned?' Questions spiraled around in my brain with no explanations. Aggravated I looked at myself. The printed dress was long and came to my knees. The red pants that came with it were a little long on me which I hadn't noticed before. Coming to the chair that I hadn't used till now, I sat on it and put my feet on the bed. The afternoon sun light had lost its vibrancy descending to the west, and now only a speck of light was illuminating the outer wall of the corridor leading to my cell. I took out one of the books Ali had given me. They were in my possession probably till I was done with them. I had gathered that much by his attitude.

Tolstoy was interesting and I opened to read it. Some of the passages held my attention but it was fleeting and I closed it carefully placing under my pillow. After learning how cherished they were by Ali, I had become more cautious in handling them. Indecision loomed as I sorted through my limited options for entertainment; the bucket had its limitations and ballet was off the table as my stomach was in no condition to take the strain. I felt better than before with my stomachache absent but I had no inclination of provoking it.

'Where was Ali?' Just like a genie he suddenly appeared, opening the door he stepped in, crutch first.

"Everything under control." My words caught him a little off guard as he proceeded. I vacated the chair for him and he nodded appreciatively.

"Yes, everything is under control." He imitated me very seriously, raising his eyebrows. His comical parody made me smile,

"I was just asking because you looked worried when you left." I waved my hand mocking annoyance. Now he smiled. I had to look elsewhere; his smile had the capability of playing mayhem with my sanity.

"You want to play another game?" I asked trying to act normal,

"I have some cards. Would you like to play that?" he asked. I was not very apt at playing cards but it was okay, anything to stay busy.

"Yeah, why not." I agreed,

"I'll get a small table too. Last time it was tricky playing with the board on the bed." The corner of his mouth curled as he said this while he glanced at the checkerboard. He left without the crutch and was back within minutes with a deck of cards and a small folding table in his hands as promised. We started playing Russian Rummy and he started beating the pants off me. The game was a mere distraction. I was very much interested in what had transpired between him and his leader, but I was sure if I asked him out right, he would avoid the subject. I had to be tactful about it.

Initially I participated in the game with feigned fervor as ulterior motives brewed in my head, but as the game progressed oddly the reality of my imprisonment eclipsed and I found myself thoroughly enjoying it....or was it because I was playing with Ali? The ease in his manner and his relaxed demeanor made me forget about my perspective escape plan.

"Ahem!" The sound positively made us both jump; Jaria was at the door.

"Oh, is it that late I didn't see." Ali hurriedly stood up and made space for her. She came in eyeing the table and placed the tray she was carrying on it.

"Your meal is in your room." She addressed Ali, sober as always.

Ali stepped out and I was left alone with Jaria. The cards laid scattered on the corner of the bed. Ignoring her, I got up and went to the bathroom. Since morning I had started working on my plan to entice Ali into disclosing the secrets of this place and till now it was going smoothly. I hoped within a few days I would gather enough info on how to escape without getting killed. By the time I came out, Jaria was sitting on the chair. The cards plus the board game were properly packed and tucked under the bed. She was particular about keeping things in order, 'I should have asked her to vacuum the room, it definitely needed that,' my mouth curled into a smile at the strange vision of her vacuuming the cell. I halfheartedly ate the oatmeal and bread, washing it down with water then suddenly something struck me,

"What did you mean these people were not honest with Ali?" All of a sudden, I realized the bizarreness of her statement,

"I don't think it concerns you." She was very direct and a bit rude, but I wasn't giving up,

"You have to tell me. I saved his life and I own part of it." I resolved to use that as leverage.

"So, you want to cash out on your good deed." She was sarcastic

"Call it what you may but I want to know and you have to tell me." I blatantly insisted. She observed me closely and sat back in the chair,

"They are not what he thinks. He works for them and follows their orders as instructed but I have heard things about their missions that are different from what Ali tells me."

"What do you mean?" I was confused; she sighed heavily and continued,

"I have heard that they are hired guns for money, but apparently they profess to everyone that they are working for the liberation and union of the country. Ali believes that and has never questioned their actions. He was promised, when he started with them, that they will help him discover the identity of his family's killers but until today they haven't done anything. They make excuses about not being able to locate them. I don't trust them, Jabbar especially; he is a relative of Daanish and doesn't like Ali at all."

I was amazed at what she was disclosing to me. At first, she was not interested in talking to me at all, but now it was like a dam broke and everything came flowing out but she wasn't done yet,

"I have knowledge that Jabbar is the one who knows exactly what these missions are really for and that he plans most of them now. This recent mission in which Ali got hurt was actually his idea." She finished,

"Does Ali know any of this?"

"No he doesn't and don't tell him anything. He would have to deal with all of them, and if he confronts them they will kill him. The only reason he stays with them is their promise to find the murderers of his family. I don't care if they work for money or anything. Ali has never done

164

anything wrong and until he remains ignorant he is safe."
Her tone changed from being secretive to assertive, like she
wouldn't tolerate anyone crossing her in this matter.

"But isn't it dangerous for him? And isn't it obvious
that they wouldn't help him find anyone. Once that is
achieved, he will be free and will leave them." I was
positive of my logic,

"That's not how it's done, once he knows who the
culprits are Daanish will assist him in taking revenge. So,
they are not afraid that he will leave them." She was also
confident of her explanation.

I looked at her with mixed expressions. Her account of
these mercenaries further convinced me about the potential
danger I was in. This group was using Ali as she had
clearly suggested but how could I be sure that his ignorance
of their real purposes was due to their trickery. Perhaps
Jaria was ignorant to the true situation and Ali was in on
everything. It was hard to comprehend who was innocent in
all this. I resolved to stay out of it; my aim was to get out of
there as early and as safely as possible, nothing else.
Whatever conspiracies were contriving here were not my
concern. Remaining silent I decided against making any
comments on her story. I noticed though that she expected
a response from me but when none came, she left.

The room was cool by this time in the evening and I
paced brooding on my options. I could turn Ali against his
troupe and use that but I wasn't sure of the validity of
Jaria's narration, maybe she was deliberately telling me
lies, leading me on so that I would try something and fail at

it. I had to stick to my original plan and make no changes; this new intelligence was of no use to me.

The fear of failing kept me thinking, 'What if I wasn't able to escape? What if Ali wouldn't fall for my lures? What if...'. Running fingers through my hair I observed the tunic loosely hanging on me. Jaria's daughter had been obviously bigger than me. All of her dresses were loose on me and this one had an open neckline, which tended to slide off one shoulder and I was always trying to correct that. It was the same way now but at the moment I didn't care if it fell off the shoulder or stayed stuck to it. I mean who was there to see. Even the scrunchy had slipped down to the middle of my tied up hair and a sarcastic laugh left my lips as I pulled it off, 'Look at me. What a mess.' Climbing onto the bed, I slipped under the sheet Jaria had brought for me and fell asleep whilst revising the angles of my plan.

Day 12

Morning was warm and bright when I woke up. I looked around to see any sign of Jaria or Ali but the room was empty. The brightness in my cell was clearly a sign that I was waking up past my usual hour. It was good that they had not tried to awaken me. It had been a well slept night after many days and I was very relaxed and refreshed. After my daily washing ritual, I took out the cards stowed under the chair in 'my room'. Patience was one of the first games I had learned and spreading the cards on the newly acquired table I started playing.

I intended later that day to ask Jaria for a new dress to change into after taking a bath along with a towel. My escape plan was going to take a few days if I did get a chance at it. I had no illusions about the success of it, but I was determined to try. There was nothing to lose. Until that happened, I wasn't going to live in squalor. The sound of the door made me look up. Ali was entering, without his crutch. He walked slowly but it was evident that his wound was healing well. He had the blessed tray in his hand,

"Good morning, I came earlier but you were asleep and I didn't wake you. How are you feeling?" He was a bit more cheery than usual. I credited it to our time playing games.

"I feel fine and thanks for letting me sleep, I was very tired and it helped. I hope you are feeling well." His eyes widened a bit with disbelief; I had not been that courteous to him before.

"I am doing well. The wound is healing and as you can see, I no longer need a crutch. I have to leave but Jaria will be checking on you." He placed the food tray on top of the cards on the table.

"Aren't you going to stay and play a round of checkers or cards?" We were conversing as if we were old friends meeting at a casual party. It was weird to hear us, even for me.

"No, later maybe. I am sorry but I have been given some assignments, and they require urgent attention." Saying this he walked out of the room leaving me with the tray. I had lost my appetite. If I was to be successful in achieving my goal, I needed him to trust me and forge a friendship, which was not possible if he wasn't going to be present. I had to try harder. Breakfast sat on the table untouched as I waited for Jaria. My thoughts kept turning to Ali, 'Where did he have to go?'. He was still recuperating from his wound so any mission was out of the question, and when I checked the compound there weren't any soldiers there. So, what was so important?

My thoughts focused on him which was the last thing I wanted. He was a tool and beyond that I had no wish to think about him. Regardless, my mind couldn't block the vision of his face from my eyes. The day passed as time ticked by slowly and I waited.

In the afternoon, Jaria came. I was relieved to have someone to divert my attention,

"Hi, I was waiting for you." The words came out before she was in,

"Why?" Her answers were back to being short,

"I need some clothes and a towel. I would like to bathe and change."

Jaria ignored what I said and pointed to the food, "Why haven't you finished it?"

I had to think of an excuse fast; to tell her that the departure of Ali had made me lose my appetite wouldn't sit well with her. But she didn't give me a chance,

"You have to eat and then I will get what you want." Simple bargaining, a little give and take. I pulled the table close and started eating.

Jarai brought the stuff I requested as soon as I was finished. I was happy that she didn't try to remove the chair and table from the cell. The new arrangement was convenient because I had something to use when playing cards or checkers.

Jaria was gone by the time I came out of the bathroom. My hair was wrapped in the towel she had provided, leaving my new clothes dry. The shirt was differently designed then the others. It had short sleeves and a shorter

169

hem. I liked it because it was easier to move in, but like the others it was quite loose on me. I sat on the bed and undid the towel from my hair making it fall on one of my shoulders as the shirt's broad neckline slipped off the other. I was trying to straighten it when I heard someone at the door. It was Ali entering with his scarf hanging on his shoulder and clothes covered in dust. He had stopped at the door with his eyes fixed on me. There was something in his gaze which made me blush and very aware of my naked shoulder. I pulled my shirt up covering my shoulder. He didn't move for what seemed like an eternity, but then he came out of his trance and stepped in, stopping in the middle of the cell. I didn't look at him. Once was enough. I wasn't ready for him waltzing into my head and creating chaos.

"Did Jaria come?" He asked, now more composed,

"Yes." It was my turn to be concise.

"Did you eat?"

"Yup."

Nobody said a word. The room was full of silence. I wanted to ask him about any news regarding the messages but I had lost my voice. A strange woozy feeling began to surround me like a haze. He stood motionless for a while then sat on the chair trying to keep his leg straight. We still didn't speak. I felt flustered. Suddenly, Jaria came in with a paper in her hand. We both were startled by her intrusion and Ali stood up once more as she handed him the paper. I couldn't understand what it said because it was in Arabic, but Ali's pallor changed as soon as he read it. Jaria was quiet but nodded at him when he looked at her. Then they both left. I was left in the cell to muse over the strange actions and circumstances. My sixth sense cautioned me that there was a change taking place in their establishment. Perhaps I could ask Jaria later, and if I was lucky, she might tell me.

I was pacing around in the cell when I heard some noise outside. It was not the usual sound of men. I got the pail and climbed on it. The scene outside was not fully visible but I could see men around some new vehicles parked in the area. They were not the ones I had seen before. Most of the others I could recognize but these guys were new and not clad in keffiyehs. Rather they were in uniforms than in black garb. I watched inquisitively. They had bags of weapons and were taking them out. Presumably to make camp here. One of them I could recognize right away, Jabbar. He was ordering the others around and intermittently looking in the direction of my cell. Did he know I was in here? He made me afraid; there was something about him that was icy and treacherous. He was standing with one foot on the rails of his jeep smoking a cigarette. As I decided to get down from the bucket, I quickly got back on when I saw Ali approach him. Ali was walking slowly and empty handed, and his scarf was still hanging on his shoulder. Jabbar didn't move from his position. Ali came near and said something to him. I couldn't hear it, but Jabbar spat on the ground in front of him and told him to go away. I could see fury on Ali's face but he turned and marched back out of my sight.

'What was happening? Was there fallout among thieves?'

I wanted to know more but how? I came and sat on the bed. Something was wrong and I was getting worried. Was it related to me? I had to find out.

Rest of the afternoon passed without event and I got really bored. Curiosity gnawed at me. I had to talk to someone. Just then Jaria came in with my evening meal, 'Was it already time for that? Where was Ali?'. I had been sulking too long.

"Oh, it's good you came. I was waiting for you." I said impulsively,

She looked at me strangely, "Why?"

"I was wondering, what was in the note that you gave Ali?" I came right out with it,

"It's none of your business." She was blunt,

"But why are there new soldiers out in the compound? One of them is Jabbar. I remember him. What's going on?" I didn't give up poking; Jaria remained silent and pointed to the food,

"I am not going to eat anything until you tell me what's going on." I said obstinately. She sighed and sat on the chair. It was coming in handy. Her face softened and she motioned me to come close,

"They are soldiers who are also part of this group but they are led by Jabbar. He sometimes comes and stays here. He was here when they brought you in and when you were sick, now again he has come back."

"Any special reason? I saw him misbehave to Ali. What was that all about?"

"Nothing new. He never liked Ali because he is better than him and the leader trusts him more." Jaria finished.

"So where is Ali? Why hasn't he come?" The words just slipped out of my mouth. Jaria observed me for a second as my face turned red,

"He is busy."

"Did they get any news from my government? Is there any progress?" I eventually was able to ask her, hoping that she would have some information.

"I am not sure about that. They were talking in the dining hall about new developments but I don't know what about." Jaria leaned back in the chair.

"Can you please eat your dinner so I can get back to work."

I had no desire to eat but to get her off my back I dug in and finished it. She was out of the door immediately. I suppose wanting to avoid any imminent questions from me. Night fall was near and I had nothing to do but to lie down and stare at the peeling paint of the ceiling. In the evenings, the cool weather made my cell comfortable. I tried to keep my thoughts from running amok with mixed images of my past and present. I had an unshakable, ominous feeling in the pit of my stomach. I wasn't in ideal circumstances but I sensed that they were about to get a lot more worse. The day had passed with idleness. My own state of health was precarious and I had no energy to do anything apart from lying in bed, trying occupy the nightly hours with sleep.

After tossing and turning for a while, I decided the next best thing to kill time was playing cards. I took out the deck and started playing Patience again. The table was very handy and I silently thanked Ali for that favor. My cell got darker as the sun set. Then door to my cell suddenly opened, during my game in full swing. I looked up and found Ali standing there. I wasn't expecting him to drop by but he had a habit of checking on me whenever he wasn't able to come at mealtimes.

He approached my bed which was a bit out of the ordinary, and it made me a little apprehensive. His ever expressive eyes conveyed his troubles. It was evident that he was distracted as he had no clue, he had almost reached my bed until I stood up. He stopped and catching his mistake, stepped back. Something was clearly bothering him. I sat back and waited for him to speak while winding up the cards but he held up his hand signaling me to leave them on the table. Next, he took his place on the chair and pulled it closer to rest of the furniture,

"You were playing Patience, right? Do you want a partner? ...... I mean do you want to play with me?" His voice was normal. Nothing could be deciphered from his tone, but his eyes had that same anxious expression. I motioned for him to start. It was a quiet game with neither of us saying much. I asked him about his leg and he inquired about my stomachache, and that was the extent of our conversation. During the second round, I asked him about the ongoing negotiations and my status in them. The question disturbed him. I saw the expression in his eyes translate onto his face,

"I have no knowledge of the situation at the moment." He had put down his cards,

"But you are assigned to take care…….. I mean watch me. Shouldn't you know?" I got frustrated. Jaria I could understand but him. I assumed he didn't want to disclose the information to me. Agitated I threw the cards on the table and pushed it away,

"How could you not know? I demand to know what is going on." Suddenly the calm in the cell was demolished by my yelling.

He looked at me helplessly. I tried to read his face, but it was difficult concentrating with my temper rising, God knows why I was this enraged but I wasn't ready for lame answers. He had met 'the leader' twice. How could he not be informed?

"I want to know right now, and if you don't tell me I will scream all night." I stood up and threatened him.

This was not the way I had planned to operate, but his complacence triggered the pent-up disappointment and annoyance in me. I was very aware of my mental breakdown, but I had lost control over it.

"Sarah please don't scream, there are men out there whom you will regret attracting to yourself. Please listen to me. I am telling the truth; you have to believe me." He was pleading, but anger ruled my judgment, and at that moment, standing down was not an option. His excuses sounded unrealistic and misleading. I believed he was playing with me. Mocking me and at that instant rationality deserted me. I ran to the wall with the window and opened my mouth to scream but before I could make a sound, he had caught me from behind and covered my mouth with his hand, shutting it tightly. I squirmed and tried to get out of his grip, but he circled my waist more securely and pulled me closer holding my mouth closed. I couldn't even have imagined the strength of his grip, but I wasn't able to move a muscle.

"Sarah, please. Don't scream." He whispered in my ear. His warm breath burned my neck. He didn't have to ask me again to stop. My breathing had practically ceased. Being so close to him, I became profoundly aware of my body jammed against his. He hadn't realized it though. The boiling blood in my veins cooled in an instant. I was breathing with difficulty as he removed his hand and turned me around to face him, still holding me by the arms. We were standing barely a foot apart. My head was getting dizzy with him clamping down on my mouth. His nearness caused my breath to come in small gasps. He soon realized the effect of his hands holding me and the closeness between us. His grip loosened but he didn't let go. His hands slid down to mine, gripping them. At that moment, screaming apart, I could barely breath. Our eyes were locked with each other. He didn't say anything, but his eyes were stormy with an intensity that flooded my body with warmth. Unable to look away, I waited for him. Pursuing his lips, he gently pushed me back and turned away.

"Sarah, Jabbar is in the camp, and he is intent on meeting you. I didn't allow him today to do so and he is itching for an excuse." Ali leaned against the wall next to me.

"What does he want from me?" I could hardly finish my sentence,

"I don't know but Daanish was here already and today Jabbar arrived. He has a very cruel nature. You should stay away from him." His logic was fine but he had to remember that I was a prisoner, and if his leader was bent on hurting me, I had no power to stop him or his goons.

"Ali, you keep forgetting the fact that I have no power to stop you or anyone. I am your prisoner." My bitter tone caught his attention and he stepped closer to me. I stumbled back hitting the rail of the bed. Another backward step would definitely land me on the bed.

"I know. But it's different with Jabbar. He has no honor or integrity. I couldn't let you give him a reason to come in here. I promise you that I will find out what's the present situation and I assure you that you will be safe." Saying this he sat back on the chair, lightly massaging his leg. I had forgotten about his wound. It was definitely hurting due to this ruckus. I felt acutely sorry for him. Quickly, I said

"Okay, let's play cards and forget about the other stuff." I picked up my hand,

I was composed by now and wanted to change tack. My outburst had upset both of us, but it had made me cognizant of Ali's protective feelings for me. I could use that.

Ali picked up his cards and we played the game silently until I asked him about his parents. His face was a flurry of expressions as he recounted both the traumatic and pleasant memories. As we delved deeper into his past, he opened up more and the happy memories replaced the hurtful ones as he talked about his sister. Hours pressed on well into the night and we became aware of how late it was when a soldier outside shouted at some imaginary enemy. Startled we paused, and Ali checking the time got up. It was time for him to leave. I wished that he wouldn't, but it was inevitable.

Before lying down, I went to the bathroom thinking about what Ali had told me about Jabbar and his refusal to give him access to me. I had a pretty good idea how that guy worked. He was the one who had pushed me on day one. He was a real jerk but the important thing to consider here was the reason of his arrival. Ali seemed edgy about the whole thing and I kind of believed him when he denied awareness of any new development.

Sleep was far from my eyes as I lay there imagining Ali holding me tightly in his grip and it made my breathing unsteady. I could still feel my curves pressed to his muscular body and his warm breath on my neck. Sleep was going to be fleeting.

Day 12 (Ali)

In the past two days I had found things that were a shock to me in many respects. First, the breach of the mission and then Daanish's sudden arrival. He did come occasionally to this camp. However, he always communicated with me prior to that, but not this time. He had just come in the middle of the night as my men had returned from the mid station camp after surviving from the potentially deadly mission. I had known of his presence, but Jaria found out later when he sent for me. At the time Jaria came to get me, I was sitting with Sarah playing a game of checkers.

Settling into my bed, I let her image fill my vision. Playing with her I discovered what a sneak she could be. Her tricks had me reminiscent of my past when I played with my father and used to cheat with him. He never minded my childish trickery. For a short period as I looked towards the ceiling, I was back in the past when I didn't have to think about my next move or have to prove anything. However, Jaria entering brought me back to the real world where I was just a pawn.

Daanish had called me in his chambers in one of the buildings farther from the main camp. His room was nicely furnished with a comfortable bed and sofas, air-conditioning keeping it cool. We all knew about his comfortable abode but today I felt agitated watching him sit in this luxury while the others toiled and lived in conditions far worse. He was cordial as always and offered me a cold drink before getting started. I declined the offer. Suddenly the pictures of kids begging in the streets crying for food dominated my conscience.

Why was my head filling up with such rebellious thoughts?

Daanish was discussing the current operations in which he was involved. He asked me extensively about Sarah and how she was faring under pressure. I didn't divulge much about her. Only that she was okay and was waiting for an update regarding her situation. Despite my persistent questioning, he didn't let on what was the status of his negotiations with Sarah's government. He didn't say much about the timetable or future plans for her either. I was aggravated by this secrecy, but I knew him. He wouldn't tell me if he had decided not to. He diverted the discussion to the recent mission where I had barely escaped with my life. He was concerned about the failure of it and the price he would have to pay for it. I couldn't understand his comments on that matter when it slipped from him that the other party was expecting a victory and he would have to return their sum. 'Why would he have to return money to anyone, it was not as if we were hired killers?' We were fighting for freedom and for the people and every mission that we fought on was for that precise reason. We didn't get paid by the people. We were doing it for the good of the nation. Weren't we? I was perplexed but I didn't confront him with my questions. My gut instinct was warning me that there was much more to this then I had seen or could see. I wanted to get out of there as soon as possible, but when his attention again turned to Sarah I had to stay and listen to what he had to say. He wanted to hand her responsibility over to Jabbar, taking me out of the picture. His rationale being that I was stuck here with her and needed to get out in the field to polish my skills because I had failed in the last mission. I couldn't wrap my mind around this excuse as I had been with her only ten days. How could my skills get rusty? This was as lame as it sounded, and I was certain that the failure was not because of me. We had been sold out. The enemy was apprised of our plan, but Daanish wasn't paying attention to that detail. I could feel that he was trying to find a reason to remove me from the base and give charge to Jabbar. I didn't want that to happen at any cost, even thinking about him getting close to Sarah drove me mad. I couldn't stand the thought. I assured Daanish that everything was under control, and he had nothing to worry. Presently he agreed to it, but I wasn't sure about the future. He seemed to be indecisive. I had known the man for years and he was ruthless as well as fickle. I didn't trust him about Sarah but then I didn't have much choice. We concluded our council after that, but I had doubts which I couldn't shake no matter how much I tried. There was something he was hiding, and I was apprehensive that it was related to Sarah.

As I had walked out of the building, my mind wandered, conflicting thoughts confused me. Should I have been so concerned about Sarah? She was after all a prisoner and with us for a short period to leave eventually. Then I would never see her again. Anything I felt was irrelevant in this. Daanish had been there for me, and I had to acknowledge that. Still the thought of her never being there made my heart constrict with sorrow. After such a strenuous encounter with Daanish I went back to her. I needed that serenity of being with her and we played cards. It was my turn to pull tricks. The game was fun. To be with her was like sitting in the cool breeze, carefree and serene.

Turning on the other side of the bed, I remembered her sitting there with the shirt hanging off her delicate shoulder and her sunshine hair bundled on the other. These new emotions wrecking my being were strange for me, but every moment I spent thinking about her made my heart race and my body tense. My mind went blank, and I couldn't concentrate. I had realized her effect on me and knew it was not the path I could tread but the way my heart and body reacted to her was nothing like I had ever experienced. For the first time in my life, I felt alive.

Till now my life had been channeled in a direction which only led to finding the killers of my family and nothing more. My existence had nothing to offer. It was a barren land with no hope, only grief and depression swept through me. Mine was not a life which could be called a life. It was on a perpetual track to destruction, of others and eventually my own. Sitting up I pressed the palms of my hands hard on my temples to reduce the pressure. I had no misconceptions about a bright future even if we won this war. We had a long way to go to achieve that and I was quite sure that any day could be my last. But no matter how I tried to block out her image it came back stronger than ever. My room felt desolate. The small fan hanging overhead turned slowly as I sat under it. My mind and ears focused on the sounds from the room next door. She was so close yet so far. Loneliness cut through my heart, and I wanted this to stop. It was agony. My eyes filled with images of a distant past where I was happy and free. Suddenly a cry outside pushed me to the present, possibly one of the new soldiers. Jabbar was back with his gang, and he had confronted me about Sarah, trying to instigate a fight. Typical tactics on his part. I didn't give him the satisfaction, but Daanish was also altering his plans, talking in riddles like him. My intuition was warning me about their intentions. I had to protect Sarah. I could sense a conspiracy, but my hands were tied. This situation was convoluted and I had to go along with Daanish and use him to deliver Sarah safely back to her people. He had come around for now and promised to stick to the original scheme, but I had a premonition that this bargain would cost more. Sarah was becoming too precious for me to just leave it in his hands. My trust was wavering, and it was because of the way I felt for her. Although I was definite that my infatuation would come to nothing, and she could never feel the same way about me. Still, I couldn't push her out of my thoughts. It was useless to suppress memories of her. I could still feel her skin rub against mine when I had fallen on her as we struggled for my books. The tangles of her hair warmed the blood in my veins. Her delicate frame holding me when I had fainted, the strength in her and her sheer courage astounded me, enticed me like nothing ever had. I got off the bed and splashed some water on my face and then went out without my crutch. Maybe a little exercise would do me good. I had to get my strength back if I wanted to keep my job. Daanish was proposing to send me to the other camp, whatever reasons he gave I had a clear idea what was the real underlying reason. Jabbar was the culprit, and he was pushing to take over my job. Even though Daanish didn't believe it. I had a strong hunch that the failure of the recent mission was because of him. He was the one who had planned it and I was supposed to execute it. He had never liked me and the feeling was mutual but now I was suspicious of his activities. I had been for some time, but Daanish didn't pay any heed to my warnings about him. The family ties they had were definitely the backdrop of that. There also might have been other factors, which were becoming apparent to me just recently.

I walked around aimlessly; my head full of random thoughts when I saw Jabbar. He was coming towards me. I stopped in my tracks,

"Hey Ali, where are you keeping her?" He asked arrogantly,

"It's none of your business." I snapped at him. He always brought the worse out in me.

"Well enjoy it while you can. I am taking over soon and then it's going to be fun." He smiled in a sinister way,

"In your dreams Jabbar. I am not letting you near her." He made my blood boil,

"We will see." He sneered at me as he walked past into the building nearby.

He always made me livid, and when he mentioned Sarah, I wanted to rip him apart but I had to tolerate him because of Daanish. And I had to serve until I could find the killers of my parents. I was stuck in a vortex of misery as everything close to me was being weighed in a balance against each other.

Sighing hard I went back to my room. It was evening and I was sure Jaria would have taken Sarah's meal to her by now. This was also by the new directions of Daanish. He wanted me to distance myself from her and get prepared for the field once again. He had heard rumors and wanted to dissuade me from extensively getting involved with her. He had hinted during our meeting and then later had sent a message. I was forbidden from taking her meals and meeting her unnecessarily. Standing in the empty room I really didn't care about his directive. I had to see her. When I went to her room, I suspected that she was happy to see me. Her indifference to her situation and circumstances astounded me. Someone else would have broken down and gone mad with fear, but she only had one episode when she was suffering from that pain and after that she had actually transformed into a more composed and calmer person. Yesterday she had asked me to play a board game or something similar with her in the morning before my encounter with Daanish. When I entered, she had asked so light heartedly if I had everything under control and I couldn't resist teasing her. We had played cards and then I found out that she hadn't had dinner by that time and Jaria was quick in pointing out that I also had to eat my meal.

186

Why couldn't I keep track of time when I was with her? Why did the whole world disappear when she was with me? I was completely sentient of what was going on and its end result, but I had conceded my defeat already. It was a lost battle. The only thing remaining was to see how I would cope with the consequences. I had a meeting with Daanish in the morning before breakfast and he was satisfied with my recovery, presenting different options to me. Most strongly he pushed for me to take an assignment in the southern district hundreds of miles from here. I had declined, adamantly forcing my position here as a better option at least until the hostage situation was over. He wasn't happy about it, but he didn't argue with me. I probed him again about the current level of negotiations, but he didn't disclose anything. This was confusing for me. Usually, he was a very organized man with everything well planned into the future. Why wouldn't he know? The question was disturbing and alarming. I could smell trouble brewing, but at present I had to sit tight and wait for new developments. As I came back to my room, I could see Jabbar's men bring in their vehicles and equipment.

I got to my room and changed. I had to do some digging today and there was a chance of me being gone for the rest of the day. I had to find Jaria. She was already coming to see me, carrying the breakfast tray for Sarah. She hadn't woken up when I left for the meeting. I had checked on her and she had been in deep sleep. I took the tray from Jaria; she was surprised by my action. I signaled her to stay in my room and took the meal to Sarah, who was up and looked well rested. What impressed me about her since day one was that she had never displayed any fear. She had this positive aura about her. She inquired about the process involving her freedom, but she was never intimidated. There was only a realization of the reality and a powerful resolute attitude.

She welcomed me as I stepped in which was a pleasant surprise. Maybe it was the time we had spent together. She took the meal and I left her in the care of Jaria. I didn't have to tell her to be careful, she was aware of the unseen danger. She had warned me about Jabbar and his gang not only for myself but for Sarah as well. She wrote a note to warn me about them lurking around the place. I fully understood the extent of mistrust surrounding us. Jaria and I had become family and we looked out for each other. She was wary of the events unfolding within our group all the way to the top. My conference with Daanish had pushed me to look for clues to find answers and for that I had to leave camp. I left to make inquiries in the nearby areas. My investigation led me to the towns close to our camp. There had been events taking place at different levels and mostly I found proof of Jabbar's handiwork, but I was searching for something else. I could explore only a few towns in the north and west. Next, I planned to reach out to the towns a little far and find answers there. My exploration had me questioning everything Daanish had told me and trained me to believe. My mind was restless; I had to find the truth. I returned late in the evening all covered in dust and more disillusioned about the cause our leader had been preaching about. The practices of his next in command had been contrary to all his proclamations of our mission.

Exhausted mentally and physically, I had to see her and that was the first thing I did. It was late but I didn't care. I found her playing cards. Seeing me she got apprehensive, probably by my state, but when I offered to play cards with her, she gladly let me. I wanted to distract myself from the pressing uncertainty in my mind which had kept me troubled all day. Then what happened next was completely out of the blue. She got so agitated due to my ignorance about Daanish's plans that I had to hold her down with force to keep her from waking up the whole camp, but that short embrace. The feel of her body pressed against mine. The scent of her skin drove me crazy. It took every ounce of my will power to stop the rising passion within me from taking over. She was also stunned and shaking. I couldn't read whether it was fear or something else? And frankly I didn't want to. To hold her once was enough to make me fully grasp the effect she had on me and I wanted to leave it there. I had to keep my sentiments under wraps. No one could ever find out. It would make things difficult for me but it would mean an unfortunate end for her for sure. Now I just wanted the negotiations to go smoothly between her government and Daanish, before he changed his plans, so she could go home safely, and I could get back to finding the murderers of my parents.

I stayed there with her after that till we both were composed, talking about my past and family. But as I laid in bed, sleep was miles from my eyes as her scent and the feel of her body took me hostage and I helplessly surrendered.

Day 13

I was awakened by the rude shouting of someone outside the wall of my cell. It was Jabbar scolding one of his men for some unforeseen complication; I could easily recognize his voice. With eyes wide open I stayed in bed, helpless in dissuading my brain from recapturing the memory of Ali's firm grip around me and his warmth. Eventually I dragged myself out of bed and washed my face to chase the remaining sleep and him out of my system. My body aches were better. Hopefully the worse days were over. I came out and found Jaria sitting on the bed. It was a first, she never got close to it. I didn't ask her to move and quietly sat on the vacant chair. She didn't greet me or anything. Just sat there mute. I saw the bowl and glass of water sitting on the tray. It was breakfast time!

I was wondering why she was so quiet,

"Jaria, why are you so down and out, something wrong?"

"Nothing is wrong." Her voice was flat. She wouldn't let on about anything even if there was a problem. I had noticed since Ali's injury; Jaria had become friendly in her own way; there was a manifested change in her attitude. I wasn't aware of what was unfolding beyond the walls of my cell, but I had a hunch that it had to do with me.

"There are changes in the nature of things. People are shifting in their loyalties." Jaria was talking in riddles again. Failing to comprehend her I got busy with breakfast. She didn't leave her place on my bed, I watched her as she sat there staring at the wall.

"Do you need more medicine?" She suddenly asked. I stopped eating,

"No, I feel much better. I won't be needing it." My answer satisfied her because she took the empty cutlery and left the room. I was alone deliberating on her riddles, 'What did she mean that loyalties were shifting? Why can't she speak in a simple language like everyone else?' I was aggravated by her puzzles. She probably did it on purpose to perplex me and get my brain in knots. I cursed her and sat on the bed, running my fingers through my hair undoing the tangles, sure of it being a mess. I kept pulling at my hair, it was frustration combined with random thoughts. The loneliness brought back every image, every memory of the past twelve days which I had spent with Ali, the peculiar thing was I had not thought about anyone else for some time, which I just realized.

Why? The question hung in the air lingering, giving way to many more poignant ones.

It was a burden I didn't want to carry; he was the enemy and I was their captive, a sacrificial lamb for their cause. I had learned his appearance was a façade, it was to deceive, I had to let go of my infatuation.

"You will lose all your hair if you keep at it." Ali's voice shocked me a bit and I was pulled out of my thoughts about him. There he was standing grander than life with a devilish smile. I took a weary breath and twisted my hair into a bun.

"You're angry?" He came a little closer, today he was walking without his crutch slightly limpinng, clearly his wound had healed to an extent that he could run around and disturb other people. I didn't want to talk to him or look at him. What was he doing to me? I was losing control; he made my head spin and my pulse race whenever he came in my cell. The orchestration of my plan was backfiring, I should have hated him, but I didn't. I was getting sick of my feeble mindedness, sick of the strange emotions taking over me, emotions that had no place in a world like this.

"Can I sit here?" he pointed to the chair,

"Yeah. Why not, I can't stop you." I said curtly, a shadow fell on his face as he heard my words; I had looked up to see the reaction and got what I wanted. He was stoic again and the smile vanished from his face. It made me a little sad, but I shrugged it off, being angry and frustrated with all of this. I was a prisoner and locked in a cell at their mercy so why should I pretend that everything was okay and why should I entertain him? Why should I oblige him or anyone? I should be a bitch and a troublemaker, so they would regret the day they brought me here. I knew my mind wasn't working on full cylinders. With so many conflicting sentiments, it was running off track and I had to bring it back in line. Ali could be my way out of here and I had to try that avenue for my own sake without falling apart.

"Sorry, for being a bit grumpy. You can sit. Would you like to play checkers? I am not going anywhere." I said rolling my eyes and he sat without saying a word. The shadow on his face persisted. Picking up the game board from the floor, he opened it and set up the pieces. I let him finish and we started the game. He didn't say anything for a while, I stayed quiet as well. We finished one game and when I started to set the board for a second one, he got up,

"I actually came to tell you that I have to leave. I have been investigating about the developments regarding your release, but I am being kept in the dark. Still, I might be able to find out something today." He said seriously. I suddenly felt guilty for so ruthlessly wiping the smile off his face. Indignation made me curse myself.

"How will you find out?" I stood up too.

"I know someone who can give me some answers."

He turned and made his way to the door. When I called him from behind,

"Will you come see me tonight?" I stuck my fist in my mouth as soon as the words were out; they were as much a wonder for me as they were for him. He paused in his position and turned around to see me. I lowered my eyes, completely mortified,

"I was thinking we could play another game of checkers or Russian rummy." I tried to hide my embarrassment.

"I will try." Replying he quickly left.

The cell felt very bleak after his departure. I got the bucket and climbed on it to take a glance at the compound. There were men in the same uniforms whom I had seen yesterday and they were lounging around playing cards or smoking cigarettes, talking and smacking each other brashly. None of them were training, which was different from the men with Ali who seemed to be always constructively busy.

It was extremely hot outside, and I could feel the warm wind on my face as it swept in through the window. I expected these men to at least sit in the shade, but they didn't seemed to be bothered by the heat. I came down from the pail and walked around the cell aimlessly. 'Ali had left the camp looking for clues; he was doing so to satisfy me.' 'Maybe I had been wrong about him, perhaps he was telling the truth.' Contradictions swarmed my mind, now I had another predicament,

'Should I play games with him and prove him right about people like me or should I be honest with him?' I couldn't decide. Not many things were in my power, but I had planned to deceive him and use him to my advantage which was against my nature and I had to really push myself to follow through. The hours I spent with him were to make him trust me, to give me the leverage that I needed to use him for my freedom. The plan was a plausible one, but the dilemma was that when I was with him it felt very real. I felt alive and complete; there was no pretense about it. I had tried to convince my heart of it being just a tactic nothing more, but it was becoming harder with every passing minute.

I sat on the chair with my eyes glued to the board game as he had left it. I wanted to wind it up but instead I started playing from both sides. It wasn't as interesting as playing with him, but it kept me occupied.

The rattling of the door alerted me to the arrival of someone. I was certain it was Jaria and I was correct. She entered with a fresh change of clothes in her hands and some food. She put both the things on the bed and sat next to it. I didn't stop playing,

"I brought your meal and some clothes."

"Yes, I saw that." My answer was blunter than I wanted it to be,

"I'm sorry, thank you." I didn't want to offend her; she had been nice to me and despite the fact that she was working for them I appreciated her help in everything. She had no obligation to do so but she had looked out for me, and I was grateful for that.

"Anything new?" I asked casually, picking up the bowl from the tray she had put on the bed.

"No, same as yesterday." She pointed towards outside, I caught her meaning. She was talking about Jabbar.

"Where has Ali gone? He told me about finding answers." I asked in a low voice, careful to keep it between us.

"He told you!" she was shocked,

"Yes, I asked him about my release and what was being done about it. He didn't know so he said that he was going to find answers to my inquiries." I said all in one breath, trying to stay casual.

"So that's why he was gone yesterday and today." She said thoughtfully, "Daanish is getting suspicious of him and can cause him trouble." "You shouldn't have."

"I didn't know it will get him in trouble. But you can't blame me; I have a right to know my fate. Today is the thirteenth day. Something should have been done by now. They sent two messages. Didn't they get any reply to them?" Anger rose in me, 'didn't I have a right to know whether I would live or die.'

"These people are dangerous and now they are suspecting Ali. You don't know what this can lead to." Her voice was wrought with fear.

"Well, if you make friends with the devil, you will have to be very careful of where you step. I didn't make him do it; it was his own decision." I was tired of this game of cat and mouse. She was scaring me now and I was exasperated worrying about Ali along with my other headaches.

"Why can't you understand he made this deal because that was his only option. His whole family was murdered before his very eyes, and this man gave him shelter and a purpose to live, to seek justice for his loved ones. You can blame him because you grew up in a house full of love and security; he grew up torn from his family holding a gun. How can you judge him? Now that he has put his life in

197

danger for you, you are the one criticizing him." Jaria's voice shook with ire.

Her speech left me wordless. She was correct, what right did I have to criticize Ali. Another thing that her lecture did was accentuate the fear already stirring in my heart for his safety. It was ironic. I was in a prison of his comrades and was worried about his safety.

"Where did he go, don't you know?" I asked anxiously.

"I don't exactly but I have an idea where he probably went, but nothing can be done now. We have to wait for his return and hope that these men are not going to reprimand him." She was pacing the cell now; I didn't blame her. I could imagine what these people would do to him if they distrusted him. Suddenly I couldn't eat another bite. I put the bowl away and watched Jaria. She was silent, angst etched in the lines creasing her face.

As I stopped, she took the bowl and left the room not insisting on me finishing my meal. It would have been futile anyway, I already felt like throwing up. I could barely swallow air. Being alone with such turbulent thoughts, waiting for something horrible to happen, was the worst part of the day. Sitting down next to the clothes on the bed, I held my head, pressing on my temples, in an effort to calm myself. The familiar rattling of the door made me look in its direction; half expecting to see Ali, but the face I saw chilled me to the bones. Jabbar stepped in, a sickening smile on his face and I jumped to my feet. He intentionally walked slowly to the middle of the room and scanned it; the smile still plastered on his lips.

"So, this is where he is hiding you. I see he is providing you with everything." His tone was sarcastic and cold. I stood in my place, praying for him to leave. He made the hair on the back of my neck stand; he was aware of the menace he caused and his smile became wider.

"What's wrong princess, can't you speak. Or you only dance for him." The way he said it made me loathe him. How dare he insinuated anything like that,

"I don't dance for anyone. Especially not for monsters like your kind. Why don't you crawl under the rock you came out from!" My voice rose with fury,

"Oh, the beauty has a beast inside. Well, that is interesting isn't it." He stepped towards me; my anger was quickly turning to alarm. I could sense the danger.

"You have to leave my cell, or I will call your boss. He promised I wouldn't be hurt and if you try anything he will be very angry." I was grasping at straws. He laughed sadistically at my feeble effort,

"Are you threatening me?"

"No, I am warning you."

His progress stopped for a minute as he deliberated on the idea and then he shrugged his shoulders and continued his advance.

"Jabbar!" Jaria's voice startled us both; I thanked God for her timely intervention,

"Daanish has asked for you." She was standing inside the door, watching Jabbar severely. He slapped his hands on the side of his leg and winking at me turned and marched out of the room. I collapsed on the bed, completely drained. Jaria quickly locked the door and left. I wanted to thank her, but she didn't give me a chance.

I just had a brush with what a real enemy was like. Jabbar opened my eyes; he made me see the light to believe Ali who had been protecting me in the lion's den. He was risking his life knowingly for me. I felt like slapping myself. Closing my eyes tightly, I tried to stop the tears welling up, but they flowed out despite my efforts. I knew my survival was a variable connected with Ali and his discretion. I lay crying on the bed unaware of the passage of time. Suddenly I wanted him to be there, incapable of imagining anything or anyone else. The plan I had been poised to follow dissolved in my tears with reality staring me in the face in the form of Jabbar. How could I be so blind and callous? I couldn't use him like these scoundrels were using him. It dawned on me that I couldn't hurt him; it wasn't possible for me even if I wanted to.

I got up and went to the bathroom, splashing my face with cold water relaxed me and cleaned my tear-stricken face. The sun was descending to the west, and I could see a glimpse of dusk over the horizon from the small window. My eyes kept turning to the cell door, in fear and anticipation. Tension riled my brain, I felt like screaming and yelling but I didn't want to. Ali was right the other night. He knew. I had been such a fool. I waited biting my lips,

"Where was he?"

Then the door opened, and I stopped pacing to watch who was entering. If it was Jabbar, I was going to fight him until my last breath or die trying, but it was Ali. A sigh of relief left my lips. I wanted to run to him, but Jaria was with him. She handed him the keys of the door and left. He was taken by surprise when I almost ran to him. Scanning my face, the color of his face changed,

"Did someone hurt you?" His voice was lethal,

"No, I am fine. A little depressed, that's it." I had seen Jaria's signal before she crossed the thresh hold of the door, her eyes cued me to keep my mouth shut, and I comprehended the danger for the first time.

"So how was your trip, did you uncover any information?" I tried to distract him with my question, for his sight was still fixed on me and it was unnerving in multiple ways.

"Yes, but it was not too much help. I will have to go again; did you eat dinner?" His eyes kept searching my face. I bit my lip; his gaze was making me hot from head to toe. I suppose he was not aware of the effect he had on me, and that was good because I didn't want him to know.

"No." my voice sounded alien to me, something was happening, and I had no conscious control over it.

Without saying a word, he left the room, but the door was not locked as he walked out. I was tempted to run but then I remembered what had happened during the day and that monster was outside with his men. I could hear them laughing and drinking. The cool breeze was not only bringing fresh air in the cell but also proof of their constant presence outside. Why didn't they go indoors and leave the area? I cursed them. In the meantime, Ali returned with dinner but he had more than one bowl. I looked at him curiously,

"The second one is mine. I haven't had dinner too so I thought I could eat with you if you don't mind." I found his statement odd 'why did he want to eat with me?' but then a lot of things he did seemed odd and who was I to object.

"Yes, why not. Company for dinner is a welcome addition." I gestured to the chair for him to sit as I checked the bowls; they both were full of oatmeal. Inadvertently it made me smile, 'where were the candles when you needed them'. He followed the direction of my sight and smiled also.

"That's the only thing we have, sorry."

"It's fine, let's eat." I picked up my bowl. I felt secure with him, and fear disappeared as we talked and ate.

Today he wanted to know all about me, the details of my family and parents. What happened to my mother, my brothers, their names and how my father spent his time? I didn't hold back anything. The past events of my life came pouring out and I told him everything, things I hadn't even disclosed to N. It just felt so natural speaking with him. I was comfortable in my skin. He was astonished when he found out my age, only one year out of school. He was hesitant to ask about my fiancé, Jake, but I had nothing to hide, the plans of our families, how things had worked out for him and me, and then his unfortunate accident. He asked if I had been in love with him and my confession that I wasn't but just liked Jake, seem to relieve Ali. We finished our oatmeal and put the empty bowls on the tray.

Our conversation was still in full swing, and he further settled into the chair as I pulled my legs up and scooted to lean on the wall behind me. He asked me about my dancing which I confessed was my mother's doing. He smiled broadly as I remembered all the times Mom had to drag me to the lessons. His expression softened when tears lined my eyes as I reminisced. I didn't want to cry and make it difficult for him but sometimes tears have a mind of their own. The memories of my family and the strain of the day ended up making me weep. He leaned forward and handed me his handkerchief, trying to console me. I wiped my tears and tried to produce a slight smile,

"It happens every time I think of them."

"I hope you are safely home in a few days. I will try to find out more tomorrow, but I am sure that it is almost over." He sounded reassuring,

I wanted to believe him, but my gut warned me of impending misfortune, at least tonight there was no danger and it was peaceful.

He wanted to know my interests and hobbies, the places I had visited and how I ended up in Iraq. I talked about my little town in West Virginia and my love of open spaces. I explained how the death of my mother had devastated the family and led to my quest to find solace eventually landing me in his country. The memories of the loving friendship I had built with N and her family flooded into my mind and drove part of my narrative. He listened in fascination as my account continued into the hours of night. He sat there focused on every word coming out of my mouth.

Eventually I got tired and laid on the bed leaning on my elbow. My back had started to ache from sitting against the hard wall. He got the hint and stood up, involuntarily stretching. A grin spread across my lips, he had patiently sat on that hard wooden chair, listening to my stories, not once shifting or letting me on about his fatigue.

'How different can people be, on one hand there were the kind like Jabbar and then there were ones like N and Ali.' I thought to myself as I eyed his back leaving the cell.

I slumped on the bed and closed my eyes. Sleep took hold of me in minutes.

Day 14

I had slept soundly for a change. Opening my eyes I looked around, strangely I thought that I was back home till I saw the empty bowls sitting on the table, Ali had forgotten to take them last night and I recalled our conversation and then comprehended the reality of my surroundings. Groaning, I sat up and rubbed my eyes. My hair was a tangled mess, brushing it with my fingers I got off the bed. The next destination was the bathroom as always, and then back to the room. I was out of the woods regarding my condition and Jaria had been a blessing in all of this. I had to thank her not only for that but for yesterday. I waited for her to come; the noise outside grew like the previous day. The sleeping cronies were awakening. I could envision them, following their sleazy leader around the area like a pack of jackals. The thought of Jabbar made me wince. I hoped that I wouldn't have to see him again but I had a premonition that hoping was not going to help.

My thought process was broken by the sound of the door opening. Jaria was there. I was joyous to see her like a child getting candy, she was a little taken aback by my enthusiasm, as she came near and put down the platter of food, I hugged her. Now she was downright astounded. She didn't push me back or hug me in return, just stood there getting hugged by me. I let her go after a few seconds; she mustered a smile to make me feel a little less foolish.

"I wanted to thank you for all your help and kindness, and for yesterday. You saved me from that perv." I moved to the bed,

"I am happy to help, and I do it for Ali and you have proven yourself to be an honorable person. I am all for justice, but I would never let Jabbar take advantage of you. I have the keys to your room, and he is not going to get them. Yesterday he stole them from Ali's room and today I will keep his too. Thanks for not telling Ali about him, he would have ripped his head off. That would have been bad. Daanish is not aware of Jabbar's exploits and he is getting out of hand, but I fear he has become too strong for Daanish." dismay lined her old face,

"Why had he come here yesterday? Hadn't Daanish assigned Ali with this job? Don't they have to follow orders?" Concern filled my voice,

"Yes, but there is a change."

"What do you mean a change and please don't talk in riddles. I want the truth." I was incensed by her vague answers.

"Okay, there has to be some trouble when so much money is involved, Jabbar has his own militia, and he is challenging the leadership of Daanish. He has grand ideas for himself, and he wants a big cut of the money." She sat on the chair tired, the creases of her face deepening,

"What money? What do you mean his cut and so much money, where did the money come from?" my head was trying to wrap itself around this new information.

"Listen, these people they work for money. Daanish and his militia are hired killers and so is Jabbar, but he is greedier and more dangerous than Daanish. He has been doing this for a long time but now Jabbar wants to be the leader. You are one of the reasons; they have been trying to sell you to the highest bidder, your government and other militias. Anyone who can make it worth their while. That's why it's taking so long." She was observing the changing color of my face,

"Does Ali know all this, and how do you know this?" my voice had reduced to a whisper,

"No, he doesn't but I think he is suspicious now. He doesn't have any particular friends that could help him. Throughout this he has never questioned Daanish's authority; he did what he was told, believing he was helping the cause of the people. I know all this because I serve here as their help, and when you are serving food to people for a long time and have been around them in situations less private you pick up information. They underestimate women like me, old and worn out, nobody pays attention to the help." Sarcasm lined her voice as she explained.

"How would Ali not know all this?" It was hard for me to believe that.

"He has been working for Daanish and as I told you Daanish is very shrewd, he has kept secrets well hidden from anyone he wanted to hide them from. All Ali wanted was to find the killers of his family and he never got more involved in anything else." Jaria sounded sincere. I sat back and sighed, I was so wrong about all of this, it was never going to end, and these men were not letting me go. Fear gripped my heart; if Ali didn't know then he was only a pawn in the hands of Daanish who was controlling him until he found the murderers of his parents and sister.

"What will happen to me? Please tell me the truth." I looked at her,

"To be honest I don't know. Jabbar has been fighting with Daanish to have you but he has not given in yet." Jaria was serious and it was interpretable from her expression that she was being honest with me.

"This is all I have picked up till now, they are being very secretive about it all." She pushed the chair back and stood up. My breakfast was sitting on the table untouched. I had lost my appetite. She pushed it towards me.

"Eat, you need your strength. This will be a long journey and you can't be weak for it."

I looked at her incredulous, what did she want me to do? This was hell for me and preserving my strength would only mean lengthening a cursed life.

"I am not hungry." I pushed it back agitated,

"Sarah, you have to understand, you have to be ready and strong for the future. The sands are shifting, and I can feel the tremors" Her riddles again, she didn't leave me until I had eaten at least half of everything she had brought. The walls seemed to be closing in after Jaria left the cell. Ali hadn't come this morning, probably had left for the place he had to travel to for information, but why did he have to go somewhere else to explore for answers. That was as confounding as the notion that he hadn't known anything about Daanish's operations. With every passing minute my heart sank, and I felt more trapped.

Walking around I focused on keeping my cool and decided to ask Ali if he could do anything about the situation. There was no guarantee but perhaps he could persuade Daanish to negotiate with my government rather than other militias. Obviously, the government could offer them far more than any local militia could, I hoped.

I stopped and stared at the window in the wall, my only access to the world outside,

"Hello sweetheart, how are you doing today?" Jabbar's voice snatched my attention to him; he was standing outside the locked door. Relief washed over me; Jaria had been a life saver again. He couldn't enter; there was no key to unlock the door.

"Don't worry this door won't hold me for long. I came to see my prize. I will enjoy having you." His words cut through me,

"You are never going to have me. You degenerate! Keep dreaming." I spat at him, my palms getting sweaty, but I had to be brave.

He laughed loudly, "You are spirited, that's very appealing. You have to make yourself boring not attractive. That's the ticket." His voice pierced my ears. I turned away and sat on the vacant chair, ignoring him.

"You can ignore me now but not in a few days. Your precious Ali and Jaria will not be able to protect you for long." His words lingered in the corridor as he walked away banging the door.

I sat there unable to think coherently, 'in a few days I won't be able to ignore him' the words haunted my mind. The midday sunlight filtered in through the window, my earlier wish to look outside, to inspect the compound was quashed. The sounds of his men outside pierced my ears, no matter how hard I covered them to block out the noise. My resolve was at the brink of shattering.

At that moment I just wanted to get out of there even if it meant running out and getting shot, but instead I lay in bed holding my head. I waited for Jaria as the minutes crawled along, but she never came. Evening drew close as the shadows settled in the cell with darkness taking hold. I was going out of my mind, sitting alone enclosed in the four walls of the cell. Night had fallen when the door opened and I sprinted behind the table as if it could stop the intruder, but it was Ali, at last. He had dinner in his hands. His clothes were dusty, and his face was marred with fatigue. He slowly made his way in and silently gave me one of the plates in his hands not even saying hi. Today we didn't have oatmeal. I stared at the food and then him; he was sitting holding his plate like an automaton. It was very obvious by his attitude and silence that he was profoundly distressed. He didn't speak and I couldn't, the relief of finally seeing him and the tension of the day had depleted my energy. Quietly I came and sat on the bed. He was still staring at his food when I asked him about his fact-finding mission. He raised his eyes to meet mine; there was a storm in their dark depths. He had definitely found something, and it clearly wasn't good. He lowered his eyes as the doubts and questions in mine got to him. I picked at my food as did he; there was a burdensome stillness in the room. I wanted him to tell me the secrets he had discovered, not that I had any ignorance of what they might be, thanks to Jaria but Ali remained silent, and we sat there lost in our thoughts. Minutes passed in slow motion, the suspense was getting to me, and I had to ask.

"Ali have you found out something about my release?" Jaria had informed me about the fiasco regarding me, but I still hoped that there might be a change of fate.

"Yeah, I did find some stuff, but I think that it might be false. I have to verify it. Things seem different then they are, and I can't give you any information that I am not sure about." His visage showed a fierce battle within him. He was not going to tell me.

"How will you confirm your discovery?"

"I will go to the source." He was determined, and I could only guess who the source was. This was all twisted,

211

I didn't want to know anymore, he was not certain of what he knew, and Jaria's narration had me scared and confused. Who was right in all of this? Maybe both or maybe none.

I shook my head to rid my brain of all the doubts and alarming thoughts. I was sick of it and just wanted to have some peace. My heart pushed me to trust Ali, he had been protecting me till now and I believed he would do the same in the future. How? I didn't know but I had faith that he wouldn't let anything happen to me. It was kind of wishful thinking, but my heart believed in him.

"What did you do all day?" Ali's voice brought me back to the real world, it was an absurd question, what could I do locked in this room, but I suppose he had nothing better to ask.

"Nothing, walked around in this cell, ate breakfast and waited for Jaria and listened to rude noises made by Jabbar's men outside." I had a scowl on my face, the long description made him smile, the tension on his face faded a bit.

"You want to play a game of cards?" He picked up the deck. I was all for it, dwelling on the length of hours and the strain of imprisonment was only self-defeating, being engaged in some activity was a better way to kill time. He probably had the same problem, I was a prisoner by force, and he was by choice, a consequence of his own demons.

We played cards and talked; it was my turn to dig deeper into his past. I knew his story, but I guessed there was more to it then he had divulged, and I intended to know it all. He went back to the days his father taught and his mother was still studying, to his childhood when he was always cherished. Then he recounted the time when his sister was born and how jealous he had become of the baby. He had plans to get rid of her but when they brought her home and he took her in his arms for the first time, he gave up on his plans. There was a light in his eyes as he got lost in his recollections, then suddenly he jumped to his feet and ran out. I was shocked by his sudden action, but he was back within a minute with the photograph of his family and a fairytale comic book. He gave me the picture, a beautiful woman holding a pretty little girl with adorable curls and a handsome man standing next to a young Ali smiled at me. He handed me the comic book, it was about a fairy princess, with small markings on some pages as I turned them.

"This was her favorite book, she asked me to read it to her that day and I had promised I would after the game. Sometimes I acted it out for her, and she loved it." Ali's voice shook with grief and his eyes were glassy with unshed tears. He jerked his head and continued with other events in his life as I held onto the picture and the comic book. He told me about how Daanish had found him on the streets lost in the slums. The story struck me as odd, because Daanish was not as powerful as he was today, and Ali's city wasn't in his domain. According to Ali's account he had expanded his area of influence in the recent years, before he was limited to his own hometown and province. Ali's father lived a little far from his domain in the south where they still hadn't been able to spread their power, then how did he end up picking Ali from there. I got hooked on that detail in all his history, critically I looked at it from different angles, I was skeptical of Ali's faith in the coincidental meeting with Daanish. He was a war lord, why would he be interested in providing shelter to Ali without reason. I suspected a hidden motive, my gut told me there was more to this then Ali's knowledge but as we discussed I couldn't put my finger on it and he shrugged it off by charting it to Daanish's mission to find and help destitute youth fight for the country, relating his days in this and other camps where he had grown up. There was a distinct feeling of loneliness in his tale, even when he joked about his first days in the local college to study chemical engineering, which Daanish had insisted on, that acute sense of isolation was discernable. Today he spoke, and I listened. Only my question about having anyone special in his life made him stop long enough to look at me in a way that made me blush. There was a fire in his eyes, and it permeated the whole space around me, enveloping me in a warm haze. I looked away and let him continue, his tale culminated in the description of the recent events.

His life had been harsh with no one to love him after the death of his family. Daanish had given him a roof over his head and food, but it had its price that Ali was paying. The hardships he faced in the time he was on his own, without any home, living on the streets and scrapping for a shred of food made my heart melt. The image of his smiling innocent face in the photograph with his family destroyed by someone's cruel hand wrenched my soul. I

214

couldn't imagine how that young boy would have felt as his world lay in ruins. I observed him as he finished, searching for something there but he had learned well to hide the fragments of his soul from the eyes of the outside world except for the few occasional displays. Hours had passed, only the silence outside reminded us of the late hour. We both had been sitting quiet after he was done, and I didn't dare address him after my last inquiry. I sat there fumbling with the folds of my dress.

"I am sorry to bore you, but I lost track of time." His voice made me raise my eyes to directly peer into his; I didn't want him to get the wrong impression of my shy behavior.

"No, you didn't I......... just was so engrossed in it, your courage and fortitude in the face of adversity. I was thinking about the little boy lost in this huge world, all alone and afraid, it just kills me." My last words made him smile. I was amazed at his reaction,

"Please don't die on me; I wouldn't be able to explain a death caused by a history lesson." The mischief in his voice made me grin amid welling tears, the thought of his lost family and my own pushed me over the edge as droplets poured from the corners of my eyes. He spontaneously wiped them as they escaped with his fingertips. The slight touch sent sparks down my spine, causing my heart to throb. As quickly as he had done it, he pulled his hand back.

"I am sorry; I didn't mean to make you uncomfortable." His apology was odd to hear because his touch didn't make me uncomfortable. Rather it was the sweetest feeling that filled up my senses. The proximity of his being made me deeply aware of my own and the extraordinary effect it had on me, but it also felt like the most natural thing in the world to be with him.

"It's perfectly fine, I am okay don't worry." I replied hastily looking at the floor as I didn't have the courage to look up at him. His touch made me remember when he enclosed his hands around to keep me from screaming before. I could feel my back against his firm chest, the warmth of his body, the slow loss of self-control. As the memories flashed through my mind I blushed incessantly. I knew he was watching, and it was disconcerting as colors danced off my face.

"I better go, you must be tired and in need of rest." He got up; I hoped he would stay, but to say that would be inviting trouble. He was nice to me, but it didn't mean that he had any interest further than that.

Oddly enough I stood up too and walked with him to the door of my cell. I had not done that before and he watched as I accompanied him the short distance,

"Sleep well. I will see you tomorrow." He stepped out, suddenly I remembered something.

"Wait." I almost shouted freezing him in his place, running to the bed I picked up the photograph and all three books, the old ones he had given me earlier and the small comic book and came to him. His expression changed from astonishment to solemnness.

"Thank you, Sarah." His voice was a little shaky,

"For what?" I asked as I gave him his possessions.

"For being so considerate, and for listening......... for being here." He stepped out and closing the door walked to his room slowly.

I came back to my bed and laid down, his story resonating in my mind, every detail, all the little incidents, the photograph, the destruction of his innocence. Reflecting on his past made my heart burst. I wanted to cry, and I did, shedding tears for the little boy whose universe was taken from him in one cruel sweep of fate. Eventually sleep brought peace to my aching heart, and as I slept, I dreamed of his arms holding and protecting me from the world.

Day 15

Finally, I woke up to a day when I could go back to functioning normally, clean up and be prepared for anything. The morning sun shone through the tiny window and a few rays of light peeped through the barred door. I sat up and tied my hair, last night's revelations and the previous days had me questioning my devious strategy. Ali had been kind and honorable to me despite being part of this band of thugs and he had not let anyone take advantage of me. The whole idea of deceiving him, using him for my own gains was becoming impossible, and moreover I could see a glimpse of optimism for my imminent release because he was going to talk to Daanish and to persuade him to negotiate a deal with the Americans. I had to wait and give it a chance, there was hope.

After washing up, I went to the door and looked out the bars. It was a first for me. I hadn't done this in the fourteen days I had been incarcerated. The corridor was empty. I had half hoped to find someone, Ali or Jaria, but the place was quiet. Disappointed I came back to the middle of the room and listened for sounds outside but there was nothing audible there. I brought out the bucket and scanned the area, the vehicles were being prepped in hushed tones. I watched the soldiers as they scurried about doing their tasks. I had noticed that since their arrival these men were left alone, the other residents of the camp deliberately tried to avoid them. I had seen them divert their route if they saw those men sitting in their paths. It was unexplainable. Why would they be so daunted by these soldiers? I concluded it to be the difference in leadership. I could understand why Jabbar hadn't been able to overthrow Daanish, it was because nobody liked him or trusted him, mostly they were afraid of him and his men. I wished he would leave and never return, coming off the pail I prayed for his demise. As I prayed, it shocked me because this was the first time I had thought ill of someone to the extent of praying for their death. I suddenly felt sad, what had they done to me? My nature was altering, I had changed, taking to deceiving and pretending but then I shook off the notion. Still I vowed to rescind my prayer but frankly I knew probably a lot of people shared my sentiments about Jabbar.

Ali's books were gone and right now I missed them, 'should have kept them to keep myself busy' I scolded myself. I planned to bathe later when the cell's heat usually became unbearable, and also after I had acquired some clean clothes from Jaria. So, I was completely at leisure listening to the whirring of the engines outside, anticipating Jaria's imminent arrival with breakfast.

Someone opened the door, I expected Jaria as she had been bringing my meals for a few days since Daanish had come to reside in the camp, but I was pleasantly surprised by Ali standing at the door,

"It's you! Good morning, so what's for breakfast, hopefully not oatmeal!" My mood lightened at his sight. He smiled broadly, his face was cleanshaven and his hair was wet. I stared at him for a minute more then I should have, he noticed, and I had to quickly look for something on the wall. He curbed his grin and came to the table then placed the tray with two bowls of oatmeal on it. A giggle escaped my lips, I just had to, it was absurd to have the same food for breakfast, lunch and dinner.

"I brought mine with yours, so you had no chance of suspecting that this was only given to you." His tone was impish; I rolled my eyes at him and picked up one of the bowls.

"I didn't, obviously the only way to keep you as his slave is through this wonderful oatmeal, this is the only thing making you 'stick around'." I said it with utmost seriousness on my face, and it made him laugh out loud, which he checked as soon as he laughed.

"You are funny. Please don't make me laugh, I will choke." He was having trouble completing his sentence,

"You mean you are not already choking on this." I pushed a spoonful of the lumpy oatmeal under his nose. He had a fit of laughter; putting down his spoon he slapped his hand over his mouth to mute the sound. It was so much fun seeing him laugh, it was like sunshine had crossed over from heaven and landed straight into my lap. He stopped after a minute or two as I made a face at him grinning. It didn't feel like we were sitting in a cell having a stale meal but rather felt like at leisure sitting in a park cracking jokes. For a short time, it made me forget where I was and what I was doing there.

Finishing, I gave my bowl to him; he put it in the tray, pursing his lips in an attempt to remain serious.

"Do you want to play one of your games?" he asked downing the coffee he had brought; I didn't drink coffee, which he had found out when I kept leaving the full cup in the tray in the beginning. I sipped water from the glass in my hand and signaled him to take out any game. He took out the checkerboard and we set it up. The game started in silence as usual. I started thrashing him once again. Then someone shouted outside distracting us from the game,

"Is Jabbar leaving?" I remembered,

"Yes he is. Good riddance." His hatred for the man was visible from his expression.

"Will you ask about me today?" I had been meaning to ask him.

"Yes, but presently Daanish is not in the camp, he went out early in the morning. He will be returning by midday, and I will see him then. Everything will be okay, don't worry." He sounded sure and I prayed that he was right to be so positive. Just then Jaria entered, she stopped at the entrance and eyed us playing the game. The expression on her face was inscrutable as always.

"Can I take the tray?" she addressed Ali.

"Yes Jaria, we are done, is Jabbar gone?" Ali's inquisition made her stop as she stepped towards the door.

"No, he is still here, but his men are ready, he was looking for Daanish I heard. You should go out more Ali, in your men, they are getting restless. They are suspicious of you spending time in here." Jaria was worried.

"Why are they suspicious? This has nothing to do with them; they can practice their skills among themselves. Can't I have some hours to myself?" He was agitated and complained like a kid, but I saw the lines on Jaria's face getting more furrowed, she was correct, Ali had to be out there for his own sake if not for theirs. I intervened,

"Ali you should go. It is about time for Daanish to return. Also, you have to meet him. Please, she is spot on; it is dangerous for you to be unaware of the proceedings in this camp." I started picking up the game pieces. Ali left his place a little confused by my remarks but went out silently. Jaria was about to leave behind him when I called her and explained that I needed new clothes and she could take all the supplies she had provided me. She nodded and walked out to join Ali, who was somber as he closed the cell door. Jaria came back later with a new set of clothes; it was a peach dress with light embroidery and lace around the neckline. I held the cloth admiring the beautiful material, she gave me the dress and took the things I didn't need any more from the bathroom, I caught her at the cell door,

"Jaria I am so thankful to you for letting me wear these clothes. I assume it isn't easy for you, but I want you to know that I will never forget your generosity." My voice

222

was sincere, I really appreciated what she was doing for me, and I wanted her to know even if she thought that it was her duty. To me her service had been a difference between life and hell.

"It's nothing. My daughter doesn't need them, and you remind me of her sometimes. Life is unpredictable; I had never thought I would end up here or that I will grow old without my husband and daughter." Her face had become pale; I could feel her grief it was like so many others who were living in misery in this country. She was alone and dragging the burden of her life holding onto some of the material memories of her long-lost loved ones, which she had the strength to share with me. She came back and slumped on the chair, tired and blank,

"I pray that you get out of here unharmed, and Ali can also have a life which he can call a life. He is like my son; I wish for him to be happy." she was staring at the pile of things in her hands. I sat on the bed and patted her hand. I knew these were not the best of circumstances for either of us and she wasn't responsible for it. We all had our own pains to endure,

"We will be fine." My voice was tender,

It was an involuntary statement, but I later realized the depth of it. She stayed with me for a brief period talking about her family and the good times. Later I went for a bath. It was a good half hour till I was out again, I heard vehicles whirring again and leaving, quickly I got on the bucket and watched Jabbar's men leave the compound. As soon as the last car was out, people started pouring out from the surrounding buildings and there was hustle bustle all over the place. It was like an unseen prison sentence was lifted. I came to the chair and sat on it running my fingers through the tangles of my hair. My hair was long, and it was difficult to brush it using fingers alone but I had nothing else to use. After struggling for a bit, I started walking around the cell anticipating Ali's meeting with Daanish. He probably was with him right that instant discussing the end of my confinement. The prospect of being free should have been joyous but when it finally was a possibility my heart sank unknowingly.

Evening was approaching, I hoped Ali would come soon, pacing the cell I kept going to the door and checking but he was nowhere. Expectation and fear both fettered my soul. I waited for him impatiently, my pacing becoming faster by the minute. In the end I got so tired that I had to sit and rest.

The door lock rattled making me jump from my place, but seeing Jaria dampened my spirit.

"Do you want me to bring your food? I also wanted to make sure you didn't need anything more. I am sorry it's a little late."

"Where is Ali, Jaria? He was going to meet Daanish and I was expecting him to come by now." My impatience was spilling over.

"He went to see him, but I haven't seen him after that." Jaria all of a sudden looked alarmed,

"I will look for him, he should be in with his men." she was out of the cell in seconds.

I sat there all alone fearful, 'why hadn't Ali come, was there a problem?' My brain was darting in different directions, building scenarios and breaking them down when the door creaked open one more time, I thought it was Jaria, but Ali stood at the threshold. Excited I jumped to my feet, he came close and the somber expression on his face made my heart sink,

"Ali what happened, why didn't you come for so long, it's late evening." I asked. He stared directly into my eyes; there was anguish in his,

"Sarah, please sit I need to talk to you." He moved closer, I sat on the bed again,

"I met with Daanish, actually he was going to call me. He has decided to take you with him to one of our hideouts near Baghdad. I have to travel to another post to take control of that area." His voice was very hollow and gloomy like coming from a well. I couldn't comprehend him, was he telling me that Daanish was taking me away and Ali was going to leave me at his mercy. He was not going to do anything! My insides twisted with anxiety and disbelief,

"What do you mean, you said you were going to persuade him to make a deal with my government so I could be free. And now I will be dragged to some unknown place with him and maybe Jabbar." Anger surged in me as I jumped to my feet and came face to face with Ali. It was an unpredictable turn of events which I had not anticipated at all. I knew that being a prisoner I had to accept my fate if I wanted to live, but then again I had no desire to live if this persisted. My expectations from Ali were probably wishful as he had no obligation to do anything for me. He had been kind but that didn't mean he would relinquish his loyalties to his group. I needed to understand that, live with it, but at that moment I felt betrayed and cheated,

"No, no, he has negotiated with your government, it's almost resolved that's why he is going there. Jabbar is gone he won't be near you, but I can't come. Daanish is sending me to the west." Ali's face was deathly pale, he looked sick, but I didn't care, how could he do this?

"You are trusting him, aren't you going to do something. He is not going to keep his word. I know it." It was hard for me to speak; fury choked my voice,

"No Sarah, he is not going to do that, you have to trust me. I can't defy him." Ali was trying to soothe me.

"Ali, if you are sending me alone with them then I'd rather die here. I am not going to stand this anymore. I am going to get out of here right now even if it kills me." I was seething with anger. I just couldn't accept this. Picking up the table, I threw it at him, which he avoided by ducking, and then ran to the door. I was blind with rage, if they were going to shoot me let them, grinding my teeth I fumed. Ali fast as lightning caught me from behind before I could reach the door. I turned around in his grip and started hitting him, clawing at everything I could get my hands on. He grunted with pain as I bumped my head in his chest and scratched him. First, he held my arms softly trying to stop the onslaught but when I hit him twice in his chest and stamped my feet on his, he wrapped his arms around me pinning my hands behind my back and my body against his, breathing heavily. I was not in the mood to be restrained, jerking my head back I screamed and writhed like crazy in his arms.

"Let me go, I am not going with your boss, you can give him some other prey." I clenched my fists trying to get my hands released but Ali's grip was very strong,

"Sarah please don't do this, it's dangerous. Don't scream, please, you will be fine. If you run, they will kill you, or worse. Please." He pleaded,

"Let them kill me. I rather die here then be played around with and be killed for his amusement." My voice broke as despair took over. At last Ali was abandoning me. I wanted him to leave me and let me die. I tried again to break his hold trying to pull my arms out, but it was useless. Leaning my head back once more, I rammed it in his chest. He groaned and pulled me closer, pressing me to him to stop my assault. Defeated and incensed, in one last attempt I opened my mouth to scream fury but before I could he lowered his face and covered my mouth with his.

As his lips touched mine, a tremor went through every fiber of my body making it numb. My legs became limp and I was enveloped in a warmth which I had never experienced before. It was like I was in water floating weightless. I should have hated him. I should have pushed him back, but his kiss was like sweet nectar flowing in, and opening my mouth I let him in. His arms eased into holding me in an embrace, encircling my waist as he released my hands. I lifted them around his neck, getting them tangled

227

in his dark hair. As our kiss deepened, he demanded more of me, pulling me even closer, sliding his hands over my back as my body arched to his. Everything faded away as he kissed me. To be in his arms was blissful beyond measure, but there was a desperation in his kiss. A hunger that made me breathless, but I didn't care about as I melted in his arms.

I had never felt like this in my entire life. It just occurred to me that the feelings I had for him were not mere gratitude or appreciation. I was in love with him and when he took me in his arms it was like I was safe, I was complete.

"Ali!" Jaria's voice snatched us back from paradise; he pulled himself away from me and gently pushed me back, his face awash in dread. The fire in his eyes was replaced with pain like that of a wounded animal stuck in a trap,

"I am sorry Sarah, I am so sorry, I shouldn't have, please forgive me." his voice was agony, I had just come out of my hypnosis staring at him disbelievingly, 'why was he apologizing.'

"Ali, please." It was all I could say before he darted out of the room leaving me standing alone with Jaria.

I was motionless until my legs gave way and I collapsed on the floor, Jaria came running to my side

"Sarah are you okay?" she propped me up onto the chair.

I was speechless, my brain incoherent, 'what had just happened?'

Everything seemed surreal and fake, like I was in a 3D movie with me at the center of it. My head spun and my eyes stung, I felt tears running down my face, but I didn't know that I was crying.

"Sarah, here drink this." Jaria pressed a glass of water to my lips, drop by drop it trickled down my throat. Cold water was like balm to my hurting head. My senses were returning slowly. I couldn't believe Ali, was I just a pasttime for him, but when did he profess any feelings for me. I had to be crazy to even speculate about any sentiments from him, I was a prisoner and nothing more. He had kissed me in the heat of the moment, but it didn't signify any real emotions, the foolishness was only on my part, and I had been corrected, how profusely he had apologized for succumbing to a moment of weakness, as if he had committed a crime, like he had corrupted a piece of merchandise. I was the property of his boss, and he was the slave of his bidding, I was only a complication which he was dumping in the lap of his master. My eyes were opened to the real facts and the real severity of my circumstances. Jaria sat next to me on the bed as my feet hung over the side and I held my throbbing head.

Time ticked by and I just sat there, with a blank mind. 'What was I going to do'. I was certain that Daanish had other plans for me then setting me free, 'why was Ali being so blind.' Jaria had been very silent during all this. I expected her to be highly critical of my behavior but there was utter muteness. I didn't want to talk and apparently neither did she. I looked up afraid to see contempt and resentment on her face but there was only sympathy. This small sign of compassion broke me. I cried for what seemed like a lifetime, Jaria never left my side, patting me gently and consoling me. I had not expected such considerate behavior from her, the one whom I had expected empathy from had turned away from me, deserting me.

"Sarah please stop crying, you will be fine. I know." She eventually spoke softly, holding my hand. I had stopped, but an occasional sob slipped out. The room was darker, and the sun had set outside. My orientation of time and space was muddled, with no assessment of whether minutes or hours had passed. Her soft words made me wonder how she could be positive of my fate. I had lost hope, it was not the fear of death or Daanish or even Jabbar, it was the loss of my soul which was killing me. I had fallen in love with a cold-hearted machine that had no will of its own, who would never love me back, never would be mine.

I had to be strong, composed. I was not going to give him the pleasure of turning me over to his master. Jaria had eventually left the cell and I sat in the dim light with my mind stumbling in an aimless pursuit of shattered dreams. A look at my hands made me furious, he had been holding them that day when he stopped me from screaming and today when he held me, I had them tangled in his hair. I didn't want to see any part of my body that he had touched. I wanted darkness and peace. Scanning the room for a possible means, I saw the table still lying next to the wall. It would work. I picked it up, and climbing onto the bed, flung it smacking the light bulb to little pieces. I threw the table on the side and sat down on the bed. The only light in the cell now was coming from the opening in the wall. I lay down on the bed and closed my eyes.

Darkness had a calming effect on me, my solitude disturbed only by an occasional sound from somewhere in the camp.

Another clinking alerted me, the silhouette of a person was visible in the meager light of the moon, it was Jaria,

"What happened? Sarah!" there were clear signs of anxiety in her tone,

"I am here, Jaria. Don't worry your prisoner is intact, good to go." I replied sarcastically,

"How did the light go out, did the bulb fuse?" she came in,

"No, I broke it." I said flatly.

"Um, I see, but how will you see. I brought some food for you." She found the chair and sat on it. "Where is the table?"

"I don't know, I threw it, and I am not hungry." I didn't get up,

"Sarah, I need to explain something to you. You have to understand Ali, he is bound by the promises he has made. He is bound by his oaths. He will not break them. These people have given him a place and they will help him find the murderers of his parents. He can't go against them. It will be dangerous for you and for his cause." Jaria said gravely, her voice was kind but matter of fact.

"How can you defend him, what promises? Which oaths? The promises and oaths to these thugs. He has given them his whole life, why can't he stop?" I couldn't comprehend her logic,

"Not his promises to these people but to his parents, to his little sister that he will get justice for them and will find their killers. These thugs are the only source of help. He has to stay with them. He has had a very hard life, don't judge him, you can't judge him. He is the only one here who has kept you safe and has made sure for the future that you stay secure." Jaria spoke aggravated,

"How is he keeping me safe? By sending me with his master, that man has no integrity, didn't you tell me that? He has me up for auction. Why doesn't Ali know this?" I responded more annoyed.

"Sarah, he has made a deal with Daanish, he will let you go."

"What? Why didn't he tell me, what deal? I am not going anywhere. I don't trust him or anyone." I screamed,

"That's why he didn't say anything. You have to go with Daanish so he can return you to the authorities. There is nothing you can do." Jaria's voice rose with anger.

My head had started to throb again. I wrapped my arms around it and tried to block out the pain, everything spun as white dots of light flickered in front of my eyes. I felt nauseous and ran to the bathroom stumbling on the way, breaking the light bulb wasn't very smart with its shards showering the floor. Throwing up whatever little food I had in my system I came out with a blinding headache. Jaria was standing outside the bathroom door waiting for me. Helping me get to the bed she left and returned a little later with a glass of water and some medicine. I took it and fell on the bed, everything that had happened until now ran through my head like a freight train, images of Ali and his parents, Jaria and her daughter, N, my father and brothers, my mother's grave, her dying hours and eventually Ali. His face a picture of the torment wrecking him and his eyes bearing the shades of storms. I pressed the palms of my hands on my eyes tightly to keep the images at bay, but they took over streaked with tiny dots of light and colors as my head felt like exploding with pain. At last, I lost consciousness.

When I awoke the light bulb was fixed and was brighter than the last one, I could actually see things, but presently it was hurting my eyes and I wanted it to be turned off. Getting up was an ordeal, my head felt like it had gel swimming in it, and I could hardly balance, standing up didn't seem to be an option. I lay in bed staring at the ceiling and hoping for a swift death. Jaria said Ali had made a deal with Daanish and he planned to release me but I had a premonition that fulfilling his word to Ali wasn't on his agenda. Everyone was using me; Ali had no interest in me. He had made sure I was out of his way so he could get back to his original point of focus. I cursed everybody, even my gym teacher. I tried to sit again and was able to, leaning on the wall I saw the food platter sitting on the table. So, Jaria had left me some morsels to keep me fed, alive and kicking for the final hunt, it made me livid.

Mustering last remnants of my energy I got up and threw the plate at the door. It was plastic but I had thrown the table with it which clanked loudly against the metal door. Pleased, I returned to the bed.

Sitting down I looked at the door and found Ali standing there, he was just standing there watching. The corridor was darker than the room and I couldn't see his face clearly but as soon as our eyes met he turned and left.

'Why had he come, was he concerned?' I knew his room was next to mine and he could hear everything that went on in mine, but I hadn't expected him to come in the middle of the night. I lay with my eyes wide open. The warmth of his embrace and the heat of his kiss still was very much alive in me. I could vividly remember the taste of his lips and the feel of his hands sliding down my back, tracing the curves of my body. I didn't want to, but it was beyond my control. Sleep was not going to be an option tonight, hopelessly I turned on the side and closed my eyes.

Day 15 (Ali)

What had I done! I couldn't believe what just happened. I had just kissed her. I had completely surrendered to the desire to have her, and God, I wanted her!

I was desperate, she was being taken away and I would never see her. Thinking of the inevitable, my heart tore with misery. The room was like a dark hole symbolizing my life. I was the victim of a pact, a contract I had made with the devil himself. It was an accord signed in blood and it would take more blood to break it. I could never risk her; never could I stand by and watch her getting hurt. She was better off gone and taken to her people safe and secure, away from me, away from this tragedy I called my life.

Past few days I had spent searching for answers, the clues to the mysteries surrounding this whole affair. It had taken me time and a good amount of traveling but I had discovered things that shattered the allegiance and loyalty I had for the people I served, leaving behind only a drive to get Sarah to safety and fulfill my promises to the ones I had lost.

Sarah had pushed me to look for the truth; I had kept my eyes closed until now trusting Daanish and his word but with every passing day my faith in him was waning and a relentless need to know the reality was replacing it. I had decided to satisfy Sarah but in fact it was a quest to convince myself of the path I had taken and the comrades I had picked or rather who had picked me. The facts were daunting, and I had to go back and confirm them a second time but still it was too much to accept, all that I had believed, every act I had committed in that fight was for a sham.

Sarah had not bothered me too much about the fact finding mission but she was concerned and I think she trusted me.

"She trusted me!" I banged my fists on the wall, 'She believed I would save her, but now she hates me, she hates me.' I leaned my head on the wall tortured and defeated. I had to give her up, if I hadn't these people would do the unthinkable. I had to make the bargain and take the word of a fiend to protect her.

I had confronted Daanish with every detail I had found out about his and Jabbar's exploits after Jabbar left, hoping for a denial and refutation, something to restore my faith in the man I had respected until now, considered my mentor and my leader. But sadly, I was mistaken; Daanish conceded to everything and tried to drag me into his pitiful demented existence by promising riches and rewards beyond imagination. 'His imagination!' I scoffed at his offer. Then he changed his tactic, bringing in Sarah. He was aware of my weakness, and he used it to get what he wanted. Sarah's life in exchange for mine. Strangely for me it was an easy decision, we agreed on the terms and then I came back to her. She was hopeful and anticipated a positive outcome of my endeavors, not the news that I was sending her with the snake. She was right he wasn't trustworthy, but I had made sure he would keep his part of the bargain. He was not going to give up his power structure for just one hostage. I was his key to defeating his opponent and squash any leftover opposition which could threaten his growing influence and power. I and he both knew it would be my last operation, if I succeeded. If not, then he would be the next target. He was fully aware of what I was capable of, so the mission was designed to put an end to both his threats.

Straightening I stared out in the darkness spreading its wings, remembering the past days spent with Sarah and the peace it had given me. We had shared our life stories with each other, and I had revealed to her facts of my private life which were a secret from every living soul around me. She witnessed parts of me which I had buried inside the depths of my heart. She had shed tears for the lost boy in the picture, a boy who had no way of going back, of returning to the safety of his home. It was her smile that had lightened my burdened existence, her consolation that gave me strength to revisit my past.

Her story was one of love and loss like mine, but it had been in the security of her home, she was at peace with it, not tormented like me looking for justice. Closing my eyes, I remembered her body pressed against mine and her arms around my neck with her hands slightly tangled in my hair. I could feel her skin under my hands, her mouth responding to mine. She hadn't pushed me away, hadn't fought me. Instead, she had kissed me back. I never wanted to let her go but I had to and forget this ever happened. She had to leave, and I had to set off on my last journey. Still, it was beyond my power to keep her out of my mind, if only she knew how I felt. She was convinced I had abandoned her, turned her over to the wolves and my heart ached at the thought but this was better, she would loathe me, forget me and never look back. Never remember the unfortunate soldier who had found a moment's peace and happiness in her arms.

Agonized I ripped the shirt off my back, finding it hard to breathe, all my senses were tuned to her, listening for anything and then there was a noise from her room. I rushed out and found her standing with the food thrown and the table lying in one corner, she had a crazed look about her, I had never seen her like this before. There was something in her eyes, an impression of resolution and loss. She stopped at the foot of her bed and saw me standing at the door in the shadows. There was nothing left to say, turning I came back to my room. The life I had dared to imagine, was lost in the dust of the future.

Day 16

Morning came like any other day of June, bright and sunny. But I couldn't care less. Everything seemed the same, I had been dealt lousy cards by fate far too many times and I was getting tired of it, 'Why wasn't the torment over? Why didn't he shoot me and get it over with?'. I had another internal fight with God, and God won as usual. Pulling myself out of bed, I went to the bathroom and then waited for Jaria. I had a notion Ali wouldn't show up, but there was this little hope in my heart that there might be a turn of events, that I was not being sent with Daanish. But sadly, I was wrong, Jaria came and was astonished by the food scattered all over the floor. I saw her and jumped on the bed, turning to face the wall but she was not the one to yield, nudging my shoulder she coaxed me to get up,

"Sarah, I have brought breakfast for you, please eat."

"No, I am not hungry and if you won't leave I will throw it in your face." I said stubbornly keeping my face towards the wall. She stood back and putting the table upright placed the fresh platter of food on it and then cleaned up the floor. I could hear her skittering about. I didn't want to be acrimonious to her, she had been so nice to me, still my temper was feral at that time. Anyone who was in my line of fire was going to get hurt; unfortunately, she was the one suffering. She was gone after a few minutes and I got up, the mess I had made was removed. Breathing deeply, I sat there trying to formulate a plan in my brain, how could I keep myself from being sent anywhere and get my freedom. There was no solution. I was getting lightheaded, not eating in about twenty hours was getting to me, water wasn't going to sustain me for long. I knew it wouldn't be long before I would collapse and if I kept this up I could be rid of this place faster than I had thought. Suddenly I was happy, this was my way out of this hell hole, I wasn't going to let any drink or food pass my lips. Taking the small water jug, I smashed it on the wall, getting rid of the last of my drinking water. Eagerly, I laid on the bed again, waiting for the final loss of consciousness. With a clanking sound the door opened and some men walked in, all of them wearing black and bearing guns. I was ordered to stand up and come with them. I complied with difficulty as my head swooned with every step. They escorted me out of the cell to the large main room. There a camera man was standing, just as before with the camera ready in hand to film me, a bout of laughter abruptly escaped my lips, startling the men escorting me. They looked at me like I had lost my mind,

"Why do you waste your time, it is absurd. How about just taking a gun and putting a bullet in my head, and

241

please don't pretend ignorance you comprehend every word I am saying." My speech fell on deaf ears as they simply ignored me and pushed me into the chair. I was silent after that. The filming was the same as always, it lasted a few minutes in which I was directed again and again to look at the lens as my eyes kept wandering to the window and the wall where Ali had stood the last time I was filmed. Their job complete, they guided me back to the cell and left, locking the door behind them. I had to give them credit for keeping a straight face throughout this, not paying attention to my outburst. They were like zombies following orders, unresponsive and unmoved.

I barely made it to the bed and fell on it, not only were my legs not able to handle my weight, but my headache was also returning with a vengeance. I had hoped Ali would be there, but he didn't show up and now that I was alone in the cell, that fact hit even harder. 'How could someone be so callous and cold; he could at least have supervised the whole process.' The thoughts crashed in the confines of my mind accentuating the pain. I lay there curled up with both my hands pressed to my head. At first, I kept my groans curbed but as the headache escalated to the level of colossal I was moaning loudly. I wanted Jaria or anyone to give me something for the pain; at that time, I was ready to make a deal with the devil himself. To my relief Jaria entered and she rushed to my side. I was not able to open my eyes, she ran out and a little later she and Ali both were in the cell, he helped her straighten me and this time she gave me a shot, probably realizing I was in no condition to take the medicine orally. The drug put me out in seconds.

The last thing I remember was the face of Ali as he watched me fall asleep.

I awoke to a cool dark room, the light was switched off, it was evening so the cell was devoid of any sunlight. The intensity of the heat reduced in the evening, making it easier to tolerate the weather. My eyes were heavy and my mind foggy, I took a slight peek around and then fatigue took over. I lay there motionless for a few more minutes but when I moved, I felt a sting in my arm. I had to open my eyes to see what it was; I was amazed to see an IV running from my arm. Jaria! She was responsible for this; I wanted to yell and stamp my feet if possible as she had ruined my plans for an early demise. Angrily I tried to rip the IV out of my arm, but a hand stopped me. I recognized the touch; I would know it anywhere in the world.

"Ali why don't you leave me alone and let me die in peace." I said closing my eyes, I wanted to avoid seeing his face.

"You are not going to die." He said quietly,

"I know, you won't even let me die with dignity. Why have you come back, to gloat about your victory over the dumb enemy, namely me." I snapped at him.

There was silence, he didn't reply, I decided to ignore him also. Let him sit there watching over the prize of his boss. I hated him. I wanted to drop dead just to spite him.

"Sarah." He called me gently, I had the fullest intention to not respond but my eyes were more interested in what he had to say then I was. He was sitting on the chair and drew closer to the bed holding the IV in his free hand. I scoffed at him, 'What was this pretense for?' I had seen his true colors. 'Why was he keeping up the sham?' He lowered his head avoiding direct eye contact,

"They took me for another message, and you weren't even there. Why do you want to keep me alive? Ali, please leave me alone. I don't need your sympathy or help." I spat out the words before he could say anything. He didn't raise his head, just sat there listening and holding my hand preventing me from ripping out the IV from my arm. Giving up, I closed my eyes and lay there. I was furious with him. I hated him but the warmth from his hand holding mine permeated my body, stirring a tingling in my belly. I wanted to remain unaffected, reserved but my heart rate was increasing by the second. I cursed my senses playing havoc with my heart due the proximity of his body. I hoped he wasn't aware of what was happening to me, it was embarrassing enough that my own body was out of control, on top of that I couldn't take his condescension.

He remained silent and I eventually fell asleep again, regardless of what my brain thought, with him sitting next to me a sense of peace washed over me and I was relaxed.

The second time when my eyes opened my cell was darker and cooler than before. I suspected nightfall, checking my arm I found the IV had been removed. My headache had vanished, and I felt better. 'Where had he gone?' The first thing to pop in my head was about him. I pushed myself up and looked around, the light was off, and it was hard to see, but I could make out someone sitting against the wall on the floor. Whoever it was had their legs pulled up to the chest. I could recognize Ali; he was just sitting there and didn't even move when I got up. I fell back on the bed, 'what did he want from me?' I had nothing to say to him.

"Sarah............ I am leaving and you probably will never see me again. You will be back with your family in a few days and then will forget about all this ..... I hope. This is the last I will ever talk to you. I am sorry if I hurt you. It was never my intention. It was my responsibility to keep you safe and I have tried my best to do so. I know it sounds strange but that's the truth. My promise to you was that you will return to safety, and I will keep it. Jaria will be here for you until you return to your people. Please take care of yourself, and please forgive me."

I couldn't see his face, but I could hear the angst in his voice, he was leaving and had stayed only to say goodbye, he was never coming back, it felt someone had cut my heart out. My next move was completely involuntary. I came out of bed and reached for him. By then, he was on his feet. I could see his face in the moonlight, and he could mine. Tears ran down my cheeks, it was the oddest thing. I had decided to ignore him, to believe he didn't exist, but when it really hit me, I couldn't take it. I didn't want him to go anywhere. The agony on Ali's face was incomprehensible. I wanted to scream at him, curse him and hurt him but I was numb, I just stood there crying as he watched me silently.

Then he turned and strode out, leaving me in the dark cell, crying, all alone.

Day 16 (Ali)

I was ordered to depart today at daybreak but I wanted to make sure Sarah was all right. Then Jaria came back with breakfast untouched and worried about Sarah's mental state. She was not acting lucidly, adamantly refusing to eat and later had broken her water jug too. I couldn't leave like this, but Daanish couldn't know that I was still there. I wanted to see her, but Daanish's men took her for another message and I remained in my room waiting for her return to be with her alone. Jaria was staying close by per my instructions. As much as I wanted to avoid it I had to speak to her, make her see sense. This was her only way out of this place, and she had to refrain from believing that I was going to stay with her. She had to believe there could be nothing between us ever. They brought her back to the cell, her video message done and over. I stayed in my room a little longer but then I heard her cry out, without thinking twice I ran to her room and was by her side in an instant. She was on her bed sobbing, Jaria had joined me also, I looked at her helplessly,

"She hasn't eaten in more than twenty hours; she will get headaches and stomach aches. She threw away her water also. I think she has found a way to commit suicide." Jaria shook her head.

"No! Please do something." I implored Jaria, "Sarah has to live!"

Jaria was already making her way to the door and within minutes she was back. I thanked God for having her, she had brought an IV and some meds with her. After giving Sarah an injection, Jaria secured the IV in Sarah's arm, as soon as Sarah was asleep. I sat there next to her, unconcerned about Daanish or his retaliation at my defiance of his orders. I was not leaving her like this. I could go get killed after she was feeling better.

She woke up after about two hours and the first thing she was bent on doing was to rip out the IV. I had to hold her down to stop her, she yelled at me and scorned my efforts, but I didn't release her hand until she fell asleep again. The second time she slept for a longer period. Jaria came and took out the IV, assuring me that she was well hydrated by now and wouldn't need it any further. I stayed there keeping watch as night fell, tired I got off the chair and sat on the floor waiting for her to wake up. Jaria checked on me a few times and the last I saw her I made her promise that she would take care of Sarah, protect her. I requested her to accompany Sarah to Baghdad after I was gone, until she was safely with her people. Jaria was already planning to do the same. Involuntarily she had grown fond of Sarah.

I sat there in the dark as the clock ticked closer to the hour of my departure. I had heard Sarah's accusations, how she ridiculed my supposedly fake concern and her pleas to let her die in peace. I had no answers for her, I couldn't tell her about the bargain made or that I had signed my own death warrant for her life. She should never know. She had to go away with a clean slate, never to look back. The last thing I wanted was to only say farewell, unable to leave without it. She awoke in the middle of the night and found me sitting there. I could tell from her demeanor she didn't want me there. I knew I had to go but I had to speak to her one last time. I said what I needed to and stood up to leave when she surprised me by getting out of her bed and coming to me. We stood there staring at each other in the moonlight. Tears ran down her face as I remained silent, restrained by the misfortune of my life from lessening her pain, checked from consoling her in any way. My chains were a burden for me to carry not hers. She had to live free. Eventually I walked out without looking back.

Day 17

Jaria woke me up early in the morning. I was in the middle of a nightmare where Jabbar was dragging me off to some unknown place and I was powerless to stop him. I had fallen asleep in the early hours of the morning after Ali disappeared. The past two days had been like an endless stretch of punishment, and I feared that it would only linger on. Jaria had some food for me, but I wasn't interested. She sat on the chair and waited for me. I remained in bed ignoring her presence. Eventually she came out with the truth,

"Sarah, they have started preparations for departure, and it is said that we will all leave before long. You need to eat to keep your strength."

"Strength for what, I am not hungry, maybe this way I can die peacefully." I said sarcastically.

"Sarah try to understand. I am not here to depress you." She was soft, but my brain was erratic,

"I don't want any food and I don't want to see you. You can leave with your precious Ali, there is nothing to

250

understand." Aggravation was visible on her face as she got up to leave. I was riled, but when she reached the door, I realized that I had to come to terms with my circumstances, and to acknowledge that she had been very considerate throughout my stay in this place and driving her away was not a wise move. She was going to be my only source of comfort wherever I was going. I had to stop her.

"Jaria." I called from behind,

She halted at the door by my sudden cry. I had yelled a little louder than I intended and I closed my mouth as she walked back to me,

"I am sorry; it's not your fault that I am in this predicament. You have shown me civility and kindness and I can't repay you for that. I will not misbehave with you but please don't force me to eat, it makes me sick." I finished with a sigh and sat on the side of the bed. She came close and patted my shoulder,

"Sarah, I am not angry with you, you are one of the bravest people I know. I would help you flee but I don't have the means. I have been praying that you are released and sent home to your family. I am hoping that they are taking you to exchange for their soldiers and money and I'll be there with you. You will be free. Ali has made a deal with them and Daanish would be foolish to break his word to him. I hope that Ali can also get out of this spiral of destruction and have a life." Jaria's hand rested on my shoulder, her tenderness had a serene effect on me, and I became calm. She stayed there for a while, and we talked.

This was the first I spoke to anyone after what happened with Ali, she narrated everything taking place in the camp except for details about Ali. She didn't ask me about that day or what she had seen. I appreciated her discretion; it would have been very difficult for me to explain. I took a bath as per her advice after she left promising to come back soon and wore the clothes, she had brought for me. Tying my hair in a loose braid I waited for her. According to her account we were leaving by noon and Daanish's party was all busy with the preparations. I wondered what kind of preparations a warlord did, probably checked his guns, bombs and other elements of mass destruction along with packing a toothbrush. I smiled at the scenario in my brain and sat back on the bed. The insanity had ended, Ali had left me, and I had to contend with that fact, he had promised me freedom and I had to wait and see if his leader came up to measure. Killing myself wasn't going to work, that much I had gathered in the past two days.

There was noise and commotion to be heard outside, now that I was paying attention. I could hear riving vehicles and men shouting at each other. Jaria returned as promised and brought a cup of hot milk for me, my first since my arrival here. She encouraged me to drink it and sat watching until I had finished the last drop. She didn't leave me after the milk was done rather sat on the chair and read a book while I played with the deck of cards, nothing passed between us. I wanted to ask her about the next leg of my journey, but silence seemed better at that moment, it was tranquil and secure.

The door was locked from inside and Jaria had the key, someone came and banged on it, she got up and opened it, two men marched in. They came close and ordered me to stand up, I did what I was told, and they took out a black cloth and pulled it over my head just like the first day. 'So, the journey has begun'. Jaria followed us as they took me out of the room. I could hear her footsteps behind me, there was no objection made on her accompanying the group. I was taken to another building after being brought out of my confinement; I suspected it to be the main residence of their leader Daanish because a few minutes later I was being addressed by him. It was the same deep voice which had greeted me on the second day of my abduction. He reminded me of all the hospitality that had been extended to me, he assured me that if the negotiations went as planned, I would be in the custody of my military pretty soon. I stood there listening to his lecture. He was right about one thing. I had been treated with care and kindness and had received every facility they could offer. But I knew deep in my gut that he was not telling the truth about the end of my journey. I had this feeling that it was all a con and I should brace myself for the worse.

This man had the air of cold dread, of being dangerous and I had no interest in finding out if I was correct about him or not. The address was done, and I was taken out of the building to a vehicle of some sort. I still had the black cloth covering my face, it was thick and almost blocked out every sight around.

"Sarah." I heard Jaria whisper close to me. She was near and that made me feel better. It was midday and the sun was shining mercilessly burning everyone under its glory. I felt my skin itching with the heat. After so many days in the cell with minimal exposure to it, I was being scorched, 'at least my face is protected.' The thought made me grin.

I walked slowly until my hands hit the hot metal of our transportation. The men who were escorting me made me stand on one side as they opened the door and guided me in. I was sitting in a car hot as an oven. After I got in, two men came and sat on either side of me. I wasn't squished but we were sitting compacted. I had no clue how long the ride would last but in the present circumstances it was of no significance.

'Where had Jaria gone?' The thought made me uncomfortable, 'Had she been left behind? Or was she coming too?'. Then I remembered, she had informed me in the cell that she was also asked to prepare for the next camp. I prayed she was there with me. No matter what was in store for the future, I just wanted to have a familiar face around.

The truck or car started and we were off. I got jerked around and bumped into my companions many times as the road got rough. I didn't remember the roads to Baghdad being so jagged, but I hadn't been out and about the country much. Still, it seemed we were more on a country road then a highway. Setting the assumptions aside, I emptied my mind. I was a captive and whatever was destined would happen, graying my hair over it wasn't going to help. After a few hours we stopped, and I was taken out of the car. A little disoriented I stumbled in the direction I was shoved in. A few moments later, I was inside a building. My escort took me down a flight of stairs in a cool room. Once in there the black cloth was removed from my head and I was able to see. It was a room better than the previous one. Made of concrete, it had no windows, but a bigger bed fastened to the floor as before. The men who had brought me in left, closing the solid steel door making me feel claustrophobic. The other room was old and in bad shape but at least there was some source to reach the outside world, this was like solitary confinement. I sat on the bed and waited. There was a sliding window in the door, which I suspected was for providing the prisoners with food. I looked around to find another door, possibly a bathroom but there was none. How was I supposed to get to one? Now I understood the true extent of my captivity. This was how other prisoners were treated, Ali and Jaria had been extremely kind to me and I appreciated that fact now. I called out from the sliding window, someone came to the door, and I asked for the restroom, he went back and returned a little later. When the door opened, I saw Jaria standing next to the guard, my heart leapt with joy, but the warning in her eyes dampened my enthusiasm. She played very cold towards me and I reciprocated her act.

'Why was she pretending to shun me? Maybe it was necessary to do that to keep these goons off her and my back.'

We were at the end of the hallway where I was directed to a door, which I found out was the entrance to the bathroom. Jaria stayed with the guard and once I was done, I was taken back to my room. Jaria left with the guard without a word.

I sat on a chair which was also fastened to the floor along with a table. I scanned the room for any possible openings and found one in the ceiling, a vent next to the socket of the light. The ceiling was high, and it would have been impossible for me to reach it. I sighed and laid on the bed, pulling the blanket over myself. It wasn't cold but the blanket felt protective. In this cell, I couldn't even guess the time whether it was day or night. This helplessness was very discomforting, and frustration set in quickly. Trying to sooth my nerves, I closed my eyes and ventured to block out every thought from my brain. But regardless of how hard I tried one image wouldn't leave my eyes, the face with deep dark eyes and an anguished countenance. In the solitude of this prison, his memories were keeping me from going insane. I gave in letting them consume me.

My rest was disturbed by a noise at the door. I heard Jaria's voice, as she addressed someone in an angry tone, probably my guard. Then there was silence, a minute later the door opened, and she entered with a platter of food. Joy filled me but I didn't show it, merely turning on my side I peeked at her and then closed my eyes. The guard stepped out, saying something.

Jaria waited for him to close the door and then putting the tray on the table rushed to my side, but she was mute. I couldn't understand the cautiousness in her behavior.

"Jaria, what's going on?" I asked in a hushed voice. I had gotten the cue.

"I am not sure, but I think that something is wrong, because we didn't go to Baghdad. We actually have come to the northern area where we used to live and where Ali's family used to live. I don't want them to know that you and I are well acquainted otherwise they might get another helper. I want to stay with you to make certain they are not going to renege on their promises," She almost had her mouth stuck in my ear, this place was not like the other,

"Where are we? What kind of place is this?", were my next questions; she looked at me as if I were a fool.

"This is Daanish's house, and we are in one of his basement rooms. Now eat because this is the only excuse I can make to come see you and it was good that Daanish has ordered to make sure that you should not lack any necessities." She was still whispering,

"What was the ruckus about outside?" I had to ask.

"He didn't want me to come in, but I told him about Daanish's orders about your meals and other stuff, he had to let me in or deal with Daanish himself." Jaria rolled her eyes,

"Now please eat."

I had to eat, if I didn't, she wouldn't have been able to see me. Chewing slowly, I took my time; the guard came in twice to check on us, he was clearly irritated. Jaria smiled slightly when he left the second time and urged me to be quick,

"He won't go back alone the third time."

"Jaria, what's going on? I have a bad feeling that Ali was wrong about this guy."

"I can't say, he has not done anything that can point to that yet, I admit this is his house and we are far from Baghdad, but it is possible that he is doing business from here. This is his stronghold, and he has no fear of interference." Jaria said thoughtfully. I still didn't believe her. To me, it was only wishful thinking, Daanish was up to something, and it wasn't good. The guard came in a third time as I finished the meal. Jaria took the empty plate and left with him. Here I was given food in proper plates and fine silver cutlery was used, not like the plastic worn out utensils of the previous camp. I had eaten after two days, warm food made me drowsy and with nothing better to do I laid down on the bed and closed my eyes. Unwittingly I fell asleep, only to be awakened by the creaking sound of the door. Someone was coming. My eyes flung open, and I sat up, a man entered with a gun and some cuffs. I was terrified, 'What was he there for?' I jumped off the bed and ran behind the table. He stopped a little far from the entrance,

"You need to come with me." His voice was thick and had a clear accent. I didn't want to go with him but to outrun him in this small room would have been useless. I stayed in my spot as he came close.

"Wait, I need to go to the bathroom." I waved my hand at him as if he was blind,

He stopped and retreated, leaving the room. I stood where I was, motionless, hoping they will get Jaria for the task but instead the guard and the same man came back and escorted me to the bathroom at the end of the hallway. I didn't really have to go but this delayed them and gave me some time to think. 'If he was taking me to his boss, I could ask him if they would allow me talk to the Americans, that would give them more leverage and I could motivate the Americans to come to terms with these guys in less time.' Thud! There was a knock at the door, 'How rude!' 'These men have no concept of etiquette'. A few minutes later I was being taken to another room which was in a different wing of the building, this was a huge mansion sort of structure with at least three wings. I had to walk through corridors lined with furnishings. There were many men about, some of them soldiers and others in plain clothes. I also saw women spread out in the house, engaged in different tasks, some of them were in uniform. The part of the building we ended up in was quite nicely done with well-lit rooms and hallways. They brought me to a big chamber, which was well furnished like a nice upscale bedroom. The afternoon sun shone through the beautiful grand windows, I looked outside at the manicured gardens visible from the windows, 'Why was I here?' with my hands cuffed I stood in the middle of that room bewildered.

I got my answer a little later as someone walked in behind me, turning I was taken aback by the sight of the person. Jabbar was standing there with a mean smile on his lips. His facial expression conveyed his contempt and sense of victory.

'What was he doing here?' 'He was supposed to be on a mission somewhere.' I tried to remember what Ali had told me but at that instant my mind was going blank. Seeing him there in that room with a smirk on his face bode ill for me. It was clear that Daanish had not been honest with Ali and there was another game at play.

"I hope your trip here wasn't bumpy." The smirk still tugging at the corner of his lips,

"You can't do this, Daanish has promised to return me, when he finds out about you, there will be trouble for you." I replied, desperate.

"Yes, he did but he needs me more than the money your government is offering him, and he bartered you for his own life and place as leader. I won't challenge him, and he will give me you and all the ransom I can get for you. Don't look so shocked. I will return you, but no one said I couldn't have some fun before that." He smiled evilly, his cruel smile making every word sink in slowly as if life had become stuck in slow motion. My suspicions had come true, we were betrayed.

I didn't want to gratify his ego any further so without saying a word I turned away from him. I heard his footsteps coming close until he was right behind me. I could feel his body inches from mine but not to show intimidation I held my ground.

"You can be stubborn all you want but it won't be long when you will be biding to my will and then you won't turn away from me." He spoke in my ear as his fingers pulled back strands of hair from my neck. His touch made the bile rise in my stomach and I felt sick to my pit. To get rid of him, I ducked away, and he laughed, a lecherous sound echoing through the room and in my ears. I was right all along; the plan was never to return me. Ali was fooled by his leader, and he didn't even know it, and when he would discover that, it would be too late.

Jabbar didn't try to catch me, he didn't have to, he knew as well as I that he was right. There was no escape for me.

My sickness was increasing, maybe it was the food after the starvation which was not agreeing with my stomach and this terrible shock. The malnourishment of the previous few days had been tough on it and now this. A pang of sharp pain shot through me and I doubled over, Jabbar was startled by the sudden change and he yelled for some help. Two women came running in and helped me out of there. I was taken to a bathroom where I threw up everything I had eaten. Barely able to stand I was carried back to my room by the same women, I noticed they were in uniform, so they were part of my host's army. Leaving me in the room, they departed to be replaced by Jaria. I was relieved to see her. Not that she could do anything to improve my situation, but it was a relief to see her. I was on the bed when she walked in,

"Sarah, I was told that you were sick." She inquired worriedly, the pain in my belly had subsided and I was feeling weak but better.

"Jaria I was right. Jabbar is here and he was the one I was taken to see. He was gloating about having me in his custody. I knew Daanish was not to be trusted." I spoke in a low voice, careful of not letting the guard outside get a hint of what we were talking about. Jaria's face turned pale, she nearly collapsed on the chair.

"I didn't think he would cross him like this. Ali will kill him and anyone who is part of this." She muttered to herself. I couldn't understand what she was mumbling about; Ali had left me in the lurch, 'Why would he care if I was in the prison of Daanish or Jabbar? He had taken his leave and had washed his hands of me, an unwelcome distraction. Wasn't that his deal?'.

"Jaria what am I going to do? He had me in his room now and it won't be long before he will get me back." My voice was shaky, no matter how much I told myself that I would fight him. I knew better. I was stuck in a predicament worse than death. If he just wanted to kill me, I wouldn't have minded. But I knew what was in store for me was a fate worse than anything I could conceive.

"I will try to get you out of here, no matter what it takes. I won't let you be sullied by his filthy hands. I will kill you myself if I have to." Jaria's lined face had absolute determination. I should have been alarmed by her

262

statement, but I was relieved, if nothing could be done she won't let me endure the devastation. I sat back on the bed and sighed, 'Where had life brought me?'. I was in the prison of a monster and the only escape was death. A weary smile spread across my face, a smile that conveyed more than just my satisfaction at being given the assurance of a savior but also the irony of this life I was living. Jaria observed my reaction but said nothing.

I shook the dismal thoughts and started concentrating on how we were going to achieve my freedom. In these circumstances, we had to come up with something plausible, something that would work because we were not getting any second chances.

Jaria had brought a medicine for my stomachache, I took it and we tried to devise a plan, something that could be put into action with minimum preparation. We came up with a rough idea when Jaria had to leave, but she promised to come back with more details and something to drink. I fell back on the bed exhausted; the vomiting and stress were taking their toll. Jaria advised me to rest as much as possible because as far as we could foresee this situation was only going to get worse. She left some extra medicine with me in case I needed it.

I closed my eyes and as soon as I had, the handsome face of the ditching devil emerged to take over my mind. I wanted to scream at him, to tell him 'I told you so' but he wasn't there and as far as I could guess I would never see him again. That realization saddened me; no matter the damage he had caused, I missed him.

'Does he ever think about me?', I wondered staring at the ceiling, 'But why would he? He wasn't in love with me.' That was only my burden. He had never disclosed any feelings for me, and I shouldn't have any expectations. Then I remembered the hunger in his kiss and the desperate way he held me, never to let me go. 'Why did I feel that he wanted to be with me as much as I wanted him? Why did I get singed whenever he was near me?' Shutting my eyes more tightly I tried to block him out, it was all in the past and likely my wishful thinking. I recalled that he had kissed me when I drove him to the end of his options; he had to keep me quiet some way. But then his touch, and the longing in his embrace, was I crazy or was he blind? I kept thinking, eventually letting his memories take over me. There was no use to fight it, these were probably the last hours of my life on this Earth, and I wanted to spend them with him.

I had lain there semiconscious, unaware of the passing hours until Jaria came back. She had some food with her. I was surprised at the lack of anything else, 'Weren't we suppose to prepare for escaping this hell hole?'.

"Jaria, what happened to the plan?" I asked her apprehensive of her response.

"I have what you will need and when that is done, we will take it from there." She spoke in a hushed tone. She had brought some kind of tranquilizing medicine for Jabbar when I was to be taken to him. The plan was to drug him via his drink and after that feign sickness to get Jaria in, who would be nearby in the waiting. We were hoping that there will be a window of opportunity for us to get out of there.

I was curious. If I was giving him a knockout medicine, why not just give him some poison to get rid of him permanently? Jaria slapped me on the shoulder. They weren't dumb, she had no access to any poison, she had made this concoction by combining some other meds. It would make him unconscious but not for long; we would have to be quick. She briefed me about everything, and I was ready for the final showdown, hoping it would work, there were no guarantees or second chances. Jaria planned to bring a gun when she would follow me, just in case the plan went awry. I was going to be free either way.

The guard banged at the door reminding us to pack it up. I had almost finished the broth she had brought in. Pressing the packet in my hand, she left. I was aware of the quazy nature of our plan, but it was all we could try. I had prepared myself for the worse, if we couldn't get out Jaria was going to end my life, I was scared but satisfied with the arrangement.

I got up and said a final prayer, I hadn't prayed in a long time. Since the death of my mother, it had been hard but today I did it to say my farewells. I didn't know what the next day would bring but I wanted to say goodbye to everyone I loved, starting from my family and ending on Ali. I was able to successfully wind up my blessings for everyone but when Ali came it was different, there was no winding up, there was no end, just a sense of being, he was there in my heart, my soul, and there were no farewells. I was going to die with him alive in me till the last moment, it was a feeling I didn't want to end. Holding his reflection in my eyes I fell asleep.

Day 17 (Ali)

I had left her alone and crying, walking out on her was the hardest thing I had ever done in my entire life, and after that I had to practically hold myself down to stay away from her room before morning, I couldn't sleep, couldn't even sit. Dim light across the horizon indicated that the hour of departure was upon me but I wasn't ready, I wanted to stay, to confront Daanish, but I couldn't not if I wanted her to live. Day break was my signal to get started on my journey. I picked up my things, tormented at the twist of life; there was not much to take except for memories. All my possessions fit in a small bag which I slung over my shoulder as I left my room. I was careful not to leave from the front where the window of her room opened. Making my way out of the base, I looked back in the rearview mirror of the jeep as the distance increased between me and the only being I had come to love in spite of myself. I drove like mad after the base disappeared from my view. What was there to wait for, if I had to die I wanted it to be quick. The drive was grueling with a tempest of memories raging within me, time passed at a painfully slow pace. Her spontaneous laughter, the way she had held me, her courage and selflessness all that she was. My tortured soul called out, 'How could I leave her like that?!'. If she had to be taken to Baghdad I should have gone with her. I could complete the operation Daanish had proposed after that, but he didn't trust me to go through with it once she had reached safety.

"Daanish didn't trust me!!" The thought struck me like a rock, if he had no trust, then why was I trusting him with my most precious possession.

Pressing hard on the brakes, I stopped the jeep and turned it around. I had to get back, I had to make sure he was keeping his word. It was Sarah's safety and her life which was on the line, 'How could I be such a fool?'. I accelerated the jeep to its maximum speed. It was almost afternoon when I got to the base and caught the last of the convoy leaving its premises. I exchanged my jeep for a car without the knowledge of anyone and tailed the convoy. There were five vehicles with one in the middle with tinted glasses. I expected Daanish was in that one with Sarah. He was not going to put her in another vehicle and separate her from him. I had to follow very carefully without getting detected. I had a bad feeling that I was going to be proven wrong about Daanish and sadly it was true. As soon as the convoy got to the main highway the direction it took was north not east and I knew they were not headed to Baghdad. There was nothing to be done except for a close pursuit. I had a hunch where he was headed. He had a mansion in the northern areas as his residence when he wasn't busy with his murderous schedule. He had built it recently as his headquarters and a base for the soldiers. It was luxurious and provided with everything one could think of, but I preferred to stay in the south closer to the desert, uneasy at the thought of enjoying when the people around us suffered. Now that I knew his route, I fell back and took a different way to approach the target. It was not a busy road and to draw suspicion was not wise. I was there after they had arrived in the dark. It was a huge house with different wings and there were cells in the lower level to keep prisoners. She would probably be in one of them. 'Maybe he was there to continue onwards to Baghdad.' I was contemplating the possibility hiding next to the outer wall. 'But why?' It didn't make sense.

I entered the building on the west side, because I remembered the layout from when Daanish gave me a tour of that part and the basement cells he had built there. This was his strong hold and he had built it to indulge all his whims. He had taken me to the east wing, which were next to his living quarters. They were lavishly furnished and didn't seem to be part of a military base, but his justification was that the soldiers needed comfort if they had to fight and die for the people. I parked my car far enough outside the wall to keep it out of sight, there were surveillance cameras at some points to keep intruders out, not that anyone dared come there. Daanish was a well-known figure in this area and people feared him terribly. Secretly, I went around the place; it was more heavily guarded and policed than usual. Evidently, they were guarding someone or something very important, presumably Sarah. I needed to find out where she was being held inside that building, but I had to wait for morning and assess the situation. I had to see what would be his next move. If he left for Baghdad, then I would follow without getting detected and then return to the western post he had assigned to me. It was a certainty that he would discover my absence from my assigned post but I didn't care. If he had any issues with it, I was ready to confront him but I was not going to leave without making sure Sarah was safe. Morning would bring the answers I needed. Coming out of the building, I hid behind crates of ammunition and barrels of oil in the side yard. The whole place was silent as the night descended into the late hours. Sitting there, between the crates of weapons, I kept watch. The number of weapons stored there gave a good measure of Daanish's increasing power.

Day 18

I woke with an ominous feeling, this was the day, I was sure of it. The day of judgment for me, there were not going to be any delays.

I got out of bed and waited, straightening my hair and pushing the random thoughts out of my mind keeping it empty. I had seen the lust in Jabbar's eyes and observed his body language. Since my abduction I had learned one important fact: a woman could sense the lust of a man without even seeing it, and he had been very vocal about his. I had a hunch he wouldn't wait much longer to claim his prize.

Jaria's medicine had done its job, I didn't experience any pain and the residual nausea was gone. This room had no window or any means to determine whether it was morning or middle of the night. I guessed that it was morning, and there was one way to find out. I slipped off the bed and banged at the door, just as I expected the guard responded by yelling. I shouted back that I had to go to the bathroom. The door opened and he peeked in signaling me to come with him. The hallway was lit with lightbulbs but at the end of it I could see the glimpse of sunlight shining from the outer door. So, it was morning, I had been correct, it was a new day.

After the restroom trip was over, I came back to the windowless room, figuring out why I was kept in this hole, probably to distort my orientation of time and confuse me. Well, I had found a way to defeat that. 'If it was morning, where was Jaria?' I wondered. She should have visited by now with the second dose of medicine supposedly and some breakfast. I was concerned about the packet of the tranquilizing medicine, 'Where would I hide it when it would be time?' My dress didn't have any pockets and holding it in my hand would be a little obvious. I was pondering on the matter when Jaria entered the room. Her face told me that she didn't have good news.

"Good morning, any new developments?" I asked before she could talk,

"I have some news about Daanish." She was grave,

"What about him?"

"Yesterday, when I found out about Jabbar I decided to see Daanish to alter his mind about you and to keep his word with Ali. I tried to get a hold of him, but I couldn't. He was not meeting anyone. I deferred it for today hoping to catch him after breakfast but he didn't show up for it. Later, I found out that he had left early in the morning with his men." Jaria despairingly sat on the chair,

"But why didn't you tell me?" I was a little angry,

"Because I didn't want you to have false expectations. I had hoped to persuade him, but apparently his decision was final. I am certain he is in trouble with Jabbar, because this is his house and he is the one who left." Her comment distressed me. If that was the case, 'How would we get out of here? How would she rescue me in the event of Jabbar's imminent summons?'.

We sat there lost in thought. Suddenly, my appetite died and I started feeling sick again. Jaria could see the changing color of my face and patted my shoulder,

"Don't worry. I was hoping to fix this by Daanish's help but I am prepared for what we planned." Her voice was reassuring.

"Jaria, what should I do when he sends for me? And where to hide this packet?" I was getting edgy and apprehensive

"Don't say anything. Just follow orders; I will stay with you. You can keep it in your hand until you get to the room and then hide it in your mouth. Its small and plastic, and it won't dissolve until you open it. I don't think he will be coming before evening. He will be busy after Daanish's departure I am sure, and then he will have time to himself." Jaria was explaining in a hushed voice, I nodded.

Time was over for the visit, and she went out with the full plater as I couldn't touch the food. I started pacing. It was hard sitting and waiting, all that we had planned was speculative, and the reality of its effectiveness or practicality would soon be tested. I wasn't dubious of its success, but we had no other alternative. 'Well, beggars can't be choosers after all'

I paced for what seemed like hours. I became so tired that walking felt quite impossible. If he had called me then, he would have had a very compliant subject, but I was spared. Sitting on the bed, I waited for the door to open and the drama to begin but I was left undisturbed for quite some time and then Jaria was back. She had brought my lunch with an extra dose of medicine. I choked down some of the food on her insistence. She had more news, Daanish's last men had departed the house and Jabbar was free. My nerves were on edge by now, afraid that I wouldn't be able to go through with the whole thing. Just to think about being with Jabbar made me sick to the stomach, but Jaria built my morale, she was sure of our plan and assured me of its success. I heard what she said but it was hard to register. In a few minutes, she was out of the room, and I was alone again waiting for the door to open, this time for the test of fate.

I didn't have to wait too long. There was a knock at the door and two men entered with their faces covered, which was strange because until now in this place I had not seen anyone cover their faces, not even the women.

I had anticipated this but still my heart jumped to my throat, it was time. They signaled me to come with them; nervous and afraid I stumbled to the door. I had to use every drop of self-confidence to keep my composure. They took me to the same part of the building as the day before. It was still lavish and immaculate but appreciation of the finesse of the household was the last thing on my mind. I was being taken to my sacrificial altar, no matter how beautiful it was. Those men walked at a fast pace with me trailing along, as we passed through the hallways of this wing, I discerned that the number of people had reduced to almost none since a day before, it looked deserted except for us.

'Where had all the soldiers and others gone?' The question popped in my head involuntarily. I scolded myself for missing the obvious, 'Why was I worried about a bunch of his people when I should be worrying about my future.'

We had stopped in front of the double doors of the grand bedroom. The men knocked and someone opened it. It wasn't visible from where we stood who was letting us in, actually letting 'me' in. The men pointed me in the direction of the open door and took their places on both sides of it. I stepped in extremely apprehensive of who might be there, but to my surprise, there was an old woman who took me by the arm and lead me straight to an attached bathroom. I hadn't expected this, but I followed her quietly per Jaria's instructions, and hid the drugs in my mouth while pretending to cough. The old woman's face was wrinkled and stern. She looked like a crooked old bat doing the bidding of her master. A glimpse in the ornate bathroom mirror reflected the face of a girl worn and tired with deep bluc cyes. I was lost in observing that face when the old woman without warning started ripping my clothes off. I was shocked by her apparent disregard for modesty; stopping her I removed them myself and wrapped a towel around my body. She said something in Arabic which sounded like an insult throwing my clothes in the trashcan. Then she pointed to the bathtub and pushed me towards it, 'So she wanted me to bathe for the heathen.' Swallowing hard I cursed Jabbar and got in it. After a hellish half hour, the bathing session was over and I was allowed out of the bathroom, smelling all rosy and frcsh. I abhorred this but had to go along. Next, she supplied me with a night gown already picked out and sitting on the huge bed. I looked at it unbelievingly, it was a very delicate sheer red chiffon and lace gown, which would rather accentuate every part of my body then veil it. Scorning I threw it on the floor, she was dreaming if she thought I was going to stoop to dressing up like a whore for her master. She simply picked it up and

275

pushed it in my face, pointing to the towel wrapped around me and the dress. It was clear I had two choices: either wear the towel or the gown. Suppressing my anger, I took the night dress and donned it. There was a crooked smile on her face. She brought me in-front of a full-length mirror hanging on the wall with copper and golden floral design around it. I looked at myself a second time and saw the changed visage of a beautiful young woman, dressed in a sheer gown leaving nothing to the imagination, with long flowing gold curls and delicate features. The bath had transformed me. Although I hated taking it, it had refreshed me and brought color back to my cheeks only to remind me who would be enjoying all of this. The thought made my mouth sour. I was hoping to give him the mixed drink as soon as he got in and be rid of him. I was in the middle of that thought when the old woman pulled me by the arm and made me sit on a settee in front of the huge mirror, now I could see my reflection as much as I wanted, but that was not her intention, she had other plans. She took a hairbrush and started working on my hair. By the time she was done my hair was a tangle of pretty ribbons and a gold head dress with thin chains woven with gold filigree hanging the length of my hair. I was amazed at the skill of this woman. She had transformed my whole appearance, but she was still not done. Letting me sit there, she raced to a small suitcase on one side and pulled out some jewelry boxes from it. Bringing them to where I was sitting, she took out different necklaces, arm bands and even leg bands. Picking them one by one, she adorned my body with them. By the end of all that, and a session of makeup, I was ready. Made up like a bride with a warped sense of propriety. Satisfied with her work, she wrapped up her essentials and left.

I was all alone in the huge room with everything for an evening of pleasure.

As soon as she was gone, I wanted to tear the garment and the jewels off and cover myself in something that would hide me. Sucking in my hatred, I had to tolerate it until I was done with my job, but I did wipe off as much makeup as I could. The asshole wouldn't be able to tell the difference. As the minutes ticked by, my pulse raced and sweat trickled down my spine making the sheer lace stick to my back. I cursed everything from the rising sun to the day I was born. But the passing minutes reduced my anxiety as no one appeared and curiosity took over. Now that I paid attention, the room was expensively furnished with crystal ornaments. A chandelier graced the ceiling of the room with beautifully carved wooden furniture. 'How were these so-called 'freedom fighters' able to afford all this?', I wondered. Thinking, I stepped closer to the French doors that lead to a balcony adjacent to grand windows that were covered with richly colored and embroidered curtains. The previous day I had seen the gardens visible from the windows, but today the curtains were pulled. I slightly peeked opened one of the French doors to satisfy my curiosity and saw the immaculate foliage. The gardens were serene in their solitude and beauty, and I kept watching as the minutes passed.

The sun had almost set, spreading a deep red hue across the horizon. I was so lost in the beautiful scenery that I didn't hear the door open. A sharp gasp made me turn to see Jabbar standing a few feet from the bed. Now it was my turn to gasp in fear and apprehension. The time for the final trial had begun. The lust in his eyes was so visible I could feel it piercing through the delicate fiber of the gown and cutting into my skin. Perspiration beaded my forehead and my hands got sweaty, 'How was I going to play the role if this continued?'. I had to brave this somehow if I wanted to make it out of there. Jaria had done her bit, now it was my turn. Pulling myself together, I walked towards the table near the bed where I had placed the filled glasses of wine. He followed every sway of my hips, every bounce of my curls. I was acutely aware of his salacious looks. It wasn't going to be long before he was going to attack me. I had to stall.

"Would you like a drink?" I picked up a glass and presented it to him, my gesture caught him by surprise.

"Why? You are not going to run or scream or curse me." He asked a little cautiously. His expression had changed; he was no fool. I realized my mistake,

"I could but then I am not dumb. You have two muscle men outside the door, and I am guessing many more around the house. If I tried to run or scream it will only hurt me. I am a realist. I know this is the way things are and will be no matter what I want, so I am going to make the best of it. I don't want to return with a swollen face or broken bones. I will have a drink too if you don't have any reservations. I don't want to feel anything." Ending my speech, I put the other glass to my lips and took a sip of the already poured wine. He was observing me closely. His shrewd mind at work; I played it cool and sipped the wine while walking to him with his glass in hand. The lust in his eyes deepened and he thrust his arm around my waist. I controlled my antagonism and placed the wine glass in his empty hand. This was proving to be difficult and was taking ages. Jaria had promised to intervene after a certain calculated time, and if I was not successful, she would take it from there. Thinking about her I pushed the glass to his lips; he had already taken a few sips holding me with the other hand. His hand was sliding up and down the curve of my back. I could hardly keep my hands from punching him in the gut. He took one more sip and pushed me on the bed. I stumbled and stopped at the edge of it. He watched me lasciviously, then setting the glass on one of the tables, he staggered towards me. A crooked smile on his lecherous face.

'He's put the drink down but if he doesn't drink the whole thing it won't work and then.......?' I couldn't think any further. The stagger in his walk indicated that the drug was taking effect, but he had to drink the whole thing for the plan to work. As he made his way to me, I ducked and rushed to the other side of the room, standing behind yet another table with ornaments. His facial expression changed when I ran to the side, suddenly realizing something.

"You drugged the drink, didn't you?" He snarled at me with a nasty smile as he stormed towards me,

"I am going to enjoy this. You little witch. You thought you could defeat me. I am going to have some real fun with you." His mouth foamed with lust and fury. The cat was out of the bag. There was no use pretending anymore.

"Yes, I did you pig! You will never have me even if I have to kill myself!" The anger and disdain I had been holding in check came to the surface in full force. If I had to fight him, I would but he had stopped not coming any closer to me. He stood there assessing my position; we were both stationary, waiting and watching. The table that loomed between us held another flask surrounded by glasses. 'If I could get to the flask, I could use it as a weapon.' It was good that he had come unarmed. I was not about to wait for him to call his goons in or grab a gun. Taking a chance, I sprinted to the table, grasping for the flask. Unfortunately, he had judged my move and like a jaguar he jumped from his place to counter it. He reached the table before me and caught me by the arms. I kicked and kneed him to free myself from his grip. Thanks to the drug, his grip loosened against my aggressive antics, and he had to let go. As I slipped away, he roughly snatched my hair, jerking it back. The sudden jerk made me fall backwards and I shrieked in pain. Trying to stand up, I clawed at his hand, but he was faster and stronger than me even in his lethargic state. He pulled at my hair harder and held onto my arm with the other, twisting it. I screamed in pain again. Pushing me forward, he threw me on the bed.

My eyes were red with fury and pain. I looked at him as he hovered over me. I kicked at him with my legs, but he caught them. Holding them tightly, he pulled me close. I tried to free myself by twisting and writhing further but his grip was very strong. The gown I had grudgingly put on was ripped in several places by now, revealing parts of my body. I desperately wanted to get away. No matter how much I kicked and screamed at him, it was no use. Tears streamed out of my eyes as I tried one last time. I hoped Jaria would come and put me out of my misery. He laughed at me callously. Pushing me down, he started grabbing at my arms. Just then the door slammed open. He was momentarily startled, and taking advantage, I pushed him off and tumbled onto the floor. At last Jaria was here, I didn't care about the noise she had made. The plan had failed anyway, she would have to kill me to save me from him.

Jabbar rose from the bed maniacally angry at the intrusion. He jerked himself to face the door to see who had barged in,

"Ali!!!" His exclamation made me jump up and stand. Ali was standing in the middle of the door with blood in his eyes. I could see fear on Jabbar's face that turned to anger. He lunged at Ali who averted his blow and punched him square in the face. Jabbar fell face down. Ali's assault and the drug in his system both had him out cold.

I was paralyzed with grief and happiness. Ali had saved me from this monster, he had come back for me...... but then it wouldn't have happened if he had not sent me with his boss. I turned away from him; with my night gown ripped, my hair all tangled, and my face streaked with tears. 'Why had he come to save me? He didn't have to do me that favor, Jaria could have done the job.'

"Sarah." He was standing inches away, his voice so gentle like a cool breeze. I couldn't bear it anymore. I just turned and hugged him sobbing. He held me caressing my hair and talking to me softly, consoling me. I cried in his arms with my face buried in his chest as the minutes became endless. Keeping one arm around me, he pulled one of the sheets off the bed and covered me with it. A sense of calm took over me, and I felt safe as the tears dried up. As soon as I pulled myself away from him, he turned his attention to Jabbar once more and drew his knife. I couldn't let him mar his hands with blood but before I could stop him Jaria called from outside,

"Ali, please hurry. You don't have much time."

Ali kicked Jabbar on the side and stepping over him, lead me to the exit. Jaria was standing outside the door with a small gun in her hands. 'Where had the guards gone?' I glanced around and wished that I hadn't. The two men lay on the floor with their throats slit. It was Ali's work. I couldn't imagine him being so brutal, but the proof was lying on the floor. Ali pulled the men inside and covered the blood with a carpet from inside the room. Having done that, he whispered something to Jaria and she took me back inside the room, where she gave me a pair of black pants and a matching shirt with a keffiyeh. She asked me to change in it quickly and handed me a bag for my stuff. She then pulled a traditional robe out of the same bag and wore it. I was soon clad in the black suit with the keffiyeh wrapped around my head and face, my entire countenance hidden except for both my eyes. Jaria stuffed all the jewelry I had been wearing in a bag. I threw the ripped red night gown on Jabbar as we stepped out. Ali was already in a black suit and now he had covered his face as well. We looked just like Jabbar's guards. Moving quickly, we reached the outer part of the mansion, there Ali stopped. He scanned the parameter and then consulted with Jaria. Quietly, Jaria pulled the hood of the cloak over her head low obscuring her face. Ali stepped in line with me once again.

"We will take Jaria back and then get out of here. They won't suspect anything for a while, and when they do. We will be far away." Ali briefed me in a low voice. I didn't want to leave Jaria behind, but there was no other choice. Jaria came close and embraced me with a teary voice,

"I had been so angry and lost after my daughter and husband died, but you helped me find peace with your integrity and selflessness. I am old with few days left to live. If I can help you get to safety, I will do it." Tears welled up in my eyes too. She had been there for me, protected me and was risking her life for me. 'How would I ever repay her?' She patted me on the shoulder and started walking to the other wing of the building where I had been held. The path continued to lead out from the mansion. Ali and I joined her; we walked beside her with our guns drawn and faces hidden. Slowly we made our way to the outer veranda, and there a group of soldiers were sitting around eating and drinking. The guard who had been on duty since my stay here came running from another room a little shocked,

"She is back. You brought her back?" He couldn't contain his amazement, Ali said something to him harshly in Arabic and he quieted down. Ali pushed Jaria forward; we all stepped out towards the main lot where the vehicles were parked. The guard followed us a little confused. He called us probably asking where we were taking the prisoner. Ali turned and started talking to him, but as he did that, Jaria seemingly released her hand from his grip and ran to a parked car. Ali pretended that he was caught by surprise, and I followed suit. Suddenly, there was chaos as the astonished guard ran after the car as Jaria drove towards the main gate. The others, unsure of what was going on, joined him. This gave us the opportunity to quietly slip away under the cover of darkness. Ali knew his way around the compound. Without talking, he led me to the rear where more vehicles were parked. Stealthily, we got to a parked jeep where he turned on his small flashlight and kneeled near it. Using a small tool kit, he picked open its lock and hopped in. I darted onto the other side of it and jumped in when he unlocked the door. He pulled off the keffiyeh off his head but stopped me from following suit. Starting the car, he drove away from the main house, taking a dirt path. I sat quietly next to him observing the lamps illuminating the entire compound all the way to the gate. Ali was grim. I wondered why, but then it became clear that he was worried for a reason. There were sentries posted at the gate. He had to get across without getting caught if we hoped to escape. Stopping at the check point, he talked to one of the guards on duty, explaining something. Ali remained seated as they engaged in a few minutes discussion. One of the other guards asked Ali something again and whatever Ali said convinced them to open the gate. Ali put the car in gear and accelerated just as the building behind that had been dimly lit got illuminated with people shouting. Someone began calling to the sentry who had talked to us a minute ago. Ali floored the accelerator, and the car flew out of the driveway onto the road. He didn't slow even when the building lights were left far behind us. I thought we had lost them but sadly I was mistaken. A few minutes later, we could see in the rearview mirror, the blinding head lights of several vehicles giving us chase. Ali revved the jeep to the max and the distance between us and our pursuers increased, but not for long. I looked at him, his attention was solely focused on the road. I peeked out of the window, it was a hilly area, and the road was winding and twisting at angles that made my heart jump, but Ali wasn't slowing down. Silently praying, I speculated on how long we could outrun our pursuers. Then Ali spoke hurriedly,

"Sarah, there is a turn coming up I am going to slow down the car a bit over there and you will have to jump out. I will too, but a little further ahead okay! When I say the word, jump." I was flabbergasted. 'Jump from the car? And without him? Was he insane?' But his face was grave. I braced myself for his cue. In the next two minutes, he continued to race the car to its maximum. Making a sharp turn, he slowed down the car to a minimal speed and shouted for me to jump. I opened the door and leapt out with my bag in hand. The roadside had tall grass that provided a cushion for my fall but still it hurt like hell. I rolled over deep into the recesses of the foliage and lay there motionless, waiting for Ali. Suddenly, I heard a loud crash that prompted me to raise my head up, but before I could stand a hand pulled me down to the ground. I was about to shriek when the other hand covered my mouth and pinned me flat to the ground. It was Ali. He was lying next to me, trying to quieten me. We remained still, counting the minutes, waiting to hear the vehicles chasing us pass by. As soon as they were gone, Ali crawled in the opposite direction holding my hand. We crawled for a long while. I turned several times to see if our pursuers were coming but the only visible thing was a distant fire. Ali stood up after reaching another bend in the path we were on. He didn't let go of me as we walked along silently. The night was bleak and gloomy, and I was afraid that those men would find us but keeping my fears at bay, I followed Ali. The path turned and wound so many times I was completely lost, although Ali was moving with the sense of a wolf. He confidently speed walked through the terrain like this was his backyard. I had no clue of heads or tails where we were. It was all the same wilderness to me, especially at night when I couldn't tell my right hand from my left.

The temperature was cool and the air fresh, making the journey bearable. Still, I grew weary after what I thought were hours. We had been walking for ages and I was hoping that we could stop and rest for a while. My day hadn't been easy earlier and I was about ready to collapse. Eventually, I asked impatiently,

"Ali, where are we going?"

He stopped to face me with the moon shining on him as he broadly smiled. 'Why was he smiling, had he lost his sanity?'

"I was waiting for you to say something." The soberness was gone, and he was in a light mood. 'How was he so happy? Weren't we in danger?' My mind was trying to comprehend the change in his attitude.

"Aren't you worried they will find us? Why are you so happy?" I was confused and a little agitated due to fatigue,

"If you want, I can become really serious. I can pretend to be afraid." It was hard for him to suppress his smile.

"Are we safe?" My question made him a little staid,

"Yes. We are for some time. We can rest until morning and then we will move again." He spoke while searching for something in the dark. He suddenly stopped like he had found what he was looking for.

"We can rest here, there is a small stream near, and we have shelter because of the mountain side." He put his bag down. I was already so fatigued that stopping was a welcome change from walking. I intentionally gazed out at our surroundings for the first time. He was right. We were in the shade of a small mountain side that protruded out like a roof and formed a small cave which could easily hide us. Now that I paid attention, I could hear the soft rumbling of the stream as well. Content, I sat on the grass. Ali came and rested next to me. I could see his weary face in the moonlight. His cheek was grazed in a few spots.

"You're hurt. Let me bandage it." I reached into my bag for some supplies, but he shrugged his shoulders saying it would be fine. Then getting up, he left me. I didn't call him from behind, assuming he would come back, and he did.

"I had to go." He explained. I was embarrassed to ask but I had to relieve myself too. When I asked, he simply guided me to one side of the mountain that was secluded. He also pointed out that my bag might have some supplies I would need. The bushes growing around came in very handy at that instant. I came back feeling awkward, but he didn't pay any attention, rather he called me to the edge of the stream and showed me how he had washed up in it. I followed his directions as if he was my scout master and I had just joined an outdoor camp. It made me laugh; he made me feel so much at ease that I wasn't embarrassed for long. Washing up in the stream, I asked him how he knew about this place. In return, he narrated a story about his monotonous days and his love of exploring so he had found many secluded places in the mountains where people normally didn't go. It later turned out to be helpful in his work.

Coming back from the stream, he took out a sleeping bag from his sack and spread it on the grass. I looked at him questioningly because rummaging through my bag I hadn't found any sort of thing.

288

"This is for you, you should rest." He waved his hand in its direction. I didn't want to take his sleeping bag and leave him to sleep on the grass,

"It's yours. Please, I don't want you to suffer on my account. I can sleep next to the tree. That spot looks smooth and clean." I pointed in the direction of a small tree nearby. His skeptical smile annoyed me a little, 'Did he think I couldn't sleep in the outdoors?' I had camped many times with my family, and I could handle sleeping on the ground.'

"Sarah, you can use the sleeping bag. I am not sleeping right now, I have work to do and someone has to stand guard also." Ali wasn't smiling anymore.

"But you need to sleep as much as me. I don't want you falling over when I need your help, so you can sleep, and I will stay awake and then I can wake you to take a turn." I was being obstinate, maybe trying to prove a point.

"Okay." He replied, raising his hands in mock surrender. He went to one side, straightening his clothes, stopping a little far from where we had made camp. I was curious, 'What was he up to now?'. Sitting next to the sleeping bag, I watched as he started to pray. I was a little astounded. I had seen N do it but to watch him engage in it was different, kind of unbelievable because of the life he led. My eyes were glued to him, there was a serenity about him as he prayed, and it was hard to look away. He was done in a few minutes and then came back to sit on the sleeping bag.

"You really don't want to rest?" He asked in an even voice,

"No, you can take the first turn." I was adamant. Silently, he slid in and closed his eyes. I sat there in the moonlight keeping an eye on the parameter and listening for any noise. There was complete silence except for occasional sounds of nocturnal animals. My thoughts turned back to the events of the day and how narrowly I had escaped. Jaria's face kept emerging in my memory, 'She would have been killed by Jabbar'. I was sure of it. The realization of that fact was too hard to bear. She had been my friend and companion who had given the ultimate sacrifice anyone could. Tears welled up in my eyes, 'How could I ever forget her or anyone here?' Even the worst of the worst moments I would remember. Recalling the night with Jabbar, my skin crawled even by the thought of it. Every flashback of the past days constricted my chest and my head started to hurt; I got up and walked around. The cool air was refreshing but the headache was getting worse. It was obvious that all the stress, malnutrition, stomach problems and fatigue were causing it. I searched through my bag for any kind of meds but there was only a change of clothes and the jewelry Jaria had stuck in along with essential travel supplies. Maybe Ali had something in his bag, but he was using it as a pillow, and I didn't want to disturb him. Walking wasn't helping; I came and slumped on the ground near the sleeping bag. He had his eyes closed but I wasn't positive if he was asleep or was just indulging me.

I kept looking at his face in the soft moonlight, it was so tranquil and peaceful with not a trace of the life he had been part of and the tragedies he had to endure. His deep dark eyes looked like they were dreaming of something beautiful, I hoped. The breeze blew strands of dark hair across his forehead with their tips reaching his eyes. I had an urge to move them on the side and leaning towards him I brushed them with my fingertips being careful not to disturb him. But as I stroked the last hair, he reached out with his hand and caught mine, startling me. He was awake, staring at me with his intense eyes, even in this dim light I could feel the heat of his gaze.

"I thought you were asleep. I was only fixing your hair. Sorry." I said abruptly. His touch was playing mayhem with my senses. I wanted to free my hand from his grip, but I couldn't. My arms were numb. He sat up, still clutching my hand. Apparently, he had forgot to let it go. Our eyes locked with each other as seconds passed without a word. His face was a mirror of the sentiments swirling within him, but he was silent as he eventually released my hand.

"It's okay. I was just surprised, that's all." He slid out of the sleeping bag, and then looking around, he started rolling it up and packing up our stuff.

'What was he doing? Was it time to move on from there?',

I was puzzled, but I got my answer when he dumped everything under the short ledge protruding out from the hill. It had more shelter, and we weren't visible from it.

291

"Now it's your turn. We will be safer in this place." He gestured me towards the sleeping bag he had rolled out on the floor. Quietly sliding in, I laid my head on my supply bag, using it as a pillow, but it was difficult to close my eyes because the headache had grown worse, and I conveniently had forgotten to ask Ali for any meds. As I lay there wincing with pain, Ali came close and knelt down next to me,

"Are you well?" He touched my forehead,

"No, I have a severe headache. I wanted to ask if you had any medicine for it and some water." I pressed the heels of my hands on my temples. He rushed to his bag and took out a small box and a bottle of water. I sat crisscrossed on the sleeping bag as he opened the box and handed me the medicine from it along with the water. I took the pills, washing them down with some water but I knew this headache would take its time to simmer down. I had to tolerate the pain until the meds kicked in, which usually took its time. Ali sat next to me with his eyes fixated on my face. My efforts to control the pain were useless and involuntarily I kept pressing my head between my palms.

"Let me." Ali came closer and sat behind me. Straightening himself, he pushed up against the mountain side. I wasn't able to concentrate on what he was up to; I just wanted the pain to be over. Still, I didn't want any more favors from him, his rescue was enough. The headache and my time alone recalling the events of the day had made me bitter. I couldn't forget the way he had just thrown me in the lap of his boss. His niceties were not impressing me anymore.

"No, you don't have to. I'll be fine." I muttered barely able to speak because of the splitting headache.

"I think I need to because I am in no mood to clean up after you throw up and I don't have a fresh change of clothes." He spoke unemotionally. I was beat, the pain was too much to argue further.

Settling behind me, he ran his fingers in my hair and started massaging the skin, working on the temples from the top then to the sides and at the nape of my neck. If he was trying to sooth my nerves he was completely misguided. Him sitting so close with his fingers in my hair wasn't helping as every fiber in my body was acutely aware of his touch. My skin felt seared from the warmth of his breath and every stroke of his fingers quicken my heartbeat. I didn't know how he felt but for me this was such sweet pain that I wanted him to stop but then I wanted more. I cursed myself for going utterly insane and to remember how easily he had washed his hands of me just a few days ago.

Incapable of coherent thought, I sat there holding my breath as he continued. After a few minutes, I realized he was calm and composed, diligently at work to relieve my pain. His ease of manner slowly relaxed me and then without knowing my eyes got heavy and I fell asleep sitting where I was with my legs crisscrossed.

Day 18 (Ali)

Day break was accompanied by the rushed activities of soldiers getting ready to depart. I was well hidden, and as far as I gathered, they were not loading ammunition from my hide out. This was reassuring, Daanish was leaving, and I could imagine that his next destination would be Baghdad. Morning hours progressed with the vehicles and men getting ready to go. In the late hours of the morning, I decided to leave my spot and explore a little. Dressed as I was, it was easy to get assimilated in the troops. Slightly covering my face, I walked around to the front and found a darkly painted, midsize truck parked adjacent to the main entrance. There was a flurry of men surrounding it. I moved closer and asked one of the soldiers, "Who was that for?" He looked at me incredulously and scornfully informed me,

"The boss' stuff and some others." I apologized for being an idiot and made myself scarce. 'So, I was correct that Daanish was planning to leave but why use that truck? Why not a car or pickup?' But I had no answer to these questions. Suspicion mounted in me, but I had to believe that there was some obscure reason why he had opted for the truck. Once done with my reconnaissance, I stepped back into the shadows and waited for the company to load up and leave. I wanted to make sure that it was Sarah who was riding in the truck; it was the only vehicle parked at the entrance of the building and was the most plausible choice for her ride. I didn't have to wait long, the soldiers started calling each other and loading into the parked vehicles. Still, no one came to ride in the truck. Minutes later, I saw the huge front door open, and a group of people loaded into the truck. It was hard for me to distinguish any faces as I had crouched further away when the soldiers had started packing into the parked vehicles.

There seemed to be five or more people who had climbed in the back of the truck. I assumed one of them was Sarah. The only thing remaining for me was to tail these guys and make sure she got to Baghdad.

Stealthily, I sneaked back to my car parked in the bush and drove behind them, keeping a safe distance between us.

The distance to Baghdad from this location was a little more than five hours. I followed the entourage but there was a nagging little voice in my head warning me. I couldn't put my finger on it but there was something wrong with this whole picture and I couldn't shake the feeling. The convoy wasn't stopping anywhere, it had been on the road for about two hours, and I was hoping they will take a break soon. I wanted to see inside the truck to confirm if Sarah was there. My gut was telling me that there was something amiss and that could only be about Sarah. At last, they stopped at a gas station and some of them went inside. The road was deserted, and I kept driving past them to stop further ahead, out of sight. The truck was parked on one side apparently unguarded. As I got closer, I saw a soldier lurking about it smoking while the rest of the party was scattered. I covered my face with a keffiyeh and got closer to the truck. Thanks to my black garb, I blended in with the others quite well. There was not a sound coming from in or around the vehicle. I tried the door and it cracked open a bit. The truck was loaded with ammunition boxes and nothing more. The soldiers who I had seen entering it were probably the only occupants, Sarah wasn't there.

"Hey! What do you want? Nobody's here. They all went to get a drink." slurred the stoned soldier guarding it. My mind was going blank with fury and anxiety. I wanted answers, 'Where was Sarah? If she was left behind, what was the reason for that?' I waited for him to stumble close enough, and then I caught him by the neck, dragging him to one side in the cover of the truck. Tightening my grip around his neck, I asked him about Sarah. He wasn't able to comprehend at first what I was asking, then I rephrased to ask about the American. He played coy until I started tightening my grip around his neck till, I nearly cut off his air then he started blabbing hysterically. What he told me absolutely shook me from head to toe. I had not seen it but according to him Jabbar had been at the mansion, and he had been staying there for a while since his departure from the base. Daanish had vacated the complex because Jabbar had threatened him, and there was some kind of mêlée between the two. I didn't need to know anymore. Jabbar was there and so was Sarah, Daanish had betrayed me. I had to get back, she was in danger, and I had to save her. Knocking the soldier unconscious, I ran back to my car. There was only one thought consuming me, she was in Jabbar's control.

'Why had I been so blind to his treachery?', Daanish had played me for a fool.

I drove madly. I was at least a hundred miles away from the house and it was a long distance to cover. Dread and fear clawed at me as I sped forward, praying incessantly for her safety and cursing myself for putting her through this. 'If anything happened to her……….' I couldn't even think beyond that. The journey was arduous, froth with despondency and foreboding. Eventually I could see the outer wall of the building in the setting sun, evening was approaching which could make my work easier but I had to find her immediately without wasting anymore precious time.

Parking the car as close as possible, I crept out and prowled in the compound. Strangely, it wasn't heavily guarded. Only two sentries were posted at one of the side entrances and some, I assumed, were in the front. Getting my weapons ready, I stole close to them. Not able to use my gun, I took out my long knife and ambushed one of the soldiers. I held his head with my arm and slit his throat. Without a sound he slumped on the ground. The other made a reach for his gun but I was on him in a second, holding the knife to his throat.

"Where is the American?" My voice was menacing. He tried to shake his head in denial, but I was not in the mood for games. Taking my knife, I cut his cheek from temple to jaw and then placed it on his neck again.

"She's in Daanish's bedroom." That was all I needed to know. Hitting him with the hilt of the knife, I pulled him and the dead sentry to one side in the bushes by the door. Thanks to Daanish's ideas of grandeur, the house was flanked by landscaped vines and bushes. The spilled blood was thankfully on the side of the steps and not visible at first glance. I knew where I needed to go. The right wing of the building was where Daanish's living quarters were and he had it meticulously decorated and furnished. I had seen his bedroom which faced the south with a beautiful garden laid out below for his pleasure. I was at the doorstep of his bedroom in two minutes. Luckily, the mansion and this wing had only a few soldiers and slipping by them was easy, possibly at Jabbar's command to enjoy his victory in private. The guards at the door were easy to get rid of. By then I was in no mood for mercy. I could hear screams coming from the room and my blood boiled with wrath. Throwing the guards on the floor, I slammed open the door to find Jabbar on the bed with Sarah who was fighting him with all her strength. The crashing sound of the door startled them both and gave Sarah a chance to roll off the bed. Jabbar stood up grumbling and was shocked to see me standing there. He yelled out my name and lunged out at me, but I was ready for him. I wanted to beat him to death, but Sarah had also gotten up from the side of the bed. She was in a fragile state. Her eyes were red with tears, and she was shaking. I left Jabbar on the floor and went to her. There was an expression of joy on her face at first, which then turned to dismay, and she turned away from me. I knew she was angry, and I deserved every ounce of disdain from her for putting her through hell, but I needed to comfort her and take her out of there. She was still crying, and her dress was torn from multiple places with her hair disheveled. I wanted to kill myself then for what I had let happen to her. If she never wanted to speak to me or see me, it wouldn't have surprised me but instead she swung around and hugged me, sobbing when I called her name. I held her and she wept until she felt a bit better. I pulled a sheet from the bed and wrapped it around her. Just then, I saw Jaria standing agape at the door with a small gun in her hands. Once Sarah was more composed, I decided to finish Jabbar off but Sarah held me back and Jaria called to us, cautioning us about limited time. I heeded her warning and went out to see what she had for Sarah. She had a small duffel bag ready with supplies. She ducked back into the bedroom with Sarah and came out in a few minutes dressed in black garb. Sarah glanced at the bodies of the dead soldiers lying on the floor and was shocked, 'I should have covered these'. The thought passed through my head, and I got a small carpet from the room and covered them. She had normalized by then and we moved carefully through the passageways. Although they were almost deserted, I was cautious. I didn't want to take any chances. Sarah was dressed in the same kind of clothes I was, a black pair of trousers and shirt with a keffiyeh covering her head and face. Jaria had been smart about the disguise. We could easily blend in with the rest of the soldiers. Coming to the main wing, I suddenly realized our predicament, 'How were we going to get out?' Sarah and Jaria were with me, and the main wing was crowded with soldiers. It would be tricky trying to take a car and simply driving out. There was a good chance we could get caught. The way I had come in was not something I expected either one of them to be able to do. We needed to commandeer a car. I stopped and gestured them to do the same. Jaria had faltered a bit behind, and I waited for her. I wanted to talk to her about the next step. We couldn't make it out of here without her help. She had paused, looking around. She probably guessed why I had stopped and stepped forward, pulling the hood of her cloak over her head. She brought her face close to my ear and whispered to take her out in the compound and then follow her lead. I trusted her and complied. Sarah didn't question us, only when she understood that Jaria might not be coming with us, she was terribly saddened. I held Jaria's hand and moved her past the soldiers at the main door. One of them called me asking something about Jaria who was presumably portraying to be Sarah. I tried to ignore his calls and kept walking next to Jaria with Sarah following suit but eventually had to respond to him. At that instant Jaria, released her arm from my grip and ran to one of the parked cars there. The soldier who had called out to me ran after her with the other soldiers following suit. I knew this was our cue to slip away. I took Sarah's hand and quickly made my way to the back of the mansion. There were more jeeps there. I picked open the driver's door and hopped in. Sarah came in and sat next to me after I unlocked the passenger side door. The gate at the back was not frequently used, and the soldiers there would have no idea what was unfolding in the front yet. I had to get out before they got a clue. It wasn't hard to fabricate a reason for leaving the compound, although one of them tried to call inside for further information and apparently got static. Probably, the others were busy thanks to Jaria's distraction. The other guy reluctantly opened the gate and let us through. I grinded the accelerator and the jeep flew out on the drive way, leading out to the road. Driving here wasn't hard for me. I had toured this area multiple times, preparing for missions or just exploring the hills in solitude. Today those trips were paying off. Even in the dark I could maneuver my way through the winding road with ease. I saw the building light up as we hurried away. It was clear we had cut it close, and the thugs would be after us shortly. As I had figured, they were on our tail within minutes, in full pursuit. I needed to shake them because our jeep couldn't outrun them for long. Suddenly, I remembered that up ahead a sharp curve was coming followed by a steep incline, leading into the valley. Sarah and I could jump out there and let the jeep run on its own into the valley and crash, giving us enough time to make our escape into the hills. Once in the hills, I could make us scarce, I knew this place like the back of my hand. Sarah was stunned when I asked her to jump but she listened and jumped when I told her to. As soon as the car hit the incline, I jumped out too, deserting our ride to let it saunter down into the valley to crash. Quickly, I crawled to reach Sarah before she'd get startled and do something we'd regret. As I had suspected when she heard the car crash in the distance she tried to stand up, but I got there and pulled her down on the ground next to me. We waited for the party chasing us to pass, and when they did, I cued her to follow me and we made our way into the hills, away from the main road. I knew we were safe as we moved deeper into the mountainous terrain. Still, I wanted to get as far as possible from the trodden paths. As we proceeded, I waited for Sarah to say something. She hadn't uttered a word since our encounter and when she did, it made me smile, relieved that she wasn't steaming mad at me. I knew a place where we could remain undetected; it was better than any other for a hideout. I could imagine that Sarah was tired, but the spot was only a little further ahead. When I told Sarah we were there, she almost collapsed to the ground, completely worn out. We washed up and ate, and then, when it was time to sleep, she stubbornly wanted to take first watch and I let her. It was callous of me, but I had to keep distant and impersonal from her. It was a pact I had made earlier to myself. Life was not lenient, and she didn't have to suffer anymore then she already had.

I had been blessed with her for a short period and that was the extent of my good fortune I knew. Still, I was thankful for that little bit of light. Before sleeping I wanted to do something I hadn't done in so many years that I had almost forgotten how. Today providence had saved her and me. I had to give thanks for keeping her safe, so I offered prayer in the solitude of the wilderness. When I came back, I saw Sarah curiously watching me, but she refrained from asking any questions, and I quietly slipped into the sleeping bag, closing my eyes. I had no intention of falling asleep but the cool breeze and the sense of her being safe drifted me off into a deep slumber.

I was in a place serene and pleasant where the trees shaded the pathways, and I strode in between lanes of green shrubs and moss. Everything looked so fresh and clean like the colors coming alive after spring rains. The peace of that place was accentuated by a lonely form at the end of the path I was treading. A figure in flowing colors of pastels with brilliant gold curls and a breeze like gait danced around. I sped to catch up with the lonesome figure but somehow the distance never seemed to reduce. I struggled to reach it but to no avail, it drifted further away. Before vanishing into the mist, the form looked back and I could see the face, it..............I caught the hand touching me, my eyes flung open as I held on tightly,

"I'm sorry. I didn't mean to startle you." The curls of my dream haloed her face as she apologized. I was mystified for a moment as the dream replayed in my head, intermingling with reality, but as I grew out of my stupor, the chasm between her and my world became starker. The distance between us could never be bridged. I let go of her hand. It was my turn to take watch and hers to slumber. She didn't quarrel this time but when she slid into the bedroll, I could see the distress on her face. She was digging the heels of her hands into her temples with her eyes tightly closed. I remembered the day when she had the headache at the base, prompting me to inquire about her condition. She was honest about it, asking for any pain killers. Giving her some from my bag, I waited as she sat up, still holding her head. It was obvious that it would take time in resolving. Regardless of the restrictions I had planned, I wanted to help. I decided to massage her head to relieve the pain, without contemplating the consequences. She wasn't inclined to take my help, behaving distantly and reserved, but I could see that the pain was escalating beyond the limits of self-control. I tried cracking jokes to convince her of my honorable intentions, which helped to soothe her a little. She didn't argue as much after my attempts at being a jester. I began to fully comprehend my mistake when I realized I'd have to sit closely behind her to massage her head. It was a tighter fit than I anticipated since I had moved the sleeping bag nearer to the mountain side with the ledge for more cover. Sitting so close to her was not a sane idea, but I couldn't back out, now that I had pushed her to accept my help. Sliding behind her as she sat criss crossed, I settled in my place, folding my legs as much as I could. Slowly, I started to massage her forehead and neck. Again, I saw, how acutely her closeness affected me. My fingertips singed wherever I touched her. Keeping my heart in check was like swimming underwater breathless. It took all of my self-restraint to contain the storm swirling wildly within me. Every instance of being close to her flooded into my head, the feel of her body in my arms, the taste of her lips and the way she looked in that red night gown overwhelmed me. I shouldn't have been imagining things like that, but I had no power over the memories taking hold of me.

'Ali, you have to control yourself, if not for yourself then for her sake.' My brain chastised my heart, and I exerted to focus on relieving her pain. Her body tensed when I touched her but as I continued, she relaxed and leaned on me. I admonished my wild heart and breathing deeply, calmed myself. Slowly, I continued later becoming conscious that she'd fallen asleep reclining on me. The pain medicine had some sedative in it probably that had done its job. Eventually I stopped and leaned against the mountain side. If I tried moving she would definitely wake up and didn't want to disturb her, also having her in my arms for this short while was perfect and I was in no hurry to remove myself from where I was. My eyes got heavy, and I knew if I stayed there I would fall asleep but then I didn't have anywhere else to go. Stretching out my legs on both sides I closed my eyes holding her from the waist and drifted off.

Day 19

I awoke to the first rays of sunlight able to shine on us under that ledge. My eyes were still heavy with sleep, but I managed to open them and peek around, 'What was this place?'. I was warm and comfortable, but this wasn't home. I saw an arm around my waist that wasn't mine. Confused, but not apprehensive, I turned to see the owner of it and saw Ali sleeping with his head back, resting on the side of the mountain with one arm resting on his side and the other around me as I leaned against him resting on his chest. Blood rushed to my cheeks in an instant. I had fallen asleep in his arms last night and he hadn't disturbed me, holding me he had fallen asleep too.

In my twisting and turning, Ali woke up. He was groggy but as he realized our positioning, he pulled his arm back and gently straightened me up. I could feel my cheeks getting hot. I sat slumped over on the bed roll as he slid out from behind me and stood up.

"I'm going to go check out the area." He walked out and disappeared behind some bush. I sat there for a while, and then feeling the need to go, got up and went to the other side of the mountain. When I came to the stream, I saw that he was already back in camp. I washed up and joined him.

"Thanks for last night." I said shyly. It was hard to even thank him. He remained silent, almost ignoring me, digging in his bag. Then he pulled out a small pack wrapped in plastic, opening it he gave it to me. There were dry fruit and pita chips in it. 'We were having breakfast!' I quietly waited for him to speak as I ate. The whole time he watched the surroundings constantly. There was complete silence around us. I wished we could stay here forever but he had other plans.

"Sarah, you have to change and so do I. You must have an extra set of clothing in your bag. Please change into that and then we can leave this place to reach our destination." He sounded urgent,

"Our destination? And a new set of clothes? Last night you said you didn't have any." I questioned him, rolling my eyes.

"Yes. That's because I couldn't take a chance of ruining them. I have to get you to safety, to the American base in Baghdad." He stopped fidgeting with his shirt and looked at me a little puzzled.

"Oh, yeah." Words slipped out slowly as I looked around, already missing the serenity surrounding us. He was taking his black shirt off to change into some normal clothes. The black garb was obviously very conspicuous. I was in a black suit similar to his that I had to get rid of too. I opened my bag, rifling through it, but I became distracted as he pulled off his shirt and fumbled with his new one, topless. Mesmerized, I stared at him. The muscles of his arms and torso were visible in the light tan of his skin. He was really handsome, and I couldn't take my eyes off of him until he unbuttoned the shirt in his hand and wore it. I quickly averted my eyes before he could catch me ogling at him. My hands shook as I stood up with one set of clothing Jaria had packed for me, leaving the second one in the bag. I raised my brows at him quizzingly, 'Where was I supposed to change?' He was outfitted in a new light blue shirt, but he still needed to change his pants. Getting my cue, he replied by raising his hands in mock capitulation. It made me giggle.

"So, genius where do we change?" I blurted out unrestrained and my hand flew to my mouth in embarrassment. Surprised by my candid remark, he smiled broadly,

"I'm going behind the bush. You can do it here or go on the side of the mountain. There's nobody here." Holding his pair of khakis, he sprinted to the bushed area. I watched him helpless, 'How did he expect me to change here?'. I was only wearing a shirt and pants without any undergarments, curtsey of Jabbar's old bat. Ali had disappeared. Grunting, I faced the side of the mountain and pulled my shirt off. The breeze which had become warm with the extending hours of morning blew against my bare skin warming it. I pulled on the long loose shirt over my head, fighting with it to settle on my shoulders. As it fell in place, I turned around to see if I was still alone and saw Ali standing a little farther behind with his back turned towards me. I blushed, 'Had he seen me? No! he isn't a peeping tom.' I rebuked myself for being absurd. I hurriedly changed into the pajama pants and called to Ali in a hushed voice. He turned around and came running,

"We have to bury these clothes and leave immediately because I am sure they'll come looking for us. Jabbar will search until he finds us." Ali's tone sounded urgent, and he had started stuffing everything in his bag including the sleeping roll. Done with packing, he took our black clothes and went to the mountain side where the bush was thick and dug a hole with his bare hands. Burying the black suits, he came back and swung the packed bag over his shoulder, and then suddenly remembering something he tossed it on the ground and snatched out a black robe from my bag, a common garment for the women in this area to wear along with a head scarf. I'd left them inside not understanding the utility. He put the robe on me covering me from shoulders to toes and then wrapped the scarf around my head. That done, he took out a small bottle filled with a mustard-colored liquid from his bag. Pouring some on his palms, he asked for my hands. I gave my hands in his and then what he did baffled me. He started to spread the liquid all over my hands, tanning them. Then, he applied some to my face. Once he was done, he took the remaining part of the head scarf and covered my face with it, leaving only my eyes visible. After completing my makeover, he washed his hands and we moved out. The path wound through the hills and bush. We trekked for a long time, meeting some nomads on the way, but other than that we were alone. Eventually, we reached a small village where Ali bought some food, water, and a pair of sunglasses. I was curious about the sunglasses, 'Why would he buy them?' But as soon as we were out of the small store, he handed them to me instructing me to wear them,

"This is to hide the color of your eyes." He whispered, and I put them on quickly, comprehending the danger. We walked around like the other gentry, inconspicuous. I saw some soldiers in trucks parked at the main square; they were watching every passerby closely. We were in a territory which had been in constant conflict, a target of different militias for occupation. Ali turned in one of the streets, and we kept taking multiple detours in different streets until we'd left the village. In the outskirts, we stopped at a small mosque to drink some water and sit in the shade. There Ali gave me the pita and fruit he had bought from the village store. We ate our fill and relaxed there. There was a small courtyard in the front where some kids sat at the door playing with their toys and their moms watching them.

"Why didn't you cover your face? Wouldn't they recognize you?" I whispered to Ali. He put his finger to his lips and shushed me,

"Please, no talking."

I bit my lip. He was right. My accent was very obvious, and we could get caught. Ali got up and we left the village. I had seen buses running but it didn't seem that Ali was interested in getting on one. We walked following the small country road leading out of the village. The land was deserted passed the boundaries of the village, apart from a man with his camels and few others with their bags in hand probably making their way home. The sun was scorching, and my head was spinning with the heat. I nudged Ali to give me the bottle of water. We reached a place where the man with the camels and the others turned away to their own respective routes, increasing the distance between us. There were fields all around us and I had no clue which part of the country we were in. Since the day of my abduction, I had been driven everywhere blindfolded. I knew that I was far from the town I had been working in but exactly where I couldn't tell. We stopped and Ali sat on the grass along the roadside. I sat next to him, and he handed me the bottled water, pulling the scarf down I drank almost half of it. Ali watched me as I depleted our rations and smiled,

"Can I have some?" He reached out with his hand. A bit ashamed I gave him the bottle, then realized I hadn't even bothered to wipe the mouth of it, but he didn't care. Putting it to his lips, he finished it.

A sedan and some vans passed us as we sat there. They were delivery and cargo vans, and Ali didn't pay any attention to them. I was worried about us sitting at the roadside in broad daylight. 'What if Jabbar's men found us?' Making sure nobody else was around, I told Ali my fears. He was staring at the grass and the fields around us,

"I am aware of that, but don't worry I asked in the village if there were any soldiers around. The shop keeper said that they had come but drove out leaving a few behind. I guess the ones in the square. I'll try to get a camel from someone because the busses can be risky. They'll definitely be checking all the vehicles coming their way. I'm planning to ride a camel or go on foot or hitch a ride from someone. That'll be the safest way to travel for us." He finished,

"But where are we?"

"We're close to Rashad. The house that you were in was near Kirkuk." He looked at me raising his brows,

"So, how long will it take us to get to Baghdad?" I wanted to know,

"I was thinking that we could go to Tikrit, and from there Samarah and Baghdad. If I had a car, I could get there within a day but I don't have one." He sounded a little agitated,

"I have some gold jewelry; can we use that to buy a car?" I asked innocently. He looked at me incredulously,

"Gold jewelry?!"

"Yes, the bracelets and anklets I was wearing at the house. Jaria had put them in my bag." I pointed to the bag in his hands as mine was stuffed in his. Ali looked at the bag as if it was an alien in his hands, then stood up not commenting on our possessions. Once on his feet he presented me with his hand, accepting his assistance I got to my feet. He prompted me to pull the scarf up and we

313

started walking again, a little far from the main road and close to the fields. There was no one on that dusty country road except us. After a while, Ali stopped and changed directions making his way through the fields, I followed. He had been quiet most of the journey and I had not tried to engage in conversation as well. The fear of being discovered weighed heavy on both of us. Ali had taken out a head scarf for men from his bag and wore it. It gave protection against the blistering sun and shaded his face. We were walking between fields going west against the direction of the sun. I was getting tired and my feet were getting blistered. Keeping up with him was becoming hard. We had been walking since early morning, and the food that we had bought from the small village hadn't gone a long way. I wanted to stop and rest but Ali didn't seem to be in the mood. I could sight a few people in the distance working in their fields as we kept walking past them. The heat and fatigue got to me at last and I had to ask,

"Ali, when will we stop and rest?"

"We have to go a little farther. When we get there, we'll rest and then move on." Replying, he kept walking without looking at me. I could understand his fear about the soldiers searching for us but we were out of the inhabited areas so he could take it easy, I guessed.

"Where are we going?" I was trying to stay in step with him,

"We're going to cross Rashad and then from there we will head for Tikrit." He stopped at the edge of a field, where was one man plowed it with an ox in the distance. Ali looked at me,

"Sarah, I know you are tired and need to rest, but we have to reach a safe place. This isn't it. I'm headed to the river where there is more shelter and water is available. We'll travel along it and bypass the town of Rashad. I was planning to get a ride from Tal-Asfar. It's still about six hours of walking if we follow the road but it might be more for us. You have to endure this a little longer." He was watching me intently, his eyes were soft, but his face was solemn. I knew his concerns, nodding I stepped forward and we were off again with the sun shifting towards the west. We pressed on until I could see the strip of water. We were at the intended river. I was happy that at last we were at the water source Ali mentioned and now we could eventually rest. The bush alongside the banks was greener and thicker than the one farther away. Ali looked relieved. Here we were all alone and I felt a bit apprehensive, the quiet of the place was serene but frightening in a way. Ali seemed satisfied, taking off his scarf he sat in the tall grass, pulling my arm to do the same. Once on the ground, he put his bag on one side. Opening it, he took out pita bread from a smaller plastic bag, handing me one piece and taking the other. The water would come from the river, it was clear. I munched on my piece of dry bread and drank some river water with it. Although it was bland and dry, it filled me up. As soon as I finished it, I became drowsy, but sleeping was out of the question.

"Ali, I wanted to thank you for coming after me. I didn't get a chance to before. I'm grateful but let me add if you hadn't handed me over it wouldn't have come to this." I had meant to say that since morning but hadn't gotten an opportunity. Now that we were alone in a secluded spot, I could speak more freely. I had pulled down my scarf, Ali saw but didn't object. The changing color of his face revealed the turmoil in him; he remained silent and kept his eyes on the river. I had touched a sore spot and I was aware of it, not that I wanted to hurt him, only wanted him to acknowledge the facts.

He lowered his head and broke off a blade of grass twisting it between his fingers. I sat watching him. The initial bout of sleep was gone, and I was more alert. Our refuge next to the riverbanks was colder than the path we had treaded. I credited it to the proximity of the water with its cooling effect on the surroundings. Ali hadn't said a word, still staring at the changing currents of the river. I wanted to ask him so many questions. Questions I hadn't asked him in captivity when we had spent time together. Those encounters were limited to exploring each other's happy memories, the memories of his merry days of a past taken from him long ago. Now I needed answers,

"Ali, why did you believe your boss and let him take me, and then why did you defy orders and come after me?" My questions made him look up for a second then he was back to studying the water. I was agitated on why he wasn't answering me, but before I could burst with impatience he whispered slowly,

"I don't know. Maybe I wanted to prove you wrong or to prove to myself that the man I had been following half of my life was honest and trustworthy."

"Why didn't you believe me when I had told you about his plans? Why did you let me be taken? You know what would have happened if you hadn't been there on time. I would be dead not by Jabbar's hand but by my own. I didn't even let my fiancé touch me and now to be violated by a foul man like Jabbar. Jaria was going to put a bullet through me rather than let me be ruined." I snapped vehemently. He was taking it so casually, as if it was nothing. This meant he just came to see if his beloved boss had taken him for a ride or not. In my fury, I had abruptly revealed some of my most intimate secrets and Ali forgot the river. His eyes were glued to my torrid face. Emotions stirred in his deep dark eyes. I could see the changing shades, but my mind was seething. I wanted him to answer my questions coherently, not the vague replies he was used to giving.

"Ali, why do you work for a man like Daanish? Why couldn't you leave him and be free? Why did you have to wait for me go through hell to figure out that he is a crook?" My questioning brought him out of his stupor, and he redirected his gaze in an effort to avoid the unabashed eye contact we had for a few moments. His fingers were twisting another blade of grass, meticulously working around the contours of it. I watched his slender but agile fingers play with it.

"I was bound by promises I had to keep. He was the only man who gave shelter to a young boy like me, took me off the streets. For almost a year I had scrounged in the gutter. I had to follow him, and I thought he was always honest with me about the missions. They were to bring the country together.......... I had nothing else." Ali spoke dejectedly, his words filled with the sorrow of ages.

"Sarah, when there is nothing, you have to hold onto whoever you find. I was given that by Daanish. He guided me through life when all I could see was darkness and misery. I had a debt to him, to give him the benefit of a doubt." His conviction spoke louder than his words. I studied his face as he said those words; the shadows on his face were visible in the bright afternoon sun.

"I know I was wrong about him. I shouldn't have let him take you but I couldn't do anything. I had to comply. I had to trust him." He kept speaking and I listened. He had saved me, but I was still angry at the way he had adhered to the commands of Daanish. I looked away to the other end of the river. 'How could I trust him?' He was their soldier. I had hoped for his help and support in the camp, but he had given in to his leader's orders. 'What if we were to encounter Daanish again? Would he protect me, or would he succumb to them?' Thoughts of the future clouded my mind, doubts and mistrust reined at that moment. The adrenaline rush of the past day had ebbed and now I was thinking in terms of the future keeping an eye on the past. We were a long way from Baghdad and his comrades would be looking for him and once they caught up with us

318

it would be a tough decision for him to choose. If it were only Jabbar, I would have felt easy and confident, but Daanish would also be on our trail by now. No matter that he had betrayed him, he could still invoke sentiments of loyalty from Ali. He could demand it as a payback for the past. 'What would be Ali's choice then, to save the life of a captive he had a moral responsibility to or to comply with a man who had saved him from the ravages of a war ridden land?' I also suspected that my feelings of affinity were one sided. I was a fool to believe that he could feel anything for me. I was the enemy after all. Even if I wasn't directly responsible for the horrors he had seen and suffered. He had been honor bound to keep me safe as his charge, but it ended there. He had always kept his emotions under control except for that one kiss, which I was beginning to believe was more to keep me quiet then a revelation of his true feelings.

"Sarah, what are you thinking?" His voice brought me back to the present. His eyes implored my face, 'Should I confront him with my concerns or try to leave him when I got the chance?' I opted for the later.

"Nothing. I wasn't thinking about anything." I replied focusing on the grass at my feet.

"I think we need to move. We will stay close to the riverbank, it's cooler and the grass is thicker too." He got to his feet, swinging the bag over his shoulder and watched me as I rose, struggling with the cloak around me, with a smile on his lips he extended his hand again. Standing up, I fixed the scarf over my head and pulled it up to cover my face. We followed the trail next to the river and kept to the side. I walked behind Ali, wondering if I had done the right thing telling him about the jewelry in the bag. I could have used it for my escape, but now it was done, and I had to make the best of it. I was a little shocked by my own change. I hadn't even thought about it, to leave him after all that had happened, but our conversation brought home the realities of the past and my mind was changed. I realized that I was living in a dream. Ali was never going to go against his own leader, there was a bond between them which was forged over the years, where he had received from him a life and he in return had earned Ali's services. Ali had been uneasy about what Daanish had done but I doubted that it would make him turn outright against Daanish. He had no such affiliation with me. He was honorable, sweet and kind to me but that didn't constitute any real feelings. I had to understand his promise to protect me, and I couldn't deceive myself with false hopes any further, it was time to protect myself.

We walked for hours; the journey was hard in the warm weather. I had a newfound respect for the women who wore this garb every day and managed it. It protected me from the heat, but it was hot in itself. Sweat ran down my back and face. I wondered if Ali's war paint would be able to withstand the constant onslaught of the heat and sweat and I touched my face many times to make sure it wasn't running. It did drip a little but mostly it held on. I suddenly got worried and asked Ali whether it was permanent or not. Ali began cracking up at my fright, assuring me that it could be easily removed with soap. We made a few pit stops at safe places on the way. Ali was mostly quiet and reserved, occasionally producing snacks from his pack. He also made sure I rested intermittently, but other than that, we covered the distance in silence, scanning the parameter and passing a few people along the river. By the evening, the landscape changed from green to somewhat barren. It had been a long journey and I was dead tired. I called Ali and sat down on a big flat rock, hearing my call, he stopped and joined me.

"I can't walk anymore. Ali please, can we rest." I pleaded,

He gave up standing and sat on the rock next to me.

"I know. Luckily, we are at the junction where we can head back to the road and find someone to give us a ride. Let's rest here for a while, then we'll head out." He glanced around making sure we were alone. This place had the river curving and turning, the bend was wide, and the water seemed static. I watched hypnotically.

"Sarah here, have some fruit." Ali placed an apple in my palm, tearing me from my spell. I started eating and quickly finished it, assuming it was our meal for that stay. It wasn't much but it gave me the energy needed to proceed with our journey. Ali was chewing slowly, taking his time. I guessed he was tired too and wanted to linger there for more rest, but I was wrong,

"Sarah, we'll get to the road from here in about ten minutes and then I am going to hail some passing cars for a lift, preferably a cargo van or something similar. You need to stay behind me at all times. I will tell anyone who stops that you are my wife and are not well, so I have to take you to Tikrit and that I don't own a vehicle. Whatever I say to you, only respond yes in Arabic, is that understood?" He was looking at me closely.

I listened very carefully until he announced that I was to pretend being his wife. I could feel my face getting flushed; lowering my eyes I shifted in my place letting him finish, happy for the paint on my face hiding the pink. Done explaining, he stood up. I followed and we set out. He was right. We were at the main road in fifteen minutes. It looked abandoned in the setting sun with only a few cars and vans passing by. Ali tried to hail them, but no one stopped, until about twenty minutes later an old man with a beat up pickup truck stopped and gave us a lift. Ali talked to him for a short while and then we climbed on the open bed in the back. He had some rations stored there and some farm tools. I was grateful for this respite; we could sit for at least half an hour without moving. The air was cooling down with the setting sun and in a few minutes, we were riding in the back of the truck in the expanding darkness. I was getting sleepy. Sitting next to Ali, I leaned on his shoulder and closed my eyes. The fatigue was killing me and I gave in. The road trip ended sooner then I hoped. We were in the outskirts of Tikrit in less than an hour. Ali nudged my shoulder gently and woke me. I had to really exert to keep my eyes open as he helped me off the truck. The driver waved at us from his window and drove off. I looked around to better discern my surroundings. We were in the outer part of the city and there were houses intermingled with small businesses and shops. It was a little after eight and the shop keepers had started winding up their wares. Ali had the scarf a little pulled down around his face and was scanning the area. I just stood there waiting for him. After a minute or so, he started walking in one direction. I quietly followed. This was a moderately crowded place and people were going about their business. I saw some other heavily clad women carrying shopping bags, making their way in the streets. Ali was reaching his destination, a small automobile workshop. He pressed on my shoulder indicating that I should remain outside as he went in. After a while he emerged from the stain ridden workshop with a short stout man. He gestured towards me, and I walked with him to an old car parked a little farther from the shop. They approached a car and the short man started talking fast. I could hear the enthusiasm in his voice as Ali listened to him patiently. After he was done, Ali said something to him which made him smile broadly and shake Ali's hand. Ali produced something from his pocket and gave it to him. His exchange secure, the short man handed Ali a key hanging on a metal ring.

So, he had bought a car. I was still standing at the place he had left me, watching not only him but other passersby. Whoever I saw on the street seemed to be in a hurry, scurrying about in a manner that was more nervous than urgent. I hadn't seen people in the village I worked at behave like this; it was obvious that something was not normal about this place. But then I thought to myself, there was nothing normal about the whole country at this time. Ali walked back to me and simply held my hand and took me to the old beat-up car. Unlocking the car, we both got in and drove off. Now that we were all alone in a noisy car, I could eventually speak. I asked Ali about the transaction and how did he pay for the car. He was driving fast, moving through streets which were completely alien to me.

"I told him my was wife sick and my old car broke down on the way here, and that I needed to buy another one. I gave him one of your gold necklaces. He was happy to remain quiet about the necklace. I doubt he would have been able to sell this car for what I paid him." Ali said, keeping his eyes on the road. The scene outside was the same, buildings on both sides with dim lights peeking through the windows and darkness spreading its wings everywhere. I wanted to ask Ali where we were headed, but finding it futile, I kept quiet, looking outside. It was about half an hour later when Ali stopped outside a small two-story building. There was a small inadequate fountain in the front lawn with grass about to quit life. Ali parked in the dirt on the side of the building. I observed that it was a little different from the rest of the dwellings in the vicinity, with more covered ground and a big dirt parking. I concluded that we were at a hotel or something similar to it. Ali stepped out of the car and opened the door for me. I got out and ascertained our location better. This area was more like a slum then a suburban neighborhood. It wasn't even at the scale of a mediocre one. 'Well, who was I to complain. At least we might have a place to rest before falling flat due to exhaustion.'

Ali led the way into the lobby of the motel. It was definitely old but clean as far as I could see. The lobby was small and lacked furnishings that could distinguish it in any way except for some evergreens in a few pots, failing miserably at bringing a little cheer to the dreary place. Ali went up to the counter and rang the bell. A woman in a hijab emerged from the room behind the counter. She was middle aged and had a disinterested look.

"Yes, can I help you?" She placed her hands on the counter and asked,

"Can we get a room, anything will do. My wife is not well and needs to rest." Ali said in a nervous voice filled with concern. She looked us over. I lowered my eyes and wrapped my arms around myself, imitating an action I would do when I used to have stomachaches. With no sunglasses on, I had no intention for her to see the color of my eyes. Keeping myself hunched, I stayed next to Ali as she checked us in. Ali took the keys and headed for the staircase in one corner of the lobby. Apparently, our room was on the upper floor.

I straightened up as soon as we got to the upper level. It was a cramped hallway with old carpet, but thankfully it wasn't dirty or smelly. Our room was the one at the end of the hallway.

'Oh goody, a corner room with all the privacy one can get.' The thought crossed my mind and made me smile under the scarf.

Ali unlocked the door and went in, followed by me. The room had a queen-sized bed in the middle with crisp clean white sheets and fluffed up soft pillows. It made my mouth water. The opportunity to sleep in a clean room in a clean, soft bed. I forgot for a minute that Ali was with me, and I just went and plopped myself on the bed sighing with relief. The sound of subdued laughter reminded me of company. Ali was obviously enjoying this with his lips twitching in an effort to hide his mirth. I abruptly got up,

"I'm sorry. I didn't mean to insinuate that it was for me or anything. I was just tired." I said, embarrassed. He'd put the bag hanging on his shoulder on the floor, standing casually with his shoes off in the corner as well. I had been completely oblivious to him as soon as I had laid my eyes on the bed.

"You can change and rest. The bed is yours. I'll sleep on the floor. I'm used to it." He was trying to be as gallant as possible. I couldn't do that to him, but I didn't see any other options in the room. There was only a chair and a table apart from the bed.

"Ah man! I forgot to get something to eat on the way here." He slapped his head which made me grin. I was hungry too, and had forgotten as well, so to simply blame him wouldn't have been fair of me.

"Wait in the room, I'll get something. Maybe that lady has something to eat." He had worn his shoes and in a second, he was out of the room. I was left alone standing next to the bed agape at his sudden departure. This was the first time since we had escaped from Daanish's lair that he had left me and gone off on his own. I stood there motionless, thinking about what was going on. The seed of mistrust started to sprout again, 'Had he gone to contact his friends, but why would he take the trouble to stop over in a motel? He could have easily taken me to Daanish, and I wouldn't have known it.' I had been thinking about a possible escape route, but nothing seemed plausible, and now that he had bought a car a new avenue had opened. I could take the car and make my own way to Baghdad.

I gathered my wits and planned a scheme for getting away when he came back. At present, the car keys were in his possession, and I'd have to wait. I off took my cloak and scarf, my hair fell around my face. Curious about my appearance with the liquid tan on, I went in the attached bathroom to take a look. It had been more than two weeks since I had entered a nice clean bathroom with my own free will. I wasn't counting Jabbar's hole and its luxurious chambers. The reflection in the mirror showed me the dirt smeared face of a girl with a dark tan. The sweat and grim had made another layer of color on my face. My fears that the color would run were unfounded, it was a pretty hard-core paint and the journey had only made it last longer. I smiled at the face in the mirror and ran out as I heard the door open. Ali was back and he had a tray in his hands, the scene made me grin.

"Your role doesn't change, does it? You're still stuck bringing my meals."

He froze in his position abashed and then he made a face at me, which I genuinely found funny. He put the food on the sole table present and sat on the chair huffing as if he had been walking a long way.

"I asked the woman we met downstairs if there was any place around here where we could get something to eat, and she offered to provide the meal for a charge. I waited until she was done and brought it up as I was the only one she could give it to. So don't judge me." He rolled his eyes like a spoiled kid, making him look so young and carefree as if he had just come home from a ball game.

"So, you were checking out your tan?" He'd observed me coming out of the bathroom, pushing my hair back, tying it in a bun.

"Yeah, it stayed. I was worried that it had been washed off by the sweat." I touched my face,

"It's designed to get more stuck on the skin as one gets sweaty and dirty, but if you wash it with soap, it washes way in an instant. So don't worry, you won't be brown for long." He said satirically.

"I wasn't concerned about that. I only wanted to see how I looked. It was interesting to see myself like this." I replied a little annoyed at his assumption.

The aroma of fresh food was making my insides rumble. It smelled like gyro, and I wanted to taste it more than anything at that moment. Coming close, I saw that the attendant had been very elaborate with the presentation of the meal. There were two gyros in two disposable plates with napkins under them and paper wrapped around them in the form of cuffs, two toothpicks stuck out of them with small colorful flags. There was a small bowl of dip next to them and two glasses with some ice and what I thought was soda. It looked delicious. Seeing my hypnosis over the food, Ali picked up the tray and offered it to me, vacating the chair also. I wasn't concerned about Daanish or anyone at that instant except for taking a bite of that gyro. I picked up one and Ali took the other and we started eating. I didn't bother to sit on the empty chair. I hadn't realized it but I was really hungry and after the first bite I just devoured the whole thing washing it down with the soft drink. Ali was eating a little more slowly than me. He still had his left over when I sat on the chair after finishing the last drop in my glass. He had retreated to sit on the bed side. When I eventually paid attention to the world outside the gyro, I found him chewing at a snail's pace and watching me. Embarrassment made my face hot, I was probably eating like a gluten and appalled him completely, 'Well who cares!' I shrugged the feeling of discomfort. He was observing my every move and smiled with his lips pressed together at my perplexed state.

"You were very hungry, why didn't you tell me?" he asked between bites,

"I didn't know." I replied simply and wiped my face with the napkin. Happy to discover that I hadn't smeared it with food. Ali finished the remaining of his gyro in silence.

"Do you want to wash that off? I can redo it in the morning." He asked me sipping his drink.

"Maybe I should. I want to clean up. I feel like a walking mud pie." I was tired of carrying that goop on my face, and the heat and dirt of the trip had done a number on me, but then I remembered my escape plan. I couldn't take that tan off my face yet.

"Why don't you go first, and I'll go later." I offered. Ali had put the empty glass on the floor next to his feet. He was in a bad shape too, with dusty hair and dirt ridden clothes, not questioning me he stood up. Opening the door of the bathroom he stopped and came back like he remembered something. Taking out his wallet, the car keys and some papers from his pockets he left them on the foot of the bed before returning to the bathroom. This was my chance to leave; I waited for the sound of the water running then quickly wore my cloak and scarf and left the room, closing the door behind me quietly. I didn't want the lady in the lobby to see me, so I made sure that I didn't make a peep passing through it. Once out of the building I ran to the car, getting in, I started it and put it in gear. The car skidded over the dirt as I turned out of the driveway and pressed the accelerator. Finally free, I raced the car but as I turned the corner of the street which I assumed was where I should be headed, I almost bumped into a jeep. The car screeched to a halt as I pressed hard on the brakes. The jeep had stopped, and four men jumped out of the vehicle. They all had automatic weapons; I froze in my spot. Backing up this old junk would have been fruitless and a mistake, they could catch me on foot. Sweat broke out on my forehead and my hands. I had to make a quick decision either I could try to outrun them, or I could just stay there and try my luck playing a mute. They were almost at the car, approaching it carefully with weapons drawn. Suddenly I recalled that I wasn't wearing my dark glasses. I'd have to keep my head low, 'What was I going to do? Maybe I should accelerate the car as soon as they came close to the windows? That should give me enough time to drive this car into some alley.' I was getting desperate as they closed in.

"Oh, you have found her. Thank God, I was going crazy. First I have a migraine and then this woman takes it on herself at this hour to go look for a doctor." Ali's voice rang through the air, everyone was startled and turned to see him, including me. He was standing at the corner of the street, huffing, with one hand on the wall and the other on his head. He stepped forward; he had changed into a jeans and t-shirt. Coming close, he smiled disarmingly and waved at the men.

"Sorry to bother you. This is my wife. She is a little stubborn. I had a migraine for two hours and she just got angry when the medicine wasn't working. She wanted to find a doctor to come see me. I tried to stop her, but you know women. As soon as I went in the bathroom to throw up, she was out in the car. I told her I could see someone in the morning, but she was obstinate about bringing the doctor right now." Ali said between deep breaths. His hands were on his sides, and he had kept them clear in sight of the weapon wielding group. The men stood in their spots, observing him. Then one of them spoke to him, he was tall and heavy set, his weapon still drawn. He had asked Ali something and Ali took out the papers he had from his pocket and handed them to the man. He looked at them and gave them back not paying too much attention, then he came close to the car window of the driver side. I started to wipe my eyes faking crying.

"She is a handful. I have to keep an eye on her. She's not very smart. Please forgive her stupidity. She sometimes goes crazy. I told her that we have to wait but seeing me in pain she just didn't think." Ali was very close to the car by now and was pointing at me as he spoke. The man who had asked for the papers stepped back and said something sharply, slapping Ali on the shoulder. Ali just laughed sheepishly and stepped on the side. As he lowered his head to the level of the window, he said something to me. I didn't understand a word he had said but I kept up the pretense of crying, wiping my eyes with my sleeves.

They all retreated and got back in their jeep and Ali opened the door of the driver's side and pulled me out. Opening the rear door, he pushed me in and got in the driver's seat. Putting the car in gear, he slowly backed it out and turned back towards the hotel. As soon as we were a little far from the corner he sighed deeply and accelerated the car. We weren't very far from the hotel and were parked in the lot within a minute. I had only been able to go as far as two streets. Once the car was in the parking lot he got out and practically pulled me out from the rear seat, not letting go of my hand he almost dragged me to our room and threw me on the bed as soon as he closed the door. Standing in the middle of the room his face exuded fury, I had never seen him like this except for the day he had broken into Jabbar's pleasure nest.

"What were you thinking?! Do you have any idea who those men were and what they could have done to you?!!" He spat the words out, breaking the silence. I sprang from the bed and faced him standing up. I wasn't afraid. He could do his worst. I didn't care. I was tired of the constant fear of being caught or being sold out.

"I don't care. I just want to get away from here, what do you care? If I leave you can go back to your trusted and esteemed leader Daanish and get back to your life. I wouldn't doubt it if you would deliver me to him if he caught up with you, for old times' sake. How can I be sure that you won't hand me over if we encounter him? He's your friend and leader and you owe your life to him. I am just a liability. Those men were simply going to shoot me and the whole drama would have been over. End of story!" Anger surged in me as I spoke. I was the victim here. I was the one whose life hung in the balance with uncertainty in every passing minute. He could be angry all he wanted but I was not listening. My heated speech had an opposite effect on him, instead of becoming madder he sighed and slumped on the chair, worn out as if he had run all the way from the moon.

"Sarah, why do you think I will hand you over to the militia?" He asked in a defeated voice. I was shocked by the sudden change in his demeanor; the fury was replaced by a weariness that was contagious. I also collapsed on the bed.

"I am a realist Ali. You have a clash with Jabbar, so you never wanted him to have me as a hostage. When

Daanish gave me over to him you probably felt a responsibility towards me and came to rescue me. But Daanish has a special place. He was your mentor and savior; you owe allegiance to him. And if he were to find us or if he sent a message to you, you would heed it. I am only a piece of merchandise for him. For you I suspect that I am a responsibility, an unforeseen complication rather than your will. I can't be sure of anything. I'm in a place where I am surrounded by countless doubts. I'm not going to hold you responsible if you leave me now or take me to him because I understand that he was there when you needed him, and you have a debt to pay." My anger had simmered down too. The words poured out of my mouth in a measured manner like I was speaking in a slow-motion movie. I pulled the scarf off my head and threw it on the side. I was done. Everything was out in the open and there were no secrets left. I looked at him as he stared at me. A stare filled with misery and grief. It wasn't what I expected.

"Sarah, the life that I lead has no friends. We live with men and fight with them. There is no bond of love or friendship. There is only a trust that exists and prevails. Daanish picked me up but I have paid him for his kindness by fighting for him without asking questions. This is not like friendship that you can conceive. There is no kiss and make up option. Once the trust is broken there is nothing left. Now I am his and Jabbar's enemy and they are mine. There is no going back. Wherever they will find me, they will kill me. And I will do the same to them if I want to survive. You are not a liability. I wanted you to be safe. To return back home and that is what I bargained with Daanish. I will make sure it happens even if it kills me. I will take you to safety. You are not a burden" He lowered his head, fixing his eyes on the faded pattern of the carpet. I sat there shocked and mortified. His revelation snapped something in me; he had put his life in danger, taken all these risks only to take me to safety. He had defied his comrades and his leader only for my sake, and the day I was secure he would have to return to a life with no future, just because of me. My head spun at this information as my eyes stung and my heart ached. Tears came burning hot and untamed, running down my cheeks. I covered my face with my hands as the dams broke and washed away every restraint. I felt a hand on my shoulder. Ali was sitting next to me; I turned and buried my face in his shoulder. I had been terribly wrong about him, my feelings for him pushed into the depths of my heart came surging to the surface. I didn't know why I was crying, why it hurt. I had doubted him, hurt him, broken his heart but it felt like I had stabbed myself, as if I had ripped my very own soul apart. He held me, comforting me until the fit passed.

We sat there as time ticked by. At last, I straightened and moved back. A giggle slipped out of my mouth as I saw his wet tan-stained shirt. He was surprised by my sudden laughter but when he saw the shirt a smile spread across his lips too.

"I think I should change or at least wash this off." He picked at his shirt, and I giggled again.

"No way, it's my turn. I'm going to take a bath. You'll have to wait." I jumped to my feet and blocked the entrance to the bathroom. He looked at me amused sitting on the bed.

"But I do have one question. How did you know that I was gone and where to find me?" I didn't go in.

"I had an ominous feeling, so I came out of the shower, and when I didn't see the car keys, I knew you had taken them. I had seen the shift in your attitude, so the next thing was me on the street following the car tracks. Good thing there are dirt roads and this car makes a lot of noise" He leaned on the headboard and crossed his arms behind his head, reclining in a comfortable pose, still amused.

Turning, I escaped in the bathroom. It was just as before, clean with washed towels hanging from the rails ready to be used. This would be heaven. Turning on the faucet in the bathtub, I removed my clothes and stepped in the warm water. I laid in the water as the grime and dirt washed away from my body and I was refreshed. Draining the water out, I finally took a shower. It felt great to be clean again. Wrapping the towel around my torso, I stepped out of the tub just to remember that I had foolishly forgotten to bring my clothes in, cursing myself and my impatience I wrapped a large towel around my body and came to the door and called Ali. He replied in an astonished voice, probably surprised at the unexpected summon. I sheepishly asked him to bring my clothes. I heard footsteps and the sound of a zipper. He knocked as he got to the bathroom door, I opened it a sliver and extended my arm out to take the clothes. Once in my grasp, I pulled my arm back and closed the door nervously. Dressing up in a peach-colored long dress, I half wrapped my wet hair in the towel and stepped out, still feeling a little self-conscious. Ali was standing at the window, looking outside with the curtain drawn a little. He turned as he heard the door open, and his eyes forgot to look elsewhere. I became nervous, 'Was there still color on my face?' The curtain slipped out of his hand, for the first time he couldn't guise indifference. I blushed under his constant gaze and my hands fumbled with the twists of the towel wrapped around my hair making it come loose and slip off my shoulder. We stood there staring at each other. The fascination in his made me warm all over. Lowering my eyes, I had to say something to break the spell.

"Is the color off my face?" I could hardly hear myself, but my question brought him out of his reverie.

"Yes, it is." His voice was a whisper. I looked up. He had stepped away from the window and was paying attention to his stained shirt. I went to the small closet in the wall and hung the towel.

"I'm going to shower and wash my shirt; I checked I don't have another and I'm not in the mood to wear the dusty one again." Remarking this, Ali went in the bathroom. I sat on the bed motionless. My heart was racing, and my head was light. I felt a little woozy, but sleep was far from my eyes. I waited, without knowing what I was waiting for. Twisting strands of my hair and thinking about the past eighteen days, every little detail playing in my mind like a movie. Ali came out of the bathroom holding his wet shirt; with nothing else available he was shirtless. I had to hold my breath just to keep from gasping. He was handsome but like this he took my breath away. I checked myself. Regardless of what havoc he was wreaking within me, I had to keep my composure. I didn't want to make him uncomfortable; averting my gaze I got up and walked to the other side of the bed, away from him. I had chosen that as my side, not that we were sharing the bed.

Ali hung his shirt on one of the hangers in the closet. He approached the bed and took one of the pillows, tucking it under his head, stretched on the carpet next to the bed.

"Goodnight, Sarah, we should sleep. Tomorrow we'll leave for the next leg of our journey." He sounded firm.

I slipped in, laying on my back on one side of the big bed, pulling the sheet up to my chest. Ali was on the floor and had nothing to cover him. I stared at the rotating fan on the ceiling, apparently neither of us had remembered to switch off the lights. I couldn't sleep first because of the darn light and then thinking about him lying on the hard floor without anything. I decided to call him up on the bed. We were both rational adults, it shouldn't be a problem.

"Ali please come on the bed. There's enough space for both of us. You don't need to break your back on the floor." I pulled myself up on one elbow and called him. He sat up. His face tense with an expression of disbelief and surprise.

"But how can we? Wouldn't that be wrong? Are you comfortable with it?" He was apprehensive. So was I, but I knew I wouldn't be able to sleep anyway thinking of him on the floor and me hogging the soft fluffy bed.

"No, I am perfectly fine with it. We're not kids. We can share the bed like reasonable adults. You sleep on your side and I'll sleep on my side, nothing to it." I said confidently. He was still not convinced; confusion was visible on his face. I pushed again,

"Please you'll be fine. I don't bite."

That did it, and he got up. Placing his pillow on the vacant side of the bed, he lied down.

"Thanks, I appreciate your generosity." He was quite formal. I didn't answer. I had asked him to join me, but now that he was here, I was acutely aware of his body lying so close to mine. Darn the lights, someone had to switch them off before he could see the rising color in my cheeks. I skidded out of bed, and he got up worried that he might have done something, but when I switched off the lights and came back he got relaxed, reclining on his elbow just like I was a few minutes ago. He looked so much at home in the sheets of the bed with his shirt missing and a smile on his face. I avoided eye contact with him and tucked in on my side. 'Damn the rationality and reasonable adult jargon. I was having a hell of a time keeping the fever in my veins from escalating.' He'd laid down on his side and I on my side of the bed. Laying on my back, with my eyes tightly closed, I tried to block out the near presence of his body permeating my senses. Opening them a sliver, I peeked in his direction and found him turned on his side with his back facing me. My eyes opened wide with curiosity to take in the sight as he wasn't able to return the favor. The sheet was loosely tucked under him covering till his lower back. The visible part of his back had marks of healed wounds. The scars of his past. It made my heart mellow. 'How hard had his life been?' And now he had made it more difficult trying to help me. 'Why was he doing it?' The answer I hoped for was a wish, a dream which could never come true, but he still made me feel safe and cozy. Serene and content, I turned on my side facing him and closed my eyes, sleep which seemed distant a minute ago lulled me into its tranquility.

Day 19 (Ali)

I had such a peaceful sleep; it was a luxury I had not tasted for long, but I was awoken by the fidgeting of Sarah. She was up and twisting in my arms, swiftly I became aware of our situation and pushing her away, slowly I got up. I didn't want to give her any ideas, we had a tough day ahead of us and I wanted to get started as quickly as possible. Also, the emotional drama was not something I wanted to handle. Sarah was shy and reserved for a while until I gave her the new dress Jaria had packed for her traveling. The prospect of changing in the open transformed her mood to mischievous as she joked about me finding her a spot for it. I liked it when she was happy and carefree, talking spontaneously and cracking remarks, but I couldn't help her in solving that problem and taking my clothes I disappeared in the bush so I could at least get ready. By the time I came back, she was in the process of changing her clothes facing the side of the mountain. I didn't want to pry but I had stumbled on her privacy by accident. Immediately, I turned and stood waiting for her to be done, but in the short glance that I had stolen I saw her standing topless fumbling with her new dress; it reminded me of the day I had intruded on her. The sensation of her skin under my hands came alive in my memory combined with all the memories of her body against mine, making my head a bit dizzy. Standing in the bush, I was annoyed at being absurd. This feebleness had to stop. I had to compose my frenzied thoughts and keep my head cool.

'This journey isn't going to be easy.' I figured that, now there were no bars separating us, I had to strictly maintain the distance between us. I couldn't tell about Sarah, but I had no intentions of losing my head.

After we both had changed, I took the liquid tan Jaria had packed in her bag and smeared it over Sarah's hands and face. I said a silent prayer for Jaria; she had thought of everything. She had stuck the things from her knapsack into mine when the escape plan had changed, and thanks to her foresight, I was confident that we could make it to Baghdad. Sarah and I emerged from the mountain trail like any other village folk, she wearing a hijab with a long black cloak and me in worn-out jeans and a shirt with a keffiyeh over my head. We had a long walk ahead of us; my view was to avoid public transport and the main highways. I knew we would have to walk long hours to get to where I wanted to but this was the safest mode of travel. Sarah didn't complain and followed me. I admired her resilience. This whole escapade was a nightmare, but she had come through and still didn't complain about the heat or the strenuous journey. Only when we had stopped to rest, she had taken the bottle of water and almost finished it without even offering me a sip, which made me smile. It wasn't her fault. This land wasn't everybody's cup of tea. We got to the river by the afternoon and there I had the hardest time answering her questions. She was irritated and disappointed in my explanations; I could see it in her countenance. Her ever expressive face with her brilliant blue eyes and delicate nose that she twitched unaware when something wasn't to her liking. I could tell my responses had not satisfied her. They were lame and I knew it. The reality was I had made a huge error of judgment and there was nothing to mitigate its effect except for the recognition of inanity on my part, which I wasn't articulate enough to do. I sat in the grass, aimlessly playing with the blades to divert my attention from the obvious. She was discontented and I wanted to soothe her beyond anything, but my brain advised against it, the disillusionment would keep a distance between us and I needed that.

The passage after that had mostly been silent and tedious with every next step becoming harder. I was tired and could imagine Sarah's condition; she probably wasn't used to this kind of torture. There hadn't been much conversation between us until we were close to the junction of roads where I wanted to hitch a ride. It was evening and the sun had almost disappeared from the horizon when we were able to get a lift. Sarah had been detached after our stop at the river. It bothered me but I had to concede to my fate. Our paths of existence were separate, and it was a fact, I had to get used to, despite the ache in my heart at seeing her so remote and formal. We got a ride, and being close to the city, we were there in less than an hour. I knew the area and where I could acquire the vehicle and supplies I needed. I used the jewelry Jaria had snuck in Sarah's bag. I had no trouble in getting the car with that kind of credit. People in the city were ruled by the ruthless military but a good bargain was never off the table. I was thankful for that because rest of the passage wouldn't be possible without a car. I drove us to the nearest safe local hotel. It was in the outskirts of the town, not anywhere near the center. I wanted to stay out of the main parts of the town as they would be less guarded and also populated with slums. That would give us the cover we needed until we left this place. The hotel wasn't too shabby, and I was happy that the proprietor wasn't very nosy. We had to rest and get collected for the next day. It wasn't going to get easier; I was anticipating blockades from not only Jabbar but also Daanish. I had been his right-hand man and knew secrets which would probably give him sleepless nights. Thinking about the next leg of our journey, I came to the room and found it to be well furnished and clean. Sarah was giddy as a child at the prospect of sleeping on that comfortable bed and it was amusing to see her happy on account of such a small thing. I had forgotten all about buying food for us but luckily, I didn't have to look too far, the hotel manager was able to provide some.

It was a relief to have a clean safe room to rest for the night, out of the reach of Jabbar or Daanish. I had picked this area carefully keeping in view, what they might be expecting me to do. Dinner finished; I was the first one to head for the shower on Sarah's insistence. I thought she was being generous but what happened later drove me mad. As soon as I got in my instincts warned me about danger and I quickly came out. To my alarm she had disappeared taking the car keys but leaving all the papers behind. I thanked my sixth sense to have warned me and ran to the parking lot to find the car missing. I stood there for a minute locating clues to her direction and thankfully the semi dirt road proved very helpful in determining her projected route. I sprinted after her, and due to the car's old engine, was able to hear its faint sound. Dread filled me, I knew this town and the people who were in control They were ruthless, and I prayed she wouldn't run into any of them. The reason why Jabbar and Daanish were not likely to follow here was because of them. I just prayed she was safe, then the sound disappeared. As I turned the corner of the street, I had to literally backtrack to keep out of sight.

Her car was stopped by a jeep, and it was surrounded by soldiers whom I knew would show no mercy if they discovered who she was. I had to come up with a plan fast, then an idea popped in my head, and I jumped out from the corner panting and calling out to those men. The story I told was quite lame, but I pretended to be of slow intelligence and to portray Sarah as the same, an illiterate, ignorant simpleton. Miraculously it worked, or else as a last resort I was prepared to fight them because there was no other option. They were going to kill her and me in any case. I thanked God for his mercy and dragged Sarah back to the hotel. I was boiling mad, 'She had been so foolish. What was she thinking?' I screamed at her for the first time since we had met, but rather than getting intimidated she confronted me and accused me of abandoning her if any of my old mates turned up. I was shocked by her accusations, but in all reality, I couldn't blame her for her suspicions. It was my fault that she had lost her trust. I had delivered her to the devil, and she had every right to be wary of me. My rage dissipated like smoke. It was time for me to come clean, for we might not be as lucky as we had been tonight if she pulled a stunt like that again. She was tired and disillusioned. I could see in her beautiful eyes the shadows of doubt and disbelief, she needed to know the truth, except for the heartache I suffered.

To tell the truth was not as hard as I once thought. She sat there dumbfounded hanging onto every word coming out of my mouth. The expression on her face changed, first she cried and then it was replaced by an equanimity which translated into her attitude elevating her mood. I felt relieved like a huge burden had been removed from my chest, and it felt peaceful beyond anything. Sarah had gone to shower and cleaned the tan off her. I took that opportunity to scan the area from the window. It was dark outside, and nothing stirred. We'd been very fortunate with those soldiers because it was late and there were only a few people out and about at that hour. The street next to the hotel visible from the window was deserted and I was sure that the other street would be the same. I hadn't drawn the curtain completely simply held one corner and kept a watch. The sound of the door opening intimated me of Sarah being done with her shower. It was a mistake for me to turn and look. She stood there twisting the towel around her wet hair which slipped out of her hands letting her hair fall on her shoulder. She was a vision. The curtain slipped out of my hand as I tried my level best to look away but miserably failed until I was brought back to the world by her question. At that moment, I cursed Jaria for giving her those dresses, but it wasn't her fault I was smitten by Sarah even when she was in her disheveled night dress. I had to control this rising tide of desire in me. We had no bars between us anymore. Answering her I went to shower and wash my shirt. Once that was done I went to the other side of the room and decided to go to sleep, even though I was utterly awake, to keep my sanity. She took the far side of the bed and I stretched out on the floor, but I had to get up because she called me to sleep on the bed, innocently suggesting the fact that we were both adults and could share sides of the bed like reasonable people without incident. 'How could I explain to her that even coming close to her drove me insane with longing?! Let alone sharing the bed.' It would be a cruel joke, but I had to comply not just to satisfy her but to assure her that there was nothing between us.

I took the other side of the bed, topless as my shirt was drying on the hanger and I had nothing to wear thanks to Sarah's water works. This made me even more uncomfortable. Still, I stayed in my spot and pulled up the sheet. Slumber was an impossibility, but I shut my eyes and pretended to sleep. I knew when she peeked at me. I was trained not to sleep even when I was supposed to sleep, and to make her more relaxed I turned on my side facing the wall. I could still feel her watching but I didn't budge and eventually dozed off into a cautious sleep.

When I woke from the sporadic doze in the morning, I found Sarah snuggled close to my back in deep sleep and me in the same position, on the edge of the bed all night very much aware of her presence.

Day 20

I held onto Ali's arms as we talked and laughed strolling around in a garden loaded with colorful flowers and evergreens. Our path was lined with a manicured hedge guiding us to a beautiful brick house with terraces and French windows. We stopped at the main entrance where he took me in his arms and kissed me then he swooped me up and pushed open the door to the house taking me in. It was huge and.......

"Sarah, Sarah" His voice distracted me. He was calling me from somewhere. His lips were not moving but his voice was calling my name, then the picture started to fade as he and the house disappeared and then the voice became louder and clearer. My eyes flung open. I was lying in bed and Ali was calling my name. He had so rudely disturbed my dream about him without knowing, but as soon as the thought passed my mind the scene in the dream made me blush. I sat up with my eyes still heavy with sleep; he was sitting on the side of the bed watching me as I tried to make sense of where I was. God knows I should have become accustomed to waking up in strange places by now, but maybe I wasn't the right material for that sort of thing.

"Sarah, sorry to disturb you but we need to get ready and leave this place." He was still watching me intently. I became very much aware of my tousled hair and clothes. I had fallen asleep on one side but apparently had spread out like I owned the bed. I had no idea how he had been able to remain on his side with me fanning out like that, but he didn't say anything about it.

"I'm sorry. I must've pushed you to the edge." I blurted out, twisting my hair into a bun,

"Don't worry, I've slept in worse conditions." He smiled. I lowered my head a little flustered. I had to desert the bed and get ready; running my fingers through my hair I slid out of the comfy bed and went to the bathroom. Ali didn't move from his spot. I took my time and when I came out, he was sitting on the chair with a tray of hot breakfast on the table. The aroma was delicious. We'd finished it within the next ten minutes. By the end, we were sipping coffee and relaxing. Applying the goop, I donned my cloak and scarf, and we were on our way, returning the keys to the same woman in the lobby. It was early morning. I saw people scampering about in the streets getting to work as our car made its way through. In half an hour, we were out of the town on the highway headed towards Baghdad. The highway was strewn with trucks and cars, and it seemed the trip wouldn't be perilous, but Ali had told me that we would be stopping on the way in Syed Ghraib at his friend's house. Access to the capital wasn't easy because of the rebels and militias in control of the peripheries. He wasn't sure about the success of our approach to the city. It was my first experience to be in the areas controlled by the militias. It was different from the government controlled areas; people were intimidated in both parts of the country only the fear had a different character on either side. I didn't see happy carefree expressions anywhere; it was as if this whole land was cursed by the worst of plagues. Everywhere I saw misery written on the faces of ordinary people, symbolistic of the ordeal they were going through. When Ali explained about the difficulty in entering the capital, I could understand. There were boundaries and check posts that would scrutinize you before granting you a chance at freedom or life. I hadn't expected it to be easy as I looked out quietly through the dirty window of the car with my sunglasses back on my nose, hiding my eyes, while Ali drove through traffic. We had passed a checkpoint without incident. I had been praying all along. The guards were suspicious of everyone, checking us closely as our car passed. I was so thankful for the goop Ali had applied to make me look tan, it had been a life saver. They kept staring at me and Ali very critically but didn't stop us. Our car maneuvered its way through the other vehicles on the road as we covered more distance. The presence of military vehicles increased on the road as the distance shortened towards the capital. Ali drove without a word, his face was expressionless, but I could see the knuckles of his hands turning white as he tightened his grip on the steering wheel. We had been on the road for more than an hour. It was midmorning and the sun shone brightly. I thanked our lucky stars because this was much more comfortable than walking. We had passed a small town where Ali got some gas along with some snacks and water. We drank and ate while he drove. I asked him how he was planning to take me into Baghdad if his old comrades would be waiting for us. He had no clear plan, anticipating getting more information from his friend we were about to meet. His friend Saad lived in a small village near Baghdad and there was a safe house there where we could hide out until we devised some way of getting past the militias and the Iraqi patrols. Ali didn't want to call the Americans directly because he wasn't sure if he could trust anyone until I was in the military facility. I had full confidence in him; he was a soldier and knew how to handle the situation. The old car was blistering hot, and our bottle of water was finished. We did pass another small town, but Ali didn't stop, explaining that we were close to the militia-controlled city of Samara, a dangerous zone for us. Here Ali drove slowly, following the local traffic, and stopping in one of the squares to buy dates and water, lazily wandering around the street venders bargaining for a better price. He seemed like a man out to buy groceries for his home rather than an escaped soldier. I waited for him in the car, patiently keeping my fingers crossed. We had crossed many military vehicles in the city and there was one in the square where Ali was rummaging through the wares of street venders. His shopping done, he dumped the bags in the back and drove off. I kept an eye on the soldiers stationed there who had stopped paying attention to him when he started to bicker with the date sellers over the price and if he could get more for a discount. I was relieved to be out of there, without asking him I knew what he had done. It was nerve wrecking but necessary for our safety. He had played a bluff and it paid off. We drove through the city without any trouble and made our way through the river valley with fields spread out on both sides of the road. Ali's friend's house was close now; he lived on his own land. Ali didn't go into the details, but he was positive that Saad was sincere enough to be trusted. Ali had a safe house which he had set up with his help. I didn't question his judgment, though I felt apprehensive. Daanish hadn't proved to be trustworthy, and I hoped Ali was right about this guy. After a nerve wrecking two-hour trip, we were on a country road leading to the destined house. This part of the land was green and visually peaceful with not a sign of the war waging in the country. The road trip had taught me a lot. Visible proofs of destroyed houses and livelihoods lay scattered on both sides of the road. I didn't feel like talking and neither did Ali. It was a quiet and solemn journey. At last, we arrived at our destination. It was a mediocre house on the edge of open land planted with different vegetables. A date grove covered the rest of the land little further ahead of the vegetables. The house had a wall around it, and Ali had to open the gate before he could take the car in. The scene inside was different than the vegetable strewn land outside, a beautiful garden in the front yard with lamps greeted us. Whoever tended it had good taste and was diligent. Ali parked the car in the driveway next to a newer sedan. We got out and walked to the main door. The gravel road scrunched under our shoes and when we rang the bell, the door opened instantaneously. Whoever lived here had very sharp ears or was already waiting for us. An older man stood at the door, surprised to see us, but then he stepped forward and hugged Ali warmly.

"Ali, my friend. What are you doing here? It is so nice to see you." He had a deep voice. I was a little surprised by his exclamation, was he Ali's friend? He could have been his uncle rather than his friend keeping his age in view.

"It is nice to see you too, Saad. I need your help." Ali hugged him back and replied, holding his hand.

"Come in, we can talk inside and rest." Saad pulled him in and Ali caught my hand and took me along with him. Saad was watching me keenly as we entered a well-furnished living room. It had earth toned sofas and chairs, backdropped by white lace curtains. The carpet on the floor had a floral pattern with beige and pink flowers. The windows faced south so there was ample sunlight in the room, though it wasn't hot. I liked the place. It felt cozy and comfortable. Staying here would be nice. Saad and Ali sat on one of the sofas, and I took a cushioned chair.

"So, what's going on?" Saad asked, his face inquisitive.

"It's a long story but the short of it is that I need to stay in the safe house and find out what would be the safest route into Baghdad." Ali leaned back on the sofa and searched the face of his friend.

"I see. It's ready. You know that, but I will have to find out about Baghdad. Let me run down there and check out the situation. You can stay here as long as you want. Does your new friend have anything to do with it?" He pointed his finger at me. I became very conscious.

"Yes and I have to get her to safety before long. Daanish and Jabbar are probably on my trail. You will need to keep safe too." Ali left his seat on the sofa standing up close to the table in the middle.

"I will understand if you can't help me. I will try to manage on my own." His eyes were fixed on Saad.

"You won't have to fend on your own. We'll be here for you." A female voice startled me in the middle of this conversation; an older woman in traditional Iraqi clothes came in the room from a door on the far side. She was about as old as Saad but had a beautiful face with her hair tied up in a braid in the back. She had a mild manner with an air of ease. Coming close, she held out her hand to me, and as I shook it, she pulled me up and lightly hugged me.

"You'll be fine here. Take off your cloak and make yourself at home. I'll prepare lunch for you both." She smiled at me, holding my hand.

I looked around. Ali was still standing in his place and Saad was sitting, both of their attention was set on us.

"Sana, thank you for your support and hospitality. This is Sarah and she'll be staying here with me." Ali went to the older woman and slightly hugged her.

"Don't thank me, you're like my son. You are always welcome in this house." She gently patted his shoulder. Ali came and sat on the sofa again, looking relieved.

Sana took me with her and asked if I had clothes and other necessities. Her house was spacious and well furnished with the kitchen that reminded me of the one back home with its cottage style décor and setting. She guided me to a bathroom and left me there. I removed the dirt ridden cloak and washed my hands. I wanted to remove the goop from my face and arms but for that I needed a bath which didn't seem appropriate at this time. Coming out, I went in the kitchen searching for her, where she was busy cooking. I offered to help, and she was glad to let me. We were busy for about two hours, and in the meantime, she gave me and Ali cold drinks and sandwiches. We talked as we cooked. She was inquisitive about my circumstances, and I had no quarrels about telling her my whole life story. She was the sort of person who could make you feel at ease in the middle of a hurricane. I felt like I had found a lifelong friend in her, and she was more than happy to oblige. She listened to every detail eagerly and kept asking me questions. Some of her inquiries made me blush. She was quite candid about asking me if I had someone special here or back home or if I and Ali had been intimate. My nervousness and utter confusion in answering her, gave her the answer she was looking for. I went as far as to suggest that Ali had no such interest in me. She grinned and cracked jokes like a teenager; it didn't feel like I was talking to a mature woman in her fifties but as if I was discussing my love life with a college mate. She made me forget where I was and the circumstances that surrounded me. I giggled and laughed at her jokes and struck back with some of my own. We hadn't noticed but Ali had come looking for me and when I paid attention, he was standing in the doorway watching me. He had come to show me the safe house where we were supposed to stay. I came out of the kitchen and went with him. Saad led the way from the back of the house into the fields, beyond the date trees. There was a broken down shed and nothing else. I was shocked to see it, and a little disappointed that we were going to be stuck in that dump for the next few days. He walked in first and then Ali and I followed. The broken building had nothing much. The roof had caved in from one side and was hanging low on the burned-out fireplace. Saad stood in front of the fireplace and pressed on a worn-out brick on the side. To my astonishment, the wall behind it parted and we could see a narrow pathway leading into the darkness. He went in first with his flashlight and then Ali and I followed. We walked on the path for about thirty minutes until it ended at another wall. Saad pressed another brick here and the wall parted like the other. We stepped out of the tunnel behind him and found ourselves in the middle of a well-furnished room, resembling a living room, and as I looked behind, the wall had closed and all I could see was a tall painting of wine country. There was a door in the opposite wall leading to a small kitchen and another one next to it, opening into a spacious bedroom. It all looked very well equipped and elaborately planned.

"You can stay here. No one will ever know." Saad sounded confident. I hoped he was right. Ali sighed in relief. I looked around. There were windows with curtains, and I could make out sunlight peeking through the crevices. Going close, I pulled one of the curtains a little, revealing the scene outside. We were probably in the middle of some kind of settlement. I could see other houses a little far away from ours.

"Where are we?" I asked. It was the first time I talked to Saad since my arrival.

"We are in a village a little far from our home in the fields. It's disconnected from us and anyone who is looking for anyone misses this because it is so obvious that it becomes invisible." Saad explained, "But please don't pull the curtains and don't turn on the lights. This house looks like rubble from outside as it was hit by mortar fire, and most of it was demolished. It's been standing in that state here with no one occupying it. The windows have slight openings to bring in light and air but other than that it remains dark and unused. There are small lamps that you can use. Their light cannot penetrate through the curtains." He continued explaining the rules of staying in the house. I had a hunch Ali already knew all this. The briefing was only for my knowledge. By the end I had understood that the curtains in the living room were always open a sliver, and the kitchen and bathroom was always stocked so we would be well supplied. We could come to the main house when we wanted and could stay here as long as we needed. Everything settled, we went back to Saad's house and to Sana.

By the time we were back it was afternoon, and she had a delicious meal ready to serve us. I had to take a bath and clean up, but she insisted on me finishing lunch first. It was clear that I was famished when I took the first bite because, after that, I didn't stop until my plate was empty. Ali and Saad were talking about ways to get into Baghdad and planning different strategies. I was bored and asked Sana how they knew Ali. She fell into deep thought and replied that it was a long story that she will narrate over tea. Everyone was done with lunch come dinner, and Sana started picking up dishes. I joined in and we were finished quickly. I was of a mind to wash them, but she stopped me and took me upstairs to a bedroom. It was not very big but had a pretty white bed with matching curtains and a sofa chair. The bed was covered with a white sheet bearing delicate floral patterns. I felt right at home in this room, it was so serene and peaceful.

"This was my daughter's room. You can take a bath and change in here. I have a dress laid out for you, and there is another to take with you to the safe house." She said quietly. I saw the long dress on the foot of the bed for the first time; it was lilac and made of delicate silken lace with embroidery. The fabric was soft and luxurious, it was definitely for special occasions.

"I can't take this. It looks expensive. You can give me any old dress. I don't mind as long as it is clean." I was apprehensive of her giving me her daughter's dress. I just remembered Jaria and the tale of her daughter. 'Oh my God, did Sana's daughter also die?' The thought made me wince.

"You can have this. My daughter is not here, she wouldn't need it and you are almost her size so it should fit." She sounded final,

"Sana, why wouldn't your daughter need it? Is she okay, I mean is she alive?" I stammered as the words came out of my mouth.

"Oh no, my daughter is fine. She just doesn't live here anymore, and we can't go as often to visit. She has kids now, so this is no more her size. She is fine, you can wear it without worrying." She was puzzled.

"I'm sorry. At the camp, Jaria gave me her daughter's clothes who had died in an air raid. I felt really bad about it, and I didn't want to offend you." I had to explain my bizarre behavior. Sana smiled and softly patted me.

"You take a bath and freshen up, don't think too much. Everything you might need is in the bathroom." She left closing the door. I was left alone in the room staring at the dress. Shrugging off my apprehension, I checked the lock on the door and took my clothes off. Throwing them on the floor, I stepped into the bathroom. It was very clean and had a white theme matching the room. I found everything to scrub myself clean lined up next to the shower. I bathed with perfumed soap and shampoo and enjoyed every minute of it. When I was satisfied with my bath, I wrapped a towel around myself and came out into the bedroom. The sun was tilting towards the west. It was close to evening. The delicious meal and the warm bath had made me sleepy, but I couldn't sleep there. Unfortunately, we had to crash at the safe house. Drying myself, I changed into the dress Sana had taken out for me. It was almost my size and looked amazing. When I checked my reflection in the mirror, I could appreciate the true charm of the dress. Its circular neckline was wide set, exposing my collar bones and closed in the front with a set of pearl buttons running down past my bust. It was very alluring the way it hugged the curves of my body. Satisfied with the fit and appearance of it, I turned my attention to tend to my hair. A small dressing table next to the sofa chair had a hairbrush and other hair accessories plus some cosmetics. I combed my hair and arranged it so it was not tied but would stay out of my face. I carefully set it with strands loose on both sides of my face and on the back, hanging in soft curls. The deep gold of my hair shone in the rays of the nearly setting sun. I savored the time I took to dress myself; it had been long since I had done this. It was surprising for me also, to take such pains to dress myself, especially in these circumstances but my heart was set on it.

When I stepped out of the room and descended down the stairs, I could smell the aroma of freshly brewed coffee. They all were in the living room. I could hear them chatting. Suddenly I felt shy, and slowly approached the open door to the living room. Entering it, my nerves were on edge. The anticipation of Ali's presence inside was making me nervous.

But I couldn't just stand there, so sucking in my breath I went in. Saad and Ali were engaged in a hot discussion of some sort standing near the window, and Sana was sipping her coffee quietly listening to them. Saad was the first to see me because Ali was standing with his back towards the entrance.

"Praise the lord, haven't we been blessed with a blooming flower!" Saad exclaimed loudly, making me blush. Ali flung around and stood there arrested in his position. Sana also beamed as she saw me.

"You look lovely Sarah. I am happy I gave you this dress." She came close and gave me a hug.

I was aware of her, but my eyes were interlocked with Ali's. There was a passion in them I had glimpsed before when he had his guard down. I was as mesmerized as he was. Saad called him and said something, a telling smile on his lips. Ali was brought back to the real world in seconds; he tilted his head stepping back and placing the cup in his hand on the table next to him. I was able to move forward and take a seat on the sofa where Sana had been sitting. She was nearly in the kitchen,

"Sarah, what flavor would you like to drink?"

"What?" I had trouble putting words together; I could still feel the heat of Ali's eyes.

"Which flavor of coffee?" She asked again, patiently waiting for a coherent answer from me.

"Anything you like. I can drink any." I was barely able to answer.

My senses were not functioning normally, the urge to dress up knowing that Ali would be there to see was not something I would do, but I had realized now that was the precise reason why I had taken so much care in preparing myself. I wanted him to see.

Saad had left his place too,

"Let me help you." He went in the kitchen with Sana.

Ali was not directly across me but he turned and faced me, leaning on the wooden trim of the window.

"Sarah, did you find everything okay?" His question was very casual, but when I peered up at him the tempest in his eyes was as clear as the sun on the horizon.

"Sana takes care of this little piece of paradise." He slanted his head towards the window and pointed out with his hand. I came and stood next to him. He gave me a sideways look and then turned his attention to the garden outside, avoiding looking at me directly.

"Do you want to go out?" I asked him.

"Maybe." His voice was dreamy, we stood there dazed with our attention focused on the garden outside.

"Would you like to take your coffee in the garden?" Sana's voice surprised me; I spun around to see her. Both Saad and Sana were in the living room. Sana had a steaming hot cup of coffee in her hand. I had no objection to her suggestion. Nodding, I confirmed approval of her offer to tour the garden. All of us walked out. The garden was not a very large but the arrangement of the flower and fruit beds was in such manner that it falsely gave the impression of being spread out. The setting sun had lost its intensity by this hour and when we strolled among the intricately manicured lanes, circling flowers and orange plants, the soft breeze felt good. I was accompanying Sana. She was an expert horticulturist with in-depth knowledge of the plants growing in her garden. I asked her the same question I had earlier about their friendship with Ali. She gave me a meaningful glance and sat on a small wooden bench near a rose bush.

"You are determined to know aren't you?"

"Yes I would like to. It's important." I sat next to her, coffee mug in hand sipping it periodically. (I still was working on getting used to coffee.)

"Why is it important? Is it to soothe your heart, to satisfy the nagging conscience about Ali and his merit?" Her tone was very somber. I instantaneously looked up to meet her eyes,

"No! No! I just wanted to know. You're not his age or in his group so it was strange for me, that's it." I had trouble making up an answer, 'How could she be so accurate?'.

"Ali saved us from people like Daanish and Jabbar. He was with the militia attacking our old village. There were opposition soldiers hiding there and they were after them. Us and the other villagers would have been collateral damage if it was Daanish or someone else but Ali took everyone who had no connection to the militia out and made sure we were safe. He saved my son who was taken as hostage in that attack and brought him to us. My daughter and other children remained safe because of him and we can't repay his debt. We sent out our kids to the south to live with my sister, and now Leah is married with one child. Ali has been our friend ever since." Sana finished her tale and peeked into my eyes inquisitively.

"Does that answer your query?"

"Yes, I am happy he has you as his friends." The coffee had cooled in my hand. I took a sip and stared at the beautiful red roses.

"Sarah, I have a request, …………please don't break his heart."

I was shocked by her comment.

"But it's not like that. I can't break his heart. He has no such feelings for me. I am his responsibility and that is the end of it." I replied in a beaten tone like I had been slapped in the face. Ali had never expressed any such sentiments for me and the passion in his eyes was a fleeting expression, which vanished as soon as it appeared. I stared at the half-filled cup.

"Sarah, even a blind man can see what he feels for you. I have never seen him so taken by anyone, so mellow and affectionate. He might not say it, but he has feelings for you." Sana spoke incredulously. Stunned probably at the sheer absurdity of my situation. I had no answer to her request except for just listening. The sun had set in the west and my coffee was cold as ice. We both headed back to the house. Ali and Saad were waiting for us on the porch and as soon as we approached, they went in. Ali gave me a look and I couldn't make out what it meant. My own brain was in disarray, 'What was the reality of everything?' The conflicting attitude of Ali was a mystery. There were moments when I saw a fire in his deep dark eyes and then it would disappear as if it never existed. Thinking about Sana's request, I wanted to scream in frustration. It was not me who was bent on breaking hearts.

Night was upon us, and it was time for us to leave for our safe house. Sana hugged me and we left for the tunnel, leading to the safe house. Saad departed at the entrance of the tunnel and went back to his house. Ali and I entered it and walked to our destination in silence, both of us deep in our own thoughts. Emerging in the hidden house, Ali locked the door to the tunnel and sat on one of the sofas heavily, the expression on his face profound. I decided to go to the kitchen and give him some space. He was in this fix because of me, and I had no way of getting him out of this. Another thing that occurred to me was the question of Ali being left behind once I was at the American camp. I wished he could stay there. 'But would they let him in? Would he want to? Would I be able to live with the knowledge of his destruction ....? or without him?' My mind was twisting in directions I had not conceived before today when we were so close to the final destination. The reality was I had to bring myself to terms with the eventual outcome of our mission, if we made it alive to our destination. The only missing key was Ali's take on the situation. 'What were his plans? Was there a hidden purpose here which I didn't know about?' Again, my mind was wandering. I banged my fists on the kitchen counter frustrated. I needed answers about his next move. 'How did he intend to survive the betrayal of his men and his own route of defiance?' The burden of choices was not only for him but for me as well. The journey of my life had brought me to a point where I wasn't sure of where home was. This new dilemma was becoming very real with every passing second, 'What would be my decision? Would I leave him and this place or ....'? I knew when the time came, I would have to choose between freedom and him. 'But was he as deep in this as I was?' I couldn't tell by his behavior. Sana might be right or maybe she was erroneous in reading him, and I was alone in this turmoil of emotions. My head was hurting, and my eyes began to sting, 'Why were tears so easy to come?' I cursed and looked through the window of the kitchen at the spreading darkness outside. We would be in gloom pretty soon without the luxury of illumination. 'But who needed it anyway?' I thought bitterly downing a glass of water. Beaten, wringing my fingers through my hair, I leaned against the counter and closed my eyes.

"Ahum! Is everything alright?" Ali's voice startled me. He was standing in the shadow of the kitchen door.

"Yes, I'm fine. But can I ask you something?" I was at the door next to him.

He stepped back into the living room, the slit of the open window brought in light from the street, and I could see his face clearly as he took a seat on the sofa across it.

"Ali, we are almost at the end of our journey, and I need to know what will you do after we are there? You have destroyed your prospects here because of me and there is no way I can repay you for everything that you have done. I can't live with the knowledge that any possibility you had for a decent life here was destroyed because of me. Will you leave this place?" I spoke with an apprehension stirring in my heart; the ache was getting to me as I sat in the shadows. I didn't want to risk betraying my poise. Saying all this was not easy for me, and hearing his answer was the real test of my composure so I waited.

"Sarah, when I came after you, I knew what I was doing. There was no doubt in my mind about my future. As to your conclusion that you have destroyed my prospects, you haven't. People like me have no prospects; we live by the day. The days we survive in this war are because of our luck and skill. I am not your ordinary man who has a life where he has the luxury to dream. I'm a soldier of fortune and my fate is the bullet, maybe not today or tomorrow but one day. To take you to safety is one good thing I can do in my destructive existence, and I have no regrets about that. You don't need to worry about me." Ali stated with an affectless face. I stared at him and just for a moment saw a hint of extreme pain in his eyes that was gone as soon as it came, in an instant. I had my answer. There was no emotional breakdown or commitments. He had been very apathetic about his future, and there was apparently no place for me in it.

My heart had slowed down to beat in slow motion as I sat there. My eyes fixated on the wall illuminated behind his chair with the streak of light. I wanted to turn on the lights and see his face more clearly. Maybe I was missing something. His stoic answer and the contradicting shadows in his eyes were tugging at my heart but we were not allowed to turn on the lights. I sat there empty and blank, twisting the loose strands of my hair. I had taken out all the bobby pins unknowingly as I tried to soothe my nerves. He stood up, isolated from my pain and emotional deterioration. I wanted to flee from there, to run and hide from myself, and from the whole world. 'Why was this killing me?' I had anticipated his answer, expected it. 'Then why was it cutting through me?' My heart had pursued a foolish endeavor and I had known that from the beginning. 'But how was I to control an untamed heart? How was I to seize my soul in chains?'

"Sarah, I have to shower. Please relax, everything will be fine." Standing, he walked towards the bedroom.

I leaned back on the sofa sinking into it. My emotions overwhelmed me, and I felt paralyzed. There were no tears. I had come beyond that, the agony of my life seeped through every vein in my body.

The room rapidly grew darker. I wasn't scared but the gloom was accentuated by my saddened heart and dread of the coming future. I wanted to sleep and wake up in another world where I had no recollection of this life. I sat there like a statue as the lights from the street fluttered and shone through the open slits in the windows. Turning towards them, I didn't expect to see the shadows of anyone nearby. Saad had been positive that this house was left as a broken and abandoned property but there were shadows outside the window. I straightened to take a better look and saw someone outside the window. Fear gripped me and I slipped off the sofa crawling to the bedroom door. The first shadow was joined by another against the panes of the window by the time I was at the bedroom door. I crept in and ran to the bathroom door knocking on it lightly. The sound of running water was audible but as soon as I knocked, it stopped, and Ali called out from inside. I softly called him out, so he wouldn't raise his voice and alert the intruders. He flung open the door standing in the middle of it, confused. I had to step back to avoid falling on him, before he could say anything I rushed forward and put my hand on his mouth. He was stunned and then alarmed. His eyes questioned me, and I gestured towards the living room. He understood at once. Crouching down, he entered the living room and grabbed his bag off the table. Quietly, he drew out his gun. I was behind him. Putting his finger on his lips, he signaled me to stay down near the table, and snuck closer to the window. He stood up in the shade of the wall, holding the gun high in his hand, ready to fire. Carefully, he peeked out. I could still see shadows through the swaying curtains. Ali kept watching and then lowered his gun. A sigh escaped his lips, slowly he came to the table and holding my hand helped me stand.

"Don't worry. It's only some kids." He spoke in a relieved voice. Keeping the gun in his hand, he went back into the bedroom. I went in behind him. He was standing near one of the windows checking outside once again. This room was darker, only illuminated by the dim light coming in from the other room. But, according to Saad, we could turn on the small lamps in this one as the curtains were designed to block light. I waited for Ali to be sure about whoever was outside. Once he let the curtain slip in its place, I turned around and switched on the lights while closing the door. The lights in this room were dim but they were enough to illuminate it to a good extent. Ali stood still near the window, firmly gripping the gun, staring at me curiously.

"I had to turn on the lights. The darkness was getting to me. I don't know but I can't take it. Please." My heart skipped a beat as I realized that I had closed us both in. All of my senses were focused on Ali. I hadn't noticed earlier but he had come out of the shower without drying himself or a shirt. He stood there in his loose black trousers, bare footed, with water droplets shining on his naked skin. My breathing became labored as my eyes took him in from his shoulders to his chest, where his scars were very visible under the sheen of water. I tried to look away, to normally step to the chair in the room and sit, but my limbs were frozen despite my brain's pleas. I opened my mouth to explain, but my lips quivered, and no sound came out. It was obvious that I was making a fool of myself and couldn't do anything about it. Ali silently watched as his expression turned from unconcern to shades of grief. My heart raced erratically. Beating so hard, I feared it would break out of my chest. I had no purpose to stay. He had made his intentions clear, and I had to accept them. Still, I couldn't leave.

'Why was I standing here? I should open the door and leave. Leave Ali alone......' but I couldn't move. My body felt like it was made of lead and my eyes stung. Defeated, I lowered my head and closed my eyes, waiting for Ali to say something or leave the room and put me out of my misery. I didn't have the endurance to take any more of this,

"Sarah."

"Sarah, open your eyes. Look at me." I opened my eyes and found him standing tremendously close, staring directly into my eyes. I was intoxicated by the scent of his body, lost in his dark intense eyes as they changed hues. The passiveness was replaced by a burning passion and then by intense heartache. I couldn't discern what was passing through his mind, but my heart ached to cry out how I felt about him and what he meant to me.

"Ali, I'm sorry, but..........I.... I am in love with you. I know it's not what you want but............" Lowering my eyes, I forced the words out as my heart felt like bursting and my restraints broke down faster than a wall of sand. Hearing my words, the gun fell from his hand, and I could see the muscles in his body strain. His chest heaved as his breathing became heavy and uneven. I raised my eyes again to meet his. I couldn't stop myself from looking at him even though the beating of my heart resonated like a thunderstorm. We stared at each other without uttering a word,

"Sarah, I don't want to hurt you." His voice was a murmur as his face reflected pain and his jaw clenched.

"I love you Ali.... I don't care about anything else." The words came out as the last remnants of my self-control vanished. I gave in. Eventually revealing my soul's truth.

A fire blazed in his eyes of yearning as the chains binding him were crushed. My love had taken down his guard, and the defenses he had built around him crumbled. Passion which he had suppressed for so long took over.

Stepping close, he softly took my face in his hands and kissed me tenderly as if he touched me any harder, I would break. I wrapped my hands around his neck, pulling him to me. Our kiss deepened and his arms pinned me to him. There was a hunger in him, a thirst as he claimed my lips. His hands held me as his mouth traced the curve of my neck, descending lower. I couldn't breathe. I felt faint as my body melted in his arms. His touch ignited every fiber of my body. It was all that I had ever dreamed. Sweeping me up in his arms, he brought me to the bed and the night turned into an endless stretch of pleasure as I slipped in and out of heaven with him exploring every inch of me. I was entirely, desperately lost in him.

Day 20 (Ali)

Shadows became long as I sat on the sofa in the living room of the safe house, contemplating on the events of the day.

Today was the final day before we reached our destination and the most difficult. I had awoken early this morning with a fitful sleep through the night, being acutely aware of Sarah sleeping next to me. She had soundly slept through the night snuggling up to me, oblivious to how it affected me. Afraid of being betrayed by my own body, I hadn't moved an inch, keeping the storm restrained within. With daybreak, I slipped out of bed as soon as I had room and washed up. The mundane activities calmed me and later I woke Sarah too. She quickly figured out how she had taken over the whole bed during the night and bashfully apologized for it. I was composed by then and dismissed it as trivial and advised her to hurry for we had to make our way to my friend's house near Baghdad from where I was planning to devise a safe route for entering the city. The fear of Daanish and Jabbar pursuing us weighed heavy on me, but I didn't want to burden Sarah about such details. We were soon out of there and quietly traveled through the war-ravaged country. There was adequate traffic on the highway, and we became invisible as a part of it in our old beat-up car. I had special permit papers for traveling through this part of the country, by courtesy of Daanish. Still, the tension of passing through the check posts with Sarah kept me fretful. I wanted to get to Saad's home and the safe house, which we had built for events like this, as quickly as possible. Sarah was reticent, alert to the danger surrounding us. She didn't question anything I did and patiently complied with everything I directed her to do. We made it past soldiers in the towns enroute and through the check posts until a small distance was left to Saad's place. I just hoped we would get there without incidence. At last, I turned into the country dirt road leading to his house and heaved a sigh of relief. We had made it. 'So far so good.' Only if we remained this lucky for the last leg of the journey. 'Lucky' that was the word which made me smirk. It was not something I had ever experienced and didn't anticipate any change in that fact in the near future. This day had been well planned and executed accordingly, the next might not be the same because I had not yet planned it.

If I only knew what was in store in the pursuing hours, I would have been baffled.

Saad and Sana were gracious as always, but I had no assumptions about their help. Only a hope that we would be welcomed by them. Their home was as I remembered it. The manicured garden in the front reflected Sana's taste and diligence, She had a knack for horticulture, and the melody of flowers in her garden showed her skill. As we drove up the driveway to the main door, the events of the past resurged in my mind, bringing back images of a time when my life was very different. The man who had brought them to safety that day wasn't the one who stood at their doorstep today. I was a desperate man with everything to lose entrusting them with the one thing that had become the definition of life for me. I prayed they could save me as I had them one day, long ago.

Sana took us in like her own and made Sarah comfortable in every possible way. Saad had the safe house in good condition. I suspected he had an intuition that it would be in use earlier then later. I could see the relief on Sarah's face as we walked through that place. It was secure and quite obviously out of the reach of Jabbar or Daanish. Later, we came back to a hot and fresh meal which was only part of Sana's hospitality. She provided Sarah with everything she needed to relax and freshen up.

Leaning back, I closed my eyes to recapture Sarah's image as she had entered Saad's living room in the afternoon. I had forgotten to breathe as my heart slowed down and then skipped beating. I had never seen her like that. The dress she wore flowed to her feet and the broad neckline accentuated her delicate collar bones and then when it dipped in the middle rounding the curves of her body, ... It could make one's heart stop. She had taken time in making her hair. It was glorious as usual but bound in a fashion that enhanced the gold in it haloing her face. I stood there mesmerized like we were the only ones alive in the whole world. At that moment, I regretted the fact that Sana had given her everything she could. If she had been a little stingy, I might have had a chance at living through this but I was never lucky.

The pounding sound in the kitchen shook me out of my stupor. Sarah was in there. I rushed to it, simply to find her agitated and hunched over the counter. 'She probably had pounded her fists there.' Something was bothering her and I could guess what it might be but I didn't want to ask. I found out soon enough. She didn't need to be asked, ducking past me she went into the living room and called for me. I had to listen to her. There was no escape from what she was about to put me through. Her questions were right to the point, and I wasn't prepared for such an onslaught. My plan was to resolve the issue of leaving her at the military base when the time came, disappearing from her life forever, but she wanted answers now. As untactful as I always was, my replies were blunt and somber. The room got darker with every word I spoke, and my heart broke within as I concluded my speech and stood up. There was nothing more. My soul was in an uproar and my mind in twists, far from rational speech. Her face reflected her feelings. I certainly hadn't given her what she wanted or expected but I was at a loss about what was there to expect. Finishing my monologue, I walked into the bedroom, excusing myself for a shower. The cold shower comforted my throbbing nerves. This night was going to be an ordeal. I knew that and rubbed water into my eyes to keep my mind focused when I heard Sarah knocking and calling from outside. She sounded scared and within seconds I was out and crawling into the living room. She had seen someone outside the living room window. Within seconds, I became completely alert and ready to take on anyone but to my relief there was no danger. In those few moments, I had forgotten everything, all the restraints and boundaries, my only focus was the threat to Sarah, and I was prepared to do anything to keep her safe. Making sure that there was nothing to be afraid of, I went back in the bedroom and checked outside its window for eminent danger, but everything was calm except for Sarah.

As soon as I was done with my surveillance, she turned on the lights in the bedroom and closed the door. This little incidence had affected her more than I had realized. She started explaining as I stood there watching her. The distress in her voice was more than just fear. She was suffering. Keeping myself isolated from her agony was like walking on the edge of a sword, every second hurt more than before. She finished and her face visibly reflected her torment as she tried her best to control the cyclone raging inside her. I wanted to console her, bring her peace and give her love, but there were restrictions I had to observe to keep her safe. I remained silent while Sarah stayed motionless looking at me. The color of her face turned pale, and she closed her eyes tightly, avoiding to look at me. My determination was at its end. I knowingly had been cold and callous with her, had tried to play the stoic apathetic soldier but her pain destroyed all the walls I had built around myself.

Stepping closer I called her name, I had to do something. Maybe I could soothe her, and we could get through the night. She opened her eyes at my beckoning, looking directly into mine. It was always difficult to keep my feelings under wraps when she looked at me like that, but what she said next went through me like a bolt of lightning.

She was in love with me. I had yearned for this, hoped for it but never believed I would be fortunate enough to receive it. For me it was a mirage disappearing at first sight. Her confession of love was not what I expected to hear. Suddenly, I was terrified. This was not for me. I never was the lucky one. She would suffer if she stayed with me, if this was pursued. 'You should stop her'. A harsh voice called from the depths of my sorrows frantically trying to dampen the surge of happiness I had felt. Every muscle in my body tensed. I wanted her more than anything I had ever wanted, more than life itself, but this fear held me confined. I was not the one, not for her. She was naïve and didn't know what she had said. I strived to walk away but my body didn't comply. Instead, I kept staring into the depths of her brilliant blue eyes and the longing in them broke down my last defenses. My attempts to heed the warnings of the unknown were useless as she tore down every shred of resistance I had. Confessing her love for me, regardless of who I was, what I was. The gun fell from my hand as my willpower gave way to the love I had felt for her since the day she had fallen in my arms.

This night became the beginning of life itself. Sarah's tender love breathed a soul into the hollow shell of a man, our love was the resurrection of me, the commencement of my life where I belonged.

Day 21

I awoke in a state of a dreamy mist, afraid that whatever
I had experienced was a blissful illusion and nothing more.
Afraid of opening my eyes, fearful that everything would
vanish, and I would be back in the world of the cold
realities of my life of refuge. But I had to respond to the
sun light shining brightly on my face. Apprehensively, I
raised my eye lids and peaked at my surroundings and as
soon as I did my faced blushed red and blood rushed into
my veins. Warmth permeated my body. I was lying in Ali's
arms under the sheets of our bed. He was asleep and there
was serenity on his face which I had never seen before. He
held me as if he let go I would disappear. My head was
resting on one of his arms and his other arm wrapped
around my body. Suddenly, I realized there was nothing but
the sheet covering our entwined bodies.

Content, I closed my eyes. It wasn't a dream, not an
illusion. This was as real as the sun shining on my face. A

sense of happiness washed over me, and I snuggled closer to Ali, closing my eyes, satisfied. Suddenly the war, the insecurity of our lives, disappeared in the splendor of our love and I didn't care about anything anymore.

A touch of lips on my forehead broke the spell of my slumber. Opening my eyes a slit, I lazily stretched. The sheet entangled with my body pulled around, hugging it.

"Wake up sleepy head." Ali's loving voice drove the residual slumber out of my system. I had fallen asleep again after my earlier awakening. I patted the side of the bed where he was supposed to be, but it was empty. Holding the sheet across my chest, I sat up. Ali was seated at the side of the bed watching me. He kissed me on the forehead as I held the sheet, trying to slow my heart rate. He leaned forward and kissed me on the cheek, the sheet almost slipped out of my grip. He smiled wickedly at his triumph on making me all nervous and flustered.

"I have to go to the bathroom." I blurted out. He was making me so nervous I was sure that I would stumble and fall before I could reach the bathroom.

"Yes, go ahead. I'm not stopping you." Mischief was visible on his face. This was a new side of him that I had never seen before. He was acting like a carefree college boy with nothing better to do then prank someone. I scanned the room to locate my clothing, but my search yielded nothing. I couldn't remember where I, or for that matter, Ali had thrown them last night.

'Last night...' My mind went back to it, making me blush again. Ali was immensely enjoying every second of my predicament. 'I should have gotten up before him', I swore silently. My only option was to use the bedsheet as a toga, and hope that it would stay without me getting tangled in its folds and falling face down. However, before I could leave the bed Ali stood up and handed me my clothes that he had hidden under his thigh. I didn't miss to slap him after I had snatched them from his hands. He laughed out loudly and threatened to take them back and run. I scowled at him and ducked under the sheet with them. Within a minute, I was out with the long shirt pulled down over my head and the pants in my hands. Ali was still standing next to the bed, amused and happy. I slipped off the bed and sprinted to the bathroom.

I took my time bathing, and when I emerged, a delicious smell hit my nose. The aroma of fresh breakfast. I came out to the living room to find Ali cooking something on the stove in the kitchen. 'Probably eggs, it smelled like eggs.'

"Oh, thank God you are out. I thought you were constructing the bathroom before using it." The mischievousness in his tone persisted. It was refreshing to hear him so lighthearted. He seemed like a whole new person. I eyed him curiously. Now it was his turn to get self-conscious. He sat on one of the chairs around the small dining table and gestured for me to sit on the other.

"Well, how rude you didn't even pull the chair for me or help me sit." I waved my hand faking a hurt look. Ali stood up anxiously almost knocking the chair down,

"I'm sorry Sarah. I didn't mean to hurt your feelings, but I'm not very good with people."

"I'm not listening. You hurt my feelings!" Suppressing my smile, I turned away from him. There was silence in the room. I wanted to see him, hear him but at that moment my impish instinct was controlling me.

"Sarah, please forgive me. I don't know how to make it up to you, please." He was behind me pleading. My patience reached its limit. I couldn't torture him anymore. Swinging around. I faced him. The joy on his face was replaced by despair. It made my heart break, 'Why was I teasing him so?',

"Ali I am not people. I was only teasing, messing with you. Please don't get sad. I was joking." I held his hands in mine. The color of his face changed instantaneously. The next thing I knew he had picked me up in his arms and covered my mouth with his. Giggling, I pushed him back and ran into the bedroom as he chased me. He caught up to me and made both of us fall on the bed. I was still laughing when he pinned me on the bed underneath him.

"Are you going to tease me again?" He asked, making a serious face which made me laugh even more.

"How will you stop me?" I spoke between bouts of laughter,

"Like this." And he pressed his lips to mine once more, taking me in. The mischief evaporated in the air as my heartbeat raced with desire and my body responded to his cresses. We were at the brink of giving in completely when there was a knock at the outer door leading in from the hidden tunnel. Ali immediately sprang to his feet and rushed out to the living room, closing the door behind him. It could only be Saad or Sana, but his quick maneuver had saved me from embarrassment. I got off the bed and straightened my clothes. Checking my reflection in the bathroom mirror, I opened the door and entered the living room where Saad was sitting at the table with Ali. He stood up and greeted me warmly as soon as he saw me. I took the chair across Ali and poured some coffee in a cup. Ali passed me the plate of eggs and toast. It had become a little cold but was quite delicious. I ate as they talked. Saad had been busy gathering information about our route to the American military base in Baghdad. He had contacted some of his people there and was waiting for further info from some of his friends in Baghdad. As far as he knew, all the main roads to the city were not safe. I got worried as they discussed different angles to the solution of this problem, but Saad was not sure who was the main man behind the roadblocks because it wasn't the military. He had called in some others who still had to get back to him with decisive information on that matter, but I and Ali were pretty sure who it could be. Ali was very sober. I could see the worry lines creeping back on his face. They sat there quietly for a few minutes and then Saad left his chair remembering that Sana had actually sent him to get us rather than sit here and talk. We both followed him and within twenty minutes we were at the grove of date trees.

Ali held my hand the entire way. It was an unconscious act on his part. When I walked beside him and squeezed his fingers as we reached the house, he looked at me surprised but didn't let go. Sana was waiting and eyed us with curiosity, but there was no expression of wonder on her face as if she had expected this and was only waiting for the final climax. I lowered my head as blood rose to my face with a telling blush. She took me with her in the kitchen as soon as I was in the house, grinning. The sun was blessedly hot and illuminated the house beautifully; I craved this peace and serenity with all its blandness. Ali sat with Saad running fingers through his jet-black hair. He was uneasy and I wanted to calm him. Assure him of a future blessed with a predictable life but I couldn't, the truth was painfully visible and foreseeably we would be walking into a trap where there was a very slight chance of making it alive to our destination. I came out of the kitchen and sat on one of the sofa chairs facing Ali. He looked up from staring at the floor and our eyes met. I could see agony mirrored by deep affection in their dark depths. I smiled at him, and the color of his face changed. The doubt disappeared and the love deepened in his intense eyes. Sana called us to join her around the small dining table where she had served breakfast. We ate silently and Saad left us as soon as it was over. Neither Ali nor Sana questioned him about his departure. I helped Sana clean up and then she also went upstairs to attend to her errands. Despite my offers, she declined my help and sent me to the living room where Ali was standing next to the window in the sunlight. He looked like the silhouette of an angel as the light fell on him and dispersed in every direction. I stopped at the door taking in the quiet gentleness of his silent demeanor. He tilted his head and called me close, aware of my presence. I joined him gazing at the garden outside,

"Sarah, I'm sorry to put you through all of this." His sudden remark was unexpected,

"Sorry for what?" I touched his shoulder and prompted him to face me.

"For all that has happened. You would have been safe and at home if it wasn't for people like me. I can't forgive myself for this. Tomorrow we'll leave and there is a chance that we might not make it." Ali had taken my hands in his, but he wasn't making eye contact with me. I could see the strained muscles of his face.

"Ali look at me. There is nothing you could have done. This is not your fault. You've been my savior rather than my doom. Please!" I squeezed his hands. He raised his head meeting my eyes and I could see the doubt and pain in his.

Pulling me to the middle of the room, he sat me down on one of the sofas and took his place next to me. I wondered what he was going to do, bringing a table closer he took something out of his pocket and placed it on the top of it. I stared at the shiny black gun and then at Ali,

"I want to teach you to use this. It is necessary. I want you to have some measure of protection if something happens to me." His attention was focused on me. I blinked unbelievingly, 'How could I use that?' I would never be able to use it on anyone.

"Ali I can't. I've never."

"Sarah, you have to. It can mean the difference between life and death." He was very serious. Peering at him, my eyes met his gentle but firm look and I knew he was not going to give up. I nodded and we both stood up. He handed me the gun, which was surprisingly light and easy to hold. He guided me to the back of the house towards a shed filled with tools and other gardening stuff plus sandbags. I didn't understand why we were in the shed. 'If I was to learn how to shoot? Shouldn't we be doing it in the open, like a range or someplace?' But within minutes my confusion was cleared when Ali took the gun and placing it on one of the sandbags fired a shot. It was muffled and barely noticeable,

"We have to keep quiet. No one should know that there is something unusual going on here." Ali shook the sand and gun powder off his hand. I was standing next to him. Turning, he handed the weapon to me. Taking it reluctantly, my hands shook with the anticipation of firing the thing. Ali lightly took my hand in his, stabilizing the weapon,

"Don't be afraid of it, Sarah. You're not the enemy here. Neither is this; it's to protect you not hurt you." His voice was soft, and in the hot shed where my clothes were sticking to my back, I could feel the heat of his body next to mine, flooding my senses, making me a little dizzy. I held onto his arm and stumbled closer. His breathing was getting as heavy and irregular as mine. The gun fell from our hands as he palmed my face in his and kissed my lips. His taste like the past night was intoxicating and I was lost.

His arms pulled me in, crushing me to his body. Suddenly, a voice jolted us from our spell and we parted. He quickly picked up the forgotten gun as Sana appeared at the door of the shed,

"I was looking for you. I was hoping you were teaching her to use that." She was sweating a bit and her whitish complexion was burning with hues of amber. Her soft brown eyes were fixed on the gun in Ali's hand and a meaningful smile spread on her face. Ali just nodded and I stood awkwardly on one side twisting the fold of my shirt. She turned and sped towards the house saying something about the heat and that we should finish quickly before it got to us. Once she was out of sight and earshot, Ali brought the gun and put it in my hands, directing me how to handle and fire it. I had to aim at the bag of sand and pull the trigger. He advised me to keep it pressed into the bag so it could muffle the sound. I was confused, 'If I was only to shoot into the bag of sand, then why all this training? Anyone could do it.' But apparently, I was wrong because when I pulled the trigger, the jerk pushed me back with such a force that I fell only to be caught by Ali. Taking me in his arms, he steadied me and helped me stand. I was shocked by the recoil of the gun, and he could assess my surprise.

"This is why I wanted you to practice. It's not easy." He whispered in my ear holding my shaking hand, "Let's try again." This time he stood behind me with his body pressed to mine supporting it. I held the gun up and he straightened my arm and held it with me.

"Now." He whispered and I fired the second shot into the bag of sand, without falling or getting jerked. His arm and body held mine firmly in place,

"Good. Now do it yourself." He let go of my hand and stepped back. I straightened my gun bearing hand and shot at the sandbag only experiencing a little jerk. Before my gun wielding hand could drop to my side, Ali instructed me to fire again, which I did without flinching, successfully. The job done I pulled my arm down to return the gun but he slid his arm around my waist and pulled me to him, burying his face in my neck. The gun fell from my hand. His warm breath burned my skin making my heart race like crazy. His arms held me firmly to him. The heat of his passion and the weather were making my head spin, and I was sure that I would faint before long.

"Sarah, I need you more than I have anyone in my life. Your closeness drives me wild. I have to use every ounce of my strength to keep myself in control. I don't know what to do." Ali whispered huskily in my ear. I was as helpless as he was. My senses were completely overrun by emotions and desire. I turned to face him, and rising on my toes, kissed him hungrily on the mouth. He responded with such vigor that I had to hang onto him to keep myself from falling. Minutes passed and we realized that we had to return. He pulled back and we walked back. Within five minutes we reached the entrance of the living room. Sana was there, waiting for us. We joined her at the dining table where she had some snacks laid out for us. Smiling, she inquired about the gun and then we remembered that it was still lying in the shed. Ali ran back to get it,

"How was your night?" Her sudden and blunt question caught me off guard, and I couldn't answer her. Lowering my head, I tried to say something but I was unsuccessful. She reached out and touched my hand slightly.

"I know you love him and so does he. I hope you two are happy and remain happy." I looked up at her with gratitude, and her smile assured me of her sincerity. Ali came huffing through the door and dumped the gun on the table.

"Any news from Saad?" He questioned Sana and she shook her head.

"We have to wait." She was quiet. My curiosity to know the whereabouts of Saad grew. It was clear they knew where he had gone and were anticipating an answer of some sort from him.

"Where is Saad?" I asked picking at the tabletop. Sana and Ali both exchanged a look, and it made me jealous for a minute, but I admonished myself silently for thinking like a crazed old fool.

"Sarah, yesterday when we got here Saad had contacted one of his friends for information about the possible routes to Camp Victory in Baghdad and how to get there. He had to find out whom to meet once we were there. His friend had asked him to come. He left in the morning for that. We're waiting for a call from him or his return. Once we have that information, I will be able to plan our next move." Ali was playing with the saltshaker on the table, and I couldn't see his expression clearly but his voice resonated with concern. I could imagine Sana's apprehension and fear. In this world of chaos and distrust, Saad had taken a huge risk gathering information for us. I said a silent prayer for him and sat there with both of them. Minutes passed and the tension weighed down on me. I didn't want to be the cause of Saad's or anyone's troubles. Sitting there with Sana became unbearable, 'What if something happened to him? How could I face her?' We had barged into their peaceful existence and toppled it. Frustrated, I stood up and left for the garden. I had to be in the fresh air, away from all of this, to soothe my raw nerves. The afternoon sun blazed but the breeze provided a cool respite. I walked in the midst of Sana's flower garden and tried to push every thought out of my head. The wall around the house and garden was more of a decorative nature then any barrier. Sana had vines climbing it and flowers hung from them, giving the impression of a hanging garden. I admired her artistic penchant. It was evident in every corner of the garden, from the hanging flowers to the lanes winding between beds of seasonal plants. There was a huge tree in one nook with its old branches touching the ground in multiple places with a wooden carved bench resting under them near its massive trunk, naturally veiled. I was attracted to it since I'd seen it but I hadn't gotten a chance to enjoy a quiet moment in its repose. Now I wanted to be there more than anything. Stepping briskly, I made my way to it. Just as I tugged one of the branches shading the bench, a hand tapped my shoulder. I invariably jumped, forgetting that I wasn't alone and this was not an isolated escape. Ali gently held my shoulders and calmed me, apologizing for startling me.

"I'm sorry. I didn't mean to scare you but I was worried. You were so distraught when you came out." Ali explained in a soft tone.

"Ali, I didn't know Saad had gone for us. Otherwise, I would have stopped him. Why should we put his life in danger? I can't bear to think about the consequences they might have to face for helping us." My face was pale with worry and fear.

"Come, let's sit. This is my favorite place." Ali held my hand, and pushing the branches aside, made room for me to pass. I sat on the cold bench as he let the branches fall back, hiding us from the world.

"Sarah, he'll be fine. He has a few good friends and they can help us. The people I worked for have no clue about him. Please don't worry." He sat next to me and held my hands in his. Ali had this calming effect on me. Whenever he was near, I felt secure and relaxed. I leaned on his shoulder and closed my eyes. I felt him circle his arm around my shoulders, holding me. I had always felt safe with him, but since last night, his touch and his nearness had a more pronounced effect on me. My skin got tingly and every fiber of my being came alive. I had to pull away from him to keep my desire at bay. I sat leaning on the bench. Peeking at him, I found him watching me intently. His expressive eyes glittered among the streams of lights dancing across his face. His gaze was mysterious and desperate, making me curious as to his thoughts, but I was tongue tied as my eyes interlocked with his. I wanted him to speak. I knew that if I kept gazing at him I was liable to straddle him, losing control. 'How did he always rule my senses?' I couldn't imagine.

He could see the turmoil within me, reflected in the irises of my eyes. Before I lost my head, his lips parted and spoke the words I only had dreamt about. As they rang through my ears, my first thought was, 'Is he joking or am I hallucinating.' Slowly, I collected myself. I wholeheartedly craved for what he had asked. For so long I thought it but impossible. With a war ravaging the country, and disaster surrounding us from every side, happiness seemed inconceivable. But it was true. I felt the heavens shine through the leaves, blurring my vision. There was nothing else I could do but to hug him and hold on. Life had suddenly done a one eighty, and I had landed in his arms.

We sat there in silence, nothing more to say or hear. Ali gently took my face in his hands, staring into my eyes,

"Sarah, I have asked you for something I shouldn't have, I guess. But I can't conceive living even a second of my life without you. I'm not sure about tomorrow or anything, and I can't guarantee we'll make it to our destination alive ……. But if I have to die, I want to die knowing I belonged to you, I was yours. I don't expect you to accept it but you delivered me. You complete me and I love you more than I can express. I need you more than you would ever need me………I know I am being selfish, but I want to be yours forever." His voice was so tender and soft.

His expression so desperate, it melted me from within. Stroking his handsome face, filled with anticipation and doubt, I lightly tapped my lips to his, sealing an unwritten and an unsaid bond. His arms enclosed around me, hiding me in him.

The afternoon sun softened. The tree's shade provided further respite, and presently it was the center of my universe. Serenity enveloped me, and I didn't want to move from there but then the lengthening shadows reminded me of the scarcity of time.

"Ali, let's tell Sana." Ali didn't loosen his grip, but my squirming made him give in, "Okay, let's go."

I held his hand, pulling him impatiently through the blooming flowers to the main door where Sana was sitting on the patio in a swinging chair.

"Sana, I have to tell you something!" I beamed at her, ignoring the apprehensive and grave expression on her face.

"Wait Sarah, I've received word from Saad. He'll be back shortly, but the situation is quite severe." Her voice was strained, but at that moment I couldn't care less. Ali, on the other hand, took a sharp breath and stopped in his tracks.

"Sana, what did he tell you? Is there……..", before he could continue I cuffed my hand on his mouth and cut him off,

"Sana, Ali has asked me to marry him. Can we get married today?" Sana stood up astonished, probably at my utter disregard for her news and my incomprehensible question. Apparently, that was not true as she was dumbstruck with joy,

"Congratulations both of you. I'm so happy for you." She hugged me first and then Ali, almost in tears.

"I'll arrange everything. God will bless you both, I'm sure." She turned to go inside, wiping her eyes.

"Sana, what about Saad?" Ali was back to his old self. Alert and dead serious, ready for anything. Except for what I was planning.

"He's coming. He'll tell you all that himself and join us for the ceremony. You won't be alone." Sana stopped midflight and came back.

"Sarah, you have to come with me. There is much to do and you can't be here." She caught me by the arm and we were climbing up the stairs, leaving Ali standing in the foyer a little confused.

Sana took me to her bedroom enthusiastically, making me a little uncomfortable. Sensing my apprehension, she sat me down on the armchair, and explained she had something she wanted me to have. Her attitude had completed transformed from gloomy to giddy in the matter of seconds. Leaving me there, she rushed into the attached changing room. I sat motionless. The background sounds of things being shifted around faded as the reality seeped in. It dawned on me for the first time that Ali wanted to stay with me, 'He was ready to leave with me.' I'd contemplated the idea of asking him about that since yesterday but didn't have the courage to pose the question. The night we had spent together was special to me, but to him, I wasn't sure whether it was love or just one night of passion but now I knew he would stay with me.

As my thoughts wandered, and then converged on one point, my heart felt heavy. I knew we both had been in love with each other for a long time, and last night was only a culmination of that love.

"At last!...... It'll finally be used by someone special. I'm so happy." Sana emerged from the room, holding a huge rectangular box. She was smiling ear to ear as she placed it on the bed and removed the lid. I could see silken white fabric in it and realized she had found something for me to wear. Without wasting another minute, she pulled it out and held it up. A beautiful white dress fell to the ground to its full length while Sana held onto the shoulder straps. I was speechless by the sheer elegance of the exquisite dress, sewn as if for a Greek goddess. It was pure white with loose folds gathering at the waist, being held in place by a beautifully embroidered belt in gold and sequence. From the waist, its folds opened up and flowed to the ground in soft ruffles. The shoulder straps were broad but it was sleeveless. The silk was feather soft and was adorned with delicate gold thread, sequence and bead embroidery all over. It was gorgeous, and to complete the look, Sana took out a lace veil with a golden headdress and placed it on my head. It's golden and lace threads reached down to the length of my waist, covering my bare shoulders and arms in a shade of delicate silk and sequence. It was beyond anything I had imagined. I was stunned. I knew that she had brought that out for me but it was so unbelievable that I had to ask her,

"Sana is this for me?", My dumb inquiry made her laugh. Not answering the obviously stupid question, she brought the dress closer and measured it along my shoulder line. She and I were almost the same height; I was only a couple of inches taller. We were both slim and the dress proved to be a good fit, hanging a little loose but perfect. She shoved me into the changing room as soon she had ascertained that I could fit into it, and she was right, it did. When I looked at my reflection in the mirror, I was astounded by the grace and style of the dress and how it transformed me. Glancing at myself, I could imagine Ali gazing at me. The memories of the past night made me blush as the sequence reflected off my skin. Composing myself, I stepped out for Sana to have a look. She was standing near the only window in the room, watching the sky. My movement alerted her to my presence and she turned around. The expression on her face was a mixture of love and grief as her eyes brimmed with tears,

"What's wrong Sana? You don't like it?", I knew that wasn't the cause of her strange manner but it was the only thing I could conjure up.

"No, my dear. You look exquisite, but some memories have saddened me." She wiped her eyes with the tips of her fingers.

"What memories?

"This dress was mine when I had married Saad. Maria, my daughter, was to be wed in it but life has been twisting

398

our paths so that she had to be sent away from us. I can't even remember for how long." Sana's voice broke with despair. My heart became heavy with the burden of the world. I had not even fathomed the shattered dreams behind the apparent beauty of the garment. My first reaction was to take the veil off placing it on the bed,

"Sana, I'm so sorry. I had no idea. Please keep it. I don't want to hurt you in any way." My voice was sincere as I. I couldn't repay her kindness by taking something she had cherished for her daughter.

"No! No! Sarah, I am so happy that at last my dress will be worn by someone I love, like I have my own Maria. You must wear it; it makes my heart delight in the thought that Ali's bride will wear this dress. He is our dearest friend and the savior of my children. It is my deepest wish that you wear and keep it." Sana quickly picked up the veil and placed it on my head, again kissing my forehead. Her love made my heart full. These people were living under such tyranny, but they still had the courage to not only give us shelter but to offer us everything they had. 'How could I repay them?', maybe there were no restitutions for such benevolence and strength. It was an aura of light that surrounded them and the ones who came in their shadow. I hugged Sana. My life had been transformed in ways I never could conceive by the darkness of the land that surrounded us and the hope which broke through that gloom.

"Now, we need to get started. The dress fits perfectly. Take it off so we can begin with the bathing and other preparations." Sana winked at me like a giddy schoolgirl, not a trace of melancholy on her gentle face. Nodding obediently, I followed her directions as the evening proceeded into the night hours. Eventually, she was satisfied with her handiwork and allowed me to have a glance in the mirror.

"I'm done. I think this will do. I hope you like it." Artificially wiping her brow, she stepped away. I gaped at the reflection in the mirror. I had known that I was somewhat good looking, but what I saw now was breathtaking. The dress flowed flawlessly to the ground from beautifully decorated shoulders in gold and red henna. My hair was twined with tiny flowers and colored ribbons with the loose strands hanging free over my shoulders, surrounding my neck. My face was delicately sculpted to rival Greek goddesses. I looked perfect.

"Just one more thing." Sana picked up the veil and placed it on my head, securing it with the delicate golden headdress.

"Now, you look perfect."

"Thank you, Sana. I can never repay you for what you have done for me." My voice was teary. I was sure sobbing was going to follow when she snubbed in mock anger, "Don't you dare cry and waste all my effort. You don't want to see me angry, it's not pretty." She scowled at me, which made me laugh, and the tears were held at bay.

"Good, let's go downstairs. Your bridegroom awaits." She stretched her hand towards me and led me down the stairs.

Darkness permeated outside as we descended. I hadn't realized how much time had passed. I had no clue what Ali had been doing. 'Probably getting pampered by the other party of the house.' A smile spread across my lips. As I entered the living room, I was surprised by the people in there. The room had a few new faces, men and women in all their finery. Sana and Saad had been busy in this respect as well. My eyes searched for the one I desired. He stood at the other end of the room. With my arrival, he turned and proceeded to greet me, leading me to sit with him. My heart raced as we made our way through the guests. The next hour or so comprised of different rituals to bind us in the ties of matrimony. When every traditional and religious rite was observed, all the guests had a toast and showered us with flowers. Food was served; Sana asked me if I would like something but I was utterly full, as if I had eaten tons. Ali had the same response as me when offered. While the guests ate and drank, Saad and Sana escorted us to the back of the house. As soon as we were alone, Saad took us through the secret tunnel and Sana returned to the guests. Saad walked in front of us as Ali and I followed on the familiar path with Ali holding my hand. Once we reached the safe house, Saad left us. Night had fallen and we were in the same place we had been a night before, but this time it was different. Ali led me to the inner chamber and closed the door.

We were alone at last. But instead of being cheerful, I was shaking from inside. Anticipation, apprehension, and joy had a hold on me as I stood near the bed with the veil concealing my face. Ali hadn't seen me. According to the tradition, I had a long veil covering my face and most of my body. It was a beautiful deception where I was all dressed up for him, but he couldn't see me until the end. Ali was there with me but he didn't come close. Rather he walked past me and sat on the edge of the bed, holding his head in his hands. I wasn't expecting this from him, waiting I didn't move. Minutes passed as he sat silently staring at the floor and I at him. Eventually, my patience gave away. Stepping close, I touched his shoulder, trying to speak but not being able to do so.

"I'm sorry Sarah. I have just realized how selfish I had been in asking you for this. I had no right. I have bound you to myself and it was completely self-centered of me. I shouldn't have done it. I didn't give you a chance to consider your answer, to think clearly and to decide when you had more choices and time." Ali's voice seemed to come from a grave, hollow and lifeless. He didn't raise his head, didn't look at me just kept staring at the floor as his words pierced through me like a sharp knife, quick and lethal. I was shocked, almost stumbling back I turned and walked to the only curtained window suddenly feeling lightheaded.

'Why was he saying that? What did he mean by that? What was going on?' I felt suffocated and the room seemed like closing in on me. First despair, then fury took over me. I wanted to rip the veil off my face and shred the dress. 'He couldn't do this to me, not now, not like this. How could he?'

"Ali!" was the only word that I managed to get out, choked by the anger and agony storming within me.

The ecstasy of union was replaced by wretchedness.

"Ali........" For some reason, I couldn't manage more than that. My words were lost, I was devastated. My body was limp and my head was dizzy. The room shrank in space and I couldn't breathe. He sat a few feet away but seemed miles away from me. I had to get out of there, I had to breathe. 'Where was the door?' I couldn't concentrate. My eyes were closing and I knew that I was going to pass out.

"Sarah, Sarah" His voice came softly in my ear as my senses were fading. His arms held me, balancing my weakening limbs. Holding me, he sat me down on the bed, bringing an ounce of energy back into me.

"Why?! Why are you holding me?! Why do you fake this?! Why?!!" I almost screamed at him; my eyes burned with anger.

"I'm not faking Sarah. I love you but I shouldn't have done this. Hold you bound to me. I've been very selfish." Ali stood up, "I love you very much and I'm the one who has condemned you to a life of strife and loss. It was wrong of me to even think this. I can't forgive myself. You'll not have a life because of me. Last night should not have happened; if I truly loved you, I should have protected you." He banged his fists on the wall in aggravation. Instantly everything was clear,

"Ali, I love you and this wasn't yours but my wish. Only God brought it true." I stood behind him.

"What do you mean?" He sounded confused, turning a little to face me.

"I have loved you Ali for longer than I can say and last night was a beautiful dream, which you are not going to take away from me." Thankfully my voice was back,

'How could he ever believe that it was him alone who had endured the longing which had pulled on our hearts since we had laid eyes on each other?' It was clear that there hadn't been a day when we weren't in love with each other.

Ali was facing me now, his stare made my cheeks turn crimson on my last remarks,

"But Sarah, what kind of life would I be able to give you? It will have no future. I've destroyed any prospects for you. You deserve better than this, more happiness and a secure life." He was staring at the floor again.

He must be blind to not see how I felt, to see how his doubts were destroying me. 'Didn't he have any faith in us?' I felt like punching him in the gut.

"I am going to kill you if you don't shut up!!" My annoyance had reached its limit. I turned and stomped towards the closed door, but before I could reach it, Ali's arm slid around my waist and pulled me back. I wasn't in the mood to accommodate him.

"Let me go! You sit here and sulk." I fought in his arms as he held me.

"I'm sorry Sarah but tonight I realized what I had done and how it would change your life for the worst not better. I'm ashamed of myself and my utter disregard for your happiness. I should be the one to look out for you. Not to take advantage of you." His grip loosened and he stepped back. He sounded wounded and his hurt made my heart break. I had to make him believe in our love, in the strength it had, and the hope it gave me.

"Ali, I love you and there is nothing else that matters. You are mine and my world is with you." Coming close, I took his hands in mine and kissed them through my veil. Ali raised his eyes to look at me, disbelief yet faith in them and before I could let go, he took my hands in his bringing me to the center of the room where the light was brightest.

There was nothing more to say, we both were acutely conscious of the tempest brewing between us and that he was fighting a lost battle.

There was not a single sound as we looked into each other's eyes, Ali's facial expression had changed, the broken desperation was replaced by tenderness. I'd lost my voice once again as he stepped closer. My breath was caught in my throat and my skin tingled. He carefully removed the decorative head dress holding the veil in its place. Taking hold of one corner of the delicate veil, he pulled it off, letting it fall on the floor. A moan escaped his lips as his eyes took me in. Feeling the same passion, I was lost in the heat of desire. Caressing my hair, his fingers ran through the soft curls and ribbons as his breathing became heavy. Leaning in, he kissed my neck and his hands encircled my waist, pressing my body against his. His mouth found mine as his hands held me, getting lost in the ruffles of the dress. My arms circled around his neck pulling him closer and crushing myself into him. He kissed me passionately as his fingers traced the contours of my back reaching the delicate straps of the dress hanging on my shoulders. Softly, he pulled away a little and pushed them off, letting the dress slide down. Taking me in his arms again, his lips descended with the dress. The ecstasy of his touch set every inch of my skin aflame and I could hear my heartbeat in my ears making me dizzy. Before I could faint with rapture, he swooped me up and took me to the bed. The rest of the night became a symphony of desire and pleasure.

Day 22

Morning was sleepy and lazy. I looked around as my eyes opened to the light shining through the window. Although the curtains restrained much of it, a few rays escaped through were enough to illuminate the room and create a bright pattern on the opposite wall. It was an interesting concoction of light and color. Turning my head, I saw Ali sleeping next to me, embracing me in his arms. The tranquility surrounding him was surreal. I wanted to cuddle up to him, but then was afraid that if I did, it might awaken him and I didn't want to disrupt his slumber. He looked amazing sleeping so peacefully. The rays got a bit brighter as the sun rose outside. I watched the forms change on the wall but the time of day wasn't determinable by those few rays of light. There was a clock that hung over the bed but I couldn't see it without turning completely. I wasn't inclined to do at that moment. Then Ali stirred and opened his eyes, all drowsy and dreamy, a slight smile dancing on his lips,

"When did you wake up?

"Just a few minutes ago." I said playfully, pulling the light blanket a little higher as his stretching was tugging it off of us.

"Why didn't you wake me?" Extending his feet and arms away, he didn't care as the soft blanket got pulled almost to his pelvis, exposing his muscular torso.

"Didn't want to disturb you. You looked so peaceful and content." I sat up with the blanket pulled to my chest. The way he was moving about, it had no chance of staying anywhere on us. Seeing my maneuvers, he smiled mischievously and purposefully pulled at it making me lean on him.

"Where're you trying to run?" His free hand caught me off-balance, making me fall on his chest. Speechless, I tried to rise again but there was no escape as he held me in place.

"You're not going anywhere." Kissing the top of my head he ran his fingers through my wild hair. I closed my eyes savoring every moment.

Eventually the clock on the wall chimed very softly, catching our attention. It was ten o'clock, I guessed. Turned out, I was correct because Ali sat up, pushing me upright as well.

"We need to get ready. Today is going to be a busy day." He wanted to leave the bed but now it was my turn to stop him,

"Why can't we just stay in today? We could leave tomorrow. I don't want to go anywhere today." I had a stubborn tone despite having plain knowledge that we weren't able to stay no matter what I said.

"We have to. You know that my love. If it were up to me, I would stay hidden here with you from the rest of the world, blocking everything and everyone out .... of our world." He held me close. We both knew what awaited us once we left the sanctuary of our room. Still, we dragged ourselves out of bed and got ready. We had travel clothes, thanks to Sana and Saad. I had a black trouser and khaki shirt with a leather jacket layering on top of it. Ali had similar colors and a jacket different than mine. The plan had been that I would dress up like a man and go along with Ali to Saad's friend near Baghdad. From there, he would take us to the military base.

Ali had changed and was in the other room, while I, disoriented and sad, eyed the clothes lying on the bed. When I washed up, only one fear occupied my thoughts, that we would probably never have these moments again. I couldn't change into those clothes. I didn't want to, all I wanted was Ali. Just then he stepped in as if he had read my mind.

"Sarah, you haven't gotten dressed, it's time." He came and sat next to me on the bed.

"Ali, I fear we will never have this again." My voice was tearful and my head was filled with premonitions of danger.

"Why do you think like that? We'll be fine." He gathered me in his arms and kissed my forehead.

It was the strangest of feelings; I sensed loss and happiness entwined together, churning within me. Desperation and fear were making me blind. I took Ali's face in my hands and kissed him, pulling him close. I wanted him, needed him before we left for our journey of no return. Ali kissed me back, wrapping his arms around me, hiding me within him. We stayed like that for what felt like centuries. Slowly the anxiety abated, and calmness surrounded me with Ali holding me in his embrace. I wasn't afraid anymore. I had him and whatever happened we were together. Looking up at him, I pulled back and kissed him again. Ali simply held my face in his hands and stared into my eyes. The deep affection in his convinced me of our abiding love, of our future. There could be war or peace around us, it was of no consequence as our lives were for each other.

"Now get ready. I love you forever." Ali let go of me, planting a kiss on my cheek.

Picking up my clothes I got dressed, for the journey which could be the beginning of a new life or the end of it all.

I tied up my hair tightly in a bun and then wrapped a turban around it, imitating an ordinary Arab guy. Ali did the same to match. I looked at my pale complexion in the mirror and the bright blue eyes staring back. Ali had the same apprehension as I did so he got some burned out oil from the frying pan in the kitchen and smeared it on my face. I wore the old pair of glasses Ali found with blurry lenses to shade my eyes and we were ready to go. In this getup, I looked like a nerdy young boy with his big brother guiding him. Focused on the journey ahead, I watched Ali getting his gear ready. He wanted me to have a gun but I wasn't very comfortable carrying one. He tactfully tucked away his weapons in his clothes, concealing them completely. It was interesting to see him practice his skills. As I stared at him, he suddenly swung on his feet and taking my face in his hands kissed it hard. I was caught by surprise,

"What? I'm all covered in oil." I stepped backed, fixing my turban.

"You look so cute in those geeky glasses and these clothes I just had to." Ali laughed and took me in his arms, the gunk on my face made me squirmy but he didn't care pulling me close he kissed me again. Pushing him back, I cleaned the few traces of oil from his cheeks and raced to the door.

"Let's go, you were the one who had us up and running, eager to put that junk on my face. So now as soon as we reach safety away from here, I am going to wash my face and then you can touch it." I stuck my tongue out at him. He followed me, laughing. He reached out to catch me with no success. It was intoxicating to hear him laugh. He had the most handsome smile and it made him look even more irresistible. I had to take a hold of my heart or else I might have ended up falling in his arms rather than running away. Together we opened the door to the tunnel, becoming serious and cautious.

As we walked through, I was sure it was midday outside but in the safe house and the tunnel it was hard to tell. 'Probably would be blindingly bright'. I was anticipating Sana and Saad's smiling faces, once we got to the house. The next leg of the journey was to the military base, and as far as my knowledge went, the distance wasn't too much. We were about half an hour's drive from Baghdad. Apprehension gripped at my heart, the thought of leaving Sana's house and its security made me afraid. Involuntarily, I squeezed Ali's hand, he stopped, and turned to look at me puzzled.

"Nothing, I am just a little sad."

"Everything will be fine." Ali kissed my hand gently and smiled reassuringly.

We were almost at the opening of the tunnel and I could see the faint light penetrating the cover of dead leaves and vines.

Ali stepped out and I followed. It was sunny as I had suspected, 'Leave it to the Arabian sun to be predictable.' Silence spread around us as we walked towards the house, entering the patch of date trees close to Saad's house. It was shady and gave a break from the hot sun. We were quiet, moving slowly, lost in our thoughts. Ali's expression was grim, although he had reassured me, but apparently, he wasn't a believer of his own prediction.

As we were about to emerge from the woods, Ali stopped in his tracks. Putting his hand on my mouth, he stopped me from making any noise. He fell to his knees and pulled me down as well. Coming close he whispered in my ear that he had heard sounds. Instructing me to stay there, he got on his feet yet remaining crouched and moved in the direction of the sounds, agile as a cat. I waited for a minute but getting impatient, I traced his footsteps. He was at the edge of the trees on the other side. I could see Saad and Sana tied up to two tree trunks a little far apart and surrounded by half a dozen men in military garb with guns. There was someone in the middle of the gathering; I could recognize that face anywhere, Jabbar! He had a gun pointed at Saad. I suppressed a scream about to break out of my throat. Ali was a few feet ahead of me, I kept my mouth shut and watched him. He made a turn and ended up a bit far behind Saad's tree. I didn't know how he would manage to free him or Sana, but he was up to something. I crouched down further and stayed put. Ali moved stealthy through the green, staying close to the ground and approached the tree where Sana was tied. The soldiers were busy focusing on Saad that Ali had the opportunity to undo Sana's ties. Reaching Saad was going to be impossible without being seen. I was startled by a loud shriek; Sana had started to cry and scream loudly. It was enough to divert the attention of the soldiers and their lecherous leader. He shouted at her to quiet down, but she kept wailing loudly and screaming at them and Saad. Jabbar turned and pointed his gun at her threatening to shoot. That silenced her but then she said something that made him lower it and walk to her, leaving Saad's side for a few minutes. His men also directed their attention to what their master was about to do. In the meantime, I couldn't see Ali anymore, he had disappeared in the trees again, just to appear behind Saad. I understood what the strategy had been; Sana had caused a distraction to make room for Saad's release. Ali crawled up behind Saad and untied his hands. Just then I heard a loud groan from

Sana's side. She had somehow hurt Jabbar. I had missed it but I saw him slap her across the face hard, making her fall to the ground. Just then Ali started shooting at the soldiers with Saad in tow, holding Ali's other gun. Sana was ready in her place. She stood up and ran behind the tree as the soldiers and Jabbar scattered returning fire. Ali stayed concealed behind one of the trees along with Saad. Together, they had took down two of the soldiers with their surprise attack. But then there was a turn of events as Jabbar, always the cunning rat, nabbed Sana before she could get any further. Holding his gun to her head, he yelled at Ali and Saad to put down their guns. Ali and Saad had no other option then to give up. All of this happened so quickly it felt like a movie playing in front of my eyes, 'But this was no movie.' Jabbar kicked the guns away from them and threw Sana on the ground. One of the soldiers dragged her near a tree, while Jabbar came close to Ali and punched him in the stomach. Ali flinched in pain but remained standing.

"You were lying. You thought I wouldn't know. He's here so that bitch would be here too. If you won't tell me, I'll kill all of you slowly and painfully. Starting with you." Jabbar shouted and hit Ali again. I could see the wrath on Ali's face but he didn't engage Jabbar.

"You want your friends to die because of you. I can easily do that." Jabbar sneered, raising Ali's face by placing the barrel of his gun under his chin. I could hardly breathe. The miserable leach had Ali at his mercy. I had to do something fast before he hurt anyone of them. Sana was in the custody of one of Jabbar's thugs, who was trying to tie her. Her face was swollen from the side Jabbar had slapped her, but she was still struggling to free herself, urging Ali not to tell anything to Jabbar. Saad stood silent with another soldier holding a gun to his head. I needed a plan to save them.

"Tell me, where you are hiding her? If you want to live or if you want these dogs to live." Jabbar spat the words at Ali who stared at him in defiance. Irritated, Jabbar punched Ali in the face, making his lips bleed.

"Okay, maybe if you're not going to speak, this bitch can wag her tongue." Jabbar gestured his ruffians to bring Sana to him. As they approached, he took out a long blade. I didn't even want to think what his intentions were, but it was now or never. Ali and Saad were quiet, and Sana repeatedly shouted that they should stay silent and not to worry about her fate.

Cursing my folly, for not carrying a gun. I searched around but couldn't find anything to help. If I only had that with me now I could have done something. The soldiers had their guns pointed at Ali and I was not taking any chances on his life. Whatever I conjured up would need to be solid. Then I saw something that made me smile.

"Jabbar, let them go and I will surrender myself." I yelled from behind a tree a few moments later. My voice interrupted him as he got ready to use his weapon on Sana.

"What if I don't? You don't have a choice. I'll kill them and you can't stop me." Jabbar raised his gun to Ali's head.

"Sarah don't come. Let him do whatever he wants. You need to go." Ali spoke for the first time since the beginning of this ordeal. "Please, you have to leave." This time his voice was pleading with me. I ignored him; I could never leave him there.

"You want me, and if you want me alive, you have to let them go." I screamed at him, Ali looked tormented. Saad and Sana were quiet and corralled to one side. Ali was in the middle, where Jabbar was surrounded by his men, seemingly to have lost his interest in Saad and Sana.

"I'll kill them if you don't come out now." Jabbar looked around, trying to ascertain my position. It was time for me to step out and bluff my way out of this.

"I'm here." I came out from hiding, holding a pistol to my temple.

I had retrieved it from one of the shot soldiers. I hoped that I could trade my life for the others.

"Ha! So, the American brat comes out. Well, your trick is not going to work." Jabbar sneered at me.

"Well, you should take it seriously because this gun is loaded and I know how to use it. If I kill myself, you have lost your bargaining chip, your prize. No consolation from Daanish and no money from the Americans." I pressed the barrel to my temple.

"Do you really want to take that chance?"

"I don't need to. I'll kill your friends if you don't put that gun away."

"I know your type Jabbar you'll murder us anyway so as I see it, once I am dead it wouldn't matter if you kill them or not. Think about it, you just have to leave them here and I am all yours." I pulled the turban off my head with my free hand to reveal my deep gold hair and wiped the oil off my face with the corner of its cloth. It was a tactic to appeal to his lust and it worked. He removed his gun pointing at Ali's head and pistol-whipped Ali with the grip. Ali fell back and Jabbar drop kicked him. The others did the same to Saad and Sana.

"No! Sarah don't do this. Shoot him!" Ali roared trying to get to his feet only to be knocked down by the other soldiers. Jabbar was approaching me,

"Stop! Don't come any closer."

"First, let them go then I'll come. No more beating." I pointed with my free hand, the other held the gun tight in its position.

Jabbar stopped while Saad helped Sana recover from the blow and fall. Ali was on his knees staring directly into my eyes, imploring me. The other five soldiers had mostly gathered around their leader, a bit distracted by the whole drama. I diverted my gaze away from Ali and fixed my eyes on Jabbar. I didn't want him pulling any stunts. He stood some distance away weighing me. Then he turned to his men and in a hushed voice gave them some instructions in Arabic. Two of them stayed with him and the other three walked to Ali, Saad and Sana.

"What are you doing?" I was confused as to how he planned to set them free. I had not thought that far.

"You want them to be left alone so that is exactly what I am going to do. They'll be left bound in the house where they can untie themselves." He smiled viciously.

It wasn't the best solution, but I had to take it. I planned to keep the gun to my head until we were far enough and sufficient time had passed for Ali and the others to escape. Jabbar came closer and the three soldiers started screaming for Ali, Saad, and Sana to move but they didn't. I was worried this might happen.

"Ali, Saad, Sana please go with them. I'll be fine. He is not going to hurt me. He can't, that would be bad business for him." I tried to assure them but Ali remained silent, ignoring my pleas and the barrel of the gun poking him in the ribs. Saad and Sana looked at me with a wounded expression. They were not ready to give up but they were powerless.

While this was happening, I didn't pay attention to Jabbar's two soldiers who had stayed behind with him. I was occupied with persuading Ali to leave, who wasn't moving an inch despite two of the soldiers pummeling him, making him double over.

"Don't! Stop!" Shouting, I was at my wits end. Jabbar stepped closer and Ali wasn't budging.

By this instant, the two soldiers I had completely forgotten about had circled quietly around me, and before I realized it, they jumped me, knocking the gun out of my hand and making me fall. This surprised not only Ali, Saad and Sana but also the other three soldiers. Ali and Saad attempted to snatch their guns from them but they managed to only knock down one of them as the other two thwarted their effort. In a matter of seconds, the whole situation changed as Jabbar caught my hair and pulled me to my feet making me shriek in pain. Ali who hadn't moved until now pounced towards him, but one of the soldiers hit him with the machine gun handle, making him fall.

"You swine! Leave him alone" I kicked and scratched at Jabbar. He tugged hard at my hair, making my head jerk.

"Don't! I won't be this soft if you keep this up." He warned me.

"You shouldn't have done this. You've given me the opportunity to have fun with Ali. He was good at concealing his love for you in the camp, but I knew it from the beginning. It wasn't about the money, Daanish was wrong. The fool! Now he'll pay for his betrayal dearly." Jabbar threw me on the ground and went over to kick Ali, ignoring my screaming and cursing. Tears flowed down my cheeks; God knows when they had started, making me even more angry at my weakness. I didn't want to give Jabbar the satisfaction.

"Stand him up." He snapped at his men who pulled Ali to his feet and stood next to him with their guns at the ready.

Ali wiped the blood off his face and looked at Jabbar menacingly.

"You better let us go, Jabbar." Ali warned. I was in the custody of two of the soldiers who had flanked Jabbar until now. One stood guarding Saad and Sana.

"I don't think you want to interfere with Daanish." Ali was glaring at Jabbar.

"Wow, you're trying to scare me with Daanish. You must be really desperate. This girl has made you soft, Ali. Daanish knows where I am and for what." Jabbar pointed his finger at Ali. Turning around, he came back to my side and signaled four of the soldiers to go and surround Ali, making a circle around him.

"You know, there is this funny story about Daanish and this college professor and his wife. This foolish man opposed soldiers like Daanish. Hmm...Where did he live?", Jabbar rubbed his index finger on his forehead, pacing and kicking dirt in Ali's direction. I saw Ali's face become ashen.

"What are you talking about?" Ali's voice was barely audible

"I was just remembering this teacher and his family. Ah! Yes, he had two kids. This guy was a pain in the ass. Always urging his students to work in peace and calling out people like Daanish. He was a troublemaker. You know the kind who thinks justice and peace should be the rule not exception. Well, it was too much of a nuisance for us and he had to be silenced." Jabbar smiled cruelly, raising his eyebrows at Ali.

"It's just that sometimes I remember things about the past which are interesting. You know what Daanish did? He went to this guy's house and shot him with his whole family except for the son. It would have been a waste because he needed soldiers."

"Where was this?" Ali's voice was a whisper.

"Can't recall everything, but the most fascinating and ironic part of the whole story is that Daanish took in the teacher's son and made him the best darn killing machine of his army. Daddy would have had a fit if he had seen his son."

"What do you mean?" Ali's whole body shook with rage, and his eyes blazed with ferocity.

"I mean fool; he killed your family and then took you in and used you for his own good. So that's your Daanish. How do you like him now?" Jabbar laughed maniacally.

Suddenly, the world went bleak. I knew what this meant. All his life Ali had been trying to find the murderer of his family, and now he discovered that he had been serving that monster, considering him his friend, his savior, his mentor. Daanish was the very person who had slaughtered everyone Ali held dear in his life. He was the destroyer of his world, of his dreams.

Ali didn't reply. He was absolutely silent. Suddenly, his face lost every expression becoming stone hard. The fury a minute ago was replaced by a cold dark countenance and an icy glare calculating the odds with cool precision. Jabbar was probably expecting a more brash reaction from him but this bored him.

"Let's have some fun." Jabbar's voice was unnerving and I didn't like the way he was standing so close to me. Slinging the gun on his shoulder, he pulled me to my feet and then touched my face. Disgusted, I pushed him back.

"If you stop me, they'll hurt Ali." He whispered, sneering evilly.

I had removed my turban to entice him for my own plan but now it was proving to be a regretful mistake. Taking his handkerchief out, he wiped my face and removed every trace of oil.

"Now you look much better. I like to kiss girls who actually look pretty." His finger touched my lips and slid down to cress my neck. The warm wind blew my locks in every direction but that didn't bother him as his hand slid further down. I squirmed at his touch and tried to slap him. Ali stood in the midst of his soldiers, his fists clenched and his face dark. I had never seen him like this; there was not a single sign there that he was a living being with any feelings. Jabbar cued his soldiers who punched Ali in the stomach. I couldn't bear it and ran towards him. Jabbar caught me midflight and twisting my arm behind my back pinned me to his body. I fought and struggled but his grip was strong and I could hear Ali grunt in pain as his men battered him, but he never called out to me or Jabbar.

"Please let him go. I won't fight. You can have me. I won't move a muscle to stop you, just leave him alone." I pleaded with Jabbar, becoming motionless.

"Where's the fun in that." Cruelty was visible from his callous eyes.

"I want to have fun." He pressed me closer and brought his mouth down on mine. As his lips touched mine, I kept my mouth closed and shut my eyes, trying to block him out. His touch was repulsive but I couldn't do anything, they had Ali.

I didn't even hear what transpired next. Jabbar had my hair in one hand with his other twisting my arm around my back. The pain of being physically twisted and his revolting kiss made me feel sick. I couldn't decipher clearly what happened in the next few moments until Ali freed me from Jabbar's grip and struck him down. 'Where'd he come from?' I wondered dazed as he took me in his arms, assuring me that he wasn't going to let Jabbar hurt me.

Jabbar tried to get up, but Ali was in his element. Quick as lighting, he kicked Jabbar's gun away and smashed in Jabbar's head, making Jabbar unconscious. To my relief, I saw the other soldiers lying on the ground in heaps. In the time that Jabbar had begun his onslaught on me, Ali had taken down his soldiers. I sat on the ground where Ali had left me, watching it all in surreal reality. Some of the soldiers got up and made the mistake of confronting Ali again, who was merciless. He cut them down without a second glance. Saad gathered the guns and Sana helped me to my feet. After disposing of the thugs, Ali came running to help Sana steady me. What happened had left me absolutely shaken. Suddenly, there was a faint noise in one direction,

"Those must be the rest of his men. He always has more." Ali shouted and looked around to find Jabbar missing. It was clear he had slipped away and probably was returning with reinforcements.

"We've got to get out of here." Ali said urgently.

"You both come with us." Saad yelled running towards the main house. I had recovered enough, and quickly followed with Ali in tow. Once at the house, Saad opened one of the cupboards and took out two guns and extra bullets. Keeping one, he handed the other to Sana, then lead us to the back shed and pulled off the cover from a motorcycle standing there.

"You two take the small path which runs from the side of the house, leading to the road to Baghdad. It runs through another patch of trees and will give good cover. Jabbar wouldn't have any motorcycles. This should help you escape." Saad gave Ali the keys.

"You're not coming? Why? I want you to come with us. We can take the car." I was frantic, desperately looking at Sana for support, but it seemed they already had their minds made up. Ali didn't question Saad; he was impassive as he nodded.

"I'll take the car and divert them. You go as soon as I and Sana take the car out." Saad gave us a hug. Sana came to me, tears glistened in her eyes and mine were flowing down my cheeks unchecked.

"Take care of yourself sweetheart. We'll be fine, don't worry." She came and hugged me tightly. My throat was choked and I was speechless. Saad gestured to her and she let me go and gave Ali a hug. After that, they were out of the shed and in a few minutes, I heard the crunching of gravel as the car skidded out of the driveway. Ali kicked the motorbike to life and then he pulled me up and placed me in front of him rather than letting me sit in the back.

"What?"

"You will be safer here, next to my heart." He gave me a hurt smile and then drove the bike out of the shed to the side of the house as quietly as he could.

I could hear the faint sound of the car and the rumble of the churning engines of approaching vehicles. My heart said a prayer for Saad and Sana. Ali drove the bike almost in neutral to make as least noise as possible until we were a little far from the house. Then he accelerated the bike. We were flying down the dirt path and it was as if life had come to a standstill. My world had been perfect in the morning but now it lay in pieces around me.

I wasn't sure if Jabbar had taken the bait or not, and I was positive the same thought was occupying Ali's mind. We were almost to the patch of trees Saad had mentioned, when suddenly two pickup trucks appeared, jumping right across us. Ali almost smashed into them. Diverting, he circled the bike and avoided them but now we were driving in the opposite direction from the woods. Ali looked back to assess the situation. The trucks were in pursuit but no one was firing at us, which seemed odd. It struck me instantly, they were corralling us back to the house, back to Jabbar. I said that much in Ali's ear. He nodded and then braking with full force pulled a 360 facing the pickups. Whirling the accelerator, he eyed the pickups as they came at us, then let go. The bike jumped to a roaring start, probably making 0 to 60 in less than five seconds. He was driving straight at them, head on. I didn't know what to expect. We might die right here or might just make it if we

425

were lucky. I hid my face in his neck and prayed. I felt a sharp curve and then we were driving straight. Opening my eyes, I looked around. Ali had made a sharp curve around the pickups as soon as he had approached them and they had almost crashed into each other trying to avoid him. They wanted both of us alive, that much was obvious, and it worked for us. We were speeding towards the trees. Once in there, the vehicles wouldn't be able to pursue us. Then the sound behind us increased in magnitude as more vehicles joined in the chase. Jabbar was here, standing on the open bed of another speeding pickup truck holding the top rail. He screamed an order and the others pointed their weapons at us and started firing. We were in trouble, but luckily, they were a little far from us and we had reached the patch of trees. It was thick and indiscriminately wooded with trees of every size growing in each direction, proving to be a refuge where Jabbar couldn't follow us on his vehicles. Unless he came on foot, it was inaccessible to him. Ali drove the bike in, leaving the party chasing us behind. I hadn't seen any motor bikes in Jabbar's party. Saad had been correct and that was one win for us. Going through the thicket, Ali stopped in the middle and checked on me.

"Are you alright?" He took my face in his palms, looking at me intently,

"I'm fine but I am so sorry about your family." I wanted to console him and comfort him. The truth about his past and Daanish's real identity was a severe blow. I knew it was the ultimate betrayal.

"I'm okay. Don't worry. I have you." He looked into my eyes and kissed my lips lightly then more deeply. I anchored my fingers in his hair and let him until he pulled back a few moments later.

"Sarah, I will try my best but I am not sure whether we will make it to safety. I don't want Jabbar ever getting his hands on you. What do you think we should do if he catches us because I don't think I can fight all these soldiers alone?" Still holding my face in his hands, Ali asked me something which I would have found inconceivable in the morning. But now our worst fears had become a reality and I had to make a choice.

"I want to die with you rather than getting caught by that slime. We will die together. I can't live without you and I don't want to." I kissed him on the cheek. "But you will have to do the job." Smiling tenderly at him, I held his hand to my heart. His eyes were glassy, reflecting an agony of lost hopes and unfulfilled expectations. Lowering his head, he took out the first gun he had and checked the number of bullets and then his second.

"Are you ready?

"Yes." One word and it was decided. I still sat facing him with my legs wrapped around his waist and my feet resting on the portion of the seat behind him. I simply tied my loose hair and encircled my arms around him.

Kissing my forehead, he started the bike again. Instead of taking the path leading out of the trees, he took the bike through the shrubs, off the treaded path. He was right to do so because as we came out, Jabbar's cars had circled around to block the path emerging from the trees. We avoided them by being a bit far on the other side, giving us the opportunity to speed towards the road. Ali was driving the bike at breakneck speed, approaching the road within seconds. Here it became more arduous as the road was open, making us an easy target. Ali pushed the bike to its limits as Jabbar and his thugs got on the road chasing us at maximum speed. Ali was trying to keep as much distance between us as he possibly could but it was reducing quickly. I could feel the bullets buzzing past. They were taking shots at us with calculated measure, intent on catching us alive.

At the moment, I had no comprehension of time and space but it was visible that we were near the city because the landscape changed. It was not patchy with a few buildings here and there. Rather the number of establishments and people along the road were increasing. Jabbar's men shot more frequently, desperately sending barrages of bullets to stop us. They had reduced the distance between us but Ali was driving at a maddening speed, carefully avoiding other cars on the road as traffic became dense. The bike was a good choice because it squeezed through the narrow alleys and snaked its way through traffic. People dispersed on the sides, scared as soon as they saw the situation. Nobody interfered or tried to help. I didn't blame them. These people had experienced so many horrors that their spirits had been broken, becoming numb to the violence. But fortunate for us, there were still some who had the courage to help. A few men came to our assistance, joining us on their bikes, returning fire to Jabbar's men. It was an open shoot out after that, but our allies were well protected wearing vests to shield themselves. Ali had nothing of the kind and I had heard him grunt a few times since we had hit the road. This escort proved more help than we could ever have asked for. It gave the precious little time Ali needed to disappear in the streets, getting off the highway. Our destination was the American military base, which was getting closer and closer. Ali had turned into the streets to avoid our attackers but Jabbar's pickup pursued us relentlessly. The others were occupied and probably diverted by our allies. Jabbar shouted at us in anger. Facing backwards, I could see Jabbar draw his gun. As soon as we were in range, he took aim at Ali and fired. Ali groaned in pain. The bullet had struck him. I was furious. Pulling Ali's gun from his side, I aimed at Jabbar and started raining him with bullets. The little training Ali had given me came in handy. I had no clue if I hit Jabbar or not, but someone had come in the line of fire as the pickup swayed and hit the curb, sending Jabbar flying off his perch. It sped out of control and crashed directly into an electric pole with full force before screeching to a halt.

Ali was injured. I checked his back and there was blood dripping from his shirt. Dropping the gun, I tried to find the bullet's entry site. Ali groaned in pain but I was able to find where Jabbar had shot him. His bullet had pierced his back on the lower right side, cutting through his flesh and exiting. Thankfully, it had missed his vital organs but Ali was quickly losing blood and I had nothing to press against it to stop the bleeding. Frantically, I folded his own shirt as much as I could and then placed my hand on it, pressing tightly to stop the bleeding.

"No one's behind us anymore Ali. Jabbar's car hit a pole. Please slow down and stop so I can find something to stop the bleeding." I begged Ali,

"No, he isn't dead. I know that and he'll come after us as soon as his other men find him. He knows where we're headed. I can't stop." Ali raced on and I held him up.

He was right. Within minutes, I heard cars coming after us apart from the general traffic that had started to skitter away as the gun laden vehicles raced after us. Ali accelerated faster. We had the upper hand as our slender bike easily dashed through the narrow streets.

"We're near the base. The university is close by. After passing it, we'll have to turn back to the main road. The base is on the other side." Ali shouted, nodding. I had no notion of where we were in the city, but I knew the main highway meant bad news. Ali had used the streets for protection and to escape the firing squad of Jabbar but if we had to go back on the highway…. 'God help us. We'd be easy targets for Jabbar.' He'd been detained momentarily due to my persistent shooting, but he was coming now. I prayed and clung to Ali as he accelerated towards the main highway. He was furiously bleeding, but my hand kept taut against his wound, keeping it under control. Still, the blood loss was heavy and I knew he'd collapse soon if he didn't get any medical attention. Dreading and praying, I held on. In a minute or two, we were on the highway,

"The street on the right, there! It goes to the base." Ali shouted to me, trying to reassure me as the roar of vehicles behind us got closer. I tucked my head into his neck just to keep the sounds from hammering into my head, but to no avail. The cars were creeping closer and closer, when Ali made a sharp right turn at full speed, nearly skidding out of control. We were on an open, dusty road sparsely dotted with buildings on both sides. Jabbar and his hooligans were right behind us catching up. The building pattern quickly evolved into uniformly built installations. Here the vehicular rumble grew. Raising my head, I looked around to find American military armored jeeps racing towards us. If they didn't know who we were, …we'd be in deeper trouble now. We were trapped in between two heavily armed groups. Thankfully, they didn't fire at us. Rather they raced towards us to provide cover. Jabbar and his soldiers hadn't given up yet, and turned their guns on the American jeeps. The armored jeeps drew fire away from us but didn't return it. I wondered if they knew who we were and why we had come. Judging from their actions, it seemed to be the case. Astonishingly, Jabbar and his men still hadn't given up even though we were nearing the main premises of the military installation. The new escort was protecting us and Ali appeared to be somewhat at ease. As soon as we were close to the main camp, the jeeps were joined in by air power. Two military helicopters appeared

431

in the sky and within seconds the vehicles chasing us were bombarded with shells.

I felt like I was in a huge 3D movie theatre watching an old military film about the Nazis pursuing the heroes only to be saved by the miraculous appearance of the Allied soldiers. It was bizarre. This whole day had been like I was floating in a nightmare, with characters materializing out of thin air and then vanishing in smoke. Closing my eyes, I wished that I would wake up to find myself in bed next to Ali, bathing in the mediocre sunlight of our safe house. But this was not an illusion or a figment of my imagination, the bullets were real and so was Ali's wound. Cursing Jabbar, I kept my hand jammed on the entry site with blood oozing out of it. One of Jabbar's trucks had been blown up by the shells, emitting a large cloud of dust and smoke, concealing the other vehicles for a brief time. Jabbar, always shrewd, took advantage of his fallen comrades and turned back with his other thugs in tow. The gunships kept shelling them only to hit one more. The last I saw was them disappearing as a speck of dirt in the distance. Ali wasn't paying any attention to the drama unfolding behind him, ignoring it like a mundane event. He kept driving the bike at breakneck speed until we were in the inner compound. Once there, he stopped. The jeeps escorting us pulled to a halt a short distance away, and soldiers jumped out of them holding their guns at the ready. Ali breathed deeply, scooting back making room for me. I looked at his face streaked with dust and blood. My hand still pressed on his wound. He smiled weakly at me, relieved and tired.

"You can let go. I think the bleeding has stopped; it aches a bit." His voice was stressed but cheerful. I shook my head stubbornly and kept my hand where it was. I could still feel the warm, sticky blood seeping through my fingers.

"They must have medical help here. We need to go in." I tried to pull him off the bike after sliding off it but he resisted and nudged me to look behind. An older man in uniform was coming towards us and the soldiers called out in reverence, signaling his seniority and position.

"I am Colonel Parker." He came close to Ali and extended his hand towards him.

"I'm Ali. I was hoping Saad's messenger had reached you. I see he did." Ali shook his hand.

"Mr. Tariqi, you need to see our doctor. Ms. Chambers, eventually it's a pleasure to meet you." Colonel Parker held my hand and patted it gently.

"No, I have to go." Ali replied, pushing the bike backwards.

"What?" I screamed before anyone was able to say a word.

"Sarah, I've got to go after Daanish and Jabbar. If I don't, they'll be a threat for you anywhere." Ali was deathly serious as he addressed me.

"Mr. Tariqi, you could stay and get the medical assistance you require and we could take care of those thugs ourselves." Colonel Parker was resigned but stern.

"No, you can't. You have no clue as to where these people are and how they operate." Ali smiled at the colonel condescendingly and then kicked the bike to life once again.

'This wasn't happening, he wasn't leaving me here, he couldn't. He had promised to stay with me.',

"Ali, you can't go. I love you. You have to stay. I'm not letting you go." I was beside myself with anger and confusion. I had to do something, stop him somehow. For the first time after removing my hand from his wound, I grabbed his arm and tried to pull him off the bike. As always, I had underestimated his strength, and he pulled me close, holding me in his arms tightly, striving to calm me. He whispered in my ear words unintelligible to me. My mind was in disarray as he explained his concern for my safety.

Only one thought echoed in me. I wasn't leaving him and he was not going anywhere until I felt other hands pulling me away. He stood there on his bike as I was taken away. For a moment, I saw tears in his eyes but then wiping them away, he turned and raced towards the city. One of the soldiers asked the colonel something but he shook his head and all the soldiers lowered their guns. I was devastated with grief. My whole existence became meaningless as the world decimated around me shattering any dreams I had. It felt like I was standing between crashing plates of the earth crushing me violently. My heart was as if it would explode and my mind was in a fog. All my attempts to break away and follow Ali were mitigated by Colonel Parker's men. Confined by this new mob, the world around me blacked out with the last glimpse of Ali disappearing on his bike in the distance.

Day 22 (Ali)

I didn't look back. Sarah's screams and pleading rang in my ears, but I kept riding that bike like a mad man until I stopped in a dimly lit, narrow alley in the middle of nowhere with no clue to where I was in the city. I had been driving aimlessly to escape the sinking hollowness breaking me. My head swam with every breath as the adrenaline ebbed and the blood loss started taking its toll. I was quite sure that without medical help, I'd soon collapse but the reason to live was lost in the dust. The street I was parked in was deserted and ragged, only a small old rusted sign on the edge of it carried its name. If I wished to live, I had to find my way back to Saad's friend's house. The place Sarah was supposed to go with me. I sighed heavily, leaning back on my bike. Suddenly, I could taste salt on my lips, wiping the corners of my eyes with my fingertips, I discovered that tears were making their way to my lips.

Silent tears had broken the bounds of my eyes without me being cognizant of it. For the second time in my conscious life, I found myself crying as my heart bled.

Standing in that deserted street, I let the tears run, lamenting the loss of my life, my soul and my love. I had nothing left. 'Did I still want to live? Was there any purpose to my life?' I questioned the legitimacy of my existence.

But the image of Sarah being held by Jabbar materialized in my mind, reminding me why I deserted Sarah and gave me the strength I needed to live. I had to survive so that she could live. The sole reason for my existence was to destroy Daanish and Jabbar. Until they were alive, Sarah wouldn't be safe and I couldn't let them get her.

Peeking at the sun shining in the sky, I got back on my bike. My next destination was the house of the only person I could trust to keep me safe, Saad's friend and confidant. Life was now a new journey with one purpose, and I sped the bike in the direction of my new reality.

Sarah was a beautiful, fleeting dream. Love had never been mine to keep, and life had proven that once again. I drove on defeated and resigned to my fate.

Day 24

I woke up in a haze. It was bright, and I was lying on a clean white hospital bed with sunlight flooding in through the large windows.

"Where was I? What was this place?" My mind was groggy and I was unable to think beyond that.

"Hello! You're awake, eventually." A cheery feminine voice greeted me,

'Sana!' was the first thing that came to my mind. Exerting to open my eyes, I looked around and found a blonde, white nurse smiling at me.

'This is not Sana' I thought. "Where am I? Who are you?" I nearly shouted.

"You're at Camp Victory hospital Ms. Chambers. You've awoken after almost two days. Thank God!" The nurse was still smiling at me,

"What is she smiling for?" I didn't like her genial disposition. Looking sideways, I avoided her as hurtful memories came flooding back in. Ali was gone, deserting me, leaving me here and returning to his old life. I felt desolate, 'Why save me if he was going to leave me in the end? How could he hurt me like this?' My mind was in shock and I wanted to die.

"Please, Ms. Chambers don't cry." The nurse came close and tenderly cleaned the tears off my cheeks with a tissue paper. I hadn't realized it but I was crying. I didn't want to, but my tears had always been rebellious.

438

"I know what happened. He did what he had to for you." She sounded so sure, why wasn't I.

"I want to be alone, please." I managed to choke out the words. The nurse turned and silently went out of the room.

I was left to wallow in my misery, surrounded by solitude. I wanted to run away and hide from everyone.

Climbing out of bed, I looked at the windows and found them to be barred. As I stumbled to the door, I was greeted by soldiers outside. It was confirmed that I wasn't trusted to stay put. The colonel was a sharp man; he wasn't taking any chances with me. Slumping back on the bed, I leaned back and closed my eyes only to be haunted by Ali's images. My head felt like it would burst, pounding with excruciating pain.

Suddenly, there were people in the room. Someone held me down, and I felt the prick of a needle as my world went dark again.

The next few days were muddled as I was taken back to the states, where I was received by multiple high-ranking officials but for me it was all inconsequential, a wasted effort. I didn't speak or respond to anyone except for when my father came to take me home. I quietly accompanied him and my younger brothers who were ecstatic to see me safe and sound. The only instance when I showed any emotions was when my father thanked Colonel Parker, who had accompanied me, profusely for rescuing me until I yelled that it was Ali who had saved me not the American colonel and his soldiers. My shouting startled my father but the colonel was quick to take him aside and explain 'my situation'. Dad had remained calm, hugging me and assuring me of the future. I was numb, tired of crying and fighting, so I listened and followed him. We arrived back home in silence, Dad tried sparking a light conversation with me, involving my brothers. But for me, speaking was a burden. My short responses and apathetic behavior discouraged him from continuing. William and Mike had grown and were more serious and observant then before. They simply hugged me and sat next to me on either side, holding my hands, saying very little. We were home in a short while as I had been flown to West Virginia on a government jet. The high brass was keeping me at a distance from anyone other than the government officials and my own family. We had our privacy as the media wasn't allowed to come near me. Thanks to my incapacity for producing coherent answers, the CIA gave up interrogating me, which was a relief.

"Here we are sweetheart. Back home safe." Dad parked the car in the driveway and opened the door for me. I stepped out looking at the old house as if it was an extraterrestrial from outer space. Will and Mike took my hands and guided me inside. I recognized the rooms and the furniture, but it felt strange and foreign. The garden outside where I had planted flowers was blooming with vines covering the side walls, which mom so dearly trimmed and maintained, still hung there. Maybe it wasn't the house, it was me. This was not for me, not anymore. But the clock ticked, as Dad and the boys got me settled in my room and life despondently began.

Day X

I was up since early morning. Day break had come later. It was tiring to have insomnia like this, but I had grown accustomed to it. My mind was far away as usual in the silence of the house. I looked out of the living room window as the sun rose in the Montana sky. Mountains shimmered in the bright rays. This place was more beautiful than anywhere I had ever been, 'Mom would've loved living here.' My coffee had become cold again. Putting the cup on the side table, I stretched on the comfy chair.

"Good morning, you're up again." Dad strode in,

"Morning, couldn't sleep." I stared out at the mountains again.

"You need the sleep sweetheart. Zain is going to be up soon and then no more peace." He smiled at me and stepped in the kitchen, probably in search of fresh coffee. I jumped out of the chair and got to the counter before him.

"Let me make some breakfast for you." I scooped up the coffee pot and started filling it with water. Dad pulled a out chair from under the small dining table, but instead of sitting, he went out mumbling to himself. He was back in a moment with a newspaper tucked under his arm. By then I had cracked some eggs and was scrambling them in the frying pan. In the next few minutes, I had the eggs, coffee and toast ready for him. Only sausages were still cooking on the stove.

Grabbing my cup of fresh brew, I joined him on the table, placing the plate of sausages next to his eggs and toast.

"You aren't going to eat anything." He raised his fork and pointed at the feast before him.

"No, dad I've got my coffee. It got cold earlier and I was left with a stale cup. This is Turkish so I really don't want to mix it with anything." My excuse was lame but he was used to it. He knew I wouldn't eat anything even if he insisted. He had given up trying a long time ago. Shaking his head, he got back to his newspaper and breakfast.

"Will's coming this weekend, isn't he?" My question was more of a statement,

"Yeah, he said something to that effect. The drive's okay now, but when the season gets more nasty, it'll be hell. I wouldn't want him driving in that kind of weather." Dad glanced at the snow outside through the kitchen window.

"Yeah, you're right but Zain just loves him being around. He misses the boys so much." I sipped my coffee.

Dad didn't answer, simply nodded. I stood up and stepped into the living room once again. The view here was different than the one in the kitchen. I stood facing our land in the front of the house and the mountains which rolled towards the sky in the distance.

'It would have been more appropriate if this scene was in the back. It's more of a backyard scene.' I thought to myself, as if it made any difference, when the land stretched acres in every direction from the house.

Flurry had started to fall. It was only October but Montana was colder and the winters here were swifter. Slowly, I sauntered closer to the window, feeling the chill of the cold breeze outside hitting against the pane.

That was when I spotted a small black dot in the distance on the long driveway, it grew larger as the distance reduced, eventually turning out to be a car coming down the lane.

'Who could this be?' I squinted to have a better look but the car had tinted windows and the fast-falling flurry was blocking the view. It looked like a taxicab. Someone new was here, it wasn't Will for sure. He had a compact SUV and he wasn't coming till the weekend.

The car approached the front of the house. I'd have to call Dad because he wouldn't have been able to hear the faint sound of the engine in the kitchen. I kept looking outside interested in the newcomer.

Someone stepped out of the rear seat wearing a long black coat with its collar turned up. The face of the person was hidden as he faced the car. It was a tall man and there was something about him, a strange feeling which made me anxious. The cab driver came out to help him with his bag but the stranger simply paid him and then turned to face the house.

My hands started shaking uncontrollably and the coffee cup slipped out of them, smashing on the wooden floor with a bang.

"What happened?" Dad called out from the kitchen,

I couldn't see clearly through the fog. My head spun as I ran to the front door and swung it open in time to startle the man standing in front of it, the cab was long gone.

"Ali!!!" I screamed.

Ali stood in front of me, in a long winter overcoat, his black hair dotted with flurry and his deep dark eyes fixed on me.

My head was dizzy as I held the door and stared at him. Before he could say anything, my legs gave way and I slumped to the ground fainting, only to be caught by him.

Slowly the haze cleared. I was in the same familiar living room of our house and the day was still brightly visible from the windows.

'It was probably a dream, like in the past.' My mind fought with my heart as I opened my eyes, recognizing the furnishings around.

"How're you darling?" I heard Dad's voice near me,

"I'm fine. Just another dream Dad, sorry." I said apologetically rising from the cushion.

"It wasn't a dream Sarah" The voice had the same deep tone and ring as the one which had graced my every waking hour and dreams for long. I sat up and saw Ali standing behind Dad.

"Ali!" My voice was lost after that. I blinked my eyes to make sure it wasn't an apparition, but he remained without vanishing or fading like so many times before. He was really here, after all this time he had come, he had returned to me.

"Ali, I missed you." Tears broke free from my eyes and ran down my cheeks. Four words made up a little statement, but it contained every note of my loneliness and love. Dad got up and let Ali sit next to me.

Ali took me in his arms and held me without saying a word. I wanted to shout at him, hit him for what he had done, for what he had put me through. But now it was just him there holding me and nothing else mattered. I closed my eyes and hid in him.

"Ma...ma," A soft sound made us all turn,

In the doorway of the living room, Zain stood rubbing his eyes as his gorgeous black hair teased him. He was in his pjs with his little teddy bear tucked safely under his arm, "Mama!...." He stressed again ordering me to come to him. I knew it was a matter of seconds before he would start crying.

"I'm here honey. Don't worry sweetheart." Leaving Ali's embrace, I got off the sofa and raced to him. He clung to my legs, hiding behind them.

Ali sat spellbound, his eyes fixed on the toddler hiding behind my legs with deep black hair, dark sparkling eyes and a milky complexion. I held Zain's hand and led him in,

"Sarah…………." Ali had left his place.

"Ali, meet our son, Zain." I calmly smiled as Zain gripped my hand with all his might.

Ali stood entranced, and for the first time, I saw tears slip past the confines of his eyes.

"Our son." He could barely speak.

"Yes, this is your son Ali." This time Dad spoke, placing his hand on Ali's shoulder. I had forgotten that he was there, watching as my life made another U turn.

Dad came close and taking my hand, led us to Ali who hadn't moved, and giving my hand in his he stepped back.

"You guys have a lot of catching up to do and I've to finish my breakfast." Wiping his eyes, Dad smiled and left us there.

Ali sat down on the sofa,

"How old is he?"

"Fourteen months." I sat next to him, "Zain look, who is this?"

I pointed at Ali as Zain uncomfortably turned away.

"Mama, no" he mumbled stubbornly

"It's okay, this is Da..da." I placed him on my lap.

"Da..da."

"Yes"

"Un han", he hugged me clinging to my shoulder.

Ali smiled broadly midst his unchecked tears, hugging us both.

"You told him about me and you named him Zain." Ali looked at me in his arms with Zain still clinging to my shoulder, hidden in the middle. He squirmed and started crying, Ali laughed.

"I love you Sarah." Pressing his lips to my forehead, Ali released us.

"I love you too, Ali." My world danced in colors as we sat there mollifying Zain together.

Ali had left his bag lying in the hallway, and his coat hung on the back of one of the chairs. Zain sat between us a little confused, hugging his teddy.

"Let me take Zain, Sarah. Come on buddy, let's have some breakfast." Dad appeared in the doorway and holding Zain's hand took him.

Ali and I were left alone sitting in the living room. Ali wiped away the tears and stood up, walking to the window. I approached him turning him to face me. His face was a reflection of tenderness,

"Sarah you're my heart and soul. You've completed me in every way, and I love you so much it hurts." His voice was full of affection as he took me in his arms and kissed me.

The next few hours zipped by as he told his part of the story and I mine. Dad would pop in the room occasionally to say hello with Zain who was slowly warming up to the newcomer.

Ali had been in hiding and I had moved from West Virginia to Montana. We both had been fighting our own battles. He had learned the truth about his parents' killer and I had found out that I was carrying our child.

The past two years had been a time of trial and success for us both. He had suffered at the hands of Daanish and Jabbar but finally had been able to settle his score with both of them with the help of friends like Saad and Sana. I had been living in a nightmare once back in the town of my birth with people shunning me because I was pregnant with the child of a 'terrorist', someone who had no moral grounds to persist in doing so. My Dad and brothers had stood by me, giving me strength. They knew the truth, the reality of what had happened. At last, my dad decided to leave and start again in Montana, far away from West Virginia. Will and Mike supported all his decisions and mine, never flinching in their resolve. I was proud of the strength my brothers had displayed, and their loyalty. Now that they had left for college, we missed them more than ever.

Ali was able to escape from Iraq with the help of friends and the American military. He had been looking for me for some weeks since his arrival in the states and at last had found where we had relocated.

We sat together content and happy, as the sun shone brightly once more with Ali holding me in his arms. Life had come full circle and there was nothing left for me to desire or wish; my world was complete.

Acknowledgment,
To everyone who believed in me.

JRY Veera

Made in the USA
Coppell, TX
25 March 2022